# EURAQUILO

# EURAQUILO

Charles D. Bass

Copyright © 2004 by Charles D. Bass.

Library of Congress Number:    2003096278
ISBN :         Hardcover       1-4134-2878-9
               Softcover       1-4134-2877-0

Illustrations by Irmgard Knoth

All rights reserved. No part of this book may be reproduced or transmitted in any form or by any means, electronic or mechanical, including photocopying, recording, or by any information storage and retrieval system, without permission in writing from the copyright owner.

This is a work of fiction. Names, characters, places and incidents either are the product of the author's imagination or are used fictitiously, and any resemblance to any actual persons, living or dead, events, or locales is entirely coincidental.

This book was printed in the United States of America.
**To order additional copies of this book, contact:**
Xlibris Corporation
1-888-795-4274
www.Xlibris.com
Orders@Xlibris.com
20098

To my wife Martha, my beloved team member whom I esteem as God's greatest gift to me on earth.

TAMESIS
(RIVER THAMES)

DOROB[RIVIS]
(ROCHE[STER])

OCEANUS B[RITANNICUS]
(ENGLISH CHA[NNEL])

LONDINIUM
(LONDON)
RIVAE
ITER)
MEDWAY
RIVER
ISLE OF SHEPPEY
RUTUPIAE
(RICHBOROUGH)
I T A N N I C U S
NNEL)
GESSORIACUM
(GRAVELINES)
LIANE RIVER
(AA RIVER)
GALLIA
(FRANCE)

*From of old I love you, so now I draw you gently home.*
James Moffatt Bible

# CHAPTER ONE

## GALLIA
## SPRING AD 43

MARCUS TRIED TO appear more self-confident than he felt as they strode across the open area toward the Praetorium. To an observer he and his aide cut classic figures of military bearing, yet his stomach was churning. He had never been in the presence of a Legion commander before.

They walked past the altar and the standards and up to the tent flap. When the aide announced him to one of the guards, the guard shouted out, "Centurion Hippalus, sir." The aide positioned himself at attention with the guards outside, and Marcus went in.

It took a moment for his eyes to grow accustomed to the semi-darkness. Numerous little flames around the tent, each reflected in a shiny metal plate, provided a measure of illumination. The atmosphere reeked of burnt oil and dampness. Small groups of soldiers milled around. Marcus had only arrived a few days before and had never met his new Legatus, Appius Drusus. He was unsure which man to salute.

At the opposite end of the tent a man arose and stepped out from behind a desk. "Marcus Hippalus," he said in a friendly manner. Quickly, Marcus swung his arm across his breast and said, "Reporting at your command, my Lord."

"Marcus, how was your voyage from Italy? Would you like a cup of tea?"

Marcus felt relieved and replied, "No, sir, but I appreciate the offer. We had a good voyage, my Lord."

Drusus said, "Do you think that your Classici are ready for the invasion?"

"Yes, my Lord," replied Marcus, "we've been in training all day, and I believe we are ready."

"Good," said Drusus. "We plan to set sail day after tomorrow. Come over here to this map." He led him to a long table where several maps were unfurled. "I've been reviewing your record. Say, you've made quite a name for yourself so young. I congratulate you. For this reason, I'm putting you in command of the legion's entire galley fleet for the invasion. I want you to lead them in an encircling maneuver on the British Isle."

Marcus rocked back slightly on his heels. He was going from the command of one galley to more than ten in less than a month. His chest swelled, and he tuned his mind to memorize every word from the commander. In build Marcus towered head and shoulders over his commander, as he did over everyone else in the tent.

"I am ready, sir," said Marcus. "I'll not let you down."

"Come to this side of the table and I'll show you the plan. If you do well in this invasion, I'll personally elevate you to be my *Primpilus*."

The instructions were that Drusus was to cross the sea with the bulk of his XX Legion by means of merchant ships and other civilian craft and land on the Kent coast at Rutupiae. He did not expect much resistance there, according to intelligence, and would quickly secure the beach, consolidate, and move inland. The area of operation of his legion would be south of the Tamesis Gulf while Legions IX and XIV would penetrate parallel to them north of the gulf. Legion II would be directly south of them. He did not expect any major encounter until they approached Londinium, and he planned to do that very rapidly.

"That's where your forces come into play. I'm aware that the specialty of your classici is to ram and board enemy ships. Frankly, though, the Brits have only a ragtag navy and no galleys that we know of. Instead," he said, pointing to a map, "I want you to sail on around Rutupiae into the Tamesis Gulf, land your soldiers on this peninsula formed by the Tamesis and Medway rivers, and rapidly march along the Medway to Durobrivae. Quickly, take that city and secure the bridge over the Medway River for us. Then, serve as a blocking action against the forces from Londinium, if they show up, until I get there. Day after tomorrow is Day One. I plan to have the legion at the bridge by Day Four. Do you think you can do it?"

"I can, sir," said Marcus without hesitation.

Following another hour of clarification and discussion, Drusus wrote out and signed a brief order for Marcus and handed him copies of coastal and overland maps. Marcus then snapped a salute and withdrew from the tent.

As he and his aide, Julius, strode along in the darkness back to Marcus' tent, he told Julius about the mission.

Julius said, "Sir, may I ask a question?"

"What is it?"

"Could you have declined these orders?"

Marcus cut him a sharp glance. The question dashed his euphoria. "Why do you ask?" His voice was irritable.

Julius hesitated to answer.

"Why?" demanded Marcus. "Should I have done so?"

"The weather bodes ill now, sir, and the Oceanus Britannicus is noted for its sudden violent storms."

"Ah, the elements. Ha! They're the least of my concerns. I

don't believe in omens. Besides, have you forgotten? My specialty is weather. You watch. These clouds will blow over tomorrow."

Julius changed the subject. "Sir, this letter was handed to me while you were inside."

Marcus casually took the scroll. Back at the tent Marcus removed his uniform, lay down on his cot, and opened it. Presently, a smile broke over his face.

Julius was straightening the tent and asked, "Good news, sir?"

"It's from a woman I met in Rome last winter," he said, still reading. "A camp follower. I might have underestimated her, though. She writes a pretty good hand. Listen to this, 'I know you will excel in this campaign. My every waking thought is of you, and I entrust your well-being unto God in prayer. I hope you will look me up again when you return. Yours, Cecilia.'" Marcus gave a rare chuckle.

"Sounds like you are being pursued, sir."

"Pursued?" he echoed. "Maybe so."

What Marcus did not read was the paragraph that said, "Since you were here, I have had a profound experience. I do not know how to explain what happened to me except to say that I met someone . . . yes, that is it. I met someone who changed my life. His name? Jesus. I'll never be the same again. Marcus, I so want you to meet him too. I hope you will let me introduce you to him when you return."

On rereading this, twin, vertical wrinkles creased his brow. *"Jesus." Sounds Jewish. Must be someone from among the Hebrews she runs with.*

And yet, the name Jesus struck an inexplicable chord in his soul. A moment of truth suddenly dawned on him, as vivid as the rising of the sun. Julius' words, "You are being pursued, sir," inspired a meaning far more profound than their original intent. *I AM being pursued,* he thought. *I feel it. But who is my pursuer? Who is this Jesus?* So profound was the feeling of a mysterious Presence in the tent at that moment that it overshadowed all concern about the coming invasion. A shudder went through his body and the cot groaned.

Julius exclaimed, "Is something the matter, sir?"

"What?" said Marcus, opening his eyes and looking around in surprise. "Oh, no. Don't worry. I must be tired."

The momentary apprehension was gone.

ROMAN TRI

REME GALLEY

*The best laid schemes o' mice and men
Gang aft a-gley.*

Robert Burns

# CHAPTER TWO

## GALLIA
## SPRING AD 43

MARCUS WAS RIGHT. By morning the clouds had dissipated, and his troops spent the day in orientations, communication exercises, training, supplying, and weapons preparation. Marcus stayed up most of both nights, planning logistics, routes, tactics, and the hundreds of other details he had to master in so short a time. His last word to the commanders of the other nine galleys at their final briefing was, "Gentlemen, be alert. The Britannicus can be treacherous."

The galley fleet disembarked soon after dawn on Day One. They were to lead the whole flotilla northward to the British coast in case they did encounter any naval resistance; then, if the coast was clear, to continue northward around the Isle of Tanatus and westward into the Tamesis Gulf.

All seemed propitious. A strong southerly wind prevailed throughout the day enabling the galleys to hoist their sails and ride the wind, giving the rowers a rest. Marcus' chest heaved with pride and excitement. He could taste victory already. Yet he was careful not to let his guard down. His mind was feverishly active throughout the voyage, reviewing plans, monitoring inter-ship communications, attending to the thousands of details incident to such a mass operation. Marcus was a detail man.

Yet a sense of disquietude kept gnawing at him.

*What is it? Oh, ho! the weather. Why is a southerly wind so strong? No, can it be? Are we being sucked into a storm?*

Marcus had a dreaded premonition. Past reports of storms upon the Oceanus Britannicus cascaded through his mind. He had sailed upon all parts of the Great Sea, but no storm in the whole Empire was said to compare with a storm on the Oceanus Britannicus.

Long before the least trace of any clouds appeared in the sky, Marcus stationed himself upon the bow of the lead ship and gazed without distraction toward the north. The wind pushed them swiftly, and by mid-afternoon the sight of the British coast appeared on the horizon. The sea was utterly placid. Soon they were cruising along with the coast on their port side, rapidly approaching the invasion site—the natural harbor at Rutupiae.

*There it is!*

Marcus signaled Drusus' vessel and watched it veer coastward with its flotilla behind. Then he turned back around to confront a nightmare! Dark clouds boiled on the horizon! A storm was bearing down on them at phenomenal speed.

"Strike the sails. Batten the hatches. Man the oars. Signal the same to the others," shouted Marcus.

No need to signal the nearby galleys. They could hear his voice!

Swiftly the fleet was readied for the onslaught. Marcus looked back and confirmed that Drusus' flotilla had attained the harbor, seemingly without opposition. They, at least, would be spared the worst of the storm.

The southerly wind gradually died away, leaving the sea as slick as glass for a few minutes. The beats of the drums of the dozen galleys resounded across the waters and curiously fell into the same tempo. Gradually the wind turned northward. An overcast sky began to darken the sea like the shadow of a titan menacing toy boats on a pond. Suddenly, the placidity of the sea changed into a caldron of waves and foam. Tall breakers fell over one another on all sides. Marcus could feel the bow of the galley rising repeatedly beneath his feet, then dropping so suddenly as to leave him virtually suspended in midair. The keel repeatedly struck the surface of the sea like a giant mother spanking her child.

"Hold her steady into the wind," Marcus shouted back to the pilot.

He glanced back to see the pilot wrestling the teller with all his might, never sure from moment to moment whether the rudders were controlling him or he the rudders. No rain was falling, though the breakers washed more water across the decks than any rainstorm could have done. After an hour the legendary mist of the Britannicus started rolling in, effectively separating the ships from a view of one another. Marcus sensed dire calamity.

"Start sounding the horn," he shouted.

A nearby soldier dropped into the hold to retrieve a battered bronze *bucina*, a curved trumpet. Tooo-uuuut! Tooo—uuuut! Then a pause. Tooo-uuuut! echoed another trumpet across the waves, then another, then another.

*I hope this keeps us together.*

The ship was continually climbing the crests and falling into the troughs of the ferocious waves.

*We're safe so long as we steer northward, but at some point we must turn west to reach our destination. But I can't turn these vessels crosswise the wind; they'll swamp.*

Unconsciously, Marcus glanced down into the open hold. Water was rising. "Bilge pumps," he shouted. Two soldiers pulled in their oars and rushed over to a series of buckets affixed to a belt. They started turning the opposing handles of a pulley, thereby pulling the buckets from the bilge to the outrigger and dumping water over the side of the galley before returning to the bilge. When this did not prove adequate, several more men formed a bucket brigade from the hold to the deck on the starboard side.

By now dusk was settling in and the storm had not abated the least. They had long since lost sight of land. Marcus began to weigh his alternatives. He finally decided to reduce the rowers to the minimum necessary to ride out the storm and let as many as possible get some sleep, sitting in place. When this order was conveyed and men let go of their oars, many of them promptly fell sick.

*There won't be much sleep for them. It's going to be a long night. Hopefully, the storm will be over by morning.*

And so it went throughout the night—some trying to sleep, some regurgitating over the side of the ship, trumpets blaring constantly, rowers alternating by shifts, drums sounding incessantly. Fatigue overcame Marcus early in the evening and he ordered the First Mate to take over while he retreated to a small cabin in the bow to rest.

"It's daybreak, sir!" Marcus was awakened by a knock on his door. Groggily he arose.

*Amazing! Slept all night. Just as well. Nothing more I could do anyway. Curse this storm!*

The gyrations of the ship were as severe as earlier. Going up on deck Marcus faced the same impenetrable mist as before. It was daytime, but he could scarcely see ten feet beyond the deck. He discerned that the sunrise was to their starboard side which confirmed they were still headed northward. Approaching the First Mate at the bow, Marcus asked, "Give me a situation report."

"Everything's under control, sir. So far. Don't know how fast the wind's blowing so don't know how far we've sailed. Not far, I fear, against this wind. Frankly, I don't know where we are."

"The other galleys?" asked Marcus.

"Think I could hear all the trumpets throughout the night. Hopefully, we're all still together."

"The crew?"

"As good as can be expected, sir. They're all strong and well-trained. They can stand a lot. I've been forcing them to drink plenty of water, especially the ill. Keep them from dehydrating."

"Good!" said Marcus. "They need salt, too. Before you retire, find the cask of salt in the equipment locker in my cabin and have someone feed a half a spoonful to each man. Also, have the mess officer distribute crackers and nut-butter to all the men to give them sustenance."

"Yes, sir. Will do!"

Little changed throughout the second day. Occasionally, the mist would lift sufficiently for Marcus to glimpse one or two of the other ships around him, but it would have been suicide to attempt to approach them. They carried no long boats, both for space and speed. Finally, about dusk, the sea began to grow calm.

"Call the ships together," Marcus said to the trumpeter.

The trumpeter blew a signal consisting of three short notes followed by a sustained note.

"Slow down but stay alert."

The tempo drum slowed its beat. Presently out of the fog appeared the ghoulish rams-head of one of the boats. Gradually, the others appeared. They coordinated their speeds and carefully came together. Danger abounded. The bronze battering rams at water level on the fronts of the galleys were made to sink enemy vessels. One slip could pierce the side of another galley. All the ships were accounted for. They all came to a halt in the water and men lashed them together, enabling the various centurions to cross from ship to ship to reach Marcus' command boat. Night was settling in. A dozen or so officers crowded onto Marcus' deck for a conference.

"Gentlemen, we're in serious trouble," said Marcus. "Here is our predicament. Day Two is already past and we must somehow rendezvous at Medway bridge within one more day. We don't even know where we are. All night and all day we think we remained on a northward course into the wind. Agreed?"

Everyone nodded in agreement.

"Good! Now we must turn westward. I will turn my craft to port immediately and resume the lead through the night.

Hopefully, I can sustain a consistently westward bearing. Stay alert for land, lest we run aground. Perchance through the night the fog will lift and we can correct our bearings from the stars."

Marcus dismissed the centurions and they returned to their respective ships. When his ship was untied from the adjoining ships, Marcus had his steersman turn precisely to port and the drumming, rowing, and trumpeting resumed. Marcus again retired for the night, with orders for the watch to awaken him for the least cause.

Marcus aroused before daybreak and went up on deck.

*Day three! Curses! The fog abides. At least there were no incidents throughout the night.*

Finally, at dawn the fog began to burn off. The sea remained calm. Hastily, Marcus measured the location of the sun and calculated their bearings: they were headed west by south. Land appeared on the horizon directly ahead.

*What is it?*

He quickly consulted his maps.

*Tamesis peninsula! Eureka! Our destination!*

"Hoist the sails," he shouted. "We're going in."

A cheer went up from the crew. All the ships were still together. They beached and Marcus gathered and briefed the centurions, posted guards on the ships, and began a forced march toward Durobrivae. Though weary, they marched southwest in high spirits, expecting to intercept the Medway River at any time. After having trod rapidly through the balance of the morning, they topped a hill and looked down to see a long body of water.

"It's the river," someone shouted.

"Not, it's not. It's the sea!" cried another.

"Halt!" Marcus ordered. "Julius, the map case."

Young Julius handed him the map case, and the other centurions came over. While Marcus studied the map, they pointed and conversed. As far as they could see, a wide body of water separated them from the opposite shore.

"That's not a river," one of them said.

"We're not where we thought we were," Marcus angrily shouted. "Our maps are not detailed enough. We're on an island—Sheppey Island."

Marcus flung the map into the air and started cursing. He jerked off his helmet, threw it on the ground, and with a savage yell attacked it with his short sword, hacking it to pieces. Then he brutally started slicing the air around him in an uncontrollable rage. For a long time he strode back and forth along the slope of the hill bitterly denouncing his fate and the capriciousness of the elements. Even battle-hardened veterans shrank from him in trepidation. Finally, he sank to the ground in a pathetic heap.

"All is not lost, Hippalus."

Marcus looked up into the face of another centurion. "What hope is there, Anthony?" Marcus said as he wearily rose to his feet. "There's no way we can cross that bay. It's over. We're defeated."

"Consider this. Why not send a runner back to the ships and have them sail around here and transport us across the bay?"

Marcus turned without comment and retrieved the map from his aide. After studying it a moment, a flicker of hope passed over his face.

"Julius," he said to his young aide, "can you run?"

"Try me, sir."

"Can you run far?"

"Yes, sir!"

"Here's what we need." Marcus began a short briefing. Finally, he said, "When you get to the coast, have the guards consolidate and man three of our largest galleys and sail here immediately. Just leave the other galleys there. Do you understand?"

"Yes, sir!" said Julius.

"Good! Then hurry!"

Julius ate a light meal, donned fresh sandals, and disappeared over the hill at an impressive pace. It was high noon.

His shoulders sagging, Marcus walked over to the edge of a bluff, flung his arms out and shouted, "Oh, cruel nature." His huge voice echoed from hill to hill.

"You are my real enemy."

Enemy! Enemy!

"You think you have beat me."

Beat me! Beat me!

"But you have not won yet."

Yet! Yet!

"I'll have the last say."

Say! Say!

The afternoon wore on. Gradually the sun sank beneath the horizon. Marcus could neither eat nor sleep. Dawn would bring Day Four and the words of Drusus rang in his ears, "I plan to have my troops at the bridge by Day Four..."

The night seemed unending. After midnight he expected the ships to appear at any moment. They did not.

As the sun was rising the cry sounded, "Here they come."

Up the channel between the island and the mainland sailed, not three, but two ships. Marcus hastened down to the water's edge. The ships had not stopped moving before Marcus shouted to Julius on the deck of the lead galley, "Blast it. I told you three ships, not two. What took you so long? This is Day Four!"

"The guards were so few they refused to man more than two vessels. Also since the wind was contrary, they chose to come the long way around the island. We were fortunate to get here this early."

"The wind! A curse on the wind. Everybody on board."

"Everybody?" said a centurion. "Have you gone insane? There's no way we can get everybody on board two vessels. I'll keep my troops here. Send them back across for us."

Marcus turned around angrily and said, "Back across? We're not going across. We're sailing all the way to Durobrivae. Whose ships are these?"

"Mine." "Mine," said two of the centurions.

"We don't have time to hassle," said Marcus. "It's already Day Four. Both of you, get your centuries on board. I'll board mine, and Anthony you also take yours aboard. That'll give us four centuries at least. We can take the bridge. Move it! The rest of you stay here. I'll send the galleys back for you. Let's go."

The Medway River had never seen the likes of the two crowded

Roman galleys sailing through its mouth that morning. The wind picked up and pushed them rapidly up the river. They had sailed for about a half hour when Marcus saw black smoke boiling up from the landscape ahead of them. His heart sank. Human bodies floated past them toward the sea, yet no clash of armies in contact could be heard. Gradually, the situation came clear. The battle was over!

Soon they were cruising past buildings along the low banks of the Medway. They were in the outskirts of Durobrivae. Destruction was everywhere. Marcus stubbornly sailed forward toward the bridge. As they rounded a curve in the river, he saw where the bridge had been, but it was now only a smoldering ruin engulfed in black smoke. It had been destroyed! Marcus could make out the ruins of the bridge abutments. Standing on the right bank was a familiar figure.

"Marcus Hippalus. You're under arrest. Get off that deck and report to me NOW!"

It was Appius Drusus.


Marcus learned that Drusus' forces had arrived at Medway bridge early that morning of Day Four. Advance word of their invasion had reached Londinium earlier, and the forces of several tribes had arrived at Durobrivae on Day Three, burned the bridge, and set up a defensive action on the north bank of the river. The Romans had to fight a major battle to break through the Brits, costing the legion mass casualties, losses that Drusus thought could have been prevented had Marcus' force reached there on time and secured the bridge. The total blame for the fiasco fell on Marcus Hippalus. Drusus was enraged. He was a man of fiery temperament, and he would not stand for excuses. Marcus explained about the weather on the Oceanus but he would not hear it. He threatened to have Marcus slain on the spot and desisted only when he learned his navy had suffered no loss of men, ships, or equipment through it all. Marcus was led away in chains.

A month later Marcus stood before the entire XX Roman Legion, assembled in dress formation on the north bank of the River Tamesis near Londinium, as the Emperor Claudius, a cripple and a stutterer, read the official charges against him.

"Centurion Hippalus, da-da-da-do you have anything to say before I sa-sa-sa-sign your court martial?"

"Your Highest, I protest my innocence," said Marcus in the hearing of everyone assembled. "I have not been guilty of dereliction of duty nor of any other charge. If anything, I admit guilt only in underestimating the significance of the wind. If I am given another chance, I can develop into a fine soldier for Rome, and I will."

Claudius looked over at Appius Drusus, who by a slight shake of his head indicated disagreement. Claudius picked up the scroll again and read, "Ba—BY court martial order I now sentence you to dishonorable discharge from the military forces of Rome."

Marcus shouted out, "You haven't seen the last of me. I'll be back."

Guards unsheathed their swords to strike him down, but Claudius waved his hand.

"Let him be. Hi-hi-hi-his sentence is enough."

Claudius bent over a field desk and signed the court martial.

Drusus stepped forward and motioned for Julius, Marcus' aide to join him. "Sir," said Julius, "must I?"

"That's an order," growled Drusus irritably.

Julius obeyed and Drusus motioned for him to stand on the other side of Marcus. As they both began unfastening Marcus' military uniform, Marcus stood erect, staring out over the Tamesis. A crude cart with solid wooden wheels, pulled by an ox, was being led down to the riverside where Roman engineers were constructing a new bridge.

Julius glanced pitifully up into his face. Marcus' eyes were awash with tears.

ROMAN CENTURION

*There is a tide in the affairs of men,*
*Which taken at the flood, leads on to fortune;*
*Omitted, all the voyage of their life*
*Is bound in shallows and in miseries.*

          Shakespeare

# CHAPTER THREE

## ROME
## SUMMER AD 43

IN ROME THAT summer a fanfare of trumpets heralded the arrival of Caesar Claudius at the city's north gate, the Porta Flaminia. A roar went up from the crowd. Thousands of people were assembled in the plaza and along the Via Flaminia, waving brightly colored pennants above their heads. Shops along the thoroughfare were all closed this mid-morning hour and banners and pennants festooned the buildings. Through the gate first came the troops of the emperor's Praetorian Guards dressed smartly in parade uniforms and marching in cadence, their hobnailed sandals loudly percussing the cobblestone street in rhythmic fashion.

Next came slaves bearing loot confiscated from the Brits—intricately woven rugs, tapestries, bronze bells, stone busts, swords, spears, metal armor. Fools cartwheeled along beside them or threw candy to the children.

Vigorous applause arose as the emperor's four-wheeled carriage rolled along the avenue led by a corps of blaring trumpets and rolling drums. Plain-faced Claudius rode alone in the carriage and waved amiably to the people. Four Legionnaires, or *legatus legioni*, commanders of the four legions involved in the conquest of Britain (among them was Appius Drusus as well as Titus Flavius Vespasianus, otherwise known as Vespasian, commander of the II Legion) rode horses on either side of Claudius' carriage. Their stiff military bearing forbade their acknowledging the cheers of the crowd.

Behind the emperor walked the prisoners. First were Caractacus and Togodumnus in chains, the erstwhile ruling brothers of Britain, passionately arguing with each other along the way. Following them were ragged soldiers, muscular youth in civilian dress, and various others, all bound for slavery. Behind them were cartloads of women stripped to the waist. Last of all came the Praetorian horsemen.

In the crowd at the plaza stood Marcus Hippalus, a valise in hand with his face half hidden beneath a straw hat. He was alone. Drusus did not see him, but Marcus stared long at Drusus with a look of hatred as he rode past.

*Why could that not be me? Just eight years his junior—with altogether as much ability.*

Long after the parade was over and the crowd had dispersed, Marcus found himself standing alone, not knowing what to do.

*Rome!*

Ashamed to return to Turris, he had come here to get lost in the crowd. His robe was long and nondescript. He wished he were not so tall. He bore a commanding presence, even in his humiliation.

*Maybe my bearing intimidated Drusus.*

Nonchalantly, Marcus hailed a horse-drawn public carriage.

"Where to, mate?" said the driver.

"Seaman Tavern." Marcus slowly slid into the back seat.

"You a sailor, aren't you?"

Marcus did not reply.

"Used to be one myself. I can always tell 'em. You looking for a good time while you're ashore? I can tell you a good spot or two."

Marcus didn't respond.

"I get it. Don't feel like talking, eh? Okay. If you need anything, let me know."

A few blocks later the taxi pulled up to a two-story building with a sign in front in the shape of a flask with the word's "Seaman Tavern" on it.

"Here we are, mate. Seaman Tavern! You must be a sailor. I can always tell."

Marcus paid the fare but did not reply.

"Suit yourself, mate," said the driver and the carriage pulled away.

As he sat alone eating dinner at the Tavern that evening, Marcus brooded over his fate. He felt lonely. It had all happened so fast. Was there any meaning to it? Had the gods something against him? He had made some judgment errors, yes, but what more could have been expected from one thrust into such responsibility with so little experience? He would start blaming himself, then remind himself that, no, he was a victim; his nemesis was the wind. It had acted against him and there was nothing he could do about it.

When he was through eating, he approached the bar to pay and said, "Give me a flask of white wine, please." Taking the flask with him, he retired upstairs to his room for the night.

When he awakened the next morning, he had a terrific hangover. Swinging his aching legs out of bed, he placed his elbows on his knees and sat there awhile clasping his head in his hands.

*What now?*

The floor was paved with crude terra cotta tiles. The sun streaming through the window slats made a stripped pattern on the tile. The clacking of horse's hooves on the cobblestones echoed from below.

*What was her name? Cecilia? Can't even remember what she looked like. Why don't I try to find her?*

"I think I know who you're talking about," said a waiter in the Boar's Head Tavern, where Marcus had last seen Cecilia. "Short, shapely, blond." Her appearance came back to Marcus as the waiter described her. "But haven't seen her since last winter. No, wait a minute. She did come in once later on, but she had really changed. Wasn't the party-type I had remembered her to be. Last I knew she had an apartment on Clivus Scauri street."

Marcus trudged up the stairs to the fourth floor of a five story tenement building occupying a whole block. He rapped softly on a door. A dog started barking within. Presently, the door opened and Marcus looked down into the face of a woman in her early twenties.

*I had forgotten how homely she is. Marcus, you really know how to pick them. Just remember, though, you're no Apollo yourself.*

"Hi!" he said.

"Marcus. Marcus Hippalon? Right?"

"Hippalus, but it really doesn't matter. Call me whatever you like."

"I'm sorry. It was just a slip of the tongue. Of course I know your name. Do come in. I heard that Claudius came back into town yesterday. You must have returned with him."

Marcus did not correct her. The fact was that he had timed his arrival in Rome to give that very impression. He was enticed by her appearance in a short house toga, revealing the entire length of her shapely white legs.

"Pardon my appearance. I've been trying to stay cool in this hot apartment. I'll go change. The dog's name is Caesar."

The small three-room apartment was hot and stuffy. As Cecilia left, the dog came over to Marcus and he petted it as it sniffed his legs curiously. It was a beautiful, long-legged, white animal with black spots over its body, and small, floppy, black ears.

From the next room Cecilia said, "Oh, Marcus, I have so much to tell you."

He ambled over to a double door that opened onto a small balcony. Fortunately, the view looked down on a park, not another building; the ancient Porta Capena stood in the distance. But the balcony faced southward and the morning sun heated the floor inside. The apartment was alive with a sweet fragrance. He could hear Cecilia singing softly.

When she re-entered, in more modest attire, she said, "Let me fix us some lunch. Come into the kitchen and talk to me."

He followed her in. The kitchen was dimly lighted by a small opening to the outside in the wall above a white moveable cabinet. None of the cabinets was built-in. A small table stood in the corner with an urn of water sitting in a ceramic bowl. A waste water pot was on the floor underneath. The white plank floor had no covering save for a woven mat in front of the small table. A dining table sat in the middle of the room, barely large enough for two people, with a single chair next to it.

"Bring in a chair from the front room, would you please?" Cecilia said.

"Sure. Then why don't I just help you?"

"Why not? Here, take these bowls and wash them in the pan in the corner."

She lit a fire of coals in a metal pot on the cabinet.

"Did you get my letter? I'll bet you were a great hero in the British campaign."

"It's not as it seems," he said. "I was court—"

"Never mind," she said. "You got back safely. That's what counts. I'm so glad to see you. And I'm so pleased you looked me up."

"I received a great honor," he said, "but before it was over I—"

"I knew you would," she said. "When I first met you, you impressed me as a man of great ability. I've never before met anyone like you."

"I hope I never have another experience like the one I had at Durobrivae. It was awful."

He felt like weeping.

"I know," she said. "All that blood and carnage. But I can tell you weren't hurt. I don't know what I would have done if you had been."

"Cecilia, I wish I could tell you..."

He could not get the words out.

"Maybe later," she said. "It's not hard to tell you what has happened to me, though, since you left. You knew that I have these Jewish friends. I brought some of them with me to the Boars Head Tavern one night. You remember? I introduced you to them." She paused and laughed. "It was comical the way they hesitated to enter the tavern because it was called the Boar's Head. They said they're not supposed to have anything to do with hogs." She snickered again, and then continued, "Well, some of them were Christians and I went to some of their meetings. And that's when it was I met Lord Jesus, whom I mentioned to you in my letter."

Cecilia talked rapidly—as if she were about to explode. Marcus could not understand half of what she was saying, but he liked to listen to her sweet voice, and her chatter set him at ease. He gave up trying to pour out his problems to her and just listened throughout the meal.

Marcus grew more relaxed the longer he was in her presence. He forgot his hangover, forgot his disgrace for awhile, enjoyed her cooking, and helped clean up the dishes. Cecilia had changed. She had a new dignity—he knew he could not bring himself to offend it. For this reason, after lunch he said, "I must be going. I don't want to wear out my welcome."

"Marcus—" She had such an unusual way of pronouncing his name. He liked it. "I've so enjoyed our time together. Could you stop by tomorrow evening before dusk? I want to fix you a more sumptuous meal; and, if you would, I would like to have you escort me to a Christian meeting nearby. Say you'll do it."

"I'll do it." He smiled.

"This is my friend Marcus Hippalus, a centurion and trireme commander in Appius Drusus' legion. He's just returned from the conquest of Britain." Cecilia introduced Marcus to several men and women of the Christian church on the Via Appia.

Marcus wondered when he might meet "Lord Jesus," supposing from the way Cecilia talked about him that her new friend might soon appear. They were meeting after dark in a mortuary in a cemetery. About a hundred people were present and everyone seemed to richly enjoy the fellowship. The setting was casual and Marcus relaxed after a few moments. Most of them, though not all, were Jews but their singing and speaking were all in Latin. There was some enthusiastic, unaccompanied singing and some Scripture reading, mixed with prayers and testimonials, followed by a lesson from a teacher known as the "pastor" or "shepherd."

When the teacher's turn came, he said, "Before he was crucified, Jesus taught mainly among the Jewish people of Galilee—"

Crucified?

"One time after he finished teaching a large crowd, he loaded his twelve apostles into a boat and sent them across the sea of Galilee while he remained behind and prayed, up in the hills—"

The allusion to sailing caught Marcus' attention.

"It was the fourth watch of the night and the boat load of men encountered a violent headwind. They couldn't make any headway, and the waves were lashing over the sides of their boat—"

Marcus sat up straight at his mention of the wind.

"Jesus could see their distress from his vantage point. All of a sudden the rowing men looked up and saw Jesus walking past them. That's right! Walking on the water! In fact he was about to pass them by. One of the men cried out, 'It's a ghost.' Jesus then said, 'Take courage! It is I. Don't be afraid.' Then Peter, their spokesman, said, 'If it's you, tell me to come to you on the water—'

*This is preposterous!*

"Jesus just said, 'Come!' and Peter climbed down out of the boat, walked on the water, and went toward Jesus. However, when he realized suddenly what he was doing, he promptly started to sink. He cried out, 'Lord, save me!' Jesus quickly reached down, took his hand, and lifted him back up onto the water's surface. Jesus said, 'You of little faith, why did you doubt?' When they climbed back into the boat, the wind immediately died down. All the disciples exclaimed to Jesus, 'Truly you are the Son of God.'"

*What does faith have to do with it?*

"Now, you know Jesus taught a lot about faith. He encouraged everyone of us simply to put our trust in him and not be afraid. Obviously, his apostles had a weak faith in him—"

*What's this man getting at?*

Marcus looked around to see if people were taking the story seriously. All eyes were glued on the pastor.

"Now you may doubt this story, but it really happened. Most of those apostles are still alive today and they all vouch for it. It happened only about fifteen years ago."

"There are several lessons for us in that incident. First, no matter how great or what kind of storm we are in, the Lord Jesus sees us in it and will bring us through it safely. Second, we never have to be afraid. And third, we must maintain faith in Jesus at all times and under all circumstances . . ."

Marcus sat dumbfounded. He had never heard a teaching like that.

*What if it were true?*

He felt a strange peace come over him.

*I wonder when they will introduce Jesus himself. I'd like to hear him speak personally. But did he say he was 'crucified'?*

After the meeting, when he was walking Cecilia back to her apartment, Marcus asked, "Why wasn't Jesus there? And what was this about his being crucified? Did he live through a crucifixion?"

Cecilia laughed. "No, silly, of course not. I've never heard of anyone surviving a crucifixion, have you?"

"Then what is his story?"

"This happened about fifteen years ago. Jesus taught only about three years and then they crucified him."

"Who did?"

"The Romans. Pontius Pilate."

"I've heard of him," said Marcus. "He was deposed as procurator of Judea only about eight years ago. But how can you say you've met Jesus?"

"Because he came back to life again."

"What? Are you serious?" said Marcus.

"It's true. After three days he arose from the grave. Those apostles were there. They saw it all. He lived in Judea about another forty days afterward and then ascended into the sky to return to God."

"Is that what they say?"

"Hundreds of people vouch for it."

"Why haven't I heard about it before?"

"I don't know. I just heard about it last year myself," Cecilia said.

"I can't believe it."

"Did you notice what the pastor said tonight? He said Jesus taught the necessity of faith in him. You say, 'I can't believe it.' That's your choice. But you have a second choice, too, you know. You can choose to believe in him if you want to."

"I'll have to think about it," Marcus said. "Here's your apartment. I'll walk you upstairs."

In front of her door Marcus said, "Cecilia, I've really been enjoying your company. That meal tonight was scrumptious. I wonder. May I kiss you?"

The dog was barking inside.

Cecilia rose on her tiptoes and permitted him to kiss her. He embraced her in his large arms and experienced a delicious warming within. She settled down on her heals and took out a large key.

"Here," he said, "Let me put that into the lock for you. There you are. Hello there, Caesar."

Cecilia knelt down and took Caesar's head between her hands, drawing it close to her face. "Good old Caesar. Have you been a good boy while I've been gone?"

The dog's rear end wagged in delight.

"Do you mind if I come inside?" asked Marcus.

"I'm sorry. I have to clean and straighten up tonight. Will you come see me tomorrow—in the morning?"

"You can count on it. Good night, Cecilia."

The next morning as Marcus came down the stairs from his room he glanced toward the bar and on impulse decided to have a drink. He just wanted a little bracer. He did not know why he was so nervous.

*Cecilia's new maturity makes me uncomfortable. Or was it that Christian meeting last night? Hmm! I'm as good as they are. What have I got to worry about?*

"Cup of strong wine, please."

Marcus downed it in one gulp and stood there a moment. He was relaxing already.

"One more please."

He paid and walked out toward Cecilia's.

As Marcus entered her apartment, Cecilia allowed him to kiss her on the cheek, while Caesar stood beside her wagging his tail. Marcus made sure to show him some attention too. Unseen to Marcus, Cecilia frowned and screwed up her nose but continued her good-natured chatter as though she had not noticed the smell of wine on his breath.

"Come over to the table. I have something interesting I want to show you."

A scroll lay furled on the table. She sat down. "Here, sit down beside me and let me show you."

Before seating himself, Marcus bent over and smelled of her hair, then raised her blond tresses and kissed her on the back of the neck.

Gently pushing his hand away, she pulled the chair out for him and proceeded to unroll the scroll. "This is my pride and joy. I don't own very many scrolls, but this is my best. I copied it down at the church. You might not can read my handwriting."

"You have sexy handwriting. Remember, I have one of your letters," Marcus said.

"This is from the Hebrew Psalms. Number two, I believe. It's very old. Probably written by a King David about eleven centuries ago. But this one's in Latin. Here, follow me as I read it."

"Okay," Marcus said, but he kept looking at her face.

"'Why do the heathen rage, and the people imagine a vain thing? The kings of the earth set themselves, and the rulers take counsel together, against the Lord, and against his anointed.'" She stopped and said, "I'll give a little interpretation."

Cecilia glanced at Marcus and saw he was admiring her. Blushing, she diverted her eyes back to the manuscript.

"You're not listening to what I'm reading."

"Yes, I am, too," he said. But he kept looking at her.

"See, 'Lord' is the word used to describe God; not a god, but the only God, the God of all heaven and earth. Now notice that it talks about 'his anointed,' who was someone special. This refers to the Messiah or the Christ, which means 'the anointed one.' Now let's see what it says about Christ. 'Saying, let us break their bands asunder, and cast away their cords from us.' This was a prediction. It was predicting that kings would take counsel against Christ. That literally happened, fifteen years ago. Pilot and Herod, both kings, you might say, took counsel together with the Jews to have Jesus crucified. It says the reason was to break his bands on them. You see, our human nature does not want to be bound by the laws of God, and we all have a tendency to want to break his laws and his constraints upon our lives."

Marcus' face grew grave and he glanced down to see what she had just read. Cecilia remained silent a moment. Then she continued, her finger pointing to the line she was reading.

"'He that sitteth in the heavens shall laugh: the Lord shall have them in derision.' You see, no matter how we may rebel against him, God is still God and he remains in control of all things. 'Then shall he speak unto them in his wrath, and vex them in his sore displeasure.' God is a mighty God and has wrath for people's sins and rebellion against him. 'Yet have I set my king upon my holy hill of Zion.' At his trial Pilate asked Jesus if he were a king, as he was accused of claiming to be. He admitted he was. But he is not an earthly king. He called his realm the 'kingdom of heaven' or the 'kingdom of God,' and everyone on earth who follows Jesus is a member of his kingdom."

Marcus was beginning to get nervous and impatient. He fidgeted with his hands and sat back in his chair.

Cecilia continued reading, "I will declare the decree the Lord hath said unto me, Thou art my Son; this day have I begotten thee.' Marcus, you may have wondered who Jesus really is. Well, it says here that he is the Son of God. You see, this is not just another religion. Not at all. It's not like any other religion that has ever been on the face of the earth. Jesus was a man who really lived—just a few years ago. But he was one of a kind. In reality he was the Son of God, come down to earth to give eternal life to all who will accept him. His Father is the solitary God of the universe, the only God, the one who created all things—you, me, the sun, the moon, the wind, the—"

Marcus abruptly stood up letting his chair fall backward to the floor with a crash.

"'The *wind*?' I've heard enough of this nonsense. Let's do something real."

He reached down, wrapped his arms around Cecilia, lifted her bodily, and carried her toward the bedroom.

"Marcus, what are you doing?"

He had an evil grin on his face.

"Please, put me down. Don't do this!"

He dumped her on the bed. Then, glaring at her, he unfastened his sash, and took off his robe. "Marcus, no! I'm not like that anymore."

Her voice was rising in panic. He leaped on top of her and began clawing at her toga. She screamed.

Caesar bounded through the doorway in a flash and made a lung for Marcus' throat. He saw the dog just in time to swing his powerful arm outward, hitting the dog and knocking it across the room and up against the wall. The dog let out a pathetic yelp and crumpled to the floor—bleeding and lifeless.

Cecilia, jumped off the bed, pulling her robe back around her, and rushed to Caesar. She knelt down beside the dog.

"Marcus, what have you done? Caesar! Caesar! Oh! No!" She screamed! "He's dead. Oh, Caesar."

She lifted his bleeding head and hugged him to her.

Marcus stumbled out of bed, put on his robe, and stood over her. Holding his head in both hands, he cried out, "What have I done? Oh, Cecilia. Forgive me. I don't know what got into me. What am I? Oh, help me!"

Cecilia huddled over Caesar crying. Then, through tear-filled eyes, she looked up at Marcus. "How could you? What kind of monster are you? Get out of my apartment! Get out of my life! I never want to see you again. DO YOU HEAR?"

Marcus staggered over, gently pushed Cecilia aside, and picked up the dog. "Oh, Caesar." Then looking around with tears coursing down his face, he said, "Oh, Cecilia. I'm sorry. I'm so sorry. Can you ever forgive me?"

He cuddled the dog in his arms and walked out of the bedroom and out the front door.

Cecilia threw herself across the bed and sobbed.

Early one evening in Seaman Tavern, a tall, slender, distinguished-looking youth approached the bar. "That drunk over there. The one sitting by himself. Do you know him?"

The bar tender in a white apron, drying a mug, glanced toward the drunk, but didn't say anything.

"I think I know him," the youth said. Does he go by the name of Hippalus?"

"That's what he calls himself, mate. Friend of yours, you say? He's been sitting at that same table morning, noon, and night the last several days. Toward closing time every night, several men have to carry him upstairs to his room."

"I think I know what's bothering him," said the youth. He walked over to the table and sat down opposite Marcus. "Marcus Hippalus, do you remember me?"

Marcus had not noticed him when he sat down. He looked

up. His eyes were bloodshot, his face pale. He stared at the youth a moment and blinked his eyes. "Gaius Plinius Secundus," he said in a mutter. "You're the first friend I've seen in a long time."

"Marcus, I think I know what's bothering you."

"You do, huh?

"Yes, Appius Drusus told me."

"Appius Drusus!!" Marcus said with a roar, slamming his palm down on the table, sloshing beer out of his mug. "That sniveling idiot."

"Calm down, Marcus. I don't agree with Drusus. I think he did you an injustice, and I told him so. He shouldn't have had you court martialed for merely getting caught in the weather. It wasn't your fault."

"That's what I tried to tell him, but he wouldn't listen. I got to Durobrivae as soon as I could. I couldn't help the delay," Marcus said.

"I want to help you. I've got an idea. But first, let's get you over this stupor. Okay?"

"Uh. I guess so."

"Good," said Pliny. "Let's get you to your room so you can sleep this off. You have a room here upstairs, don't you?"

"Uh."

"Good. Come on, let me help you."

Marcus stood up and reached down for a flask of wine.

"No," said Pliny. "Why don't you just leave that here? You need to dry out, don't you think?"

"Uh."

With Marcus' arm over his shoulder, Pliny helped him up the staircase and to his room and dumped him into bed. No sooner had his head hit the pillow than he was fast asleep, snoring.

The next morning when Marcus came downstairs into the bar, Pliny was already sitting there. "Here, Marcus! Good morning. Let me order you some breakfast."

"Let me order a drink, first."

"No, you're going to need to be fully sober for what I have to say. Why don't you just lay off the flask for awhile?"

"Okay, I guess," Marcus said.

It took several more such days before Marcus finally got his senses back. Then, at a noon meal Pliny said, "Let me tell you what I have in mind and see what you think of it. How would you like to get into the Alexander-Rome grain shipping trade?"

"Tell me about it," Marcus said.

"I know a man who owns a ship, who's going to be needing a skipper pretty soon. Now, it's an old ship, mind you, but he's having it completely refurbished at the present time. I could give him your name, if you like."

"Perhaps so," Marcus said. "I'd at least like to talk to him."

At noontime the next day Marcus and Pliny were sitting together in Seaman Tavern making idle conversation. "Tell me where you are from," Marcus said.

"I was born and raised in a small town in northern Italy. Near Verona."

"What are you doing in Rome these days."

"I'm a lawyer."

"You've done pretty well for yourself at such a young age. Being acquainted with Appius Drusus—working as a lawyer. May I ask how old you are?"

"I'm nineteen. I've just been lucky, I guess. Excuse me."

Half rising Pliny motioned to someone at the door. "Decius, over here."

A middle-aged man walked over. "Marcus, I'd like you to meet Decius Commodus. Decius, this is Marcus Hippalus."

"You're not the younger brother to Felix Hippalus, are you?" asked Decius.

"None other than," said Marcus.

"He's a freight captain down south, plying the Mare Arabian between Egypt and India. I met him once in Alexandria. He told me about you," Decius said.

"That's right," replied Marcus, "he's—

Pliny cut in. "I told you this is one of the finest upcoming skippers on the Great Sea. He's had a misfortune lately, though. Marcus led the vanguard in the conquest of Britain recently. Appius Drusus himself put him in charge of all the warships of his legion. Unfortunately, while he was sailing toward his rendezvous point, a vicious storm struck his fleet and delayed his arrival. Drusus got so mad he had him discharged from the military."

"You were on the Mare Britannicum when a storm struck?" Decius asked Marcus.

"Yes."

"How many ships were in your command?"

"Ten triremes and quadriremes."

"How many did you lose?"

"None."

"None, huh? Not bad. I've never been to England before, but storms on the Britannicum are reportedly the worst in the world. Would you be interested in plying the calmer waters between here and Alexandria?"

"I might," Marcus said. "Tell me about your ship."

"I just acquired it recently. My first. It's called the *Syracuse*. It's early Tiberius, so it's not as sleek and modern as today's vessels. But it will hold a lot of grain, and that's what I'm concerned about."

"Where is it now?" asked Marcus.

"At a shipyard in Puteoli near Naples."

"Before I make a decision, I'd like to see the ship. Do you mind if I go there first?"

"I'd be happy for you to do so," Decius said. "Let me write out a letter of introduction for you so you can board the vessel. If you decide to accept the offer, let me know by post and you can just stay down there and take command of the ship when it's finished. It should be ready any time now. Send notification to me when it's ready and I'll immediately journey down there and join you. I will stand the expense of the crew and pay you per each successful shipment. Okay?"

Marcus nodded in agreement.

"If you do not choose to accept the job, please let me know posthaste. I'll leave the offer open for two weeks."

"Agreed," Marcus said. "I'll leave for Puteoli tomorrow."

Decius went to the bar and borrowed an inkwell. Then he lifted a satchel to the table, pulled out a blank sheet of papyri and a pen and wrote out a letter of introduction for Marcus.

That evening Marcus walked over to Cecilia's apartment. When he knocked on her door, a woman stuck her head out the door of an adjacent apartment and said, "If you're looking for Cecilia, she doesn't live here anymore. She moved out several days ago."

"Do you know where she moved?"

"I have no idea. She didn't say."

*I can never get away from my God! If I go up to heaven, you are there; if I go down to the place of the dead, you are there. If I ride the morning winds to the farthest oceans, even there your hand will guide me, your strength support me. If I try to hide in the darkness, the night becomes light around me. For even darkness cannot hide from God; to you the night shines as bright as day. Darkness and light are both alike to you.*

Living Bible

# CHAPTER FOUR

## PUTEOLI, ITALY
## LATE SUMMER AD 43

"THEY'VE DONE A good job fixing her up," said Marcus. "But before you accept it, I recommend you have them make other changes: first, have them add an *artemon* (a foresail)."

Marcus and Decius were in the Puteoli shipyard examining Decius' newly-acquired freighter. The 175-foot-long ship, moored in repose beside the dock, was banana-shaped, its stern ending in the *aplustre* in the form of the head of a swan kissing its neck. A balcony with a fancy bannister around it protruded behind the stern, cantilevered—an afterthought—containing the captain's tent. Lashed to the ship's sides directly in front of the swan's neck were two paddle rudders. On the deck in front of these was a deck house with bannisters around the top of it, the officers and passengers cabins. A single mast was mid-center of the ship, and the ship's boat sat on the deck forward of this. The sides of the ship met at the prow and swept upward into a square surface on which was carved a helmeted head. The name *Syracuse* was painted on either side of the deck house.

No one was around the ship at the time, but men were working on various other ships, some in the water, others propped up on land, throughout the shipyard. Coastal clouds drifted lazily inland.

Motioning with his hands, Marcus said, "It would have a shorter mast, leaning out over the prow like this, and would be rigged with a smaller sail, square, similar to the mainsail. This would add to the steering ability and enable me to maneuver better in a harbor. Also, it would add considerably more cloth—you know, increase the speed."

Decius' face brightened at the mention of more speed, as Marcus had hoped.

"I'll see," Decius said. He started walking up the gangplank followed by Marcus. Together they toured the deck, chatting casually. Next they lighted a torch and went below deck to walk through the windowless crew billets, latrines, ship's store, and mess facility. Then they climbed down into the cavernous hold where the grain would be stored. The area was surprisingly clean and dry.

"It will hold 1,300 tons of grain," Marcus said. "The first thing I examined down here was the foundation of the mast."

The flickering torch illuminated the massive timber of the mast, descending from the ceiling and anchoring at its lowest point to the keel.

"This one looks very secure. Obviously it's never been through a big storm before. But a setup like this, by Jove, has been the death of more ships than any other single factor I know of. In a storm the constant swaying of the tall mast continually exercises the keel and its surrounding boards, until the hull eventually starts to leak. That's the main reason they sink in storms. I contend they need to build ships with two masts, to reduce the stress and distribute it to other areas. Possibly, even three for the larger ships. Anyway, I recommend you have the ship smiths add some heavy cross members between the keel and the adjoining longitudinal ribs in this vicinity, just in case. You wouldn't want to lose a valuable cargo."

"I see your point and I'll give it serious consideration. Any other recommendations?"

"No, that's all. Let's talk terms."

They climbed back up on deck and discussed Marcus' employment. Decius concluded his offer, saying, "And I'll pay you a retainer fee through the winters between sailing seasons—beginning immediately. We're virtually at the end of the season now so it wouldn't hurt just to leave the ship here for the additional repairs you recommend. Would you be willing to remain with it and oversee the work? If you would, I'd authorize you to inspect it and accept its final delivery. I have other investments in Rome I need to oversee and probably won't be back down here this winter. Would you accept these arrangements?"

"It's agreed," said Marcus.

"Fine. I'm glad to have you, and I think we can have a good working relationship."

They shook hands.

"Why don't you just hire a good crew from this Naples area," Decius said. "It's the shipping capitol of the world and you'll have plenty of qualified men to choose from. You may proceed on to Alexandria from here next spring at the earliest possible shipping date according to the almanac. I'll leave that to your discretion."

The sky over Ostia was as angry as a lioness robbed of her cubs as the *Syracuse* sailed into harbor one summer morning the next year. Clouds tumbled violently over one another, winds whisked erratically, lightning like titanic arrows crashed to the ground. Marcus, drenched to the skin, stood atop the deckhouse shouting directions to the helmsman. It was not raining at the time, but they had obviously just come through a shower.

Slowly the *Syracuse* threaded its way through the array of other ships which were moored or anchored at Rome's harbor city. Decius, wrapped in a weather coat, was standing alone at the grain wharf, watching. As the ship approached the wooden dock and bumped gently against it, Marcus nimbly leaped over the railing onto the pier while the crew tied up the vessel. He strode over to Decius. "Sir, your first grain shipment," he said and waved his hand toward the ship.

"Marcus Hippalus! What's taken you so long?" Decius shouted in anger. "Do you know what day this is?"

"Sir, it's—"

"It's July the first! You should have been here at least six weeks ago! I'm not pleased with you one iota! I've been coming out here every day for the past month watching for my ship! I've seen new ships and old ships, big ships and little ships, but mine . . ."

"Sir—"

"Do you realize it's been a year since I've even seen you? I entrusted the *Syracuse* to you to sail to Alexandria because I thought I could trust you. But no! You come dragging in here the middle of the summer. What do I get? One shipment for the *year*! At this rate you don't even have time for a second one. I haven't even made enough profit to pay the crew."

A bolt of lightning struck a nearby warehouse causing them both to jump.

"Sir—"

"I may relieve you of command. Direct the unloading tomorrow while I think it over."

"Decius Commodius, if you'll just listen to me. The wind was against me all the way . . ."

A look of awareness came over Marcus' face. *The wind! The wind! Always the wind! Woe is me!*

Decius ranted on. Finally, he stopped and said, "Are you listening to me?"

"I'm sorry. You're right. I've been cowed by the wind. It'll never happen again. If you'll only give me another chance."

"I hope I can get top dollar for this shipment. I don't know. I may have to sell the *Syracuse* if I don't. Go on and get in line for unloading. Then come to my office right afterward."

A cloudburst sent the two men scurrying for cover.

Later, the port authorities told Marcus the *Syracuse* could unload the next morning. Promptly, he turned the ship over to the first mate and caught a carriage into Rome. That night he slept above the Seaman Tavern.

That night Marcus sat alone in a desk chair in his room while the thunder rumbled outside. He thought back over his cruise to Alexandria. He had waited until mid-April to leave Puteoli because he had heard about storms in the Peloponnesians. Skirting far south he had reduced his speed near Cyrene lest he encounter the Syrtis Major sandbars. After loading in Alexandria, he had waited several days to sail. When he finally got the nerve, he had started eastward, sailing along the coast for safety, and had put in at both Tyre and Antioch to get the latest word on the weather.

*I've been a coward. I've let the wind master me. That does it! Never again! Marcus Hippalus, you've got it in you. Take control of your fate. To arms, big boy!*

Later, as he climbed into bed, the thought occurred to him that it was Sunday and the Christian church would have met that day. They could have told him where Cecilia had gone. Too late now.

*How I long to see her. To hear her forgiveness.*

In the middle of the night Marcus woke up with a plan. He sat up, lit a candle, and thought it out. He would execute it the next day.

Early the next morning, Marcus was back at the *Syracuse*. The clouds had past, and the atmosphere was cleansed and pure. A scent of freshness was in the air.

Marcus told the First Mate, "Cancel all shore leaves. Order all crew members to help the longshoremen unload the cargo. Prepare to sail for Alexandria immediately afterward."

"What? Half the crew has already gone ashore."

"Send someone after them. But don't waste time. Hire extras in their place if they don't show up by noon."

"Yes, sir. Will we winter in Alexandria? We may not have time to return. The westerly winds begin in August."

"We'll beat them."

"Aye, aye, sir," the First Mate said. He seemed challenged by the daring plan.

In late July Marcus burst into Decius' office in Rome and said, "Sir, shipment number two is in Ostia."

Decius rose from his table and stormed at Marcus, "Hippalus, where have you been? I ought to kill you! What did you do with my ship? I have arrest warrants out for you all over the empire! I told you to be at my office immediately after unloading!"

Marcus had a smile of confidence on his weathered face. When Decius had vented his wrath, Marcus said, "Did you hear me?"

There was a long pause. Decius finally said in a low tone, "I heard you." Gazing fiercely into Marcus' eyes, he said, "But I don't believe you. What kind of shenanigan are you trying to pull?"

"None! Your second grain shipment *is* in Ostia."

"Impossible!"

"Come and see for yourself."

As they rode along in a carriage, Marcus told the story. "The reason I didn't go to your office after the unloading was that I knew you would fire me."

"I was going to." Decius' knuckles were white as he gripped the reins. He whipped the horses with a fury. "I may yet. I've been unable to collect for that shipment. Did you forget I needed the receipt of delivery. I'm in financial distress."

"Oh, yes. Sorry. Here's the receipt. With two shipments to collect for, you won't be in distress any longer."

"It's a good thing. The crew members you left behind have threatened to take me to court." Waving the receipt, he said, "This will get me off the hook temporarily, but it's not enough to cover the rest of my expenses. You'd better be telling me the truth or I'll have you thrown in prison for the rest of your life."

Marcus told the rest of the story. Leaving Ostia he had sailed with both sails full in a mad dash for the straits of Rhegium between Italy and Sicily, hoping to catch the west wind that had plagued his westward crossing before. He succeeded and had flown across the Great Sea in only nine days. In Alexandria they had been able to load quickly, then had taken a daring risk. Suspecting that it was time for the wind to reverse itself, he had sailed out to sea due westward. Most ships from Alexandria, when carrying a heavy load, sailed north to Cyprus or Asia Minor first, lest they be caught at high sea with a contrary wind or a storm. But Marcus had taken the calculated risk of sailing straight toward Rome. The wind was still westerly when they left the port at Alexandria. Miraculously, though, it immediately reversed itself and boosted them again with a brisk tailwind.

"I hoisted both sails and let her run. We were in Ostia this morning—eleven days after leaving Alexandria."

"Incredible!"


When they reached the dock, Decius saw a jubilant crew. All the members were topside—some dancing in loin cloths and twirling their togas overhead, some picking goodnaturedly at one another, some singing nautical songs, a group milling around on the dock.

"Hey, Centurion," one of them shouted to Marcus in the carriage, "you really know how to sail."

"Three cheers for Hippalus."

"Hip, hip, hooray! Hip, hip, hooray! Hip, hip, hooray!"

"Come aboard," Marcus said to Decius, "and look at your precious cargo."

Marcus led the owner aboard, had a man open a hold door, and showed Decius the packed grain shipment.

A few days later Marcus dropped by Decius' office and handed him the receipt of shipment. This time the ship's owner was smiling broadly.

"Marcus, you've really made a name for yourself. Everyone's talking about your incredible turn-around to Alexandria. Twenty-three days, wasn't it?"

"That's correct. Please don't expect that consistently. The gods were with me this time. Had that wind not reversed itself when I left Alexandria, we'd still be on the deep for weeks to come. We were just lucky."

"That's alright. It shows what you can do. You've got plenty of courage. Yep, plenty of courage. Want to try again? It's still just July."

Sailing out of the busy Ostia harbor a second time, Marcus felt like a new man. He stood tall atop the deckhouse. Effortlessly, he guided the *Syracuse* past several inbound and outbound ships. Most of them were grain ships. With both sails full the *Syracuse* overtook and passed the gigantic *Castor and Pollux,* so named for the twin Roman gods who were the patron gods of sailors. The figurehead on the bow was in the form of two bearded faces, one behind the other.

"Hey, Hippalus, twenty-three days turn-around? How did you do it?" shouted the Captain.

"Pure luck, friend."

Sailors on other ships waved, rang bells, or blew horns as they passed. The crew members of the *Syracuse* basked in the glory.

"Maintain full cloth on both masts," said Marcus as they headed down the coast.

Marcus said to the First Mate, "I hope the westerly wind has begun by the time we reach Rhegium. We can then make another quick dash to Alexandria. Getting back, though, will be another problem. Will have to sail north to Asia Minor, then cut past the

Peloponnesians or south of Crete. I hope I can get one more shipment to Rome this season, plus a return to Alexandria for the winter. Then we can be ready to load and sail quickly next spring."

He was not disappointed. The wind was turning westward when they reached Rhegium.

One calm, clear afternoon on that voyage Marcus was sitting on a coil of rope near the front of the deck with a sheet of papyri in his hand, writing. The First Mate walked up to him and said, "May I ask what you're writing? Looks like something other than the ship's log."

"You're right," Marcus replied in a grave tone. "I'm keeping a personal journal. Right now I'm writing observations about the ocean depths. See Claudius over there at the railing. He's sounding depths for me."

"Why? We're nowhere near land. What difference does it make?"

"You know, you're right. It really won't make much difference at all. But then, who knows? Maybe there are mountains down there. Maybe cliffs or valleys or river beds. Maybe at one time that was dry land; maybe we're sailing in the sky of the people of yore. Maybe Atlantis is down there somewhere. Maybe also one day I can piece my notes together and discover something significant."

"Makes sense to me," said the First Mate.

"I also write down observations about the wind patterns, the ocean current, the sun, the moon, the stars. Someday I'm going to master those elements."

Marcus stood to his feet and with a sweep of his arm said, "That's my obsession. Take the wind, for example. I've been whipped by it more than once—but never again. I'm greater than all the elements together."

He held the papyri sheet above his head. "With these data I expect to discover their key, and when I do, they'll be at my service."

Claudius had just pulled his sounding weight up onto deck.

"What's the reading?"

"152 fathoms, sir."
Marcus wrote it down.

As they neared Alexandria, Marcus was in his tent reading back over his personal journal. He was especially interested in reviewing his nighttime observations. Noteworthy to him was the following:

> *August 3, 44. Night 3 out of Rome. Spent the night on my back atop the deckhouse observing the heavens.*

Marcus remembered that night well. The sail, gridded by the seams where the canvas pieces had been sewn together, had blocked much of his view. The huge cloth had flapped all night in the breeze.

> *Especially interested in the movement of the stars across the sky through the night. The navigational star remained still; those nearby travelled in an arc in relation to it. It soon became obvious that all the other stars also moved in an arc in relation to the navigational star, like the ripples made by a rock in a pond. I now see why the ancients believed the supreme god dwelled at the navigational star and the lesser gods dwelled at the other stars in subservient orientation to the supreme god.*

Another entry read:

> *August 5, 44. Night 5 out of Rome. The new moon arose after dusk. I think I can almost see pock marks on the moon, maybe craters.*

He thought of the thick glass cup he had looked through that made the moon look larger.
*Can the moon be a vast ball—a globe? If so, it might be floating freely in the sky, ten thousand miles away. The sun appears round like*

a globe too. Maybe the stars are globes but are so far away they appear as points of light. I wonder if our world itself is a globe.

> *August 7, 44. Night 7 out of Rome. I lay watching the moving stars again. I have watched them so much recently they now appear to me like a disk above me rotating around the navigational star. In my fatigue I fell asleep and had a dream: I was lying down watching the stars when the ship got caught in a giant whirlpool. Around and around it spun, faster and faster. It gave me the impression that the stars above me were spinning faster and faster around the navigational star. Of course it was I who was spinning, not the stars. I awakened with a bold new thought: in reality the stars are not spinning around the navigational star. It is our world that is spinning, making the stars only seem to spin!! Eureka!*

As Marcus sat in his tent pondering these observations, he made a further leap of logic. *Both Roman and Greek religions tend to associate their gods with the stars. The sun is Apollo; two stars in the constellation Gemini are Castor and Pollux. Yet if the stars are really globes and worlds, then they are material substances, not gods. Perhaps men are mistaken. Perhaps what they thought were gods are nothing but ordinary material objects. Perhaps there is no god. It is an illusion.*

Marcus realized his plan for three grain shipments to Rome that year as well as a return to Alexandria by the end of the shipping season. Early one evening in Alexandria that autumn Marcus sat in his second-story apartment reading. There was a knock at the door. He arose and went to answer it.

"I thought I would catch you home at this hour," said a tall, lanky, older man in the darkened hallway.

"Felix!" cried Marcus and rushed to embrace his older brother. "I shouldn't be surprised you're in Alexandria. One of your shipping points is not far from here, is it?"

"No, the port of Arsinoe, is a couple of hundred miles southwest. Not much to it. Just a remote sea-land transfer point. I always winter in Alexandria. Isn't that what you're doing?"

"Yes, this year at least. I'm in the Egypt-to-Rome shipping trade now. It's my first year," Marcus said.

"Shipping? I thought you were commanding a galley."

"I was, until last year ago. That's another story. But I'm anxious to hear about you. I now work for Decius Commodius of Rome. He told me he once met you—wasn't it here in Alexandria?"

The flame on the small lamp dish on the table flickered and died and Marcus got up in the darkness to refill it with oil. "Go ahead while I relight this," he said.

"Describe him to me," Felix said.

"Oh, about your age. Medium build. Somewhat wealthy."

"Seems like I met him in a tavern here years ago. Think he was trading in Roman silver and coral—trading them for Eastern gems and silks. I didn't have any business with him. I don't get into the actual trade. I just transport the cargos."

"Same here," said Marcus. He lit two more tallows in reflective holders on the wall. A wailing sound from an eastern flute floated through the open window from down below. "All I do is pick up freight here—usually wheat from the government dock, sometimes smaller articles too—and deliver them to government warehouses in Ostia. All I get for it is a paper receipt."

They both laughed heartily.

"No, actually," said Marcus, "I get a hefty year-round salary, plus so much per delivery."

"Year-round! Not bad. I have to exist through the winter off what I make in trade seasons. My return season from India is mid-November. I just got back last week. Say, you may be interested in something I discovered last year. It's revolutionizing the Eastern trade."

"What is it?" asked Marcus. He pulled over an ottoman, sat back down, and placed his feet on it.

"They call it trade winds. We used to have to hug the coast all the way to India and back. I would sail down the Gulf of Suez, across the

Red Sea, along the Arabian coast, past the opening to the Persian Gulf, and finally to India. Whew! It would take months, one way.

"Well, I started studying the winds. I discovered that they reverse themselves seasonally. A southwest wind blows from July to September; then in November a northeast wind sets in. The local Arabs verified that those wind currents can be depended on consistently. So last year I left here in September and risked simply running across the Arabian Sea before the wind. You know what? It took me directly to a part of the Indian coast that I was familiar with, and I just coasted on down to Malabar. Then in November I set sail from there and again ran before a northeasterly wind right back to the Arabian coast and home. It worked! We sailed both ways in record time."

"Amazing!" said Marcus. "Isn't the distance from the Red Sea to India about the same as from Spain to Syria?"

"Exactly."

"Did you have clear skies?"

"Often not. Those were monsoon winds—"

"And frequently rainy," said Marcus. "Out of sight of the navigational star. Wasn't that highly risky?"

"Not really. I made certain the wind was consistent, never deviating significantly. What could go wrong? Going eastward I would inevitably hit the Indian coast. Going westward I would hit either the Arabian or the African coast, and I was familiar with all three coasts. I sailed it again like that this season, with no problem. Several other ships have also tried it successfully. I predict that within five years the India trade will expand tremendously. Which is fine by me. There's plenty of room for more ships there. Why don't you come down and work those waters?"

"Frankly, I don't have any love for the East. The Great Sea is my sea."

"I'd love to have my kid brother sailing alongside me."

"No, thanks," Marcus said.

"Then why don't you experiment with trade winds on the Great Sea?"

"You know yourself, Felix, that sailing trade winds are ancient history on the Great Sea. Even the Phoenicians did it. But you gave me an idea when you talked about sailing in monsoons, without a view of the navigational star. We have a wind in the autumn that always closes down traffic. Called the Euro Aquila. A northeaster. It's usually associated with overcasts and storms. I wonder if a ship could risk running before it . . . I guess not, though. The trouble is, we might miss Sicily and run all the way to Spain. It's maybe something to consider though. Say, brother, why don't we get an apartment together this winter. You're not married, are you?"

"Not yet," said Felix. "How about you?"

"No . . ." He removed his feet from the ottoman and bent forward. His eyes moistened. "There was a girl in Rome . . . . But I lost her."

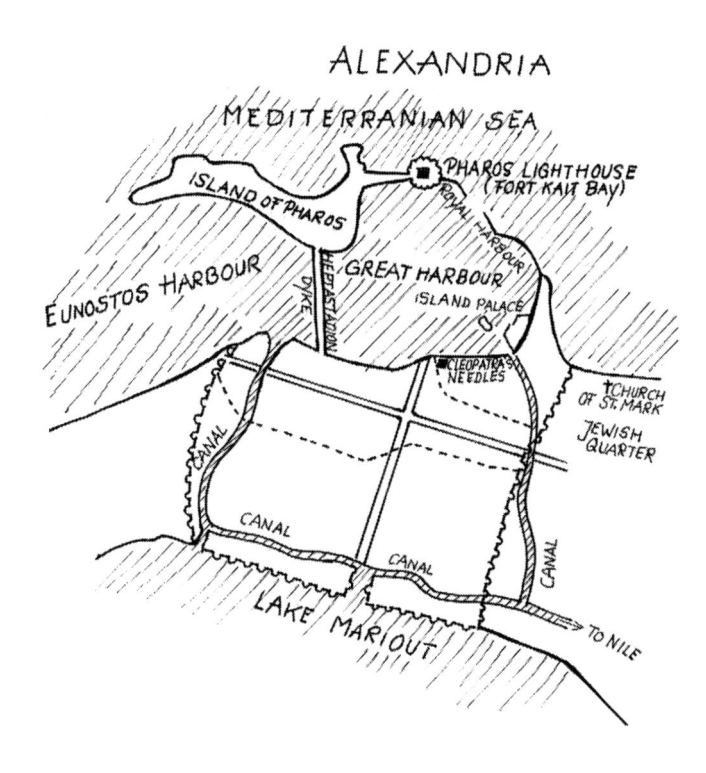

*Chief of all thy wondrous works*
*Supreme in all thy plan,*
*Thou hast put an upward reach*
*Into the heart of man.*

                                        Harry Kemp

# CHAPTER FIVE

## ALEXANDRIA
## AUTUMN, AD 59

FIFTEEN YEARS HAD passed. Today cool, blustery winds whipped the waters of Alexandria's Great Harbor, gently rocking the dozens of idle frigates moored around its rim. Leaves blew onto the pier from the access streets. The only activity to be seen anywhere was around the ship *Bacchus*, where crewmen were busily at work on the mast, the yard, the deck, and the dock.

In a heavy, gilded chair atop the deck house sat Marcus, overseeing the battening down of the ship for the winter. His hairy legs were largely visible below a centurion's *pteryges*—the heavy leather strips suspended from the front of a military belt. His feet were shod in the thongs of hobnailed sandals (*caliga*). A two-foot sword sheathed in a fancy wooden scabbard hung from his belt.

Marcus yawned, took off a laurel from his head, and smoothed his short, graying hair. His pocked face was beardless and leathery. Spotting a man approaching the ship, he hastily put back on his laurel. He yawned again but watched the man out of the corner of his eye. Presently, a seaman came up the gangplank and shouted, "There's a man down here to see you, Captain."

"Who is it?"

"He says his name is Agabus Ben Uri."

"Show him up."

"Aye, aye, sir."

The seaman led the man up to the edge of the deck house and showed him the steep steps up to the top. He started up the steps, stumbling often from stepping on his shin-length robe. Finally, he pulled himself up past the bannisters and stood before Marcus puffing. He was of medium build and wore a black-striped *tallit*— a shawl with tassels on it—identifying him as a Hebrew. His bearded face appeared gentle and kindly, his manners affable and extrovert. Marcus refused to rise. "State your business," he said.

"Ah, I can see you are a man who does not waste time on formalities. You are speaking to Agabus Ben Uri." He made a flourishing bow. When Marcus refused to reply, Agabus asked, "Could you be the illustrious Captain Marcus Hippalus?"

"I am. What do you want?"

"Ah, Captain. You are a man of wide renown. I note the fresh laurel upon your head. Might I be privileged to congratulate you upon some noble deed?"

"That's my business. What is yours?"

"My business? Why, kind sir, I have business that might interest you personally. I have come to offer you a much larger and more modern ship—the *Kibotos*."

Marcus looked up into the man's face with renewed interest. He rose to his feet and said, "Now that's different. Why don't we go below to my cabin. First Mate! Take control!"

"Aye, aye, sir," said a man on the deck.

The two descended the steps and entered a door in the side of the deck house. Marcus stepped over behind a desk and threw his hulk onto a chair, flippantly motioning his visitor to another chair.

"I see you have converted the entire deck house into very commodious quarters for yourself," Agabus said.

"And should I have the same prerogative on the—what did you call it?—the *Kibotos*—if I assumed command."

"Aye. That can be arranged. The *Kibotos* is a brand new ship of the largest class made today—1,500 tons capacity. Time and again as large as this ship. Is this not about 800 capacity?"

"900," replied Marcus

"Ah, yes . . . Hippalus, you have the top reputation on the high seas—the fastest man alive! But I've studied you. I perceive you to be a man of principle. Shipping, to you, is a matter of calling. You're not just a transporter of goods. You are dedicated. To you, the sea's a personal challenge. Yes, consistently you deliver more shipments in a season than anyone else—and have a lower record of loss. And yet it's not just shipments that concern you, is it? I perceive that you're motivated by a different kind of obsession. To put it bluntly: you're obsessed with a desire to conquer the elements, aren't you? Am I right?"

Marcus gazed at Agabus with a raised eyebrow. "I see you have investigated me thoroughly. Go on."

"That's why I want you. Mind you, I am nothing other than a lowly businessman myself, striving to keep food on the table for my family. What I want is very simple. I want the largest possible shipments to Rome, the largest possible number of shipments, and the least possible loss per season."

"I think I understand you," Marcus said. He picked up a stick and tapped on the desk. "What you want it seems is the largest possible *profits* per season."

"Ah, I would not put it such crass terms. My desires are modest."

"Very well. Then what's in it for me?"

"Simple. I'm offering you the most modern ship, of the largest capacity, with the standard remuneration per shipment, *plus* 2% of my net income."

Marcus toyed with the stick. "Only 2%. Make it 10% and I'll talk further with you."

"My friend, you drive a hard bargain. Yet my income per shipment is so small I can go no higher than a 4% commission."

"Sir," said Marcus, halfway rising to his feet. "I must bid you good day unless you can promise me at least 6% of the profits."

"Ah, sir, I wish I could be so generous, but the risks I assume on the cargo are so great. I am afraid 6% is beyond my means."

"Ben Uri, you doubtless know my record. I've never lost a shipment. Nevertheless, if it will ease your mind, I'll tell you what I'll do. I will agree to split with you the cost of any shipment I lose, if you will grant me 6% of the profit."

"You would do that? Then, my noble friend, let us talk further."

Eventually, these were the terms agreed upon, though Marcus delayed his final commitment until he could examine the *Kibotos*.

"That can be arranged," Agabus said. "The crew is bringing it down from a shipyard in Tyre next month."

ROMAN WHEAT SHIP

Marcus stood on the pier with Agabus, watching as the mighty

*Kibotos* approached through the breakwaters of the Great Harbor. In spite of its huge size it maneuvered easily toward its berth.

*Now that's my kind of ship.*

As soon as the ship slid up to the dock, Marcus, disdaining protocol, grabbed the first mooring line tossed from the ship and pulled himself up the eight foot height to the deck. A startled crewman quickly assisted him up and helped him over the railing. Casually, Marcus walked across the deck inspecting the new ship. It was spic and span and exuded the odor of new lumber.

A bearded man hastened over to him from the stern and offered his hand, speaking in an unfamiliar language. Taking his hand Marcus replied, "I am Captain Marcus Hippalus."

"Hippalus!" said the man with a wide grin on his face, and he continued his strange speech. The way his beard framed his large teeth reminded Marcus of a camel. Marcus kept moving as the man hustled along behind him. He stopped several sailors along the way, among them the First Mate, and asked them questions in Latin. When they each replied in Greek, Marcus broke off conversation and moved on.

In a few minutes Marcus and the bearded man were joined by Agabus. He said something in the unfamiliar language to the stranger, then turned and said, "Captain Marcus Hippalus, I would like you to meet Captain Meshach of the Tyre Shipbuilding Company. Captain Meshach, this is Captain Hippalus. I will be glad to interpret for you."

Meshach began speaking. Agabus said, "Yes, I have already met the great Hippalus. We were just inspecting the ship."

Marcus asked, "How does she handle?"

Meshach replied, "As smoothly as a well-bred camel."

Marcus smiled in spite of himself. "Did you find any major problems?"

Meshach replied, "This was the maiden voyage of the *Kibotos*, as I am sure you know. Yes, of course, we found some kinks to iron out: hawsers needing tightening, kitchen flues not drawing well, some areas left unpainted. I have workers with me from the shipyard who will remain here as long as necessary to make the needed repairs. Also, I must inform you that there is very little furniture on board. Only what's built-in. You will need to acquire bunks, tables, chairs, and so forth."

"Did you go through a storm on the way?"

"No, there was one reported over Cyprus when we left and we could see a cloud bank, but it did not come our direction."

Marcus then addressed Agabus directly with a list of changes he required. Last of all he said, "And I want to replace the First Mate with one who can speak both Latin and Greek."

Agabus agreed to all the changes, then said, "Will you then take over the *Kibotos*?"

"It's agreed," said Marcus, and the two shook hands.

Marcus hired Gaius Erastus, a Greek from Corinth, as First Mate. He was a pleasant, slightly short, beardless, barrel-chested man in his mid-twenties. Immediately, Erastus very ably set about assisting in the readying of the ship—overseeing the repairs of the shipyard workers, buying the furniture, stocking the ship's store, training the crew.

Soon after his arrival, Marcus had him assemble the crew—some one hundred ten men—on the deck of the *Kibotos*. Usually, Marcus dressed in the pteryges, sword, and sandals of a centurion, but on this occasion he added the breast armor, head laurel, and greaves. Thus attired, he stood atop the deck house facing the crew below. Despite Erastus' efforts to line up the crew in a military fashion, the rugged seamen slouched in a curious array of formations and postures.

"Gentlemen," said Marcus, with Erastus translating from the deck, "I am Marcus Hippalus, Captain of the Emperor's merchant fleet. This is your new First Mate, Gaius Erastus, a very capable and experienced officer from Corinth, Greece. You are privileged to be the very first crew to operate what will prove to be the finest sail ship on the Great Sea, the *Kibotos*."

So powerful was Marcus' voice that people on the beach of the Island Palace three hundred yards away turned their heads his direction.

"Her new owner is the worthy Agabus Ben Uri of Alexandria." He motioned toward Agabus standing by the deck railing. Agabus smiled proudly and waved.

"I have one ambition: to sail faster than anyone has ever done before. This year I intend to set a seasonal record of six deliveries to Rome."

Murmuring arose among the seamen and they shifted their postures restlessly.

"My success will depend upon you. I will test every mettle in you. We will sail night and day. We will sail in stormy weather as in fair weather. We will sail when you are tired to the bone. We will sail when you are sick, weak, and discouraged. We will sail when even the most hardy crew has already put in to shelter. But we will sail on to historic records. And if I succeed, you succeed. The glory will be yours."

He paused to let his words soak in. They hit the crew like a typhoon. Men moved restlessly, looked at one another, commented under their breath. Momentarily, someone said in Greek, "We can do it."

"Yeah, let's go for it," someone added enthusiastically.

"Whoop, whoop, whoop!" someone yelled. Gradually, a noisy ruckus arose all over deck: "We can do it!" "Yeah, we can do it!" "Let's do it!"

Marcus motioned for silence. "Word is out that the Nabataeans will be pirating this season. With their smaller warboats, they can outrun us. If we are attacked, we must be prepared to *fight*! Therefore, as part of your preparation I shall be leading you in combat training. That will begin soon.

"To succeed in my ambition we must sail early. Therefore, I have already requested an early scheduling for grain loading. I have asked for loading to begin on March the first. That's just six weeks from today. I challenge you to be thoroughly ready by then."

Marcus' oration that day had its desired effect. After that, the crew took to the preparation for the voyage in high spirits. In those days, seldom was there a single part of the large ship without activity. Battle training began promptly. The clang of swords in mock duels was frequently heard. Twice, in wind and rain storms, they put out to sea overnight in shakedown and training missions. The crew worked diligently alongside the shipyard workers to repair leaks and make the vessel tight and seaworthy. Everyday the big voice of Marcus could be heard barking out orders in Latin, echoed by the voice of Erastus in Greek. The two men were a propitious mating.

During that time, Marcus did not socialize with Erastus—not with anyone, for that matter. Several times they ate the noon meal together at the Sailor's Cove, a small cafe fronting on a block-long wall of warehouses set back about seventy-five feet from the water and within sight of the *Kibotos*. But as they ate Marcus never discussed anything but business. Nevertheless, as he hunkered over his food, he tolerated Erastus' garrulous jabber about every subject under the sun.

One day Erastus said, "You know, there's a rather remarkable speaker these days over in the Jewish Quarters, not far from here. Goes by the name of John Mark. Speaks to a sizable crowd every Sunday. Anyone can go to his lectures. Most of the time he's teaching about a Jew named Jesus Christ."

Marcus flinched.

Erastus continued, "He claims that earlier in this century Jesus actually arose from the dead. A new era has dawned, he says. I've been to hear him several times myself. He's quite interesting. You ought to go sometime."

Marcus kept eating without comment.

Marcus roomed in an apartment with his older brother, Felix, as he had done every winter except one for the past fourteen years. He had usually chosen to remain in Alexandria through the winter in order to get a jump on the shipping season the next spring. The one exception was when he had stayed in Rome searching for Cecilia. He had finally coaxed from the Christians the information that she had left Rome for good and was residing in a small town near Venice. He had traveled there to find her but was unable to do so.

In Alexandria when he found the time Marcus walked the streets alone. It was a metropolis boasting a million population and was a sight-seers paradise. Galleries and porches abounded, as did courts, halls, walks, groves, libraries—the largest library in the world was there. Marcus frequented it, doing research on such diverse subjects as ships, astronomy, religion, even science. Some of the world's top scientific and technological progress was being made in Alexandria. He enjoyed staying in Alexandria more than in Rome.

Early one Sunday evening in February while the sun was still low on the horizon and the crew was still busy, Marcus changed into a long, plain, Roman toga and left the harbor. He walked eastward across the narrow peninsula where the Royal Harbor was, past the Royal Palace, to the opposite shoreline. There he turned southward to the mainland where he soon entered the area known as the "Jewish Quarters," a large, neat ghetto filled with attractive homes and shops. Twice as many Jews lived in Alexandria as in Jerusalem. All around were indications of prosperity and civic pride. The shore road along which he walked was one of the main roads through the Quarters and was lined, on the inland side, primarily with shops and businesses, most of which were still open at that hour and busy with activity. The seaward side of the street was entirely open save for sidewalks and trees. Bathers played along the sandy beach. Crowds of people roamed the thoroughfare with him.

He turned down a side street and walked another two or three blocks before he stopped in front of a rather nondescript building— single story, white, flat-roofed, Grecian-style—sitting alone on a square-block-sized lot surrounded by a low stone wall. A small sign by the gate said in Greek, *Christianos Ekklesia*, "Christian Assembly." A small cluster of adults, youth, and children were casually milling around the front door of the building, which stood open. Trying to remain inconspicuous, Marcus walked slowly past the wide open gate and crossed the street to sit down and watch from a park bench under a shade tree. More and more people arrived at the Ekklesia, but he waited until enough people had entered the structure to conceal his own approach. Then he walked confidently across the street, up a sidewalk, and into the building. The sun was just setting.

A truly sizable crowd was gathered there just as Erastus had reported, perhaps two hundred fifty people. Most of them were Jewish, although no small number of Gentiles was also among them. Marcus found a place on a bench near the back and sat down. The quiet music from several stringed instruments gave him a relaxed feeling. Several people were engaged in quiet conversations around him, but by and large the atmosphere was still and reverent.

Soon a short, Jewish man arose and identified himself as Annianus. "I want to call us to the worship of our crucified, risen Savior, the Lord Jesus Christ. Let us pray."

After the prayer, he said, "First, this evening, let me share my testimony. In AD 45 I was a humble shoemaker here in the Quarters when our brother, John Mark, made friends with me and eventually led me to faith in Jesus."

He turned toward a man about Marcus' age sitting in a chair on the platform, and numbers of people in the crowd said quietly, "Amen."

The man continued, "Since that time I've been immensely happy and have devoted my life solely to the propagation of the Gospel. But enough about me. Now let's all sing the praises of our blessed Lord."

There followed several songs, accompanied by the stringed instruments, in which the whole assembly joined together as in one great voice.

After the singing, Annianus said, "Before we hear the teaching of God's Word, is there anyone who would like to give a testimony?"

At that moment Erastus entered the back of the auditorium. With a grin on his face, he pushed past Marcus and sat down beside him. Erastus whispered, "I thought this might be where you were going when I saw you change out of your uniform."

Marcus frowned reproachfully.

A middle-aged, bearded man arose from among the congregation and said, "You all know me. I used to be the scourge of the synagogue. I never attended; and whenever I had the opportunity, I spoke against the synagogue and those who attended. I had no principles. I lied and cheated. I never prayed or worshipped. I claimed I didn't even believe in God. But I was lying. Down deep in my heart I knew there's a God, but I was afraid. I wanted to live my life my own way, without regard to the dictates of another. I wanted just to be independent. Truly, I got by with a lot. But actually I suspected that time was running out for me and one day it would all catch up with me and I would be held personally accountable for the godless life I was living.

"Then it was that a man from this church, Janus over here, started making friends with me and slowly started telling me about Jesus and how good he was—and *is*. He showed me that no matter how bad my life had been in the past, none of it would be held against me if I were to put my faith in Jesus Christ. In other words it wasn't too late for me. That really excited me, because that was one of my main hindrances. I used to think, 'If I'm going to hell anyway, I might as well enjoy my sinful ways.' I think most of you were here when I went up to the altar and gave my heart to Jesus. I'll tell you, I'm more delectably happy now than I ever thought I could be. Praise His name!"

"Praise the Lord," echoed several people.

At that time a young woman stood up and said, "I'm not a Jew, but I understand that it doesn't matter to Christ Jesus. We're all one in him. I never knew anything about the Jewish faith. I followed Isis. But it felt empty, like my whole life had been. Since I've found Christ, my life has been wonderfully full."

More "amens" followed and then John Mark stood up. He spoke in a friendly manner in the Latin familiar to the people of Alexandria. "I have here with me a part of a letter written by my esteemed friend, the Apostle Paul, who, as you know, is now in prison in Caesaria—a letter which he wrote to the church in Corinth two years ago. Listen to what he said, 'Though we have known Christ after the flesh, yet now henceforth know we him no more.'

"I think I know what he meant. The fact is, I knew Christ Jesus when he was in the flesh. We thought very highly of him, but in actuality we really didn't know who he was. It was not until his resurrection from the grave that we found out who he is—the very God of the Godhead—and so now I too can say, 'Henceforth, I know him no more after the flesh.'"

John Mark proceeded to tell what it had been like to know Jesus personally when he was on earth, and what it was like to know him even better, now that he was in heaven "at the right hand of the throne of God."

Marcus found Mark's style easy and appealing—it was like face to face conversation. As Mark spoke he answered questions that arose in his own mind, just as they came up. He liked Mark and decided he would try to talk with him in person after the service.

When the assembly was dismissed, after about two hours, Erastus said to Marcus, "Come on, let's go to a nearby inn and I'll buy you a mug of wine."

"Not now," said Marcus. "You go on. There's someone I want to talk to. I'll see you tomorrow."

"Who?" asked Erastus, and waited. Then said, "Not John Mark?"

"Who knows?" said Marcus, and he started walking toward the front of the auditorium. In the crowded aisle several people smiled at Marcus, introduced themselves, asked his name, told him how happy they were that he was in the service, and generally were friendly to him.

At the front Marcus asked an attendant, "Excuse me, can you tell me where John Mark is?"

"Sir, he has an office through that door over there. He might be in there."

Marcus went over to the door and cautiously cracked it. Seeing Mark inside talking to two other people, he quietly pulled the door closed. While his hand was still on the door handle, he felt a tug from the opposite side. He released the handle and Mark himself opened the door. Mark said, "If you don't mind waiting about five minutes, I'll see you then."

"I'll wait," said Marcus. Mark gently closed the door.

A few minutes later the door opened again and the two people emerged, commented briefly to Mark, smiled at Marcus, and walked up the aisle.

"Come in, I'm John Mark."

Marcus found Mark as personable and approachable as he had imagined him to be. After their introductions, Marcus said, "Your religion has some very curious teachings. I'm reserving opinion concerning your claim of a resurrection, but—"

"I was there," Mark said. "I saw it. What else do you need to know about it?"

"Perhaps so. I'll certainly accept your testimony at face value. However, what I'm concerned about more than that are your religious teachings. I take it you worship the God of the Hebrews. Let me get to the point. At what star do you claim your God to reside?"

"I'm sorry. I don't think I understand your question. Could you elaborate?

Given this opening, Marcus launched into the attack for which he had been preparing. "My own observation has been that worshipers in all religions have historically located their god or gods at some star or planet in the heavens. That's why most talk about 'god in heaven above.' For example, the Babylonians located their god Marduk at the navigational star, where also the Canaanites located Baal. The Greek god Helios is located at the sun, as was the Egyptian's ancient god, Aten. Ashtar was at Venus. And so forth. So far, in my research, though, I've been unable to locate the star where the Hebrew's God, Jehovah, is said to be located, but you probably know the answer to that. His location is not really my main concern right now anyway.

"My concern," said Marcus rushing forward, "is that mankind's belief in the existence of God is flawed, due to the fact that the stars cannot be religious abodes. I'm a world navigator by trade and an astronomer by hobby. My direct observations of the stars and planets show me that they are all merely physical worlds like our own, suspended out in space. Why, if you could stand on the surface of one of the stars, you could look up and see our own world as nothing more than a star in your own sky. These are not gods. Yet since this belief has always been mankind's sole explanation for the existence of God, then there is no God. Do you follow what I mean?"

John replied, "What you say is curious and novel. I don't understand much of it. All I know is that I once met a man named Jesus. Not a star, not a legend, not a myth, but a man. And he claimed to be God. He said, 'I and the Father are one.' Then one day he died—truly died—yet three days later he resurrected from the dead—truly resurrected. I say that his resurrection gave complete credence to his claim to be God. So I have discovered God to be, well, a real person. Not a thing, but a person. And when you have known him personally as I have, what a wonderful person he is. Today, anyone can come to know God personally, by repentance of his sins and faith in Christ. You too can come to know him like this."

Together they talked long into the night, and a sense of comraderie grew between them. But when they parted, Marcus went away frustrated that his carefully researched and reasoned assumptions found so little acceptance with this Jewish preacher. Mark's simple distinction between God as a person and God as a thing knocked the props out from under his most prized defense against God.

Late in their conversation, however, a mental image of his humiliation at Durobrivae had flooded Marcus' memory. His final comment was, "I cannot accept the existence of a God, who, by his petty caprices, uses nature's elements to overwhelm and defeat helpless humanity. I stand opposed to such a God, yea, and henceforth will stand opposed to him."

Mark said, "Before you leave tonight, may I have a word of prayer with you?'

"If it's all the same to you, save your prayers for those who have lost their morality and integrity, like the poor man who testified tonight. I don't need them."

The moon shone full on the deserted streets of the Jewish Quarter as Marcus walked home that night. So deep in thought was he that he was oblivious to his surroundings. He did not notice, for example, that he had passed the boundary of the Jewish ghetto. The environment had become markedly different. The homes and lawns and shops were not so neatly kept. Trash lay in the streets. Dogs rummaged through piles of garbage. Bunches of men caroused or lay drunken in ditches. Marcus did not notice. He struck his fist into his palm and tilted his face toward the night sky. A black cat chased a rodent across the street. Marcus moaned, "Durobrivae! Durobrivae!"

Of a sudden the swing of a five-inch-thick post struck him in the back of the head, and he crumpled to the ground. Two men quickly tore into his toga for his money and possessions. Just as suddenly they ran away leaving him unconscious on the street.

Marcus awakened. It was daylight and he lay naked on a bed. No other furniture was in the room except one chair pulled up to the bed. The walls were white and bare, the window undraped. Stark Egyptian sunlight flooded the room. A man was moving about. "Where is this?" Marcus asked.

"So you have at last awakened. This is the Alexandrian School of Medicine. My name is Apollonius. What is your name?"

Marcus reached up and felt a cloth wrapped around his head. Caked blood stained the bed sheets. He halfway raised himself up but fell back with a groan. His head ached terribly. He said, "I am Captain Marcus Hippalus. Where is my toga? What day is this?"

"Your toga is hanging over here. This is Wednesday afternoon. You've had a terrible blow to the head. Someone brought you here Monday morning and left you. He said he found you unconscious in the street. What happened?"

"I don't know. The last thing I remember . . . I think . . . I was walking down the street at night—Sunday, I think. Yes, late Sunday night."

"We have been washing you and administering certain salves

to your scalp and certain medicines by mouth. We suspect your skull was crushed. How do you feel?"

"My head hurts terribly. I'm also hungry. Has anyone who knows me come here?"

"None so far. You had no identification on you and we didn't know whom to notify. Here, let me adjust your bed covers."

"Could you possibly put new sheets on for me?"

"Sure. I'll bring you something to eat too. After that you get some more rest."

Marcus again awakened at dusk that day to receive more nourishment and medicine, then again the next morning. This time two other men were in his room. Marcus said, "Is this Thursday morning?"

"That's correct," answered one of them. The other man left the room. "How do you feel today?"

"I feel better than I did yesterday."

"Good. Our physicians are preparing to open your scalp this morning to determine the extent of damage to your skull. Then, they will repair it."

"Not my scalp, they're not," said Marcus.

"We'll see," said the attendant.

"May I ask a favor of you, kind sir. Would you mind bringing me some food?"

"Certainly," he said, and left the room.

When he returned, Marcus was gone!

On March the 1st, workers began loading grain on the *Kibotos* and on March the 3rd she sailed out of Alexandria. Marcus sat in a special chair atop the deck house, feebly calling orders. His head was wrapped in a white towel. A long-legged, black-and-white spotted dog lay at his feet.

*These are the sins I fain would have thee take away*
*Malice and cold disdain;*
*Hot anger, sullen hate;*
*Scorn of the lowly, envy of the great;*
*And discontent that casts a shadow gray*
*On all the brightness of a common day.*

          Henry van Dyke

# CHAPTER SIX

## ALEXANDRIA
## AUGUST AD 60

THE ROYAL HARBOR bustled with activity. A half dozen large ships lined the long wooden pier awaiting their turns at the massive wheat warehouses. Each was preparing to make one more dash for Rome before the season ended. Already the winds had turned westerly, making any further voyages westward across the open sea impossible this year. From now on they would have to sail northward to Cyprus or Asia Minor, thence to beat their way toward Italy as best they could.

A young beardless man, tall, broad-shouldered, slim-waisted, threaded his way through the freight cluttering the dock. His build was that of a classical Greek athlete, with a straight-bridged nose and leonine black hair. He wore a short, pale-red robe, opened to his chest hair, a royal blue sash, and open sandals.

"Ho! Erastus! Gaius Erastus!" he called.

Erastus, going up the gangplank of the *Kibotos*, saw him and exclaimed, "Why, Playboy Hermes! What a surprise! What the heck are you doing out here in the working world? Your father's money hasn't run out, has it?"

"Not yet! But you'll be the first to know when it does. I'll come hitting you up. I was just out here looking at the ships. Not surprised to see you here though. I trust you're still in the navy."

"Make way! Coming through!" said a stevedore carrying a burden up the gangplank.

Erastus nimbly leaped down to the dock and grasped Hermes' hand. "Not *the* navy. The merchant marines. Have you got a few minutes? Come on, I'll show you the sights."

He took Hermes by the arm and led him away from the harbor. They went down a wide roadway, between warehouses, which led to other, more luxurious, tree-lined streets. Hermes was relieved to get away the noise and foul aroma of the docks. As they walked along talking, they approached the large, fenced grounds of the magnificent palace.

"This," said Erastus, "is the Emperor's Palace, formerly the palace of the Ptolemies. Maybe you've already seen it."

"No, I've seen much but never been back here before."

"How long have you been in Alexandria?"

"I came here in late winter," said Hermes. "Came to study at the university."

"You know, the last time I saw you was back home in Corinth—I guess right after we got out of school. Did you come here directly from Corinth?"

"Yes, and your parents there were doing well the last time I saw them."

"Father's still building buildings, is he?"

"Still Chamberlain of the city. When I left, he was laying a new pavement at the Theater—paying for it out of his own pocket."

After awhile, the two friends came to the bay behind the Palace grounds. A row of palm trees lined a gravel beach.

Erastus stopped and said, "Look across the water at those buildings facing the bay."

He was pointing toward the Jewish Quarters. From where they stood it did not appear as densely settled as the rest of Alexandria.

"What is it?"

"Well, it's just the Jewish Quarters, but back up in there is a small building called an *ekklesia*. A rather remarkable man—he sort of reminds me of you—speaks at gatherings there every Sunday. It's a public assembly and anyone can go. His name is John Mark."

"Sounds like you've been there?"

"Several times."

"What is his thesis? Some philosophy?"

"Most of the time," said Erastus, "he teaches about a Jew called Jesus Christ. Earlier in this century, he claims, Jesus actually arose from the dead. He says it's the dawning of a new era."

"'John Mark,' you say. Must be what they call a 'Christian.' Isn't that what your father, Erastus, is—a Christian?"

"Yes, he makes no secret of it. He talks to me about it every time I see him."

"I know," Hermes said. "He regularly invites me to attend their meetings too. I've never gone. They meet in someone's home back in Corinth. On Sunday, also."

"Well, I've gotten quite curious about them. It's pretty interesting. Some of it makes sense."

"I, too. I've wanted to read some of Jesus' writings, but the library here doesn't have any. Me? Basically, I'm a follower of Philo, and Philo never subscribed to the teachings of Jesus that I know of."

"Philo was Jewish too," Erastus said.

"I know. A 'skinless.' He used to live and write here in Alexandria."

"Before I sail next," said Erastus, "how about accompanying me to one of their meetings? Come to think of it, it will have to be next Sunday. We sail next week."

"Why not?" replied Hermes.

When they returned to the Harbor, Erastus said, "Look, it's after noon. Let me buy your lunch. I don't have anything else to do. Our crew is standing down for the day. Let's stop in here at Sailor's Cove—that is, if they've cleared out last night's drunks."

As they entered the tavern Hermes asked, "Have you been back to Corinth lately?"

Erastus selected a grungy table near the large paneless window at the front of the tavern. "Not in several years. I've been at sea most of the time. I've really prospered in the merchant marines. In fact, when I came on board my present ship, I was made First Mate for the first time. It was last winter."

"Not on the *Kibotos*?"

"Yes, Why?"

"I'll be on it myself this voyage."

Erastus cocked his eyebrow. "Not as a sailor. You're not on my crew list. How so?"

"As a passenger. I'm going to visit my brother in Naples."

Erastus looked skeptical; then a broad grin broke over his face. "Aha! You've heard the owner's daughter will be on board. That's it." He laughed jovially.

"So what? She'll have a companion with her too."

Erastus responded dryly, "Yeah. Her maid, the hag."

"No, not just her. Kore."

"Who?"

"Kore, a comely young damsel. They both worked at the university."

"You're jesting."

"No, seriously. I know."

"Hmm!" said Erastus. "We'll see about that." He paused thoughtfully and looked out the window. "That's the *Kibotos*, alright—the 'ark'."

"I know. What could you expect from a Hebrew owner but a Hebrew name? Let's hope it lives up to its name."

"It's done alright so far. We've already made five easy trips to Rome and back this year. This will be the sixth. If we get there before winter, we'll set a new record—six deliveries in one season. She's fast! Also new. This is her first season. She was made in Tyre last year."

Through the window they could see the *Kibotos* positioned as the third ship in line. Sitting stem-to-stern the ships were deceptive in their sizes. Similar in design to the smaller vessels in the harbor—that is, single-masted, save for a smaller mast at the front—they looked rather ordinary. Their truly colossal size could only be appreciated by the diminutive appearances of the men carrying bags of grain up the gangplanks of two of the ships. Brown-skinned bearers, clad only in loin cloths, formed an ant-like stream from the warehouse, up a long gangplank, and across the deck to a cargo hatch. There they dumped their sacks onto a palate where, by means of a derrick, they were lowered to the hold of the ship. The bearers would then return down another gangplank to the warehouse. However, few workers were around the *Kibotos* at the time.

"Uh, oh," Erastus said, "Watch this."

A fancy Egyptian litter, a *lectica*, borne by four husky Ethiopians, was coming rapidly down the wharf. It created a stir among the dock workers. As it approached a tight line of bearers, a voice roared from the litter, "Don't stop, you naked nincompoops. Push your way on through. Over to the *Kibotos*."

The litter bearers pushed through the line and ran on to the next ship.

"Right here! Stop! Let me out!"

The bearers gently lowered the litter to the ground, and one of them pushed back the curtain. A short-haired, spotted, back and white dog on leash leaped out first. Then what seemed to Hermes like a giant unfolded from the cramped litter.

"Hercules!" he exclaimed.

The passenger was crudely ostentatious, making every move for dramatic effect. When he straightened to his full height, the litter appeared to shrivel beneath him. For a moment he stood with his legs spread apart and his hands on his hips, looking at the ship. Only the huge size of the vessel dominated his appearance, but even it seemed to shrivel before his mighty hulk. He wore a military uniform, including hobnailed sandals and greaves.

"Who in the world?" said Hermes.

"That, my dear friend, is our glorious captain."

Hermes burst out laughing, and Erastus ducked back behind the window frame. The captain looked their direction and scowled. Hermes had quickly raised his hand over his face and appeared to be only a drunk sitting in the tavern. The captain turned and dismissed the litter bearers, then regally led the dog up the gangplank and began an inspection of the ship.

"You could have gotten me in serious trouble," Erastus said. "He's my boss."

"I know," replied Hermes. "I'm sorry, but he's a pompous ass. What's the matter with him?"

"Well, seriously, he's not the fool he appears to be. In fact, he has the reputation for being one of the best captains in the merchant fleet. He's quite in demand for getting cargoes across the Sea rapidly. He's broken all records for speed between here and Rome."

"What's his name?"

"Marcus Hippalus. His dog is Caesar."

"Never heard of him."

"He's something else! You've got to admire the man though. He knows his job. He can get more grain to Rome each season than anybody alive. You're aware that that's basically all the Royal Fleet does, aren't you? Just ships wheat to Rome every summer. It's to feed the populace there—to pacify them, especially the slaves. The authorities fear a riot. Anyway, the Nile valley is its main source of grain; they call Egypt 'Rome's Bread Basket.' You see, ship owners are paid so much per shipment. The more shipments they deliver, the more profit they make. Agabus Ben Uri is real lucky to have Hippalus."

"Run those names by me again."

"Who? Marcus Hippalus? That's who you just saw. What other name?"

"Agabus something."

"Oh, Agabus Ben Uri. He's the owner. Ben Uri plans to be on this voyage with us, along with his daughter, as you know."

"Oh, I didn't know her fathers's name."

"Of course," said Erastus and smiled. "Do you happen to know why she and her father are going along? I haven't heard. It's unusual to have a female on board a grain ship."

"She said they're going to visit her grandfather in Rome. He's critically ill. She lives here with her father. Her mother is deceased. Apparently, they're quite wealthy. Tell me more about Hippalus, though. Why does he wear a uniform?"

"It goes back to his days with the Roman military. He used to be a centurion over a galley," said Erastus.

"A centurion," said Hermes. "Whew!"

"The story is that he was commanding a trireme in the invasion of Britain about fifteen years ago. But something happened and he was court martialed. They kicked him out of the military. He's been trying to prove himself ever since."

The two young men conversed together in the tavern throughout the afternoon.

Midmorning the next day, Hermes arose leisurely and returned to the harbor to see his friend. When he found Erastus busy aboard the *Kibotos*, he went into Sailor's Cove and sat down at the table by the window again to watch the action. One grain ship had already sailed and another was about to do so. Hermes surveyed the commodious Alexandrian harbor—the Great Harbor—looking for the Roman galleys he had heard so much about. A squadron of them was supposed to be stationed here. He was not disappointed. Several triremes and quinqueremes were anchored across the harbor. One was moving slowly toward the Great Sea. He could hear its drum beat.

He was also intrigued by what was taking place aboard the *Kibotos*. It was a cauldron of confusion. Marcus was shouting orders in Latin, Erastus was shouting orders in Greek, Caesar was barking, and men were running everywhere.

*What's going on? A mutiny already?*

He chuckled to himself.

Swordsmen on deck were vigorously matching sabers with one another. Men were tugging at taut ropes. Some were hoisting large empty urns by hand to the railing of the ship and tipping them over as if pouring something over the side. Some were in a longboat beside the ship. Hermes watched in fascination as others climbed up ropes dangling from her side.

At noon the activity broke up at the sound of a bell and several sailors came hustling toward the tavern. When Hermes saw Erastus come through the door alone, he hailed him.

"Gaius Erastus, over here."

A sweaty Erastus came his way with a big grin on his face. "You wonder what we are doing?" he said, his voice mocking Marcus' grave tones. "We are preparing for combat." He laughed. Seating himself and resuming his own voice, Erastus said, "What else could you expect from a centurion?"

"What were you doing?"

"Just that," Erastus said. "Combat training."

A waiter appeared and said, "What can I get for you?"

Erastus said, "I believe I'll have a plate of sea bass."

Turning to Hermes, the waiter said, "And what'll you have?"

"Make mine lamb—let's see—green beans, asparagus, and leeks. The pie-of-the-day for dessert. Water to drink."

"Bring me a mug of water too, please," Erastus said.

"Why combat training?" Hermes asked.

"Who knows? Part of Marcus' compulsion, I suppose." Erastus glanced around to see that none of his subordinates could overhear him.

"Tell me about it. What were they doing?" asked Hermes.

"Oh, the swordsmen were training to repel boarders. Some

were practicing boiling of oil and dumping of it over the side of the *Kibotos* onto smaller attacking ships. Others were learning to disengage grappling hooks and board pirate ships."

He paused to take a swig from the mug which had just been delivered.

"The old man's serious," continued Erastus. "Some vessels leaving Alexandria this season have been rammed and boarded by Nabataean raiders, he says. He doesn't want us to be victimized. Mainly, what he wants to avoid, I think, is being slowed down. Notice how he has modified the ship: the side railing has been filled in between posts. That's to cut down on an attacker's view of the deck. We can hide behind it and they can't reconnoiter our strength. Also, he's mounted huge timbers around the outside of the hull at water level. To protect against ramming. I questioned whether that might retard our speed, but Marcus said it wouldn't make much difference."

The waiter set their plates before them and they began eating.

"What do you think about all this training?" asked Hermes.

"Personally, I think it's a waste of time. In my ten years on the sea I've never once seen an attacker. There *is* such a thing as the *Pax Romana*, you know. Rome has ruled these waters since the days of Augustus. But Marcus says it takes just one attacker. The crew resents it. They say, 'We're seamen, not soldiers.' They also resent that he can't, or won't, speak Greek to them. Most of the crew are Greek or Greek-speaking. That's why he engaged me: I can speak both Greek and Latin and he uses me to interpret for him."

"So that's what you were doing," said Hermes.

"Incidentally," said Erastus, "I'm to inform the passengers that departure is now scheduled for five days hence. We're next in line at the warehouse, which will be in three more days. Then it will take us two days to load our grain. So, be here at sunrise next Tuesday. Have you ever sailed on a grain ship before?"

"No," replied Hermes, "this will be a first for me."

"Well, you need to understand that this is a cargo ship, not a pleasure cruise. You may have to share a bay with others. That cabin on the deck is the captain's. All the other berths are on the first deck. Down there the owner—you know, Ben Uri—has a large cabin amidship. He doesn't usually accompany the cruise. Since his daughter will be along, accompanied by her maid, and—yes, a friend—By the way, I've checked that out; you were right."

Hermes smiled.

"Anyway—" Erastus cleared his throat. "They have modified his cabin to enable the ladies to stay in there with him. I don't blame him; they will need protection. Marcus is taking a personal interest in their safety himself and has sternly warned the crew to leave the ladies strictly alone. He really put the fear of the gods into them. Of course, I'll reinforce it too. Take note, playboy!" He grinned.

"Me? Never, never, never. I wouldn't think of bothering them."

"No?" said Erastus. "Well, anyway, forward of the owner's cabin are cabins for officers and passengers. So far as personnel are concerned, we're only about half full. I have a cabin to myself for a change. You might too. From here we cross over to Rhodes. We might pick up passengers there; sometimes do. Might have to double-up then. But we'll have it relatively comfortable on the first leg of the trip.

"One other thing," continued Erastus, "you know, don't you, that we're starting rather late in the season? We're near the last grain ship out of here this year. Marcus is determined to get to Rome—to set that record—six shipments in one season. Ben Uri needs to get to Rome while his father is still alive. 'Course it's money in his pocket, too. To tell the truth, though, we could get stranded midway. We may have to winter in some port en route. That's the reason we have so few passengers. Most people fear having to spend the winter in some strange port. Even if we do get to Rome, we'll probably have to winter there. 'Course, with Marcus' reputation, we'll probably not only get there but return also in this season."

Erastus pushed back from the table, arose, and said, "Got to call the crew back to work."

"Understood," said Hermes, also standing. He placed a friendly hand on Erastus' shoulder and said, "I'll see you again next Sunday for the trip to the *ekklesia*."

Sailor's Cove was open uncommonly early Tuesday morning. The proprietor always courted the trade of the seagoing crowds on departure days. Most ships did not bother to fire up their messes for breakfast the first day. He even opened a special room next door, with benches, for the convenience of the passengers and their baggage while they waited, hoping the smell of cooking might draw in some of them.

Hermes was at his place by the window before the sun came up, sipping a hot apple drink. The tavern was filled with noisy sailors eating and drinking. An hour after sunrise he saw Ruth arrive with her party and enter the anteroom next door. All were dressed in robes and cloaks of Syrian vintage.

Ruth was incredibly beautiful by any standard—one in a million. She was tall and comely proportioned. Neither the layered clothing nor the floor-length robe could fully hide her long legs, her slender waist, her uplifted breasts, or her narrow, rounded shoulders. Her posture was proud and self-confident, her every move naturally full of grace. Despite a hood which she wore for modesty this morning, copious tufts of auburn hair of an unusually dazzling brilliance could be seen framing her lovely face. Her complexion was rosy and clear. Her features, evenly balanced, revealed innocence and kindness. Her face bespoke an inner purity, tranquility, intelligence, and maturity.

Every time he saw her, Hermes was drawn to her like a cold wayfarer to warm shelter. This time, though, he hesitated; Ruth's hand was upon the arm of another man. Puzzled, he thought he should prepare a good strategy before approaching her.

A few minutes later Hermes got up and walked outside and over to the anteroom and stopped a moment in the doorway to adjust to the dim light within. The stance he assumed in the doorway was casual but studied—perhaps even a trifle dashing. Glancing around, his eyes fell on the two damsels.

"Ruth, Kore," he called out, with a student's disdain for formality. "How are you?"

The two had already spotted him, but had discreetly awaited his first move. Kore's excitement at seeing him was unguarded and she burst out, "Hermes, you're not going on this voyage too, are you?"

Ruth, with a greater reserve, arose, lifted the man seated beside her by the arm, and said, "Solomon, I would like to introduce you to a friend from the university."

Somewhat startled, the man awkwardly stood to his feet and followed her to the door.

"Solomon, this is Hermes. Hermes, I'd like you to meet Solomon."

The two men exchanged greetings with one another.

Solomon was tall and startlingly thin, bearded, with a long, narrow face. His appearance was like the elongated image of a man in a bent mirror. Long curled sideburns identified him as a member of the Assideans or "Pious Ones," whose center was in northern Galilee.

Ruth then said, "Hermes, come over here and I'll introduce you to my father."

Hermes was surprised at how friendly Agabus was, for one who controlled such wealth and power.

The fifth passenger in Ruth's party was Miriam, her maid, an older woman whom Ruth obviously regarded with deep affection. Ruth also introduced her.

Kore, in the meantime, had inched her way to Hermes's side and was gazing eagerly into his face, leaning toward him like a school girl on tiptoes awaiting a kiss. While not as strikingly beautiful as Ruth, Kore had turned her share of male heads in Alexandria. About Ruth's height and build, she was graced with medium-brown hair and unblemished features, save for a slightly crooked nose. Her demeanor was very cheerful and vivacious.

"It would be my pleasure to host you all to breakfast if you would like," said Hermes. "Sailor's Cove serves excellent food, despite its sordid appearance."

"That is very kind of you," Agabus said, "but we had a meal before we left home."

"Then, may I buy you a cup of wine or perhaps some fruit juice?"

"That does sound interesting. Would you all like to join him?" Agabus asked the group.

They were willing, though Ruth found it necessary to mildly coax Solomon to participate, Hermes being a Gentile. Hermes led them outside and into the tavern. His front table was still open, and he invited them over to it and pulled up additional chairs for the party of six.

As they awaited boarding, a pleasant conversation ensued, animated by the witty exchanges between Agabus and Hermes. Agabus, seemingly unaware of Hermes' interest in his daughter, explained how, when Ruth was a little girl, he and his wife, before her untimely death, had pledged her to be married to Solomon.

The conversation soon turned to the *Kibotos*. Agabus told how Marcus Hippalus had captained his ship throughout the season and performed extraordinary feats of daring that earned the *Kibotos* the reputation for being the swiftest grain ship in the Royal Fleet. He expressed pride in having him as captain and told how he had come to allow him vast leeway, even permitting him to adapt the ship to his own unique designs.

"Notice the captain's cabin on deck," said Agabus with a twinkle in his eye. "Do you notice anything different about it?"

"Not me," said Hermes. "A ship's a ship."

Solomon said, "It's taller than normal."

"Exactly," said Agabus. "Do you know why?"

"Could it be because you have Goliath for a captain?" said Solomon. He laughed awkwardly.

"No, the doorway itself is not oversized. But notice the roof," said Agabus.

"I see something on top," said Hermes. "What is it?"

"Marcus calls it his 'Seeing Glass,'" answered Agabus. "It's an exceptionally large and thick piece of glass which Marcus had specially molded by the Phoenicians in Sidon. He's secretive about it, but I've been inside and you can hold a special piece of glass in your hand and gaze upward through it and can see faraway ships as though they were near. I've never seen one like it before. That's just one of his many eccentricities, but I allow it because he produces results."

"Come aboard! Come abo—ard!"

They heard the jangling of a bell from the ship. Passengers from the tavern began to move to the anteroom to get their baggage.

In the anteroom Hermes saw Ruth looking in dismay at the excessive amount of baggage at her feet. He walked over and asked, "May I help you carry your baggage?"

Behind him Solomon said, "That won't be necessary. I'll help her."

"I'll let you help me with mine," said Kore nearby in a cooing voice.

Hermes picked up Kore's baggage and led her out to the gangplank while she chattered to him all the way. A short line had formed at the foot of the gangplank where the First Mate, Erastus, was greeting passengers. As Hermes and Kore passed him, Erastus said to her, "You must be an exceptional lady, mam, persuading *this* man to carry your luggage. He's never done a lick of work in his life."

"Pay no attention to him, Kore. He's the cabin steward. Anything you need, just ask him." Hermes laughed, then added, "Seriously, this is the First Mate, Gaius Erastus. Friend, I'd like you to meet Kore."

"How do you do? Hermes had told me you were coming. We're glad to have you aboard. After you get all the baggage to your cabin, please return to the deck for the Captain's briefing. And—ah—don't forget to tip your porter."

After leaving Kore at the owner's cabin, Hermes returned to the anteroom to get his own luggage. As he was loading up, he saw Ruth and Solomon come in to get one last parcel. Standing in line at the gangplank a few minutes later, he glanced back and saw Solomon bidding Ruth farewell.

*Is he NOT going on the voyage? Marvelous!*

Solomon obviously wanted to kiss her, but Ruth, seeing Hermes, only permitted him an embrace.

At the briefing on deck, Captain Marcus Hippalus was all business. His fierce intensity was unsettling. He began the greeting in perfect Greek but shifted to Latin in a few moments while Erastus interpreted. Hermes wondered whether Marcus actually might, in fact, have excellent control of the Greek, but deigned to use it. There did appear a certain deviousness about him. Certainly, he did not appear to like people. Hermes took note of the Roman short sword at his side. This was Hermes' first opportunity to see Marcus up close. His face was scarred by childhood pox. Despite their intensity, his eyes looked sad, having a complex mixture of defeat and determination, of anger and sorrow, of strength and independence. The briefing was quite short; just the essentials. Marcus appeared to want to get back to his first love—sailing. Hermes never again heard him speak Greek.

When the ship got underway, the passengers—some score in number—crowded the railing to see the sights of the harbor. The deck of the sail ship proved an excellent place from which to view the city, and Alexandria had plenty to view.

After awhile Erastus came over to the passengers and described to them some of the sights—Cape Lochias, the Island Palace, the Caesareum where Caesar Augustus was worshiped—with its twin Cleopatra's Needles, the Theater, Alexander's Tomb, the groves of the Mouseion, the famous Library surrounded by buttressed walls, Pompey's Pillar, the Temple of Serapis, the Park of Pan, the Temple of Isis, the Shrine of Pompey, the Heptastadion Dike, and Pharos Island. The *Kibotos* sailed slowly along the placid waters of the crescent-shaped Great Harbor, affording them a prolonged view of the city at its height.

THE PHAROS AS BUILT BY
SOSTRATUS

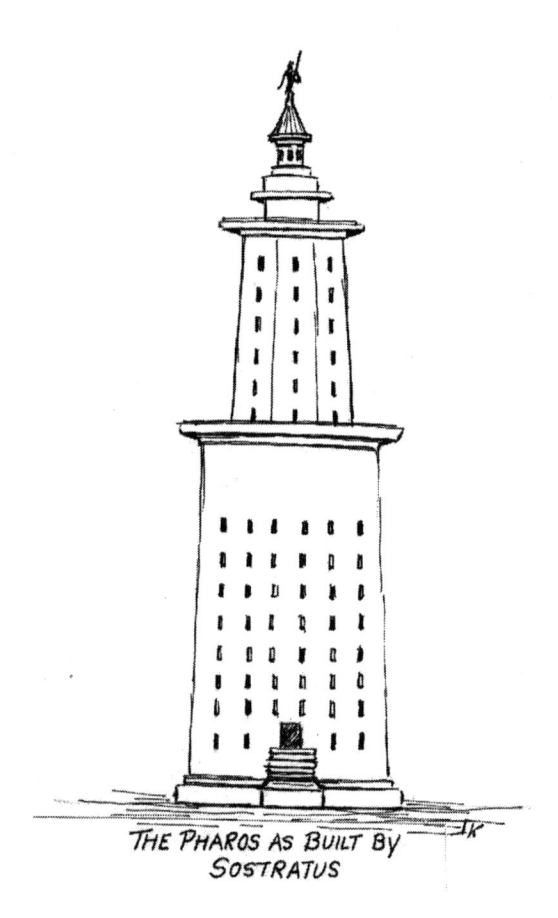

Erastus said, "Ahead on your left you can see the most incredible sight of all—the famous Pharos Lighthouse. One of the seven wonders of the world, it has already stood for over three centuries. A Grecian architect by the name of Sostratus built it on commission by the Ptolemies in 279 B.C. It stands over four hundred feet tall. The statue on the top is Poseidon."

People had to strain to see Poseidon, with his harpoon in hand, on the very crest of the lighthouse.

"Notice that it consists basically of four stories, or better four buildings—a building on a building on a building topped by the lighthouse."

While they sailed along, Agabus sought out Hermes, and found him standing at the railing, Kore at his side and Ruth on the other side of her. "What do you think of that colossus?"

"It's stunning," replied Hermes.

"It's especially stupendous at night," said Agabus. "The blaze of an oil fire magnified by reflectors can be seen by sailors three days out of port. All through the day workers are inside, hoisting oil to the top by means of a hydraulic lift. Furthermore, occupants in the Lighthouse can also *see* ships three days out of port, by means of something they call 'The Mirror.' Marcus got the idea for his 'Seeing Glass' from The Mirror."

Marcus did not mix with the passengers. No sooner had he dismissed the briefing, than he absorbed himself in the task of sailing. He was a master sailor but he was also single-minded. At this time of his life little else mattered to him but sailing.

*I cannot find Thee! Still on restless pinion*
*My spirit beats the void where Thou dost dwell;*
*I wander lost through all Thy vast dominion,*
*And shrink beneath Thy light ineffable.*

*I cannot lose Thee! Still in Thee abiding*
*The end is clear, how wide so e'er I roam;*
*The Law that holds the worlds my steps is guiding*
*And I must rest at last in Thee, my home.*

Eliza Scudder

# CHAPTER SEVEN

## FIRST DAY OUT OF ALEXANDRIA, AD 60

ON SAILING FROM Alexandria, the passengers were guests at the Captain's Mess for their first evening meal. The mess hall was located next door to and toward the stern from the owner's cabin which was midship on the first deck. Long tables were arranged throughout the mess hall, with the Captain's table on the exterior wall and perpendicular to the others. Approximately one-fifth of the tables were set with white linens. Captain Hippalus was not present; but seated at his table were the First Mate, the owner, and several junior officers. Mess personnel dressed in white togas served.

Following the meal Erastus left the head table and came over and visited with Hermes, Ruth, and Kore at their table. "Hello, folks, did you enjoy your meal?"

"It was very good. The beef was—Umm!—tender," said Hermes.

"The longer we sail, the less likely we are to have meat. We have no ice with which to pack it. When sailing out of Rome, we sometimes have ice—you know, brought down from the mountains—but not out of Alexandria. We do have a small amount of meat on hoof: a few lambs and hogs. Also some laying hens, fryers, fish, and lobster. So we'll fare pretty well. Now, if you'll excuse me, I must mix among the rest of the passengers."

Turning to leave, Erastus leaned over and whispered to Kore, "May I take you for a stroll on deck after dark?"

"What?—oh—why yes, I would love to."

"I'll knock on your door a little after dark."

When he walked away, Kore shyly looked up and the eyes of everyone at her table were on her.

"What did he say?" asked Ruth.

"Oh, nothing. I'll tell you later."

As dark settled in, Erastus knocked on the hall door of the owner's cabin. Kore opened the door. "Good evening! Ready to go?" he asked.

He could see Ruth and Agabus within. Several lamps were burning around the walls.

"Yes, let me get a shawl."

Erastus took her arm and led her down the semi-darkened hallway and helped her ascend the steep steps. The sky was gilded with brilliant stars against a pitch black background. The ship was gently swaying from side to side.

"Speak softly," whispered Erastus. "The Captain must not know I'm with you."

"Why not?" asked Kore.

"For my neck! He gave orders strictly forbidding anyone to have anything to do with you ladies. I'm responsible to enforce it."

"Why?"

"For your protection."

"Aren't you afraid he might come upon us?"

"Not really. This time of night he's in his cabin, over there, studying his charts."

Quietly, he led her past the cabin toward the stern.

"Good evening, First Mate," said the helmsman as they walked past.

"Good evening, pilot," said Erastus.

When they reached the railing, Kore said, "That glow on the horizon. Is that Alexandria?"

"Sure is. Look above the glow."

"What is it? A star? I know—Venus!"

"No, Venus is the morning star this month. That's the Pharos Lighthouse."

"Oh! It's so high."

"It is that. And just as we can see them, they can see us, through The Mirror—in the daytime, that is. We keep all the running lights out at night for protection against pirates."

They both stood together in silence for awhile, enjoying the view and the companionship of one another. The Great Sea was relatively calm. All they could hear was the bow slicing through the water, the constant groaning of the vessel's structure, and an occasional sea gull. Erastus glanced up at the billowing sail and said, "We're getting a slow start. That's a westerly breeze."

Kore turned around to look up at the towering mast and leaned back casually with her elbows on the railing. Erastus looked down into her face and she smiled at him.

"I'm flattered that you should invite me like this," she said. "Tell me, though, why didn't Hermes ask Ruth also?"

"I don't know. I haven't had time to talk with him this afternoon. Knowing him, he probably didn't think of it. Was she disappointed?"

"Well, she was certainly envious of me."

The two casually conversed awhile longer before Erastus escorted her back to her cabin.

After breakfast the next morning, Erastus pulled Hermes, Ruth, and Kore aside and said, "Let me take you to tea at the mess hall later this morning. I'll take a break about midmorning and knock on your doors."

Agabus was seated at a desk in his suite studying some manuscripts. At the sound of three bells he arose and knocked on the ladies' door. His cabin had been large enough to divide in two, enabling the ladies to enjoy the privacy of their own quarters within the protective enclosure of his cabin.

"Ladies," he said, "it's time for morning prayers."

Miriam answered the door. Inside, Kore said in a husky whisper, "Ruth, what about Erastus and Hermes?"

"Father," Ruth said, "Can we hurry? We had something else we wanted to do in a few minutes."

"Come on then. I'm ready to go," said Agabus.

"We are, too," answered Ruth.

Agabus led the party down the hall, up the stairs, and across the deck to the stern. On the fan deck Miriam spread out a small rug. Agabus pulled his tallit over his head, and the ladies placed kerchiefs on theirs. Then Agabus led their united recitation in a sing-song voice, saying, "Hear, O Israel: The Lord our God is one Lord: and thou shall love the Lord thy God with all thine heart, and with all thy soul—"

"Silence!!" boomed a deep voice, like a tuba in a cavern, behind them. It was Marcus. "What you are doing is forbidden on this ship! Roll up your mat and return to your cabins. Do there whatever you were doing—not here."

He towered menacingly over them, anger flashing from his face.

"What do you mean by this?" said Agabus, struggling to his feet.

"I mean you cannot do that on this ship. There will be no public religious services here. Playacting, that's all it is, anyway. Who knows whether or not there is a god? Not I. Not you. Not anyone. You just want to impress others with your self-righteousness. I'll not allow others on this ship to be shamed by your example. That's it."

Marcus turned and walked away. Agabus pursued and grabbed him by the arm. "See here now."

Marcus abruptly shook his hand loose and looked down belligerently into his face. "What is it?"

"You have no right to do this," said Agabus loudly. "This is not your ship. I will not permit you to tell me what I can or cannot do on my own ship."

"While we are at sea," Marcus said in measured tones, "according to Roman maritime law, I set the rules on this ship. If you don't like it, fire me."

He walked away again. Agabus stood shaking with rage. The ladies hurriedly gathered up their belongings and fled down the stairs, weeping aloud. Agabus followed, stomping noisily, and slammed the cabin door loudly behind him. He was so livid he could not speak.

At that moment there came a soft rap on the door.

"Who is it?" shouted Agabus.

"The First Mate, sir."

"Don't bother me."

Kore came running out of her compartment and opened the door. "Oh, Erastus, come in and help us."

Erastus and Hermes entered. "What in the world's wrong?" asked Erastus.

Kore and Ruth were crying. Each blurted out such incoherent bits and pieces of the story that Hermes interrupted and said, "Slow down. Let me try to get this straight. The four of you went up on deck to pray? Then Marcus came up and demanded you quit? He said it was forbidden on this ship? That's preposterous."

Agabus arose from his desk chair, where he had been seated with his back to them. He walked over to Erastus. "Gaius Erastus, I am here and now relieving Marcus Hippalus of command and making you captain of the *Kibotos*. I shall write out orders for you."

Erastus looked dumbfounded. Agabus said no more, but returned to his desk and began writing. Erastus followed him saying, "Sir, I beg you not to do this. I'm not ready for command. I can't control this ship, this crew. Sir, with all due respect I think you're overreacting. The incident is not that serious. I beg you to reconsider. You need Marcus."

Agabus arose from his desk and with a trembling hand offered him a document. "The deed is done. Here is your authorization."

"With all due respect, sir, I refuse to accept these orders. I'm leaving your quarters now; I shall return to talk with you after the noon meal, after you've had time to think this over."

Erastus turned and walked out. Hermes said to the ladies, "I'll be back," and ran after Erastus. "Just a minute," he called. When he caught up with him, he said, "Let's take the ladies into the mess hall as we'd planned and talk this over with them. We might can be of help."

"Alright. Get them and I'll meet you there."

Hermes went back for the three ladies.

As they sat down at a long table Ruth was in tears. "Why did he have to be like that?"

"Your father?" asked Erastus.

"No, Marcus."

There was silence. Hermes said, "It's because he's not a religious man."

Ruth looked up into his face and searched his eyes for a few moments. "Well, are *you*?"

"Ah—, yes, in a sense. I believe there's a god. Not like the Greeks, though. I believe there's just one god, like some of the old Egyptians did."

"Or like the Hebrews do?" she asked.

"Oh, I don't know. Maybe not. I haven't given up the Greek's gods just to accept some other national god."

"I know what you mean," said Ruth. "I tire of the idea of a national god, too. And yet the Hebrews, when you get right down to it, don't actually believe in a national god either. I know in practice many of them do. But we don't. At the time Marcus interrupted us, we were reciting a statement of our faith called the *Shema*, which starts out like this, 'The Lord our God is *one* Lord.' Actually, we believe in one *universal* God."

The ladies were no longer crying.

Erastus said, "Do you people believe in someone called a Messiah?"

"Do we?" said Kore. "That's our highest hope—the hope of his coming."

"Well, I know of a group who believe he's already come—in the earlier part of this century. They say his name was Jesus. In fact they call him Jesus Christ or Jesus the Messiah."

"Oh, them," said Ruth. "I know who you're talking about. But the problem is, we believe Elijah has to return first. The Messiah can't come until Elijah returns."

She sighed aloud.

"I've heard that," said Erastus. "But they say Elijah has already come—in the form of John the Baptist. You've heard of John the Baptist, haven't you?"

Ruth looked startled, as if in a moment of truth. "Why, yes . . . It does make sense. So that's who John the Baptist was. I've often wondered what his mission was. It's all beginning to make sense now. I never thought of that."

She lifted her eyes again and looked intently at Erastus and asked, "Are you one of them—a follower of Jesus?"

"Yes, Erastus," said Hermes, "I've wondered about that myself. Tell us. Are you one of them?"

Ruth cocked an eyebrow at Hermes and turned again to Erastus. "Seriously, Erastus, I want to know," she said. "I'm eager to find out more about Jesus if I can."

"Don't look at me like that. No, I'm not. I've just gone to some of their meetings. Hermes and I went there together last Sunday," Erastus replied, glancing toward Hermes.

"Where?"

"Where? Well, right there in Alexandria—at a meeting place in the Jewish Quarters. Over near the waterfront just east of Cape Lochias."

"I'm going there when I get back. Kore, let's go together."

"Wonderful!" said Kore.

"Hermes, would you take me—er—us," Ruth said. "I'd be a little afraid to go alone."

"Why, yes. Ahem. That is if I return to Alexandria."

Ruth looked hurt. "You are coming back, aren't you? . . . You have to complete your studies, don't you?"

Kore spoke up. "If he won't, Erastus can take us. You will, won't you, Erastus? Say you will."

"Sure. Why not?"

"We could all four go together," said Ruth.

"Ahem," said Hermes, "That brings up another subject. What about old longlegs?"

"Who?" asked Ruth.

"Solomon."

"Oh, him?" Ruth said. "He wouldn't be found dead in that place."

"Ruth," said Hermes, "could I ask you a personal question?"

"Mmmmm?" she replied.

"Are you, how do they say it—'betrothed'—to Solomon?"

"No, I'm promised to him but not betrothed," she replied, placing her hand upon Hermes' hand. "I won't tell you what I think of him, though."

They talked on—no one noticed that Ruth did not remove her hand from atop Hermes' hand—no one but Hermes, that is.

After they left the mess hall, Erastus knocked on the door of Marcus' cabin.

"What do you want?" said Marcus loudly from within.
"It's the First Mate, sir. May I speak with you a moment?"
"Come in."

Erastus had been in the Captain's cabin several times before and was familiar with its layout. This time, though, he was mildly distracted by the glare of the sunlight through the Seeing Glass overhead. Caesar was lying curled up in a corner. The dog acknowledged the visitor by opening one eye and wagging its tail slightly. Marcus was standing on a chair beneath the Seeing Glass peering upward through a handheld glass piece. He looked down briefly at Erastus when he entered, then resumed his viewing. "Make it brief," he said.

"Sir, I want to report a conversation I just had with Ben Uri."

"Go ahead."

"He told me about an encounter he had with you this morning. He said you interrupted his prayer time and prohibited him from ever praying on deck again. He said you claim total control of the ship so long as it's at sea."

"So?"

"Then he handed me a set of orders relieving you of duty and making me captain of the *Kibotos*." He paused.

Marcus continued looking upward. "And?"

"I told him I refused to accept the orders."

He paused again and waited for Marcus to speak. Marcus dropped the glass piece to his side and looked down at Erastus. His eyes looked weary. "Do as you wish. I'll not fight you. There are plenty of other owners begging for me."

"Sir, I remain steadfastly loyal to you. I will not undermine your leadership. I will *not* accept Ben Uri's offer. You can count on me."

"I can? Then just where were you when you talked to Ben Uri?"

Erastus felt trapped. He stammered, "I—I was in his cabin, sir."

"Why? Did he call you in?"

"No, sir."

"Then why were you in his cabin?"

"I had gone there to talk to the ladies."

"You what?" Marcus shouted. He stepped down off the chair. "I gave strict orders against all familiarity with the ladies."

He started backing Erastus toward the door, leaning over him shaking the glass in his face.

"You're the First Mate. It was up to you to post those orders. Little man, have you forgotten your role? Didn't you realize that you're the enforcer of the captain's orders? Then why do you behave like a swabbie. You think this is just a game? You think you're somebody special? You think my orders don't apply to you? You say you remain steadfastly loyal to me. Then why do you break my orders? You boast about being offered command of the *Kibotos*. You couldn't command a row boat. You haven't got it in you. You walk in here dreaming of being captain, but you've come close to walking out of here as a seaman. I insist on obedience. You follow my orders! Leave those ladies alone, do you hear?"

"Yes, sir!" said Erastus, snapping to attention. "It will be as you say. If you have nothing else, sir, may I be dismissed."

"Go!"

Marcus turned and stepped back onto the chair while Erastus hastily exited.

Erastus was stung by the scolding—but not demoralized. He knew that he had risked repremand by seeing Kore. At least he had not lost his job. Now he had to go confront Agabus one more time. He felt caught between two giants.

After lunch Erastus returned to Agabus' cabin. He was impressed that Agabus was again reading scrolls. Ruth was sitting nearby doing needle work. He saw the commission naming him captain of the *Kibotos* open on the desk. He felt a brief moment of indecision.

"The offer is still open," said Agabus warmly. "Have you changed your mind?"

"Sir," he said, "I promised this morning I would return to talk with you after lunch. Having had time to think it over, I must say that I'm all the more convinced I did the right thing in refusing the commission. Personally, I feel honored—and tempted to no small degree. But I am convinced it would not be in my best interest at this time, nor in the best interest of the ship."

"Father," said Ruth, "it's not absolutely necessary that we go on deck to pray. We can pray right here in the cabin, can't we?"

Agabus turned toward his daughter. "My dear, I'm doing this for you. I saw how stricken you were with the captain's words this morning."

"I'll get over it. But I think Erastus is right. Keeping Marcus on would be best. Do what you like, but you don't have to fire him on my account."

Erastus said, "Sir, if you would accept a suggestion, why not wait until the voyage is over to fire Marcus. There's no real rush."

"If I do, then what about this?" Agabus said motioning toward the commission. "Shall I file it for future use?"

"Why not destroy it, sir?"

Agabus looked at Ruth, then back at Erastus. "Very well," he said. He picked up the document and tore it three ways and dropped it into a waste basket. "It's done."

*Howsoe'er I stray or range,*
*'Whate'er I do, Thou dost not change.*

Arthur Hugh Clough

# CHAPTER EIGHT

## FOURTH DAY OUT OF ALEXANDRIA, AD 60

HERMES ABRUPTLY SAT up in bed. A bell jangled violently. He heard a cry, "Everyone on deck!" The *Kibotos* was listing strongly to port.

*Swerving! Must be a crisis!*

Hurriedly, he threw on his tunic and stepped into the hallway, the first passenger out of the cabins. Light from the stairwell indicated the sun was up. At the opposite end of the hallway sailors were scurrying topside.

"What is it?" he called out to one of them.

"Don't know. The Captain's called an emergency meeting of everyone on deck."

Hermes walked over to the door of the owner's cabin and waited a few moments. Presently, Agabus stepped out. Seeing Hermes, he said, "Do you know what this is?"

"The sailors say it's an emergency meeting on deck."

"Ben Uri," bellowed a voice behind Hermes, "we need to have a quick talk."

Hermes turned to see Marcus striding quickly down the hallway. "Let's step inside," said Marcus.

The three ladies were just coming out the door and Marcus stepped back to let them pass. Hermes started to follow the two men into the cabin but Marcus put his arm across the doorway and said, "You go topside!"

Marcus closed the door behind them. Hermes then led the ladies to the stairwell.

On deck Erastus stood facing the assembling throng. Hermes sidled up to him and whispered, "What is it?"

"Pirates." He shrugged his shoulder toward the west. Hermes glanced that direction but could see nothing. Momentarily, the Captain and the owner came up on deck and joined Erastus.

Marcus spoke a sentence in Latin and several in the crowd looked to the west. Erastus then translated, "We're being approached by two unidentified ships from the west." The rest of the crowd also looked westward. Marcus continued, "I have reason to believe they are attackers. We have changed our course to the northeast to try to veer away from them. They may not have seen us yet."

After gazing futilely westward, several of the sailors looked at one another. Others looked up and saw that the crow's nest was empty, though men were at that moment scampering up the mast. A strong westerly wind was filling the sail.

"We're also unfurling the topsail and foresail," continued Marcus, "to try to outrun them. Chances are, though, they will catch up with us by midafternoon. I'm calling an immediate alert. The Second Mate will issue weapons from the quartermaster store following the briefing. Then prepare your fighting positions. After the crew has been armed, we're asking each passenger to secure a weapon for his—or her—own safety. Passengers, remain in your cabins. We will have the lower deck sealed off if an attack occurs. Tar squad, begin heating the tar immediately. Off-duty crew members, return to your quarters with your weapons. Duty crew, go about your normal activities in the meantime. When you hear another alarm from the bells, everyone report promptly to his battle station. Any questions?" There being none, he said, "Dismissed."

What followed was an orderly, well-organized procedure. Men hastily lined up in the hallway outside the quartermaster store to receive swords, spears, knives, bows and arrows, ropes, and other combat items. Others scampered to and from the mess hall carrying firebricks and large urns to the deck.

Ruth, Kore, and Miriam hurriedly worked their way through the crowd toward their cabin. Ruth was ashen. Kore trembled. "What are we going to do?" she said.

"I don't know. I'm scared," said Ruth.

Miriam was wringing her hands. Just as they were entering their cabin, Hermes came up behind them. Ruth saw him and cried, "Oh, Hermes, what are we going to do? I'm terrified."

"Try not to worry. Marcus Hippalus has been training the crew all summer for just such an event as this. He's an army veteran. He knows what he's doing. We'll come through okay. You'll see."

Kore said, "What do pirates do to women? I think I'm going to scream!"

"Calm down, Kore," Hermes said. "They haven't even seen us yet. We might get away without being seen."

Agabus appeared in the doorway. Softly he said, "We must not fear." He walked over and withdrew a scroll from a cabinet. "Come over hear and listen." He unrolled the scroll and began to read:

> He that dwelleth in the secret place of the most High shall abide under the shadow of the Almighty. I will say of the Lord, He is my refuge and my fortress: my God; in him will I trust. Surely he shall deliver thee from the snare of the fowler, and from the noisome pestilence. He shall cover thee with his feathers, and under his wings shalt thou trust: his truth shall be thy shield and buckler. Thou shalt not be afraid for the terror by night; nor for the destruction that

wasteth at noonday. A thousand shall fall at thy side, and ten thousand at thy right hand; but it shall not come nigh thee. Only with thine eyes shalt thou see the reward of the wicked because thou hast made the Lord, which is my refuge, even the most High, thy habitation; there shall no evil befall thee, neither shall any plague come nigh thy dwelling. For he shall give his angels charge over thee, to keep thee in all thy ways.

When he finished reading, he led the group in a simple prayer.

"I must look a fright," Ruth promptly said.

"I'm famished," Kore said. "Will they be serving breakfast this morning?"

Hermes was impressed even though he had not been able to understand the Hebrew language. *Amazing! Such tranquility! And all from reading a passage of scripture. I even feel calmer myself.*

"I'll go check on breakfast," he said. "But first, Agabus, I'd like to ask a question. How does Marcus know that pirates are approaching?"

The ladies went into their compartment.

"He could see them through his Seeing Glass."

"I thought so. I wish I could look through it."

"I doubt that will be possible. He seldom allows anyone in his cabin."

"One other question," said Hermes. "Do you believe in angels?"

"Angels? Yes, I do," replied Agabus. "They're in God's Word. They are, as their name implies, 'messengers' from God to help us in our extremities."

"Do you believe that the Messiah will be an angel?"

"Well, no. Most believe that he will be a human being—with mighty powers—and will deliver the land of Israel from . . . well, from the yoke of Rome. He will set it free again. He might be a king or maybe a mighty priest or perhaps a new prophet. A few believe that God Himself will be the messiah."

"Hmmm. You believe that there is only one God for all the earth, that he is *your* God, and that he will send a mighty deliverer to you or that he might even come himself to rescue you. That's pretty audacious. When will this happen?"

"Soon, we think," said Agabus.

"Could he have already come—the Messiah, that is? Some Jews claim that Jesus was the Messiah."

"I don't think so. Jesus died in Jerusalem about twenty-five or thirty years ago. The Romans crucified him."

"Crucified? Oh! I didn't know that. I hope you don't mind all these questions."

"Not at all," replied Agabus with a smile.

Hermes excused himself and went next door to the mess hall. In a few minutes he came back and knocked on the owner's door. When Agabus opened, Hermes said, "Erastus said he will be down in a few minutes and take us to the mess hall. It will have to be a cold breakfast, since the fireplace has been removed. May I knock on the ladies' door and tell them."

"Of course," said Agabus returning to his desk.

When he knocked, Ruth opened the door a crack and he gave her the message. Hermes then left again.

Hermes was alone in his cabin following breakfast when he felt an unusual movement of the ship. He went topside to see what it meant. He still saw no other ships but he did see the foresail being turned and the huge yardarms and mainsail being rotated by the crew. Erastus was directing the operation. Hermes went over to him. "What's up, Erastus?"

"The Captain said the pirates have spotted us and are in pursuit. The lookout hasn't see anything yet though."

The Captain himself was not to be seen. Hermes glanced at the thick glass atop his cabin and imagined Marcus inside monitoring the approach of the two vessels.

Shortly after noon a shrill cry came from the crow's nest, "Pirates! Pirates! Here they come!"

The ship's bell started clanging violently. Sailors poured out of their cabins, weapons ready, and scurried throughout the ship. Hermes dashed topside to see two specks approaching from the west. Erastus saw him, ran over, and said, "Back below. Help me scour the cabins for stragglers."

They ran throughout the crew's bays. Then Erastus said, "Here, let's secure the hatches."

Together they pulled closed the hatch at one staircase and slid a rod through metal hasps. Then they both dashed down the hall to the other staircase. Erastus said, "Stay down here and care for the rest of the passengers. We can't open the hatches from above. Don't open them unless you hear a slower jangling of the bells indicating 'all clear' or else a series of three bells, like ding, ding, ding, pause, ding, ding, ding, pause, indicating 'abandon ship.' And, Hermes, —pray! After I go up, bolt this hatch behind me as we did the other. Okay?"

"Understood."

Erastus dashed up the steps, and Hermes securely bolted the hatch closed. He glanced down the semi-darkened hallway and saw several passengers standing in their doorways. He walked down to them and told them the situation. Then he knocked on the door to the owner's suite. Kore answered the door. "Hermes, come on in and stay with us if you can."

The three ladies were in the outer compartment—Agabus' cabin—seated close to him.

Hermes pulled up a low stool and they made room for him. He said, "I could see two pirate crafts closing in on us from the west."

Although Agabus' cabin was on the west side of the ship, it had no porthole through which to view the action. Lamps mounted on the walls burned constantly and the space reeked of spent oil.

Ruth said, "Pirates? In this day and age? Who are they? What do they want?"

"They're Nabataeans," Agabus said. "The desert people. Their capitol is Petra. I've been there before and I found them to be a highly developed people. You ought to go there sometime and see their architecture. The city is well named *The Rock*. It's located within a barren, rocky canyon south of the Dead Sea. Whole buildings are carved out of the canyon walls. The place is impregnable—and wealthy too. A Nabataean king once held a banquet in Rome in the days of Tiberius and gave away gold crowns as gifts. Oh, and incidentally, Herod Antipas had a Nabataean wife before he married Herodious."

"If they're really so wealthy," said Ruth, "why are they pirates?"

"Maybe that's what makes them wealthy," said Kore. Ruth and Miriam laughed nervously.

"The pirates are probably just renegades," Hermes said. "I understand they have hidden ports on the Sinai coast."

The sound of feverish activity on deck carried down through the ceiling. Hermes asked, "Have you each gotten weapons yet?"

"I have a spear," said Agabus, pointing to a shaft tipped with a shiny steel point, standing in the corner.

"How about you ladies? Do you have anything?"

"I couldn't use one of those things, anyway," said Kore.

"How about swords or knives?" said Hermes.

They shook their heads.

"Let me go see if I can get you something. The stairwells are locked and we're sealed off down here, but it's better to be armed just in case."

He left and returned shortly with short daggers and gave one to each of the ladies. "Now I must go check on some things." He left the cabin again.

Hermes was stewing around in his cabin when he heard the slow mournful beat of drums wafting across the sea. *Galleys!* As the sound grew louder, the beat grew more rapid. Soon he knew they were extremely close. His cabin being on the west side of the ship, he braced himself for a jolt.

Meanwhile, topside, all the crew members of the *Kibotos* were in place, in readiness for the attack. Both attack ships were moving extremely fast, being driven by the force of the oars and the high wind. They were approaching from the port side and toward the bow of the *Kibotos*, shrewdly calculating their point of impact the way an archer does who shoots arrows ahead of a moving prey. The *Kibotos* was too large to take evasive action.

BOOM! A ship struck them broadside. When it hit, the pirate vessel literally bounced backward and the impact threw the rowers from their seats.

Hermes was thrown all the way across his cabin. *Must have hit directly against my cabin!* The crash was deafening.

The top of the *Kibotos'* mast heaved violently to starboard but slowly righted itself as the momentum of the grain ship carried it past the pirate's vessel, which was now dead in the water. The second vessel barely missed the stern of the *Kibotos* and then turned northeasterly in hot pursuit. Marcus quickly sent seamen down into the hold to inspect for damage. The grain bags had shifted radically toward port, but no evidence of leakage showed—the side timbers had effectively dissipated the force of the blow!

Now the second pirate vessel was catching up on the starboard side. When it drew directly alongside, a dozen grappling hooks simultaneously shot over the railing of the *Kibotos.* Just as quickly, crew members of the defending ship hoisted two large urns to the railing and poured boiling tar down upon the startled pirates. Two large urns of lamp oil followed. Without delay flaming arrows from the deck of the *Kibotos* struck both the oil-soaked deck and the billowing sail of the galley, instantaneously setting a massive fire that destroyed the sail and swept uncontrollably across the deck from prow to stern. With methodical efficiency, trained crew members aboard the *Kibotos* moved up to the railing and disengaged the grappling hooks, allowing the flaming Nabataean vessel to fall behind in total disarray.

The other attack ship was again moving up on the port side. On the *Kibotos* a daring action was underway. At the starboard bow Marcus and another seaman tied long ropes around their waists, slipped over the side of the ship, and rested their feet on the timbers which had protected them against the ramming. They then walked the timbers over to the bow. When the first pirate ship caught up with the *Kibotos,* the two dived into the water out of sight of the attackers. Clinging to the timbers at water level, they worked their way around the bow, then submerged and reeled themselves out along the port side of the *Kibotos* and moved toward the stern of the attacking vessel.

Meanwhile, having witnessed the cunning tactics used against their sister ship, the pirates remained just far enough away from the *Kibotos* to be out of reach of the hot tar. A rain of arrows drove the *Kibotos* defenders back from the side of the ship as the grappling hooks again shot up and snagged on the railing. Urn bearers who attempted to hoist their tar and oil containers to the railing were felled by sharpshooters. In an instant the side of the huge *Kibotos* was awash with Nabataean attackers pouring over the railing. A fierce hand-to-hand battle broke out on deck.

Below deck Hermes heard a scream. He flew into the hall from his cabin and saw a Nabataean pirate poised in the open doorway of Ben Uri's cabin. Hermes did not stop running until the spear in his hand penetrated the back of the enemy. He jerked his spear out and heard a shout behind him, "Look out." He dodged sideways just as a sword bypassed his head and struck him in the right arm. He grabbed his arm, dropping his sword to the floor, and turned to see another pirate fall dead at his feet, a thrown knife in his back. Erastus was standing on the steps several feet away. "Check on Kore and Ruth," he shouted, pulling the hatch cover back down behind him, relocking it, and starting down the hallway.

"Ruth, it's me, Hermes," Hermes said as he stumbled into her cabin. "It's okay, now. They're dead."

When he came through the doorway, Ruth ran into his arms while Kore dashed to Erastus behind him. Neither woman was hurt.

Ruth drew back from Hermes with blood on her hand. "Hermes, you're hurt."

Hermes looked down at his forearm and sat down. "I don't think it's bad." He flexed his fingers and wrist. "It's just a flesh wound."

"You poor man," said Ruth. "Here let me help you. Miriam, bring us some water and rags. Hurry."

While Hermes was being treated, Erastus went out to check on the two Nabataeans, then dragged their bodies away from the door. When he returned to the cabin, Hermes was on his feet again with his arm wrapped in a cloth.

Erastus said, "They broke the hinges of the hatch above and forced it open. Quick, I've got to get back topside. Follow me and secure the hatch behind me as best you can. I'll post several defenders above it to prevent this happening again. You might do well to stand at the foot of the steps with your spear handy just in case. Agabus, close your door and put some furniture in front of it."

Erastus dashed back topside, his sword flailing.

Underwater, reeling out the ropes that pulled them through the water, Marcus and the other sailor maneuvered to the pointed stern of the Nabataean vessel. They had to risk surfacing briefly for air, but the juxtaposition of the two ships prevented their being seen. They removed curved metal bars from their sashes and again submerged. At the stern, they inserted their bars into the seam where the ship's planks came together and began prying, bracing their knees against the barnacled sides of the ship. They pulled with all their might but nothing happened. It appeared at first the tactic might not succeed. Marcus was on the port side of the stern, the other man on the starboard side; but the forward movement and rocking motion of the ship made it difficult to exert enough pressure on the planks. Finally, with a herculean effort, Marcus wedged his bar deeply enough into the seam to be able to pry away the end of one of the boards. Quickly, he thrust his bar through the hole and against the back of the board on which the other man was working. With the butt of his hand, Marcus struck the end of the bar and broke the board loose, at which time his partner quickly pried the end of it the rest of the way off. Marcus then pulled himself around the stern into view of the sailor and motioned upward with his finger. The two resurfaced.

Gasping for air, Marcus said, "We're . . . making headway. Once more . . . should do it."

He could hear the clang of sword against sword above. He turned bottom up and resubmerged, followed by the other man.

Both resumed their positions at the stern and this time began to make rapid progress. Planks started splintering and breaking away on both sides of the keel until two severe gashes the size of large urns were created. Seawater poured into the very hold of the ship with a vengeance.

When Marcus started to swim back around the stern to resurface, the powerful surge of water into the hold caught him and sucked his legs through one of the openings. He grabbed hold of the keel and his partner caught his rope. The pressure on him was overpowering. It was a critical moment! Marcus' grasp was loosening. One hand was forced off the keel. His partner tried to maneuver himself toward Marcus without being sucked into the current himself. Blindly, Marcus thrust his free hand outward through the current. Instantly, his partner grasped it, just as Marcus' other hand lost its hold. At grave risk the man stood up, positioning his feet on either side of the gaping opening and tugged with all his might. The effort was successful and Marcus emerged from the opening. He rolled himself out of the opening and around the ship's side, away from the flow of the water, and headed for the surface, followed by his partner.

The two then drifted over to the side of the *Kibotos* to await the results of their work. From their vantage point they could see an almost immediate lowering of the pirate vessel. In the excitement above, the sinking effect was not obvious to the attackers at first—

not until it was too late. The boarding ropes between the two ships began to snap one by one. The thicker ropes that tied the smaller vessel to the *Kibotos* grew taut and held the starboard side of the low-slung pirate ship up out of the water while the port side tilted below water level, swiftly flooding the deck with seawater. Seeing what was happening, a specially trained *Kibotos* sailor broke contact with the enemy on deck, dashed to the railing, and swiftly cut the ropes of the grappling hooks just in time to prevent the swamping vessel from pulling the *Kibotos* underwater with it.

The hand-to-hand combat aboard the *Kibotos* ceased as the warriors of both sides turned to see the swift sinking. Then, quickly, the tide of battle turned. Many Nabataeans dashed to the railing and dived overboard. Some who could not get to the railings were quickly surrounded and summarily executed. It became only a mopping-up exercise. The repeated cry, "Spare me!," resounded across the deck; but in the exhilaration of their victory over the superior foe, the novice warriors abandoned all mercy and finished off the pirates to a man. Some even shot arrows at the hapless strugglers in the sea.

As the situation on deck came under control and the noise abated, Erastus noticed the barking of Caesar from the captain's cabin. He ran to the port side. "Help me find the Captain," he shouted.

"Here they are back here," came the reply.

Erastus ran to the stern and leaned over the railing to see the two exhausted men being pulled along by the ropes. Marcus had a bloody dagger in his teeth, having been forced to defend them against several Nabataeans in the water. Neither of the two was hurt. By now the ship's forward movement had carried them beyond the danger. Erastus could see scores of pirates afloat in the sea behind them and a longboat picking up survivors. The smoldering hulk of the first pirate vessel lay further back. Marcus withdrew the dagger from his mouth, sheathed it in his loincloth, and shouted, "Throw down some ropes."

Erastus grabbed two nearby ropes and tossed them down and

pulled the two men up onto deck. When their drenched captain emerged into view over the railing, the seamen let out an ear-splitting cheer.

A hero's cheer from these people meant nothing to Marcus Hippalus. He shrugged it off as though it were merely the clamor of children chasing a candy vendor. What need had he for them? He had walked with Centurions, Prefects, Tribunals, even an Emperor. Was he not on a first-name basis with a world famous author? Had he not once led an entire squadron of galleys into combat. This latest feat meant little more to him than a fool's entertainment for the rabble between gladiatorial events.

Sailors and passengers alike were clapping their wet, barefoot, half-clad leader on the back, clasping his wrist, hugging his waist, shouting their gratitude, praise, and adulation to him as he walked across the wooden deck. Yet not a smile broke his grim face, not even a slight nod acknowledged their praise. His broad shoulders shuddered at every touch as though he resented being approached so familiarly by this mob.

Suddenly, he turned and roared at the crowd. The people around him fell back. "What did he say?" asked someone on the fringe of the crowd. Someone else translated, "He said, 'Get your filthy hands off me!'" He was brandishing his knife. The crowd grew quiet.

They watched as he walked over to his cabin. When he opened the door, his dog came bounding out, jumping up on his master and yelping with excitement. Marcus bent down and fondled the dog's ears, then straightened and looked up at the pilot. "Untie the rudders. Reset our course northward. I'll be up in a minute to check the direction. Second Mate, have this mess cleaned up. First Mate!" He paused a second and looked around. "Rastus," he shouted.

Erastus said, "Here, Captain."

"Follow me," said Marcus. They entered the cabin.

The subdued crowd on deck began milling around. A loud yell came from the stern, "Three cheers for Philip!" A knot of people began shouting, "Hip, hip, hooray! Hip, hip, hooray! Hip, hip, hooray!" The rest of the crowd turned to see a band of men lifting to their shoulders the sailor who had assisted Marcus in the water. The man was grinning with delight. A wave of jubilation swept over the deck. A rousing Greek song broke out, accompanied by the rhythmic stomping of feet and clapping of hands, as they carried their new hero back and forth over the deck.

When they heard the bells ringing "all clear", Agabus and the ladies in his cabin began shouting for joy. There was a loud bang on the door, and they heard Hermes's voice, "It's me. Hurry up. Open up." They pulled furniture out of the way, and Hermes burst through the door and yelled, "It's over. We must have driven them off."

Ruth rushed into his arms and clung to him with her feet dangling behind her. Hermes grunted with pain.

"Oh, I'm so sorry. I forgot about your wound."

She fell to her feet and Hermes sat down grasping his arm. Ruth said, "As soon as we can, we need to have that seen to. It might get infected. There's an orderly on board."

"I'm in no hurry. He'll have so many others to tend to now. There's no need of rushing."

Agabus said, "Ladies, come listen to the Scriptures."

Hermes arose and said, "I'd better go release the hatches."

"No, stay with us awhile. Someone else can do that," said Ruth.

"Alright," said Hermes and sat back down.

Agabus began reading.

> O give thanks unto the Lord, for he is good: because his mercy endureth for ever. Let Israel now say, that his mercy endureth for ever. Let the house of Aaron now say, that his mercy endureth for ever. Let them now that fear the Lord say, that his mercy endureth for ever. I called upon the Lord in distress: the Lord answered me, and set me in a large

place. The Lord is on my side; I will not fear: what can man do unto me. The Lord taketh my part with them that help me: therefore shall I see my desire upon them that hate me. It is better to trust in the Lord than to put confidence in man. It is better to trust in the Lord than to put confidence in princes.

Hermes again found himself transfixed by the reading. *They see this delivery as occurring strictly for their benefit. It was done for them. They allow no credit to the sailors—to Hippalus. Their "Lord" rescued them.*

Erastus walked the decks and halls the rest of the day and through half the night. Since most of the crew were so keyed up they could not sleep, he permitted those off-duty to raid the wine stock and throw a wild party in the mess hall. It was pandemonium.

After dark he knocked on the door to the owner's cabin.

He heard Agabus' voice, "Who is it"

"The First Mate, sir. I'd like to talk to Kore."

The door opened and Agabus said, "Come on in, Erastus. I'll get her."

Agabus tapped on the ladies' door and said, "Kore, you have a visitor."

Kore appeared at the door and said with excitement, "Oh, Erastus."

"Care to go for a stroll on deck? I saw Ruth and Hermes up there."

"Sure, I couldn't sleep with the uproar next door anyway. Let me get some wrap."

They joined Hermes and Ruth who were seated on a bench at the bow. Hermes' arm was in a sling.

"Are you in charge tonight?" Hermes asked Erastus.

"Yes, the Captain's sleeping. He's not likely to catch us. He retired right after the battle."

"You must be weary too," said Kore to Erastus. "You haven't had a break all day, have you?"

"No. I am pretty fatigued."

"I heard Hippalus pulled a knife on the sailors today," Hermes said.

"That was shocking. It really upset the crew. They were just slapping him on the back in appreciation, but he didn't want them touching him. Thought he was too good for them. Then he called me 'Rastus,' right before the whole crew."

"Boy, that was the wrong thing to say. You used to hate that nickname when we were growing up."

"Yes, it's made me pretty discouraged. You know, I had charge of the whole crew while he was underwater scuttling the pirate's craft. That's alright, but what thanks did I get for it? None. Not from the crew... They were beside themselves over Philip, but no one said an iota to me. Not from Agabus... He kept saying over and over, "Didn't I tell you I had the best captain on the Great Sea?" Not from the Captain... He just congratulated himself. You know what he said?

"He said, 'Ha! I won again!' But when I congratulated him on the victory, he said, 'I'm not talking about the Nabataeans. I'm talking about the wind, the elements.' He said the wind pushed the enemy toward him. He believes the elements have been out to conquer him all his life. While he was talking to me, he suddenly got this crazy look in his eyes and jumped up from his bunk and violently put his hands together as if he were choking somebody and said, 'I beat you this time, you vile foe. And I'll beat you the next time too.'

"You know what I think? Don't tell anyone I said this, but I believe he's getting so obsessed with the elements he's going crazy. He could get dangerous some day—you know, pulling that knife on his own crew like he did. Maybe I should have taken the command when Agabus offered it to me. Perhaps it's not too late... We'll see."

His voice trailed off, and his head dropped down while the

four sat in silence for awhile. Then Kore said, "You poor boy. You need a little tender loving care. Come with me."

She lifted him by the arm and led him away, clinging closely to his side and whispering into his ear.

Ruth, Kore, and Miriam spent the next week and a half in a leisurely pursuit of handcrafts, table games, and conversation. They especially enjoyed the company of Hermes and Agabus, as well as of Erastus, when he was not on duty. The two couples eagerly looked forward to their meals together, their clandestine rendezvous in the mess hall, or their occasional trysts on deck after dark. The females never could adjust to the constant tilt of the floor from the crosswind. They laughed often as they staggered down the hallway. The tilt kept Hermes from practicing his discus throwing out to sea from the deck, as was his daily practice, but he did manage to do daily calisthenics.

> *My brain is full of the crash of wrecks,*
> *and the roar of waves,*
> *My life itself is a wreck, I have sullied a*
> *noble name,*
> *I am flung from the rising tide of the*
> *world as a waif of shame,*
> *I am roused by the wail of a child, and*
> *awake to a livid light,*
> *And a ghastlier face than ever has haunted*
> *a grave by night.*
> *I would hide from the storm without, I*
> *would flee from the storm within.*
>
> Alfred Lord Tennyson

# CHAPTER NINE

## FIFTEENTH DAY OUT OF ALEXANDRIA, AD 60

"LAND HO!" CRIED the lookout.

It was mid-morning. The passengers rushed up onto deck. To the north they could see a hazy mountain range. Marcus came out of his cabin and went up to Agabus, who was standing at the railing. They spoke a minute, then Agabus followed him back into the deck cabin. A few minutes later Agabus came out and walked over to where Ruth, Kore, and Miriam were standing on deck. "Ladies," he said, "We're turning into port at Myra."

"Myra?" said Kore. "I thought our next port was Rhodes."

"It was. But we're having to make a change. The westerly wind is too stiff to enable us to turn toward Rhodes. We could eventually make it by tacking, but our water and store are getting slim and we need to restock. Myra is the closest port. Those peaks are the mountains of Lycia, above Myra. We'll be turning northeasterly this morning to get there. You should appreciate that. With the wind more to our backs we'll speed up, and the deck should become level."

"Hallelujah!" said Kore. "Maybe I can now walk without looking like I've been too long at the wine cups."

They all laughed.

Agabus added, "We're still fifty knots out, but we should arrive this afternoon."

Ruth ran downstairs to tell Hermes. Kore stayed on deck to watch Erastus order the rigging changes necessary to effect the new bearing. She could feel the gradual leveling of the deck. The sea was smooth on into Myra and everyone was heartened at the prospect of going ashore.

Finally, the *Kibotos* drew near to Myra. Passengers crowded the port railing and watched the coastal hills and mountains drift lazily past. Presently, they rounded a promontory and turned into a spacious bay. Myra was not to be seen at first since it was another two miles up the Andriaki River which emptied into this bay. Marcus and Erastus in their respective languages shouted, "Strike the mainsail," and the mainsail was hoisted to the yard. Slowly they sailed up the wide river, propelled by the topsail and foresail. Marcus, in near-full military attire, stood beside the pilot. Soon they were passing prominent structures on both banks of the Andriaki. Ahead they could make out a stone quay with several crafts docked at it, among them a sail ship half the size of the *Kibotos*. It appeared as graceful as a swan, a figure suggested by the fore cheniscus, which consisted of a swan's head, and the aft cheniscus, which appeared to be tail feathers.

"Strike the topsail," shouted Marcus echoed by Erastus.

Hastily, sailors hoisted the sail above.

As they drifted slowly past the other ship, they could make out a name carved on a large wooden plaque on the deck cabin, the "*ODYSSEY.*" The passengers hurried below to retrieve their purses and satchels.

"Uh, oh, trouble!" said Agabus Ben Uri as he and his party walked across the deck preparing to disembark. He was eyeing a Roman centurion and his aide, standing at the foot of the gangplank.

"What is it?" said Ruth.

"That centurion. He just looks like he's trying to get to Rome. If he chooses to do so, he can commandeer our ship. He probably just got off the *Odyssey*. Did you notice the number of soldiers around it when we went past? That's probably his century."

Agabus stopped and watched as the centurion spoke to a crew member who was working the hawsers on the *Kibotos*. After the exchange of a few words, the sailor pointed up at Agabus.

Agabus walked down the gangplank and the centurion approached him, saluted, and said, "Sir, may I have a word with you, please?"

"Of course. Just a moment. Hermes, would you mind escorting the ladies into town. I'll meet you in a few minutes at that restaurant down the street." He pointed toward town.

"I'll be glad to."

Agabus followed the soldier over to one side. He was a typical centurion, tall, big-boned, muscular. His face was clean shaven, his jaw bold, his appearance strong yet reasonable and lenient. Even a child would have felt comfortable in his presence. He said, "I am Julius Priscus. I understand that you are the owner of this ship. Is that right?"

"Yes. I am Agabus Ben Uri."

"I assume this is a grain ship. Are you perchance bound for Rome?"

"Yes, if the weather permits."

"I saw a Roman officer on deck. Do you presently have a military contingent on board?"

"No, there are no military personnel on board. Perhaps you saw our ship captain. He frequently takes the liberty of wearing a uniform. Was he standing at the helm?"

"Yes. What is his name?"

"Marcus Hippalus."

The centurion looked startled. He paused for a moment, then resumed questioning. "How many passengers do you now have on board?"

"One hundred thirty-one on the manifest."

"No, not including the crew, how many do you have? I have not seen very many passengers disembark."

Agabus hesitated. "Only twenty-one."

"Allow me to explain my situation. On the *Odyssey* now I have a century—one hundred fourteen soldiers, including myself, to be exact—along with thirty prisoners. Oh yes, and one doctor. We are on our way to Rome. We have come from Caesarea. The *Odyssey* is only a coastal frigate and will terminate at Adramyttium in the Aegean. We arrived in port here yesterday to wait out the wind. You should have room for a hundred forty-five more persons aboard the *Kibotos*."

Suddenly, the centurion snapped to attention. "Agabus Ben Uri, in the name of Caesar, I hereby commandeer your ship to transport us to Rome."

Agabus groaned. "I was afraid of that. Of course as a centurion, that's within your power. However, I'm sorry to say we cannot accommodate you. Our total capacity is only two hundred fifty persons."

"Never mind that. You'll just double up. You can easily crowd on two hundred seventy-six people. Take me to your captain."

"Follow me, then" said Agabus curtly.

The two men walked up the gangplank followed by the aide. On deck Agabus knocked on the captain's door.

"Who is it?"

"Ben Uri."

"Come in."

Agabus opened the door for the centurion, while the aide positioned himself outside the cabin.

Marcus was at a desk filling our the ship's log. He neither rose nor looked around.

"What is it?" he said.

"Marcus Hippalus," said the centurion.

Marcus wheeled around. He looked questioningly at the centurion a moment and said, "Do I know you?"

"You don't recognize me? I am Julius."

Marcus stared up into his face. Suddenly he grew rigid. "Julius," he said coldly and turned back to his desk. Flippantly, he said to Agabus, "This was my aide in Turris, Italy."

"That's right," replied Julius softly. "In Turris," tactfully refraining from mentioning Briton too. "Captain Hippalus, you've earned a worthy reputation for yourself on the Great Sea since I last saw you."

At the sympathetic nature of Julius' remark, Marcus turned back around, sighed, and said, "Not the name I might have had."

"Friend, you were treated most unfairly. They had no right to do to you what they did."

"I blame no *man*. I lay all the blame on the elements. They were against me... and I did not even know it. I realized it too late."

"Ah, I see. You don't blame humans. You blame the Fates."

Marcus frowned. He said somewhat roughly, "No, I don't believe in the Fates. I'm not a religious man—never have been." He paused. "It's nature that's my enemy—the wind, the elements, call it what you will—this earth is against me. I don't know why. But it's true. It happened again on this voyage, like before. Pirates were blown to us by the wind; they were upwind from us and the wind blew them to us.

"Ha! But I defeated them easily. So far I've defeated everything it's thrown at me. There was just that once. You were there. You saw it. You saw how the wind turned on me—trying to annihilate me. It won because I wasn't expecting it. I didn't know it was my enemy. But I learned. Since then it hasn't won another battle. But enough of that. What's on your mind, Julius?"

"I'm bound for Rome from Caesarea with a century of soldiers, plus thirty prisoners—"

Agabus broke in. "He has commandeered our ship."

"What?" Marcus jumped to his feet. "I won't have it!" He moved menacingly toward Julius. "Get off my ship."

Julius refused to budge. His hand moved to the hilt of his short sword.

Agabus rushed between them and pushed them apart. "It's no use, Marcus. We have no legal choice but to comply."

Marcus sank back into his chair. He bent forward, bowed his head, and started running his hands through his hair. Just as quickly he stood up again and said, "Get yourself another captain. Get 'Rastus."

He started toward the cabin door. Agabus seized him by the arm. "See here, now. I don't like this any better than you do, but I don't have any choice. You know Roman law. Look, I don't want to change captains now. Will it help any if I say I want you to stay on?"

"Marcus," said Julius, "When I heard you were in command, I looked forward to sailing with you again. It will work out well. I too have no choice. The ship we're on will terminate in the Aegean—at Adramyttium. We must change ships. I've got to get to Rome before winter. I can't leave my century in port for long. Not with thirty prisoners. You know what I'm facing. You've been there."

"How the tides have turned," said Marcus. He paused long and thoughtfully. "Alright, then. But we're going to have an understanding from the very beginning. *I'm* in command on this ship. Is that understood?"

"To the extent of the law," said Julius. "I won't sail your ship for you. I've got enough to do to manage a hundred forty-five men. I'll work with you."

For the next hour the three men hammered out the details. The Second Mate would prepare the cabins, consolidating and doubling up where necessary. To allow time for preparation, the new personnel would not board until the next morning. Julius offered his soldiers to assist the First Mate in acquiring extra provisions, solemnly promising remuneration to Agabus from imperial funds when they reached Rome. Marcus would visit the captain of the *Odyssey* to gather information concerning the coastal winds and currents. Departure time would be set for daybreak of the second day hence—Thursday.

Julius Priscus returned to his cabin aboard the *Odyssey* after supper and opened the door to find a roomful of men. Several had scrolls, partially unrolled, which they were discussing. Flickering candlelight dimly lit the room. Julius recognized some of the men—Paul, Luke, Aristarchus, several passengers and several crew members. But others he did not know. *They must be from the city.*

Paul was speaking. He was an aged man, roughly sixty, but he exhibited the liveliness of youth. Mentally he was fully present. He was slight of stature and his head was oversized for his body, but his face was handsome and distinguished. A prominent scar was evident under his left eye. With hair and beard white like snow, he might have been taken for a rabbi.

He was saying, "I'm afraid we will have to end our discussion for today. If someone could possibly gain us entry into the synagogue, I will be glad to take up tomorrow where we leave off today. Is that possible?"

"I can get us in," responded one of the men. "What time?"

"Say, the second hour. How does that sound?"

"Fine by me," the man responded.

"I cannot be there. I have to work," said another, echoed by several others.

"Those of you who cannot attend during the daytime, be alert to the possibility of my assembling with you tomorrow evening or on future days." He turned back to the first man. "Why not line up several more of your friends to be there tomorrow morning? And now grace be to you from our Lord Jesus Christ."

Paul led everyone out into the hallway where affectionate farewells were exchanged. When he reentered the cabin, Julius said, "You don't waste any time, Paul."

Solemnly Paul said, "I am moved by the persuasion that the Lord Jesus may return very soon and time is short. I would love to plant the seeds of a church while I'm here."

"Your time here indeed is short. We sail day after tomorrow."

"I take it you were able to arrange passage on the *Kibotos.*" Julius nodded.

"I am thankful. I had prayed God to provide another ship at this very port of call. I still feel strongly that he would have me to stand and witness before Caesar, and the Lord is in control of my life."

Julius said, "I had a remarkable coincidence on the *Kibotos* this afternoon. I discovered that the captain is a longtime friend of mine. His name is Marcus Hippalus. Today, he is one of the foremost seamen on the Levant—on the entire Great Sea for that matter. But he's also known for his eccentricities. Years ago he had a tragic experience that changed his life. I believe it would be well for you to know his background in order to understand him. I'll tell you the story if you're interested."

At that moment a tall, clean shaven, middle-aged man, entered the cabin. Paul said, "Grace to you, Dr. Luke. If you have the time, take a seat. Julius was about to tell me about the captain of the *Kibotos*. They're old friends."

"Well, the story begins on the coast of Gaul long ago . . ."

As Julius was beginning his narration aboard the *Odyssey*, Hermes was groping his way down the dimly-lit hallway of the *Kibotos*. He knocked on Erastus' door.

"Come in," said Erastus.

Hermes stepped in and collapsed on one of the bunks. "Whew! I'm fatigued."

"Where have you been? Hitting the taverns?"

"I've been out shopping with the ladies all day. I didn't know what I was getting into. You wouldn't believe all the packages they acquired. It took all four of us to get their loot back to the ship."

"You volunteered for that?"

"Never mind. I learned my lesson. I'll never do that again. I was hoping I could find some time alone with Ruth, but no! Kore and Miriam were always right at her side. I fit in like the fifth leg of a horse."

"I would have *loved* to have been there with you. I had to work all day, though. I could at least have relieved the group of Kore."

"And of Miriam."

"Oh, no! Not this Greek."

They laughed boisterously.

"What ever happened with Agabus?" asked Hermes. "The last we saw of him, he was talking to a centurion on the dock. He rooked me into the shopping expedition. He told us he'd meet us shortly at a restaurant. Never showed up. After an hour, Ruth insisted we see the town.... What happened?"

"The centurion commandeered our ship. Tomorrow he's boarding his century and some prisoners for the trip to Rome—a hundred forty-five more passengers."

"Ugh! Agabus told us he suspected that," said Hermes.

"We've been stocking up and readying the empty cabins. We're having to double-up to get everyone on board. While you were gone, I took the liberty of moving your gear over here to my cabin. I wanted to choose who would be in here with us. I invited the centurion—he seems like an affable chap. Then, before I could name any others, the centurion—Julius is his name—asked if we could billet three of his group in here too, a doctor by the name of Luke and two of the prisoners. One is a political prisoner—or something like that—and is older. The centurion seems to be fond of him. His name is Paul. The other is named Aristarchus."

Erastus went on talking about the meaning of this new development and of the hardships he anticipated because of it. It would be a real test.

The next morning after breakfast, the *Odyssey* crowd marched aboard the *Kibotos*. Erastus and the Second Mate oriented them and with the help of the centurion's aide directed them all to their various cabins and bays. The prisoners were all in chains.

After awhile, Erastus opened the door to his own cabin and ushered in three men. Hermes, who had been sitting on his bunk writing on a papyrus, arose.

"Hermes," said Erastus, "I would like you to meet Julius. Julius, this is Hermes."

"How do you do?" said Julius. "I hope we're not crowding you too much."

The two men clasped wrists in a friendly way and looked each other over. Hermes admired Julius' athletic physique.

Julius said, "Hermes, I'd like you to meet Dr. Luke, our physician. Also, my friend, Paul of Tarsus."

Hermes walked past the slight Paul with his hand outstretched to Luke.

Paul seized the conversation. "Hermes, is it? What is your position on the *Kibotos*—an officer?"

"Just a passenger," replied Hermes without further comment.

"I see," said Paul. "I'm interested. I assume you boarded in Alexandria and are bound for Rome too. Is Alexandria your home?"

"No," replied Hermes uncomfortably, glancing around at Erastus, Julius, and Luke. *What a skinny weakling!*

"I see," said Paul. "I've never been in Alexandria before. Would you recommend it as a place to visit?"

"If you'll excuse me, I have things to do," said Hermes. He rolled up his papyrus and left the cabin.

Paul looked quizzically at Julius, who merely shrugged his shoulders.

Erastus said, "I'll help bring up the rest of your baggage." He left, followed by Julius.

Paul sat down on one of the bunks and wearily fell over. Luke moved from bunk to bunk, pressing on each one with his hand. "Julius never bothers to tell anyone who you are. Just let's each one find out for himself."

"Who am I?" said Paul without opening his eyes. "Nothing but a prisoner of the Lord Jesus Christ."

"I thought Aristarchus was going to be billeted with us," said Luke.

"He was invited, but he said he preferred to stay with the other prisoners—to witness to them. He'll meet us at the synagogue in a few minutes."

The ship bell rang twice.

"Speaking of the synagogue," said Luke, "we're supposed to meet the local Jews there right now."

Paul sat up, rubbed his eyes, and said, "I'm ready."

Paul and Luke returned to their cabin from the synagogue at noontime. Julius was just leaving. "The First Mate," he said, "has arranged for us to eat at the Captain's Mess. It convenes in just a few minutes. I was just going there myself. If you would like, come on down."

"Thank you, kindly," replied Paul. "We'll be there momentarily."

The mess hall was filled when Paul and Luke entered. Many of those from the *Odyssey* arose respectfully when they saw Paul. Paul waved a friendly greeting over the room. After being seated, Paul and Luke bowed in prayer, and numerous others did likewise.

After the meal Agabus approached Paul and Luke and said, "Pardon me. I am Agabus Ben Uri, owner of the *Kibotos*. I understand one of you is a physician."

"I am," said Luke. "Can I be of help?"

"No, thank you, not now. I just wanted to welcome you and make you feel at home among us. The only medical person we have on board now is an orderly. I hope you will be available to us if people need medical attention. Are you a military physician?"

"No, I'm not, but I will be happy to be of service whenever I'm needed. I accompany this man to serve him personally."

Agabus' right eyebrow lifted and he looked carefully at Paul.

"May I introduce you to Paul?" said Luke.

"My name is actually Saul. I'm very happy to meet you, my brother."

"Ah, so, a fellow Hebrew." said Agabus bowing slightly. "I am honored to have you aboard my ship. You may be interested in some scrolls I have with me."

"Of the Scriptures?"

"Indeed."

"Of course I would. What books do you have?"

"The Psalms, Isaiah, and Jeremiah."

"In the Hebrew or Greek?"

Luke spoke up, "This man can read either one. Latin too."

"Wonderful. A scholar, no less. My scrolls are in Hebrew. And now, if you will excuse me, I have things to do. Do stop by my cabin this afternoon and spend some time with me."

"You can count on that," said Paul. "May I bring a friend to read for me? My eyes are almost gone."

"Of course. I will be watching for you."

Paul and Aristarchus were about to knock on Agabus' door, when Agabus opened the door to leave.

"Oh, Saul, my brother, come right in."

"You were just leaving. Please excuse me and permit me to come on another occasion," said Paul.

"It's no bother," said Agabus. "I can delay my errand a few minutes. I'll show you the scrolls and if you desire to read some, you're welcome to remain here for awhile in my absence. Why not?"

"I am grateful to you. Where I have been, I haven't had much access to Scriptures."

"I understand," said Agabus. "I pay honor to my countrymen who rebel against Caesar. When you are through, simply replace the scrolls where you found them. Good day."

When they were alone, Paul said, "Please read for me the passage that begins, '"Who hath believed our report?"'"

Aristarchus found the long scroll of Isaiah, unrolled it, and began.

> *Who hath believed our report? and to whom is the arm of the Lord revealed? For he shall grow up before him as a tender plant, and as a root out of a dry ground: he hath no form nor comeliness; and when we shall see him, there is no beauty that we should desire him . . .*

As Aristarchus read, Paul's dim eyes gazed far away. Unexpectedly, there was the sound of female voices nearby. Three ladies, chattering excitedly, were walking out of a door within the suite.

Paul and Aristarchus arose. Ruth heard them and wheeled around.

Paul said, "How do you do? I am Paul and this is my friend Aristarchus. We didn't mean to startle you. Ben Uri invited us in to see his scrolls, but he had to leave hurriedly. He permitted us to stay here and read for awhile."

"Please pardon my start. I didn't know you were here. I am Ruth, Agabus' daughter. This is my friend Kore and my maid Miriam. I'm happy to meet you."

Kore stepped forward to Aristarchus, extended her hand, fluttered her eyelashes, and cooed, "I'm very happy to meet you, Aristarchus. My name is Kore."

"How do you do? And this is my friend, Taul of Sarsus. Ahem!" Aristarchus cleared his throat, closed his eyes, and paused. "I mean Paul of Tarsus."

A slight mirth passed over Paul's face.

"We're on our way—shopping again," said Kore. "Bye bye."

At mess that evening Erastus sat at the head table with Kore, Ruth, and Agabus. Marcus had not shown his face there since they landed. As they ate, Agabus nodded in the direction of Paul and said to Erastus, "I am favorably impressed with the new man, Saul."

"You mean the prisoner?" asked Erastus.

"Yes. But the centurion said he's a political prisoner. He's bound for Rome to stand trial before Nero."

"Actually, he might better be called a religious prisoner," said Erastus.

"Why?" asked Agabus. "What is he charged with?"

"Well, in addition to the usual charge of insurrection, he's also charged with desecrating the Temple in Jerusalem."

Agabus lowered his eating utensils to the table and squinted his eyes. Very deliberately he said, "Is . . . this . . . man . . . Paul . . . of . . . Tarsus?"

"Yes, that's his name," said Erastus.

Agabus' fists came down on the table. Bam! He struck so hard several goblets were upset. He got up and angrily left the hall. Every eye turned to look. Ruth got up and ran after him.

"Father, what is it?" she asked in the hallway.

"Why didn't someone tell me we had a traitor in our midst?"

"You mean Paul?"

"He deceived me. Do you know who he is? He's Paul of Tarsus."

"So? I like him. He seems very nice, to me."

"He's the one who has turned the world upside down."

"What are you talking about?"

"Don't you know what he's charged with? Desecrating the Temple. I've heard about him for years. For a long time the High Priest has been trying to have him put away."

"Father, how do you know the charges are true? How do you know he desecrated the Temple?"

"Because the Sanhedrin condemned him."

"Oh, father. The Sanhedrin? So what? Didn't they condemn John the Baptist too? Didn't they also condemn Jesus of Nazareth, before Pilate had him crucified? How has Paul turned the world upside down?"

"Ruth, don't you see? This is the man who's been trying to change our basic traditions. He's been going all over the Great Sea saying people don't have to keep the law any longer. This is that infamous Apostle of Jesus. You can't support a person like that. I'll not have him on my ship."

"Oh, father. You're an Assidian bigot. You sound just like Solomon."

"Do I really?"

"Just listen to yourself. You don't know whether these charges are true or not. Even the Romans are saying they're trumped up. Maybe the priests are jealous of Paul. Maybe they're scared of him, scared they'll lose their pompous positions. Maybe Paul's not like that. Did he seem that way to you, before you knew these charges? Why don't you give him the benefit of the doubt? Ask him his side of the story? You might be surprised. Doesn't the Scripture say,

'Thou shalt love thy neighbor as thyself: I am the Lord.' Is that love—to condemn Paul by hearsay?"

Agabus walked on down the hallway. "Still, I don't have to transport a man with his record on my ship. I'm going to Hippalus."

Marcus sat at his desk while Agabus stood. "A religious fanatic, you say? Paul of Tarsus? Never heard of him." He twirled a ruler between his finger tips. "This is none of my business. I didn't want any of this riffraff on board anyway. I didn't permit them. You did! Do you have anything else?"

"I suppose not," said Agabus. He turned and left the cabin.

*I might try the centurion. . . . No, I suppose that wouldn't do any good either.*

At sunset Hermes answered a knock on his cabin door. It was Ruth. "Is Paul in? I want to talk to him."

"I'm sorry, Ruth. He's gone to the synagogue tonight. Won't be back till late." He hurriedly slipped on his sandals. "Let's go stroll through the town."

"Swell," said Ruth.

As they walked over Myra, all Ruth could talk about was Paul and Agabus' outburst at him and her growing curiosity over Christianity.

"What do you see in that old shrimp, anyway?" asked Hermes.

"It's not Paul himself I'm interested in. It's what he stands for. Father said he represents Jesus of Nazareth, that he is an Apostle of Jesus. And I'm wondering if Jesus might be the Promised One, the Christ, as you say."

"Why all this 'Messiah' talk? What does he mean to you folks, besides a conqueror to throw off the Roman yoke?"

"Hermes," she said sweetly, "you know about our Scriptures. Long before either the Romans or the Greeks came along, they were predicting the coming of a Messiah. There are hints of it in stories as far back as the dawn of mankind. So it's not just to throw off the Roman yoke. I've never lived in Israel and could care less whether it's free or not. However, I come from a strain of Jews who see more in the promise of a Messiah than just a national deliverer. Somehow, his coming gives us hope for the future—hope for the prospect of a permanent peace with God. Personally, I mean. More than that. Hope for a warm personal relationship with God—at all times. Does that interest you?"

"Sort of," replied Hermes. "What interests you interests me."

"That's sweet of you. You see, we believe also that the coming of the Messiah will be of benefit to the Gentiles too, that he is not just coming for the Jews but for the Gentiles as well, to draw us all closer to God. Since there is just one God, and he created all mankind alike, it's not reasonable to assume that the benefits of his goodness are for one race alone. God might be planning to send the Messiah for all mankind."

"You don't sound like the typical Jew I've known."

"I know," said Ruth. "But that's the way some of us believe. Now then, people like John Mark and Paul come along and tell us the Messiah has already come and has left wonderful blessings for those who believe in him. That's what I wanted to talk to Paul about tonight."

"It's going to be a long trip," said Hermes. "You'll have plenty more opportunities to seek him out. I don't care about him myself. But if I can, I'll help you arrange a meeting with him."

Late into the night they walked and talked together before returning to the ship. At the door of her cabin, Ruth squeezed Hermes' hand, gazed into his eyes, smiled enchantingly, then ducked inside.

*I fled Him, down the nights and down the days;*
*I fled Him down the arches of the years;*
*I fled Him down the labyrinthine ways*
*Of my own mind; and in the midst of tears*
*I hid from Him and under running laughter.*
*Up vistaed hopes I sped;*
*And shot, precipitated*
*Adown titantic glooms of chasmed fears,*
*From those strong Feet that followed, followed after.*
*But with unhurrying chase*
*And unperturbed pace,*
*Deliberate speed, majestic instancy*
*They beat—and a Voice beat*
*More instant than the Feet—*
*"All things betray thee, who betrayest Me."*
From "The Hound of Heaven" by Francis Thompson

# CHAPTER TEN

## FIRST DAY OUT OF MYRA, AD 60

EARLY THE NEXT morning, while crew members were scurrying around, readying the *Kibotos* for sailing, Marcus stood at the stern suspiciously watching a group of strangers approaching the gangplank. They stopped and from the dock initiated a conversation with two of the newcomers up on deck, one a gray-bearded man, the other somewhat younger. The younger man then left the railing, went to the lower deck, and returned in a few minutes with a group of soldiers. Together, they all descended the gangplank and greeted the strangers on the quay with handclasps and hugs. He watched as the gray-bearded man then led the crowd over to the far edge of the quay. Marcus had to move his position to see what they were doing. They were kneeling. Marcus just shrugged his shoulder and went on about his work.

An hour later he looked down again. The crowd was still kneeling. "First Mate," he called.

"Aye, aye, Captain."

"See that crowd down there. What are they doing?"

"It looks to me as if they're praying, sir. The white-bearded man is Paul of Tarsus, one of the prisoners."

"I don't like the looks of them. Are we about ready to sail?"

"Aye, sir. We can sail within the hour."

"Good. Proceed to call the passengers on board. I'll see what happens."

A few minutes later Erastus cried out, "Come aboard! Come abooooooard."

The men and women on the quay started getting up from their knees. Marcus could not hear what they were saying, but he could see many of them embracing the gray-bearded man. Those who were passengers then moved toward the gangplank. Later, when the ship cast off, Marcus saw the strangers still standing on the dock waving fondly to the passengers.

The *Kibotos* resumed its journey. Because the wind was adverse, she had to be towed down the river by a small galley in order to reach open waters. When she attained the bay, she hoisted sail and headed west toward Rhodes. The wind had shifted to northwest while they were at Myra and they found themselves facing it almost head on. By staying close to shore they were assisted by occasional coastal breezes and a three knot current, but still Marcus found it necessary to tack. Sailing was painfully slow and boring. Marcus' temper was not the most pleasant for the delay. Besides the wind, he had other things to provoke him as well.

At the noon meal Marcus deigned to attend the Captain's Mess for the first time in recent days. Seated with him at the head table were Agabus, Erastus, Julius, and others. Marcus started baiting

Agabus. "Ben Uri, I understand you have some fellow Jews on board now."

"We renounce those of our blood who break the laws of Caesar," said Agabus.

"Ah, but the main offense of Paul of Tarsus, I am told, was profaning the *holy* temple in Jerusalem. Is that an offense sufficient to turn you against your brother? Indeed, I personally honor those who do sacrilege to the false god of Israel—*or* of Syria *or* of Greece *or* of Egypt either, for that matter." Marcus gestured toward Paul. "I honor this prisoner by permitting him to eat with me."

Agabus was infuriated and barely managed to keep his temper. He said, "But that's not all he's charged with. He's also been indicted for causing factious disturbances around the world."

"Ah, yes," replied Marcus with a smile, "but who brought those charges? Not the Romans. They come from your own Sanhedrin in Jerusalem. You Jews do not defend your own. Indeed, you turn them over to the occupying power—whom you hate—to punish them for you."

Agabus was flabbergasted. He did not know what to say, having been bested in the very sophistry in which the Jews considered themselves so skilled. He had taken the bait—hook, line and sinker. Marcus had won the battle, but to Agabus the war was not over yet.

That afternoon at the ninth bell, Marcus glanced out the door of his cabin and saw Agabus and his party setting up to pray on the stern. He burst forth and said, "I warned you there would be none of that here."

"We defy your order," said Agabus.

"You what? You know the law of the sea, Agabus. While at sea, I *am* the law. Get up and get out."

By now Marcus was shouting, his voice like a bass horn at full blast. Agabus had intentionally delayed his worship until he had seen Julius on deck so the centurion could witness the confrontation. Surely enough, Julius walked up behind Marcus and said, "Excuse me, Captain, I couldn't help overhearing your words. Why not permit them to pray on deck? There's no law against their practicing their religion on board. I just came from Judea, and I know that the ninth hour is one of their traditional hours of prayer. To pray facing Jerusalem is also customary."

"This is my ship," said Marcus, "and I will not permit open displays of religion on board."

"Marcus Hippalus, what's happened to you? You know this is not your ship. This ship belongs to the very man you're persecuting. Now hear me! I'm hereby overriding your order. I'm granting these people the right to exercise their religion according to their customs!"

Marcus wheeled around and shouted, "First Mate."

Erastus ran over.

"This soldier is threatening mutiny. Call to arms."

Erastus shouted, "Call to arms." In a matter of seconds two dozen armed sailors surrounded Julius and the four frightened Jews at his feet.

"Captain," said Julius, "do you forget that a century of crack legionnaires is on board this ship." He was speaking in steady tones. "Do you really want to risk your future—your very life—over this incident? And will you toy around with the welfare of all those entrusted to your care?"

"My future? Bah, I have no future. All I have is a past! Ahoy, pilot, abandon the helm!"

By now a crowd of spectators had gathered nearby. The action was taking place at the stern not far from the helm. The pilot looked over in astonishment and said, "Captain, you want me to leave the teller?"

Marcus was looking straight at him. "Abandon the teller—*right now!*"

The *Kibotos* was steered by two large paddles on either side of the stern, connected by a pole or teller across the deck. The pilot started to tie the teller in place.

"Imbecile, don't tie it down. Abandon it."

"Yes, sir," replied the pilot, releasing the teller. The paddles promptly flopped to one side and the bow of the ship turned toward the rocky coast. If Agabus and the Jewesses had intended to pray toward Jerusalem, they now found themselves facing Alexandria.

"Now what are you going to do, Centurion?" said Marcus.

"Marcus Hippalus, is this really what you want? Is this what you dare? I don't think so. I'm leaving you to your own conscience."

Julius pushed his way through the sailors and started below. Agabus and the females rolled up their rug and hurried after him through the crowd.

Marcus looked around in confusion. "First Mate," he said resignedly, "Dismiss the sailors. Pilot, return to the helm. Resume the former course."

He hung his head and returned to his cabin.

That evening Ruth knocked on the door to Hermes' cabin and he came to the door. "Is all arranged? Will he see me?" she asked.

"It's all arranged. Just a minute."

She waited in the semi-darkened hallway as Paul came out of the door followed by Hermes.

"Dear Ruth," said Paul. "Hermes said you wanted to talk to me."

"Yes, I do. It's urgent. The Captain won't permit men to fraternize with us ladies so I had to see you in private."

"Follow me," Hermes said. "Erastus has given me a key to one of the storage rooms where you can have some privacy. I'll stand at the door until you're through."

He led them down the hallway to a door, unlocked it, and opened it, handing Paul a lantern he was carrying.

They stepped into a dark closet crowded with tools and weapons—mops, spears, long swords, bows—as well as shelves filled with various items. Hermes closed the door behind them. The smell of seawater was especially pungent in the crowded space. Ruth looked into Paul's eyes and said, "Oh, sir, I've been wanting to talk to you ever since I first heard about you. May I ask you a few questions?"

"Certainly you may."

"Are you really guilty of desecrating the Temple as they say you are?"

"Dear friend, I would not lie to you. I am not guilty of that. Two years ago I was visiting the Holy City during the Feast of Pentecost accompanied by several men from Greece, Asia, and Galatia, some of whom were Gentiles. They were going there for business not related to the Temple. The Gentiles never entered the Temple, but I did. When I entered it, I had with me four other men, all of whom were Jews and residents of Jerusalem. I was paying their expenses for a Nazarite ritual in strict accordance with the law. It so happened that some Jews from Ephesus, who were already hostile toward me, saw me inside the Temple that day and might have assumed that I had brought in the Gentiles. But I had not. They started shouting aloud that I had desecrated the Temple. A near riot ensued in which a mob threw me out of the Temple, intending to kill me; but Roman soldiers quelled the riot, rescued me, and imprisoned me in Jerusalem and eventually in Caesarea. I stood trial thrice but never was convicted. Yet to appease the Jews, they wouldn't release me either. Now I'm on my way to Rome to stand trial a fourth time. That is the true story."

"Are you guilty of leading an insurrection among the Jews?"

"Absolutely not. I myself am a Roman citizen. I was born a citizen of Rome, in the city of Tarsus. I have tried to avoid nationalistic politics. My purpose is much different from that."

"What is your purpose?"

"My purpose? It's to open people's eyes. To turn them from darkness to light—from the power of Satan to God—that they might receive the forgiveness of sins and a place among those who are sanctified by faith in Jesus Christ."

"I will confess that I feel moved by the teachings I've heard about Jesus. But my question now is, was John the Baptist Elijah?"

"Hum! Well, Jesus claimed he was. He might have been speaking metaphorically. However, we do have reason to believe that John was the intended fulfillment of Malachi's prediction of a messianic forerunner. You know how John answered the Pharisees when they interrogated him, don't you?"

"No, what?"

"He said, 'I am the voice of one calling in the desert, "Make straight the way of the Lord."' That's one of the messianic prophecies. Later John pointed Jesus out to his disciples, and said, 'Look, the Lamb of God who takes away the sin of the world.' "

"Then whatever happened to Jesus? I heard he was crucified."

"He was. He was slain like a sacrificial lamb for our sins, as John predicted. But that's not the whole story. After he died and had been entombed for three days, he miraculously came back to life again. God literally raised him from the dead. Many people in Judea and Galilee saw him alive after that. Then, later, he ascended on high and today he sits at the right hand of the throne of God. Subsequent to all this, I saw him myself."

"You have seen him?"

"Yes, I have. That's why they call me an Apostle of Christ—a 'sent one.' But that's another story."

"I am amazed and deeply moved by all this," said Ruth. "But I have another need I want to discuss with you also." She told Paul what happened on deck that afternoon. She added, "I blame my father for the whole thing. When we first left Alexandria, Marcus prohibited us from praying on deck. It wasn't really essential that we pray on deck anyway, was it? You seem like a devout Jew and I haven't seen you praying on deck. But Father knew that when Julius came on board he officially usurped Marcus' authority on the *Kibotos*, so Father took advantage of the situation and started praying again. Was he right or wrong?"

"He was wrong. That was not the loving thing to do. Jesus once said, 'Blessed are the peacemakers, for they will be called the sons of God.'"

Paul paused and Ruth mulled that over. It gave her a warm feeling inside. "Thank you so much for seeing me. I hope in time to learn more about Jesus. May I talk with you again later?"

"I shall welcome that, sweet Ruth. Before you leave, though, I have a question for you. Why did your father suddenly become so cold toward me? At first he was very warm. He allowed me to read from his scrolls. But all day today he's avoided me. He's denied me the use of the scrolls. When I knocked on his door this morning, he said, 'I don't have time,' and slammed the door in my face. What offense have I committed?"

"Sir, . . . my father at first thought you had only committed insurrection against the Romans and that was the reason you were a prisoner. That impressed him. He's very nationalistic. He applauds insurrection against Caesar. However, yesterday Erastus told him the Sanhedrin had condemned you—said you were guilty of profaning the Temple. When he heard that, he suddenly became aware of who you are. 'The infamous Paul of Tarsus,' he called you. He said your name's an abomination among the Jews—all over the world. So he's now imposed Hebrew sanctions on you. He won't have anything to do with you. I personally don't agree with him. I told him he ought to talk to you personally about it—give you a chance to explain yourself."

Paul nodded. "That explains his outburst in the mess hall last night, doesn't it?"

"Yes."

"Well, I love Agabus and respect him. I wouldn't do anything to cause him offense. I hope, though, that he'll come to understand that I'm not the rebel people make me out to be. I used to be a leader of the Pharisees in Jerusalem myself. I persecuted Christians. But after I met Jesus, I saw things differently. I came to see that Christ didn't come to destroy Judaism. He came to fulfill it. That is what I teach everywhere."

The next day, at three bells, Agabus Ben Uri asked the ladies to accompany him on deck again for prayer. This time they refused, so he went alone. No sooner had he unfurled his rug and begun praying than he heard the unmistakable voice of Marcus right above him, shouting, "First mate, reverse tack."

Agabus, his head still bowed, peeked through his eyebrows to see the crew quickly swarming over the deck changing the rigging. "That's it," bellowed Marcus. "Loosen the ties. Reverse the boom. Helmsman, reverse the teller for southwest tack. That's it."

Through it all Agabus continued trying to pray. Soon the action and noise subsided. Agabus patiently turned his position so as to continue praying toward Jerusalem. No sooner had he settled down than he heard the enormous voice of Marcus again. He was obviously still standing right at his heels.

"Swabbies, all out, swab the deck."

There was a lull in the commands, during which Agabus could hear sailors scurrying around him with urns, dashing water and slinging mops.

"That's it. Lower your urns over the side! Retrieve that seawater! Don't spare the water! Drench the deck! Sling those mops!"

Marcus kept up a constant jabber. Agabus steeled himself but would not budge. By now all devotional thoughts had gone the way of the wind. All he could concentrate on were the words of those commands.

*How idiotic! He's speaking Latin. The swabbies can't understand a thing he's saying. I don't hear the First Mate repeating his commands in Greek.*

It was true. Erastus had discerned the absurdity of the situation and had withdrawn to one side. Caesar, Marcus' dog, playfully nuzzled Agabus' clasped hands. He dared not open his eyes. The mops were close by. Water doused his face every time he heard a swishing sound.

*Glory! My robe's getting wet. My rug is drenched. The Captain's gone insane.*

Marcus never said a word to Agabus, never touched him; but his game continued the full hour of prayer. Neither Agabus nor the Captain would move, and the Captain never stopped bellowing the whole time.

When Agabus returned to his cabin, he was soaking wet. Ruth said, "Father, what happened?"

Agabus plopped down at his desk, looked up at her with sad eyes, and said, "Darling daughter . . . I'm too tired to talk about it."

Ruth started to leave the room.

Agabus said, "I'm glad you were not with me," and sighed long. She looked down at him and started to leave again but he said, "Do you know what the Captain did?"

"No, what did he do this time?"

Agabus paused and looked down at the floor. "He didn't forbid me to pray. . . . But when I started to pray he started shouting orders to the crew. He stood over me—the full hour—shouting."

"No!"

"Yes . . ." He looked up at her pleadingly.

Ruth did not know what to say.

He said sadly, "Cursed be the man who steals alms."

Ruth did not understand how this proverb fit the situation, but she said, "Perhaps, Father, but, 'Blessed are the peacemakers, for they will be called the sons of God.'"

Agabus thought about that a moment, then looked up at Ruth with tears in his eyes. "What have I done? I've sown seeds of contention. I've provoked Marcus and Julius to conflict for no good reason—to their hurt. What am I?"

Ruth went over, knelt beside him, and put her arms around her him. "Abba, I still love you. And God loves you. And he will forgive you."

"Will he?"

Ruth just hugged him harder.

In the meantime, at three bells, Paul and Luke were in the hold of the ship praying. Paul always preferred to pray alone, or at least only in the presence of those who understood his intense communion with the Lord Jesus. Their dim candlelight scarcely penetrated the darkness of the cavernous hold. They knelt on top of wheat sacks.

After an hour Paul said to Luke, "The Lord is sending me to witness to Captain Hippalus. I must go."

"Very well. Let me help you up the ladder."

Paul struggled to get up from his knees. The dankness of the place had settled into his bones. After much exertion Paul finally exited from the hold through a door at the end of the hallway where their cabin was. Luke led him down the hall and stopped before their cabin. He opened the door slightly and looked in. Paul paused behind him.

Luke turned around and said, "There's no one here. I'll stay and pray for you."

"Alright."

Paul resumed his long trek to the upper deck, alone. On deck he paused again and caught his breath. Then he went over and knocked on the door of the deck cabin.

"Come in," boomed Marcus from within. He had just returned from his experience with Agabus. Caesar started barking.

As Paul opened the door, Marcus turned around from his desk and said, "Why Paul of Tarsus. Do come in. I'm so happy to see you. Quiet, Caesar. Sit."

The dog walked over to a corner and curled up.

Paul was surprised at his reception. Knowing Marcus' reputation for rudeness, Paul blessed the Lord for a providential intervention.

"Captain, I hope you can grant me a few minutes of your time. I merely wanted to make your acquaintance while I'm aboard your ship. Am I intruding?"

"No, no, I'm very happy to see you. Do sit down, won't you. I've been wanting to meet you too. I saw you on dock yesterday morning. You seem different from the other Jews I've met . . . and I honor you for it. If I may be frank with you, you don't flaunt your religion as others do. Indeed, I think it is to your credit that you have differed so thoroughly with the powers in Jerusalem that they turned you over to the Romans to punish." Marcus chuckled to himself. "What makes you so different from the other Jews?"

"You ask what makes me different. It's due to a traumatic

experience I once had. I used to be like any other Jew. In fact in Jerusalem I rose to power among the strictest sect of Jews, the Pharisees. I too used to persecute my fellow Jews. Perhaps, Captain Hippalus, you've heard of the followers of Jesus? I used to persecute them."

Marcus beamed. "Yes, yes! Oh! I'm sorry. Won't you take a seat."

Paul pulled a stool over and sat down. He continued, "I put many of them in prison. I voted to put them to death. Many a time I went from one synagogue to another to have them punished. In my obsession, I even went to foreign cities to persecute them. But Captain, I wasn't happy with myself. Something about this life of violence bothered me. Something seemed to be prodding me. I grew jaded with the life of a Pharisee."

Marcus nodded approvingly.

"Then one day I was traveling to Damascus under the authority of the chief priests. About noontime I was on the road. Suddenly, I was blinded by a bright light from above. I didn't know what it was. It blazed all around me and my fellows. I was blinded for days afterwards. We all fell down. Then I heard a voice speaking to me in Aramaic, saying, 'Saul, Saul, why do you persecute me? It is hard for you to kick against the prods.' I said, 'Who are you?' The voice said, 'I am Jesus. I am the one you are persecuting.'"

Marcus abruptly put his hands behind his head, stretched his long frame out, and tilted his chair backward.

Paul continued. "The voice said, 'Stand up. I have appeared to you to appoint you as my servant. You are to witness to what you have seen of me and of what I will show you. I am sending you to the Gentiles.'"

Paul looked deep into Marcus' anguished eyes. He said, "Marcus, that which may be known of God is manifest to you, because God has shown it to you. The invisible things of him who created the world are clearly seen, even his eternal power and Godhead. They're innately understood by those he created, so that people are without excuse. Indeed, the wrath of God is now revealed from heaven against all our ungodliness and unrighteousness.

Marcus Hippalus, God loves you, loves you as a person, loves you totally. He wants you. He wants to give you peace and happiness and joy. God has come to you today calling you to repent and call upon his name. Listen! "Whosoever will call upon the name of the Lord will be saved." My friend, aren't you ready now to make your peace with God?"

Marcus suddenly arose, letting his chair fall backward beneath him with a crash. He backed away to the opposite side of the cabin. He said, "What have you to do with me? Have you come to torment me again? I've heard this before. You don't fool me. I know who you are now. You're the wind. You attacked me in the English channel. You blew the pirates toward me. You're our impediment toward Rome. You've plagued me all my life. And now you've finally come to me face to face. What do you want from me? What have I that's yours? Why do you torment me?"

"Marcus, listen, I'm not the wind. I'm just a man like yourself. Nor do I mean to torment you. Instead, I've come to offer you a solution. There is hope in God if you will only yield yourself to him."

"You may mean well, Paul of Tarsus, but it's too late for me! I've resisted and resisted and resisted until I have no hope left. See that dog over there. I call him Caesar."

The dog perked up his ears.

"A woman I knew in Rome many years ago also had a dog named Caesar. During the time of our friendship, she became what she called a 'Christian.' She took me to church with her several times. One day in her apartment she tried to persuade me to become a Christian too. I remember that day so well. We were sitting at her dinner table. I resisted her efforts, but I felt extremely uncomfortable. Finally, I had enough and I playfully arose and tried to force her into bed with me. She screamed and her dog attacked me. I didn't mean to, but I hit the dog with my fist and knocked him across the room and up against the wall. It killed him. She was devastated. She loved that dog. She never forgave me. I tried to reconcile with her but she moved to another city and I never saw her again. There is no hope for me."

"Yes, there is, Marcus. God is still pursuing you. He still loves you and wants to reconcile you first to himself, then to others. Won't you yield to him this time?"

"Paul! Please, please, please, just leave me alone. I want to be by myself."

"I understand, and I am leaving. But may Christ Jesus in his marvelous love for all men have mercy on you and deliver you from the thralldom of Satan."

Marcus was standing in a corner. As Paul got up to leave, Marcus took his face in both hands and wrung his head back and forth from side to side several times, looking upward in bitter pain. Paul left the cabin.

Luke saw Paul come back into their cabin. "How did it go with Marcus? I've been on my knees praying ever since you left."

"I offered him the Savior but he turned him down." After telling Luke the story, he added, "This is a very complex soul. You know that Julius told us how Marcus has been warring against the elements ever since his court martial. Strangely enough, I think he sees me as the personification of the elements. I believe he's transferred his resistance against the elements over to me personally."

"That's because his real war is with God," said Luke. "You and I know that our God is the ruler of the elements. Inwardly, Marcus knows that, too, but he won't admit it to himself. You come along as a living representative of God and now he's out to defeat you too."

"You may be right," said Paul. "Well, the Master said, 'This kind goeth not out but by prayer and fasting.' I'm going to fast for him."

"Paul," said Luke urgently, "think twice about that. You know how your stomach is. The voyage across the Aegean and the Adria will make you seasick. You need to conserve your strength. Now is not the time to fast."

"Though the price for Marcus' salvation be that high, I will pay it. My God will take care of me."

Marcus was absent from the Captain's Mess both at noon and in the evening that day. That evening when Luke and Paul sat down at a table, they prayed; but when the dishes were served Paul declined to accept anything. Instead, he stood up, picked up his cup of water, and began visiting cheerfully among the diners. Seeing an empty place beside Erastus, who was eating with Kore, Hermes, and Ruth, Paul sat down backwards, without swinging his legs over the bench. Ruth greeted him warmly, but Erastus only grunted, and Hermes turned to talk to the person on the opposite side of him.

Unshaken, Paul said to Erastus, "In all my travels I've personally met only one other man by the name of 'Erastus.' He's now the Director of Public Works in Corinth. He told me proudly that he has a son on merchant ships. Is he a relative of yours?"

"Why yes! He's my father! How did you happen to meet him?"

"He's active in the Christian church in Corinth. Have you heard from him lately?"

"Not for several years. Hermes told me he saw him last year." Hermes flinched slightly but refused to turn around, raising his shoulder between them even higher.

Erastus continued, "Next time you see Father, tell him I've been attending a Christian church in Alexandria some myself. Might make him feel good."

"That's interesting. You must have gone to John Mark's services."

"Yes, that's right. Do you know him?"

"Very well. We've been on a missionary journey together. I see him from time to time. I think a lot of him. He's a preeminent minister of the Gospel. Erastus, I perceive something about you. You may have attended the Christian assembly, but you're not yet a believer, are you? You're thinking about it though, aren't you? I'll tell you one thing, I've never yet met anyone who became a Christian and lived to regret it."

Paul clapped him on the shoulder and got up to walk away.

"Nor have I," said Erastus.

Ruth and Kore had been following the conversation attentively. When Paul was gone, Erastus called down the table, "Hey, Hermes."

"Yeah."

"You don't like Paul, do you?"

"Does it show? He's too puny for me. I've got a prejudice against weaklings. Can't stand to be around them."

"I know, *Hercules!* But it depends on your definition of *weakling*, doesn't it? I find Paul quite strong."

"I, too," said Ruth.

"Me, too," said Kore.

A few days later Paul entered his cabin followed by Luke. They were returning from their morning prayer session in the hold. Hermes was changing clothes.

"Morning, Hermes. Say, I remember where I've heard of you now," Paul said. "You're the famous Olympic discus thrower from Corinth, aren't you?"

Hermes tied his sash and started toward the door. "Erastus told you."

"No, no! No one told me. I watched you once. You set an all-time record—seven and a third cubits. I was there. I remember—"

"You're right, but when was that and where did it take place?" Hermes had stopped in the doorway.

"Let's see, if I remember correctly it was seven years ago last spring at the Isthmian games. I lived in Corinth at the time."

Hermes closed the door, walked back over, and sat down on his bunk. "Are you a sport's fan."

"I am that. In addition to the discus, I enjoy boxing, footracing, wrestling. I especially enjoy the pentathlon. Discus throwing is a part of that—as, of course, you know. I remember you competed in that, too, but actually you won your laurel in the special event for the discus. I well remember when they placed the garland on your head. You were the youngest athlete there and your victory was the talk of the Posidonium. You were hailed as 'Hermes of

Corinth.' I heard you were competing again at the Isthmus three years ago and I desperately wanted to attend. Almost did. I was traveling from Ephesus to Macedonia that spring and came by ship to Athens, but my time didn't permit me to stop at the games. I—"

"Pardon me, but that hundred thirty-three feet wasn't my best distance. I competed in different games over Greece every two year after that and my distance improved every time. I won them all—the Olympian, the Isthmian again, as well as the Nemean. Well, I take it back. I was there in Athens at the Olympics, but I didn't actually participate in the discus event that year. Did you hear that Nero himself wanted to compete in discus throwing that year? The best he could do was only about a hundred feet. So they made all the contestants secretly swear not to throw farther than a hundred feet. I refused to take part. Everybody knew what was going on, including, I believe, Nero himself. I resented turning the ancient Olympics into a farce. Then, he's emperor, so what were they to do? . . ."

*Can you pull in the liviathan with a fishhook
or tie down his tongue with a rope?
Can you put a cord through his nose
or pierce his jaw with a hook?*

>                                              Book of Job (NIV)

# CHAPTER ELEVEN

## SIXTH DAY OUT OF MYRA, AD 60

SAILING ON TACK had a curious effect on the passengers. For hours they would watch the gradual approach of the Lycian mountains only to have the ship change positions and leave the range behind. The next day they would see the approach of the identical scene, its position relative to their viewpoint changed only slightly. They were zigzagging, and progress was very tedious.

On Wednesday of that first week out of Myra, Ruth met Paul again in the hallway closet. She was saying, "Sir, may I make a bold request of you?"

"What is your request, dear friend?"

"Would you conduct a synagogue service for us this Sabbath?"

Paul thought a minute, then said, "I would delight to do so, but you know Captain Hippalus' directive against religious activities on board. I pray that someday such activities will be protected by law for all people everywhere. But I'm sure you would agree with me that in the meantime we all must strive to get along peaceably in our cramped little world."

"Oh, that's right. I had forgotten."

"I will offer another plan, though, if you're interested. On the Sabbath I could give a lecture. If Scripture and prayer happen to be a part of it, that would only be incidental. What would you think?"

"I can't believe that would be objectionable."

"Then give me a day or so to arrange a place and time and to prepare some material and I'll get back with you."

The next day in the mess hall Paul whispered to Ruth, "It's all arranged. Erastus gave us permission to use our cabin and coordinated it with the other occupants. They say they have no objection if we don't stay too late. Many will probably attend because people are always looking for diversions on a long voyage like this. We've set it for Friday evening about dusk in order to comply with the Sabbath requirement as well as to allow the day crew to attend if they wish. You spread the word. I'll contact those soldiers and prisoners whom I know would be interested—those you've seen praying before their meals? They're Christians. Oh, yes, and I've chosen the topic, 'The Claims of Jesus in Relation to the Scriptures.'"

Friday evening Paul's cabin was almost full. A dozen and a half people were in attendance. People were sitting on the bunks and on the floor. Since the windowless room was so stuffy, it was thought best to leave the door slightly ajar but to post a watchman in case the Captain came down.

Paul began, "'Hear, O Israel, the Lord our God is one Lord . . .'"

The Jews among them joined in the recitation.

"This meeting tonight is not a worship service as such. We will, nevertheless, engage in a preliminary prayer."

After prayer Paul announced his topic and spent his time in a general introduction to the life of Jesus, frequently quoting Jesus' own words. He cited references for his anecdotes, most of which were from eyewitnesses he had personally interviewed. He quoted from memory a profuse amount of Hebrew Scripture to prove that Jesus had fulfilled ancient prophecies. Midway through his presentation, out in the hallway Agabus slipped up to the door and stood listening for awhile. Seeing him, the guard discreetly opened the door a trifle wider.

Two hours passed, yet no one lost interest. They found what Paul had to say unusual and well presented. The air in the room was pungent with burnt lamp oil. Eerie shadows danced upon the walls and ceiling.

Finally, Paul closed the lecture, entertained questions, and led in a brief discussion. After awhile he said, "The hour is late, and I must draw our time together to an end. Thank you for coming. If you would like to attend again, we will have more discussions like this in the days ahead. I must remind you before leaving that Christ is alive. He is willing, out of his love for everyone, to enter into a personal relationship with anyone who desires, the kind of relationship with Him that I have long enjoyed. The way you can receive Christ into your life, as he is in mine, is to accept the claims he has made—both the claims concerning himself and his claims upon your own life. Let each one bow his head now and, if you will, pray like this, 'Dear Lord God, I admit that I am a sinner in need of a Savior. I accept the claims of the risen Jesus to be the Messiah and to be the Savior of the world. I now accept him as the Savior of my soul. Please give to me eternal life.' We will remain with bowed heads for a few moments to give you a chance to pray this prayer if you wish."

After a few minutes of silence Paul said, "Now, after a closing prayer, we shall be dismissed. I ask that those who prayed this prayer remain behind for a few minutes. I'd also like to announce that, the Lord willing, I shall give another lecture here tomorrow evening, on the subject, 'Did Christ Have to Die?' Like others of you on this voyage, I have plenty of time on my hands and will be happy in the meantime to converse on these subjects with anyone who is interested. Do feel free to approach me at any time."

Most people lingered after Paul's prayer and conversed with one another. Luke and Aristarchus mingled among them, searching out especially any who might have prayed Paul's prayer. When Paul approached Ruth, she said, "Paul, I prayed as you asked us to."

Her beautiful face was more radiant than ever.

"Marvelous! Then why not pray and thank God for what he has done for you?"

"Now?"

"Why not?"

"Alright." She lifted her eyes and said quietly, "Bless the Lord, O my soul, for he has sent our Redeemer and has heard the humble prayer of his lowly maiden. Amen."

"Now, dear Ruth, you must begin a walk with Christ by daily prayer, righteous living, and frequent fellowship with other believers. Would you also be willing to do one other thing?"

"Whatever you ask."

"This evening, or in the morning, tell someone about what Christ has done for you tonight. Would you do that?"

"I will."

Ruth returned to her cabin. She had become separated from Kore and Miriam and they were not there yet. When she entered the room, Agabus was sitting on his bunk reading a scroll. She had not been aware that he had observed the meeting that evening.

"Abba, you're still up."

"Yes, my daughter. How did Paul's meeting go?"

"Wonderful! You should have been there. I have some news I want to share with you. Tonight I accepted Jesus as the Messiah. I prayed to become a follower of his. When I did, I felt the most wonderful joy in the world. I wanted you to be the first to know."

"Have I been such a poor Hebrew that my own daughter should leave our fold?"

"Father! Please! I'm not leaving Israel. If anything, I feel as though I've become a—well—a fuller Israelite. Tonight I literally met the God I've heard proclaimed for so long. Father, it's wonderful—this peace that has come to me."

He looked at her in wonder for a few moments, then shook his head sadly.

The next morning Agabus and Julius arrived at the Captain's door at the same time. Agabus knocked and heard the booming command, "Come in."

They entered and Marcus said, "Sit down. I've asked you to come because we have a decision to make. The port of Rhodes is directly ahead of us. We should reach it tomorrow. Do we or do we not stop? I recommend not."

"I see no problem with that," said Agabus. "We took on enough provisions at Myra to last us till Rome. We have no passengers to unload there. And we certainly don't have space to take on any more passengers. I see no reason to stop."

"Nor do I," said Julius. "Let's keep going and not lose the time."

"Then it's agreed," said Marcus. "But another decision regards our route. The usual route is due westward from here, across the Aegean, through the Peloponnesians, across the Adriatic Sea, and up to Rhegium at the southern tip of Italy. However, I anticipate that the head wind we're now facing will continue for several more days. My friend Pliny writes that it begins in August and lasts for forty days. Perhaps it will subside sooner but at the rate we've been sailing since we left Myra, we'll never reach Rome before winter sets in. For that reason after we pass Rhodes I recommend we turn southwest, away from this wind, pass south of the isle of Crete, and take advantage of the coastal shelter of that land mass. That's what we're now doing with the continental land mass. Who knows? By the time we pass Crete, the wind might turn favorable."

"You have my approval," Agabus said.

"Then it's agreed?" said Marcus.

"Not so fast," said Julius.

He bent over the chart for a few minutes and mumbled something to himself. "No," he finally said, "it increases the distance too much. Besides, the route from Crete would be across open sea and in this season I'd be hesitant to drift too far from land."

"I violently object!" said Marcus, slamming his fist down on the desk. "I know this wind! We'll stall in the Aegean!"

"I want to get to Rome as fast as you do, Centurion," Agabus said. "My father's there in grave condition. But Hippalus is the top captain on the sea. I trust his advice."

"It will be as I have decided," said Julius.

"You're just being stubborn," said Agabus.

"You're not a seaman. What do you know about sailing?" said Marcus.

"But I am a soldier and I know how to make a decision. We'll continue on the normal course. Are there any other decisions to make?"

"With the wind against us, we can't just strike out across the open Aegean," said Marcus his voice rising.

"Centurion, regardless of your rank, this is still my ship," said Agabus. "This is my wheat. You've got your prisoners to think of but this is my livelihood. It's not right for you to take over my ship."

"Gentlemen," said Julius firmly, "if you have no further arguments, I must dismiss myself. Good day!"

He left the cabin.

Marcus picked up an inkwell and threw it violently against the door.

That evening at Paul's lecture, the room was more crowded than before. After leading a recitation of the Shema, Paul said, "Before I begin this evening, Ruth, daughter of Agabus, would like to say a word. Ruth."

Ruth said softly, "I just want to let you know that last night I accepted Jesus as the Messiah. I feel . . . I feel as though I've risen to the third heaven. I was reared in a devout Hebrew home, but in spite of all the prayers, sacrifices, and pilgrimages I've made, I've always had the feeling that my sins were still with me—that they'd never been quite forgiven."

Several people nodded their heads in agreement.

"Last night for the first time in my life, my sins were all forgiven. It's wonderful. Now, I'm starting a new life. From now on it will be a life of service to others, like Jesus lived. I want to announce that my first act of service will be to darn socks."

Several people chuckled.

"You may laugh, but seriously, if any of you have any socks with holes in them, please bring them to me and I'll be happy to mend them. My only stipulation is that you wash them first." Laughter filled the room.

Ruth sat back down on the floor and several people reached across and touched her on the arms and shoulders.

"Shhhh!" said the watchman. He gently closed the door.

The room got deathly still. They could hear the unmistakable sound of Marcus' hobnailed sandals on the staircase.

"Erastus!" Marcus' voice exploded in the hallway.

Erastus sprang to his feet. "Aye, sir, be right there."

Several people doused their lamps. Erastus carefully worked his way across the roomful of bodies, opened the door just enough to pass through, and closed it directly behind him. The people in the room remained still and listened to the muffled sound of voices right outside the door. Presently, they heard Marcus leave and ascend the stairs. Erastus reentered the cabin and said, "It was nothing. Just business."

There was a sigh of relief. Paul then began another lecture and followed it with discussion and another invitation. In dismissing, he announced that there would be another meeting the next night. The subject would be, "How Christ Jesus is the Fulfillment of Judaism."

The next day the *Kibotos* passed through the straits of Rhodes. The sea was crowded with fishing vessels, which made it necessary for a seaman to stand at the bow of the *Kibotos* and blow a horn to warn boaters of their approach. They were on a starboard tack and therefore were sailing directly toward the harbor of Rhodes. Passengers crowded the bow to catch a glimpse of the famous old city. Rising from the sea in the shape of an amphitheater, it still had the remnants of its classical glory.

At that moment Ruth and Kore came up through the hatch from below deck. Kore was dressed in an unusually short toga that revealed the length of her legs. Men whistled when they saw her.

Erastus passed by and said, "Ooloo! Look at you. You're gorgeous this morning."

"Thank you, Erastus. Come join us. We're going to view Rhodes."

"Wish I could but got a lot going now. I'll see you after awhile."

He walked away but took another look back at her. The ladies went over to the crowd at the bow. The brisk wind was roaring in their ears. Someone shouted, "Paul, do you have any information about this island?"

"Why don't we ask Dr. Luke?" said Paul. "He's a frequent traveler on the sea."

Luke worked his way to the front of the crowd. "I'll be happy to share with you what I know about it. I've been here often. My family used to vacation here when I was a little boy—"

"Speak up! We can't hear you," someone shouted.

The sail was fluttering loudly, drowning him out.

Luke raised his voice. "I said, 'I've visited here often.' You're looking at both the island of Rhodes and the city of Rhodes. This is, of course, one of the great cities of the ancient world. It's not what it once was, though. About a hundred years ago the people here refused to submit to Roman taxation, and, as a result, it was besieged by Cassius, conquered and plundered. It's been in decline ever since. You'll notice the ruins of the famous colossus of Rhodes lying beside the harbor. This was one of the seven wonders of the world."

"Glory!" exclaimed Kore. "Second of the seven wonders we've seen on this trip. Turning out to be quite a voyage for a wheat ship."

"Excellent observation," said Luke. "This colossus was

constructed over three hundred years ago by a sculptor by the name of Chares from Lindus. It's made of bronze and was originally a hundred and five feet tall. It stood for only fifty-six years before it was toppled by an earthquake."

The fallen statue, broken into several large segments, lay on its side. Its huge face, clean shaven and boyish in appearance and framed by long curly hair, stared back blankly at the passengers. A crown on its head had rays projecting outward. The statue was adorned in a long robe, its bronze surface green with oxidation and pitted by corrosion.

Kore shouted into Ruth's ear, "Look at that face and nose. Doesn't that remind you of Hermes?"

Hermes glanced over at Kore and smiled.

Ruth replied, "Reminds me instead of Hippalus. See how pocked its face is."

Both of them glanced back at the stern toward Marcus. He was standing beside the helmsman nattily dressed in his full military attire. With his feet spread apart and his hands on his hips, he did look like a colossus. They looked at each other and tittered.

"Notice," said Luke, "where the statue originally stood. See its base."

A pedestal, topped by jagged remains, could be seen beside the bronze fragments to the right of the harbor entrance. "Obviously, the common idea that the colossus stood astride the harbor is wrong. The statue represented Helios, the sun god. See the rays projecting from his head like the rays of the sun. The Rhodans used to worship the sun. They were the only Greeks ever to have done so. Paul, maybe you have something to say about that."

"Make that the 'alleged' sun god," Paul said. "Today we know that God is not the sun, the moon, the stars, or the planets. Indeed, these are the mere products of his creation, as is everything else we see in the heavens or on earth.

COLOSSUS OF RHODES

"My friends," he continued, "I've been teaching you that human beings are fallen creatures. We've all come short of the glory of God because of our sins. This statue is a good illustration of that. Even in its ruin it seems magnificent, doesn't it? And we, even in our ruin, appear magnificent too. But still, this statue is fallen. Humans are fallen too. We are not what we were made to be. Not what we could be.

"Do you think anyone could ever rebuild this statue? No? But

God can restore a fallen human. Christ Jesus came into the world to rebuild fallen man."

"Oh, look!" someone shouted.

Two boats with children aboard were sailing up to the *Kibotos*. The passengers went over to the port rail and started tossing coins for the children to dive after. A man on one of the vessels was hawking flowers. Hermes tossed down some coins and the man swung onto the side timbers of their ship and handed a large red rose up to him.

"Here, Ruth," Hermes said, "Let me pin this in your hair."

The bright red rose against her auburn hair, plus the wind's action on her hair and robe, made her exceptionally beautiful.

"Erastus," called Kore.

Erastus came over. "Shh! shh!" he said. "The Captain might hear you."

"Would you get me a flower?"

He leaned over the railing and exchanged a coin for a rose from the vendor. As he was pinning it into her hair, he heard a voice shout, "Get off this ship."

The Captain was leaning over the railing at the stern looking forward at the vendor. Whether the Greek could understand Latin or not, he obviously caught the gist of the command. He dove into the water.

About that time a harbor galley was approaching them, apparently intending to assist them into harbor, thinking they intended to dock at Rhodes.

Seeing it, Marcus shouted, "First Mate. Reverse tack."

"Excuse me, gorgeous," Erastus said, "Got to go."

When they changed the rigging, the *Kibotos* sluggishly turned away from Rhodes and gradually left the city and its inhabitants behind.

That night Paul's lectures were held in the mess hall since the crowd of listeners had grown too large for a cabin. The mess hall was halfway full. Agabus attended openly out of curiosity over the evening's subject, "How Christ Jesus is the Fulfillment of Judaism."

When Paul spoke, he elaborated on Hebrew history in story fashion since the audience was mostly Gentile. As he quoted profuse amounts of Scripture, Agabus's brow furrowed at Paul's memory.

*He's a more formidable adversary than I thought.*

"God's original commission to Abraham," said Paul, "was this, 'In thee shall all families of the earth be blessed.' Notice he did not say merely, 'Thy seed shall be blessed,' but 'all the families of the earth shall be blessed.' Nor was this just a promise; it was a command: 'You *will* bless all the families of the earth.'

"But what have we seen? We have seen the Hebrews closing themselves up, hoarding their blessings for themselves and their seed, and treating the rest of the world with contempt..."

Agabus was stung by the denunciation, but he admitted it was true. It fit even himself.

Later, Paul quoted some of Jesus' words. Agabus felt stirred by the quotes, the same way he was always stirred whenever he read Scripture.

*Could the words of Jesus be the Word of God too?*

Paul let drop the quotation, "Blessed are the peacemakers for they will be called the sons of God."

Agabus sat up with a start. The very words of Ruth that had moved him to tears a few days before.

*Amazing! They were the words of Jesus. Did my own heart recognize them as the words of God?*

Paul ended by saying, "In city after city all over the Roman Empire, churches, made up of all sorts of people, are leading both Jews and Gentiles to believe in Christ. They are obediently giving service to their neighbors, even to 'all families of the earth.' It is the Christians who are fulfilling the commission that God originally gave to the Jews."

After the service that night, Agabus returned to his cabin in deep meditation.

Early the next morning the sea was unusually turbulent. Paul stood at the starboard railing watching the coast ahead of them. Julius passed by.

"Julius, come here a minute."

Julius walked over.

"Look. That's the Triopian promontory. Beneath its heights, the Persians beat the Spartans in the famous naval battle of Cnidus four hundred fifty years ago. We're heading across the Aegean, aren't we?"

Julius nodded.

"Think what that means. We're headed into open sea. We've left the smooth sailing. This turbulence will continue from here on. We won't have the westward current to help us any more either. I've been by here before. I know. I recommend we turn back to Cnidus and stay there until the wind changes—possibly even all winter. The sailing season's almost over anyway."

"I don't think so. We need to get to Rome."

"At least think about it. Cnidus has an excellent port. It's sheltered from the northwesterly wind. Also, they have all kinds of commodities there. If we had to winter there, it wouldn't be that—"

A messenger interrupted. "Centurion, you're wanted at the Captain's cabin."

Julius excused himself and walked over to the cabin. Inside, Marcus and Agabus were already conferring over a map.

Agabus said, "Julius, we have a new development. You've noticed the turbulence? It's because we've moved out from under the shelter of the land into open sea—the Aegean. We've also lost the boost of the three knot current. The result is, we've ceased all progress. We're stalled! I strongly recommend we turn southward and sail with the wind, then fall under the lee of Crete. You see our dilemma?"

Julius looked at the map for a few minutes. Then he said, "I see the problem. But we also have another alternative. We could turn back to Cnidus and wait out the wind there. Then if the wind changes, we have the advantages I outlined before: we wouldn't have as much open sea to cross as we would if we sailed from Crete. Furthermore, if we get stranded at Cnidus—which I pray the gods we don't—at least it would be better than one of the Cretan ports. Cnidus is sheltered from the 'northwester,' fully supplied with stores, and *well* suited for wintering."

Marcus asked, "Where did you learn that?"

"Paul has been along this route before."

"Paul!" thundered Marcus. "That upstart, that charlatan, that deceiver! He's led you down a Pharisaical path. What does that Tarsan know about the sea? Nothing! Why do you take his wisdom over mine? Am I not a sea master? . . ."

He paused, his rage temporarily spent, and looked intently at the centurion. "Julius," he said somewhat softly, "will you punish me forever? . . . Isn't Briton the real reason you resist me?"

Julius calmly said, "What part of my information is wrong?"

"What part is wrong?" Marcus was shouting again. "The whole thing. There's no way we can turn back to Cnidus. Look at our location. We'd be sailing directly into the wind. Our only means of propulsion is wind power. There's no way we could maneuver into that harbor from the south."

"Makes sense, I suppose," Julius said. "But if we reach Crete and get stranded, is there a good port there for the winter?"

"Indeed there is," said Marcus. "Look at Phoenix. I know that port. It would be perfectly suitable. It's on the south side of the island. It has a deep enough harbor, which is protected by an island. The only winds that could threaten it would be the southwest and northwest, neither of which blows in the wintertime. The city of Phoenix itself is large—has plenty of room and board. You could even set up a cantonment in the hills above the city—if it comes to that, which I don't think it will. I think by the time we get there the wind will have turned eastward and we can proceed on. What about it? Shall we turn south."

"Under the circumstances, I will agree."

"Then it's agreed?" said Marcus. "I'll give the order."

Marcus started toward the door, at which time Agabus and Julius stepped in front of him and exited. Marcus stepped out onto deck and shouted, "First Mate."

"Aye, aye, sir," said Erastus nearby.

"Set the course to *Auster Africus*. We're headed for Cape Salmone, Crete."

"Aye, aye, sir. . . . Adjust the rigging."

As soon as they adjusted their course from westward to south-southwestward, they came under a quartering wind and the ship leaped forward in speed.

With a favorable wind the *Kibotos* sailed the distance to Crete in short order and arrived at its eastern tip, Cape Salmone, the next morning. Rounding the narrow eastern end of Crete, they began beating their way westward along the southern coast. Since the wind was still from the northwest, they experienced the same sailing conditions they had encountered along the coast of Lycia—sailing into the wind but with the advantages of a weather coast—which meant smooth waters and a forward current. Again, they had to tack.

Meanwhile, Paul continued his lectures each evening. The night crew asked him to conduct sessions in the daytime, so he also arranged for lectures in the mess hall after the noon meal. With the help of Luke and Aristarchus he also conducted special classes for new converts. Ruth attended these and helped out by providing Agabus' scrolls.

Ruth heard a knock on the door one afternoon. She was sitting in her father's cabin on his bunk, her legs crossed beneath her, darning socks. "Who is it?"

"Hermes."

"Oh, come in."

Hermes entered and said, "Hello, little hermit. I've been missing you lately. What's up?"

"Oh, I've been busy with socks and scripture study. Please don't think me rude for not standing. I'll dump everything if I do."

"You're missing a lot these days. We've been up on deck

admiring the Cretan coastline. It's virtually uninhabited, but really pretty."

Hermes stood looking down at Ruth a moment. "Do you know how much you've changed lately? You're not as fun-loving as you used to be. You're always so busy. You seldom give me any time any more."

"Don't I? I'm sorry. I hadn't noticed. Here, sit down on the bunk by me." She patted the bed. "I guess I got carried away. I've been enjoying the Christian life so much the time has gotten away from me. I'm sorry."

Hermes sat down.

Ruth said, "Now let me ask *you* a question? Hermes, why haven't you accepted Christ too?"

She held a white sock up to the candlelight and studied it.

"Oh, I don't know. I'm just not the religious type, I guess. Never have been. My parents weren't either. You come from a religious home, so it's natural for you. But it's not my cup."

"Me religious?" She laughed softly. "I'm not religious. I used to be—you know, with rites, ceremonies, rituals, prohibitions, festivals, abstinences—all that sort of thing. It was a family thing, a social thing, maybe even racial. But one thing it wasn't—it wasn't personal between me and God. It was between my family and God or my race and God. It's different now—my experience with Christ Jesus—well, it's direct, it's immediate, it's—ah—personal. I feel his very presence with me, something I never had before. No, what I'm experiencing is definitely not religion—it's a relationship."

"I just don't understand."

"Hermes, I've been thinking. You know what I might do? I might look for a good Christian husband in Rome."

"In Rome? Hey, what about Solomon?"

"Solomon!" She put down her mending. "I had almost forgotten about him." She sighed. "Oh me, just as well I guess. When I marry, I'll let Father go back and break the news to him."

The hall door burst open with a bang. It was Kore. "Ruth, Ruth, come look. There's a wonderful hill ahead."

"Must be Matala," Hermes said, rising to his feet. "It's a major promontory. Come on, take a break. Let's go watch it."

"It does sound interesting," said Ruth. "Just a second." She lifted her pile of mending from her lap and placed it onto the bunk, then unfolded her legs, went into her cabin, and got a headscarf. As she came out, she was tying her hair up in the scarf. "I'm ready," she said.

When they emerged on deck, they saw passengers crowding the starboard railing. The ship was approaching a long sloping treeless hill. Beyond the hill, the shoreline receded sharply to the north. People watched in fascination as the *Kibotos* sailed past the hill and started out across open waters.

"Look far across the water in front of us," said Hermes. "You can just barely make out some land way over there. We must be headed toward it."

On the horizon Ruth could make out a coastline that was almost completely obscured in mist.

Abruptly, a brisk wind whipped across the starboard deck. The ship's mast tilted sharply to port. Ruth's headscarf went flying. Hermes took off after it. It caught on a baluster on the port side. Just before Hermes reached it though, it blew out into the water.

Passengers dashed for the hatch to the lower deck. Sailors went scurrying across deck. Hermes walked back over to Ruth.

"Sorry I couldn't reach it in time."

"Darn, that was my best scarf."

Hermes looked up at the heavily billowing sail. "Something's up. We're veering. I think there's trouble."

The *Kibotos* was drifting away from the coast. The Captain bolted from his cabin. "First Mate," he shouted in a foul tone. "To the mast. Reef the sail. Prepare for corrections."

"Reef the sail," cried Erastus in Greek. "Urgent."

The sailors sprang into action and the square sail began to rise. Gradually the ship straightened, but the water was exceptionally turbulent and the ship was tossing violently.

"Strike the foresail," shouted Marcus above the howling wind. "Now, reef the mainsail at half mast. Swing the boom abeam."

Erastus shouted, "Strike the foresail. Reef the mainsail at halfmast." He turned quickly to Marcus. "Sir, did you say abeam?"

"Aye, man. Abeam."

Erastus shouted, "Bring the boom abeam."

When the boom of the mainsail was swung perpendicular to the fore-and-aft line of the ship, the northwest wind caught it full blast. The ship shuddered like a stubborn mule and began an erratic movement backward.

Marcus dashed toward the stern where the helmsman was struggling with the tiller. Erastus ran after him to hear the confusing orders.

Marcus shouted, "Don't follow me. Go fetch the other pilots. All of them."

Marcus reached the helm and shouted to the pilot, "Get the paddles out of the water. Come on, I'll help."

Marcus and the pilot together hoisted the large, heavy starboard paddle out of the water. By that time Erastus and three other pilots had joined them and together they hoisted the portside paddle. The *Kibotos* was now careening backward uncontrollably.

At that moment Agabus approached the stern and stopped to watch the action.

"Greeks," shouted Marcus. "We're going to maneuver to aft. This will be tricky. First, separate the two paddles from the tiller so we can handle each one separately. You two, handle the starboard paddle. You two, the port paddle. Then do as I say."

Erastus transmitted the orders and remained closeby to help. The ship was swiftly careening toward the rocks of Matala.

"Reef the sail to quartermast," shouted Marcus.

"Quartermast," cried Erastus.

"Lower the starboard paddle," said Marcus.

Two helmsmen started to drop the paddle overboard.

"Slowly, man!" cried Marcus.

When the paddle touched water, the two sailors almost spun around from the force of the current on the paddle. Marcus jumped over and lent his might to the paddle. The ship slowed and straightened out its course. Things then calmed down for a few minutes.

Passengers came back up on deck and again crowded the starboard railing, watching in fascination. With the ship proceeding astern, Marcus stood still, alert to any eventuality, with Erastus at his side. Agabus walked up to him. Marcus was still panting.

"What's happening?" said Agabus.

"We came out from under the lee . . . of the island when we passed Cape Matala . . . back there . . . . When we did, the northwest wind hit us full blast . . . . I couldn't buck it . . . . We were drifting out to sea."

"What are you doing now? We're sailing backward. Are we out of control?"

"I dare not try . . . to turn the ship around in this wind . . . Everything's okay, though."

Marcus offered no further explanations. The three stood in silence awhile. Agabus then turned and walked off. Near the hatchway, Julius and Paul came up to him.

"Excuse me, Agabus," said Julius. "Can you tell me what's going on?"

"Well, when we sailed past Matala, the wind hit us full force. Marcus couldn't buck it. He's now backing us away from the wind flow."

"Kind sir," said Paul, "the coastline turned northward at Cape Matala, permitting the northwest wind to hit us head on. It's the same wind we've been bucking since Myra. While we were sailing westward along the coastline, we were under the shelter of the land. We lost that shelter when we passed Matala."

"Phoenix is across that open bay," said Julius. "I wonder what Hippalus' intention is now. We're sailing aft. I've never seen anything like it before. He owes us an explanation. Let's check it out."

"Julius," said Paul, "perhaps a little restraint would now be in order. He's overtaxed now. Why not let him get us out of trouble; then question him?"

"Perhaps so. It can wait. Excuse me. I need to check the other prisoners."

Ruth was still on deck, standing close to Hermes, shivering. Her long tresses trailed in the wind. Kore had joined them.

"Look at that little island back there behind us. I'll bet that's where we're headed," said Hermes. "I've never before heard of a ship sailing backward, especially one of this size. Leave it to Marcus Hippalus. He's a whale of a captain."

"Look at Erastus too. I think he's a whale of a First Mate," said Kore.

"He is," said Ruth and snuggled more closely to Hermes.

By means of continual adjustments to the sail and paddles, the mighty *Kibotos* soon came abreast of the small island Hermes had pointed to. It was two knots east of Matala. On the landward side of the island was a large lagoon with quiet waters. A smaller island was situated to the east of the first island which helped define the boundary of the lagoon.

"Adjust the boom for forward movement," shouted Marcus. "We'll move into the bay."

The boom swung around, the paddles were returned to normal, and the prow of the ship turned into the lagoon. The surface was placid, but a sandy bottom rose rapidly as they sailed forward. When they reached a position midway between the island and the west end of the bay, Marcus shouted, "Drop anchors."

Windlasses wailed like whistles as two large anchors on either side of the bow fell into the water.

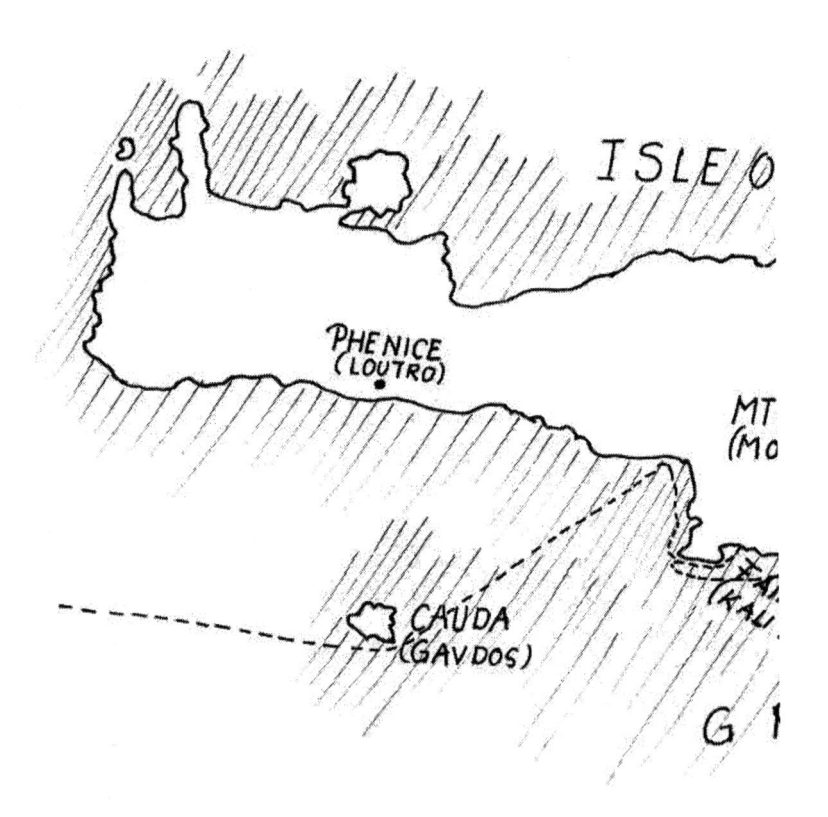

CRETE

IDA
(NI VRONDISSI)

LASEA
(LENDAS)

HAVENS
(LIMINES)

GREAT SEA
(MEDITERRANEAN)

*They all were looking for a king*
  *To slay their foes and lift them high:*
*Thou cam'st, a little baby thing*
  *That made a woman cry.*

*O son of man, to right my lot*
  *Naught but thy presence can avail;*
*Yet on the road thy wheels are not,*
  *Nor on the seas thy sail.*
            George MacDonald

# CHAPTER TWELVE

## NINTH DAY OUT OF MYRA, AD 60

ON THE SEA chart the name of the lagoon where the *Kibotos* anchored was Calolimonia, which means Fair Havens. Despite its auspicious name, no pier was to be seen anywhere upon its shores—only a few huts scattered among palm trees. The sole center of population in its vicinity was a coastal city by the name of Lasea which the ship had passed five knots to the east and to which Erastus had sent a reconnaissance crew immediately upon anchoring.

Everyone else remained on board since Erastus had said they might sail again at first light. They found the ship's stillness and quietness refreshing for a change.

That evening was idyllic. The ship rocked gently in the swell. At dusk passengers and crew members strolled the deck to view the palm trees gently swaying in the breeze and the full moon rising above the sea. Even Marcus lounged in a deck chair atop his cabin.

Miriam came up to Ruth and Hermes and whispered, "The lecture is beginning in the dining hall."

Reluctantly, the two left the railing and started below, joining a stream of people at the hatch. Apprehensively, Ruth glanced back to see what the Captain's reaction would be to the commotion. He was watching intently. Since the duty crew had been reduced to a minimum, more than the usual number of sailors were attracted to Paul's lecture.

The mess hall was filling to capacity. When Ruth went through the door, she saw and waved to Paul, who was casually leaning up against a serving table at the front. When everyone was inside and the doors were closed, he began, "Hear, O Israel, the Lord our God, the Lord is one," and many people joined in.

Immediately, the watchman at the double doors said, "Sssshh! He's coming."

The crowd grew quiet. They could hear the sound of several footsteps—more than one man was approaching. Suddenly, the doors burst open and Marcus entered. He stopped at the threshold and assumed a menacing stance—his feet spread apart and his hands on his hips. His huge hulk filled the passageway. "Who gave you permission to assemble like this?"

Several of the roughest of the seamen, wielding clubs, pushed in past him and took positions along the back wall.

"I did," said Julius, rising from his position at the front of the room. "This is a lecture."

"And you said nothing about it to me?"

"I should have. I assume full responsibility. Won't you join us?"

"This is not a lecture. This is a religious gathering. Why else would Paul of Tarsus be leading it? Why do you persist in resisting my authority? In no uncertain terms I specifically forbade such gatherings on this ship. Centurion, are you deliberately countermanding my orders?"

Julius started toward the back of the room and a number of soldiers rose to their feet. The air grew tense.

"Remain in your positions, men," said Julius.

The crowd drew back, permitting Julius to confront Marcus from a few feet distance. Neither man was armed.

"Marcus Hippalus," said Julius, "I did not perceive of myself as countermanding your wishes. This is not a religious gathering. Do you see any icons? Any bowing? This man's a highly respected scholar, a student of the best schools in Tarsus and Jerusalem, trained in several languages. He's a Roman citizen. He himself has denied repeatedly that he intends to teach religion. Even the Jews do not perceive him as a religious person. Was it not their religious leaders who charged him with impiety? Though a Jew, he is neither Pharisee nor Sadducee, neither Zealot nor Essene. In fact, his lecture this evening is on the subject, 'The Unknown God.' Why not remain with us? Give him a hearing."

"Not religious?" Marcus sneered. "This man bleeds religion. He's the most religious man on earth. I despise him. I'd rid the earth of him if I could. He's come on board to destroy me. How do I know this gathering is not his ploy to plot a mutiny against me? Where is Agabus Ben Uri?"

Everyone looked around. Julius replied, "I don't believe he's here."

"Not here, eh? Does he approve of this meeting? If so, why isn't he here? Julius Priscus, are you, my friend, also plotting against me?"

Marcus, for a moment, appeared sincerely hurt.

"No, my old friend, I'm not plotting against you. Believe me, this meeting has nothing to do with you. It's for the entertainment of the passengers. In the long boring hours aboard ship, ought they not to be allowed a diversion like this, not to mention the food for their minds that it brings? They enjoy it. See how many there are here. Paul is a resource. Should we not use him to advantage while we can?"

"Paul is a deceiver. I will not permit him a voice on this ship any longer. Julius, if you respect me at all, you'll honor my wish. Erastus!"

Erastus stood to his feet at the front. Marcus scowled at him for a moment, then said, "I charge you to find other diversions for the seamen. I'll leave that to you. This assembly is dismissed."

Marcus left with the ruffians behind him. Julius looked back at Paul who was rolling up his scroll. He nodded to Julius in the affirmative, and the people slowly departed the room.

By the next morning it was obvious the ship was not preparing to set sail. As Paul and Luke stepped through the door into the hallway from the hold where they had been praying, Julius saw them and said, "Ho! Paul! People are looking for you. There's a stranger on shore who wants to see you. Would you be interested in going ashore to talk to him? We can't allow visitors to come on board."

"I wonder who it could be," said Paul, turning to Luke. "I know no one on this part of Crete. What do you think?"

"The change might do you good."

"Come on, then," said Julius. "They're keeping a crew on duty all the time at the longboat. It's waiting beside the ship now. Are you ready to go?"

"Certainly. With Luke too?"

"Certainly."

Hermes called down the hall from his doorway, "Would there be room enough for Ruth and me to go?"

"Of course," replied Julius.

Hermes promptly went down the hall, knocked on Agabus' door, and was admitted. Julius, Paul, and Luke went up on deck. A few minutes later Hermes joined them with Ruth and Kore. Kore sidled up to Julius, flashing her eyelids, and said, "You don't mind if little old Kore goes along too, do you?"

"That would be fine," he said gravely.

Descending the rope ladder to the longboat was not easy for Paul, weak from age and abuse as well as from fasting. As they settled into the boat, Luke said, "Perhaps we can get some fruit juice or milk for you on shore. I'll try."

They pulled away from the *Kibotos* and headed for the west shore, only a few hundred feet away. In front of them was a narrow sandy beach backed by a stand of tropical trees. Steeply rising hills, rocky and sparsely vegetated, provided the backdrop to the shoreline.

Julius said, "The little island we're anchored near is called Anchorage Island. The one at the east end is Trapho Island. We're headed toward that fisherman's wharf over there."

A man was standing in a boat at the wharf working his tackle. As the longboat approached, he glanced up and said, "Hello, welcome ashore."

He stepped out of his boat, caught the mooring line thrown from the longboat, and pulled the boat up to the dock. His face was tan, heavily lined, and alive with mirth and good humor. "Centurion, Epictetus is up at the house. All of you can come on up."

Julius said to the passengers, "I'd like to introduce you to Tatius. This is Paul of Tarsus, Dr. Luke, Hermes, Ruth, and Kore."

"You've come to the right place. My wife is the best cook in the Levant. You'll have to sample some of her fare. She's expecting you up at the house now."

"Just a minute," Julius said and turned to the longboat crew. "Return to the ship. The First Mate wants you to string hawsers from the ship to shore and from the ship to the island, to help secure the vessel."

"Aye, aye!"

The fisherman led them through the trees to a humble cottage, chattering all the way in a strange Grecian dialect difficult to understand. In front of the house was a large farm wagon with two horses hitched to it. A matronly woman appeared at the door accompanied by a tall, beardless, distinguished-looking, middle-aged man.

"This is my wife Sybil and my friend Epictetus from Lasea," said the fisherman.

Epictetus walked out of the house right up to Paul and embraced him warmly. "So you are the mighty Paul of Tarsus."

"Not mighty at the moment—as a prisoner of Rome. But kind sir, how is it that you know me?"

"I'm sorry. I've caught you at a disadvantage. You see, I'm from the city of Lasea. Yesterday, some sailors from your ship showed up there asking questions. We welcomed them and in the midst of their conversation they mentioned an elderly political prisoner on their ship, calling him Paul of Tarsus. We were surprised to learn that you were here. Christians everywhere know of you and hold your name in reverence."

Paul's eyebrow raised. "Thank you kindly. But are you a Christian?"

"Yes, I am. We all are—all of us at the synagogue, that is. We all believe in the Lord Jesus Christ."

"Why, that's wonderful! I've never heard of a church in Lasea before."

"An *ekklesia*?" said Epictetus, stressing the Greek term Paul had used for *church*, which also referred to town meetings. "I don't know what you mean. The city council holds them frequently. Is that what you're referring to?"

"You don't know what a church is? You said that your synagogue is made up of Christians, didn't you?"

"Yes. All of us. I'm not a Jew myself. But when I met Christ Jesus, I joined the synagogue."

"That's amazing! Never before in all my travels have I heard of a synagogue completely committed to the Lord Jesus."

"That's the way it should be, should it not?"

All the time he had been talking, Epictetus had been embracing Paul and speaking right into his face. He now released him and turned to the others. "I am Epictetus of Lasea. How do you do?"

He courteously greeted each one and then turned back to Paul. "Now then, let me tell you what we desire of you. We want you to come and speak to our synagogue tonight at the sabbath service. I have come out here to take you back to Lasea when you're ready."

Paul turned to Julius. "What about tonight's lecture? In light of Marcus' threat last night I personally believe it would be impolitic to risk any more lectures. But would you object to my being away, perhaps overnight?"

Julius replied, "I think the situation with Marcus is now self-evident, unfortunately—no more meetings! I have no objection to your going into Lasea if you wish. In fact, I would like to accompany you."

"Fine," said Paul.

Luke and the fisherman's wife came out of the hut with pitchers in their hands.

"Master Paul," said Sybil, "You must be famished. I hear you are fasting. Why don't you at least drink some fresh milk and some freshly squeezed orange juice? Here, come over and sit down on this log under the tree."

Kore said, "May I have some too. I love fresh milk."

"Of course, dear child. Let me get more cups. Also, I have some freshly baked cakes. All of you come over and sit down. There's plenty for all."

While Sybil went back into the hut, the group went over and relaxed themselves in the pleasant shade. Fall was in the air, and the breeze, which had so hampered their sailing, now proved a blessing. Epictetus and Hermes started preparing the wagon for the trip.

Soon they were on their way—seven people crowded up on benches on either side of the open wagon bed. Kore had arranged to sit beside Julius and when the wagon started moving she began nonchalantly kicking his sandal. He paid no attention. Ruth, sitting to her left, nudged her with an elbow and whispered, "Pst!" and frowned disapprovingly.

A few minutes later Kore said in a cooing tone, "Julius, this is a real honor. I've never been this close to a centurion before. This is exciting!"

Ruth rolled her eyes in disgust.

Getting no response, Kore began to play with the handle of his short sword, gently attempting to withdraw it from his scabbard.

"Careful, young lady, this sword has cut off the heads of damsels younger than yourself."

"Oh! I'm frightened. Julius, where are you from? Are you from romantic Rome?"

"My wife and children live in Puteoli, Italy. I have a daughter your age."

Julius spoke across the wagon to Luke, "Dr. Luke, would you mind changing places with me?"

"Not at all," said Luke.

As the two exchanged places, Kore stuck out her lower lip.

Epictetus with the reins in his hand said to Paul, "Tatius and Sybil are not yet Christians. They're business associates of mine. In town I market their fish for them. I'm seeking to win them to Christ. We're winning people all the time. Many Gentiles are now in the synagogue—indeed, more than fifty percent of the members are non-Jews."

"How did a Christian group like this originate in such a remote area?"

"Thirty years ago a man and his wife from our community journeyed to Jerusalem to celebrate the Feast of Pentecost. While they were there, they fell under the preaching of Simon Peter and were converted to Christ. As a result they stayed in Jerusalem to have fellowship with the new Christian congregation and while there shared many great experiences with the apostles and others. Later an incident occurred in which a cripple at the Temple was miraculously healed, after which there began a persecution of their leaders. Then it was that the couple decided to return home. Their unending zeal for the Lord Jesus in Lasea turned the synagogue into a Christian assembly."

"You're a truly historic group. You haven't had much to do with other Christian groups, though, have you?"

"Rarely. See those mountains to the north. That's the Messera range, and it's some twenty-five hundred feet in height. We've always been separated from the more populous northern part of Crete by that barrier. Lasea is largely isolated. We seldom see other Christians. That's why we feel as though God has sent you to us."

"How about Jews? Have you been visited by Jews who've tried to persuade the Gentiles to be circumcised?"

"No, we haven't."

"Have you yourself been circumcised?"

"No, we all feel that circumcision is unnecessary if you accept Christ's crucifixion for your sins. Should we be circumcised?"

"Certainly not, if you're a Gentile. Not that it would hurt anything if you were. So far as being saved is concerned, circumcision is immaterial."

"Well, I'm glad to know that. We haven't had very many teachers, and sometimes I wonder whether we're on the right track or not."

"From what I hear, you're on track alright. I think you're abiding by the essence of the faith already."


The horse-drawn wagon creaked and groaned as it rolled along the stony trail, up dry stream beds and along high paths overlooking the Great Sea. The roadway was little more than a footpath. As they drew near the city they passed scattered residences beside the road. A traveler on foot shouted, "Hello, Epictetus. Been on a journey?"

"Just been down to Fair Havens. You won't believe who I have with me. Look here. This is Paul of Tarsus. Come to the synagogue at dusk. He'll be speaking."

On their right they passed a rocky hill that jutted out into the water. Epictetus called it Cape Leona, or Cape Lion, and it did resemble a crouching lion. Just beyond, they arrived at the edge of Lasea, a surprisingly modern Greek city with many marble-columned buildings, including two temples. Fronting on the sea, the city was perched mainly on a low cliff, except for a quarter-mile length of beach backed by a seawall. At last Epictetus reined the two horses up in front of a posh atrium-style home on the edge of the city.

"Come in to my humble abode and I'll introduce you to my

family. My wife should have noon meal ready soon. We have room enough in our home to host all of you for the afternoon and evening."

After lunch Hermes, Ruth, and Kore went shopping and exploring while Julius went into town to get acquainted with the civic leaders. Paul and Luke retired to a room in the home. Occasionally, friends of Epictetus would drop by to meet Paul, and Paul would courteously greet each one; but Luke insisted the visits be short to allow Paul plenty of time for rest and study.

A crowd filled the synagogue to overflowing that night. Before the service began, Paul genially moved among the people, with Epictetus always at his side.

Paul said, "I would like to meet the official leader of the congregation."

"Of course," said Epictetus, "follow me."

They nudged their way through the crowd until they reached an older man.

"President Simeon, I want to introduce you to Paul of Tarsus."

Paul said, "Kind sir, I take it you are the leader of the synagogue. You're 'president.' Is that correct?"

"Paul of Tarsus! I've longed so much to meet you. Yes, I've been president for many years. How long has it been now, Epictetus? Fifteen?"

"Something like that."

"Simeon," said Paul, "have you felt comfortable leading a synagogue made up primarily of Christians and Gentiles?

"I must confess I had some reservations at first, but the idea quickly grew on me. We've always had proselytes and they've never been disruptive of the order. As to our Christian orientation, I've felt that the acceptance of Jesus Christ as the scapegoat for our sins made a very natural addition to our ceremonies. You'll see. But then, you, Paul,—if anyone—must have had many experiences with Christian synagogues."

"No, this is my first."

The president called the assembly to order. He placed a shawl over his head and had a sacred scroll of Scripture taken from the tabernacle. Paul followed the entire ceremony with a familiarity inbred from childhood. He found little deviation from orthodox Hebrew practice save for the ending of all the prayers with the phrase, "In the name of thy holy child Jesus, we pray. Amen."

The president said, "Brother Epictetus will now come and introduce our distinguished guest."

Epictetus came to the front and said, "Dear brothers and sisters in Christ. You must agree with me that the unexpected arrival upon our remote shores of the Apostle Paul can be nothing other than the moving of divine providence. Today has been one of the rare experiences of my life, as I have been privileged to fellowship with this mighty man of God almost without interruption. Without further word, I now bid you give to Paul the undivided attention such a man of God surely deserves."

Paul stood, had a shawl placed over his head, kissed the scroll, and opened it to begin reading, "The Lord says to my Lord, 'Sit at my right hand until I make your enemies a footstool for your feet.'" When he got through reading, he handed the scroll to an attendant and sat down. He began:

"Your Jewish-Greco assembly stands as a prime example of the unifying effect the Lord Jesus Christ is having upon mankind. Surely the middle wall of partition between Jews and Gentiles is being broken down . . ."

He chose to speak in Greek and an official scribe transcribed his entire discourse. Several in the assembly also took copious notes. Following his message, Paul again mixed among the people. Epictetus said to him, "There's another individual you need to meet. Pease come with me."

He led Paul to a very ancient woman in the women's section who was still seated.

"Paul, this is Sarah. This is the widow I told you about. She's the one who went to Jerusalem with her husband and brought back the news of the Gospel."

Epictetus raised his voice as he spoke to the woman. "Sarah, this is Paul. He's the one who knows Peter."

"Dear Brother Paul, I'm so pleased to meet you," she said in a weak voice. "You know Peter? Where is he now?"

Paul leaned over toward her. "Peter and his wife moved back to Galilee. They make their home there now. But they're usually away from home on mission trips like myself."

"That's so nice. I liked him a lot. Mary was such a dear friend too."

"Mary passed away recently. You know she used to live with the Apostle John."

"I'm so sorry to hear that. You tell Peter and his wife that Sarah sends her love to them when you see them again."

"I'll surely do that," said Paul. "Dear lady, I honor you and your husband for your faithfulness to our Lord Jesus Christ over these many years and for your effective witness that has led so many people in Lasea to Christ."

"Thank you. I give all the praise to the Lord Jesus Christ. My husband went home to be with Jesus ten years ago."

Finally, at midnight, the people disbanded and Paul and his friends went home with Epictetus for the night. The next morning they returned to the *Kibotos*.

The northwesterly wind continued to blow for a week. On Monday morning Hermes came out of his cabin and encountered Erastus walking down the hallway.

"Morning, Hermes. Finally pulled yourself out of the bunk, did you? You missed breakfast."

"I know. I spend a lot of time sleeping these days. The weather's like springtime. Besides, there's so little to do."

"You could have come to my lyre concert at the mess hall last night."

"Oh, yeah. I forgot about it. How did it go?"

"Go? It was a flop. Not a dozen people showed up. The

sailor's resent it because I didn't bring in girls. I tried to, but couldn't find any. Man, Lasea is a staid place. Then, in addition, the Christians boycotted it because of the cancellation of Paul's lectures. Marcus insisted I bring in some type of entertainment, but I'm plumb out of ideas now. Say, where are you going with that towel?"

"Swimming. Want to go?"

They started walking together toward the staircase.

"Wish I could, but I have work to do. Maybe this afternoon. I'll see."

"I tried to talk Ruth into going but she was too shy to swim in front of the men. Kore spoke up and said she would go, but Ruth wouldn't let her."

"Did you ask Miriam?"

"Ha! You and your feeble jokes." Hermes tried to trip Erastus and the two wrestled goodnaturedly on the staircase.

When they reached the deck, they saw Marcus tending some instruments atop his cabin.

"What's he doing?" asked Hermes.

"Monitoring the weather. He watches it like a midwife tending a woman in labor. He's very anxious to sail. Don't blame him. The season's wearing on and we can't even get out of the Levant."

"Funny thing," said Hermes. "The mess personnel tell me he pops his head into the mess hall sporadically. Keeps expecting to nab Paul lecturing again. Here's the longboat. I have to go."

Paul was also on deck at the time intently watching Marcus. In his prayer session that morning he had felt led to try to witness to him one more time. Standing there alone, he formulated his approach, prayed silently for help, then walked toward the deck house. Marcus was atop the house monitoring a wind gauge and a sun dial and writing figures onto a small scroll. Caesar was walking around the roof sniffing things.

Paul looked up and said, "Good morning, Captain. Do you foresee any soon change in the wind?"

Marcus, without looking at Paul, merely grunted and moved across the roof out of sight. Caesar came over to the edge above Paul. He pulled back his ears, then waged his tail, then stopped wagging, pulled back his ears again and growled a low guttural growl.

Paul walked around the cabin to where he could look up and see Marcus again and said, "Sir, I would really like to make friends with you. If I have offended you in any way, I wish to apologize."

Marcus stood up and looked at him. He started to speak, then changed his mind and walked out of sight again.

Paul followed him around and said, "Did you know that Jesus of Nazareth once made an observation about weather casting? He said, 'When evening comes you say, "It will be fair weather, for the sky is red," and in the morning, "It will be stormy, for the sky is red and overcast."'"

Marcus was not looking at Paul, yet he let his scroll fall idle in his hand and stared aimlessly ahead. He mumbled to himself, "That only occurs in the wintertime. The Levant has very little rain except in winter."

Paul did not hear him. He continued speaking, "The point he was making was that his enemies could interpret the signs of the weather but couldn't interpret the signs of the times. Captain Hippalus, there are forces at work in your own life of which you are unaware. God is directing circumstances to draw you to himself, if you will only yield to him."

"Never!" shouted Marcus. He rapidly walked to the ladder, descended, went to his cabin and closed the door with a bang. Caesar had followed him to the ladder but couldn't get down by himself. Suddenly, Marcus burst from the cabin and went to the foot of the ladder.

"Come on, boy. Jump down."

The dog leaped into his arms. Marcus dropped him to the deck, returned rapidly to the cabin with the dog in pursuit, and slammed the door behind them again.

Paul watched the quick scene in astonishment.

Thursday was Yom Kippur, the Day of Atonement, an annual Jewish holiday. Five different services were held at the synagogue in Lasea throughout the day to accommodate the crowds. All the services were packed to capacity. Almost all the passengers, soldiers, prisoners, and crew members not on duty, attended. Most of them walked to Lasea, a two hour trip. Each prisoner was chained to a soldier. Julius marched with his soldiers. Epictetus had sent his wagon early for Luke and Paul, and the ladies and Agabus had also ridden with them. Paul spoke at each of the services.

In Lasea, Agabus, Ruth, Kore, and Miriam walked the streets until time for the afternoon service. The shops were closed but they found a park and rested beneath its trees. Yom Kippur was a day of fasting so at noon they sipped some water and then headed for the synagogue. At the front door Agabus separated from the ladies and went to the men's section. Inside, he found a seat.

Someone said, "Pardon me, friend. Are you Agabus Ben Uri?"

Agabus looked up and saw a silver-haired elder.

"Why, yes I am."

"I thought so. People from the ship often speak of you. I am Simeon, president of the synagogue."

Agabus was impressed at how Jewish the president seemed. He had a robe with tassels, phylacteries upon his brow and left arm, and ashes atop his head. Yom Kippur was a day of repentance. Agabus felt relieved.

The man continued. "Master, would you be so kind as to read from the scroll in this service?"

To do so meant to occupy a place of prominence throughout the service.

"Why, I would be delighted to do so."

He followed the president to the front, facing the crowd, and was seated. As he made himself comfortable, he looked to one side and was chagrined to see Paul seated next to him.

With a twinkle in his eye, Paul said, "Good afternoon, Agabus. Did you bring your *Isaiah* scroll?"

Agabus saw the humor. "And carry it five miles?"

"Seriously, that's what you will be reading from this afternoon—*Isaiah*. I recommended you as reader."

"Hear, O Israel: the Lord our God, the Lord is one," intoned the president. The service had begun.

Soon it was Agabus' turn. The scroll was taken from the tabernacle, a text was assigned to him, and a shawl was draped over his head. He began reading, "All we like sheep have gone astray; we have turned every one to his own way; and the Lord hath laid on him the iniquity of us all."

When Agabus sat down, Paul began speaking from his seat of prominence. "From the days of Moses the Hebrews have practiced a strange ritual. Annually, they select one goat. Then the high priest places his hand on that goat, prays, and confesses all the sins of the people over the past year. After that he leads the goat outside the gate of the city and releases it into the wilderness. It is the people's scapegoat. God had prescribed this ritual for them. It symbolized the putting away of sin. It is taking place at this very moment in Jerusalem on this Yom Kippur or Feast of the Atonement."

Agabus knew the ritual well. Once he had been in Jerusalem to witness the solemnity of the event. Now, however, he was uncomfortably close to Paul. He could lay his hand on his arm.

Paul continued. "It was no coincidence that Mount Calvary, where Jesus was crucified, was outside the walls of Jerusalem. God planned it that way in order to fulfill the symbolism of the release of the scapegoat. You see, Christ is our scapegoat. The Hebrew scapegoat typified Christ's coming death, and in his death Jesus completely fulfilled the intended symbolism of that event. On the cross Christ Jesus took away all our sins once and for all. Jesus is the fulfillment of Yom Kippur."

Agabus was once again stunned by Paul's words. His logic was impeccable. The truth of his comparison irresistible. Agabus felt as if he had been struck.

Friday morning Paul and Luke were in the longboat on their way back to the ship.

"Look," said Luke. "The hawsers have been removed from between the ship and shore."

"Something's up," said Paul. "I hope Marcus isn't intending to move the ship. It's too late in the season."

The boat pulled alongside the *Kibotos* and Paul struggled up the rope ladder to the deck. Luke then helped him down the staircase to the lower deck. They found the door to their cabin ajar and heard voices inside. Opening the door, they saw Marcus sitting on a bunk beside Julius with a sea chart unfurled on their laps. Agabus was standing over them. Marcus shot Paul an ugly glance as he entered.

Marcus was saying, "This is not a good harbor in which to winter. There's no dock here. It's also susceptible to storms from the south. Nor are there any supplies within a close proximity. If I lay off the crew here, I can't expect to find another one next spring. And Agabus doesn't want to pay the crew to remain with us all winter. No other seagoing vessels anchor here as you can see. And so forth. Let me show you an alternative."

He pointed to the chart.

"Here we are. Over here, just forty miles away is Phoenix, which I know to be perfectly suitable to winter in. It has all that this site doesn't have. I suspect you could even find a military contingent there—or at least could establish a bivouac site nearby for your—"

Julius broke in. "That's where we were headed before, isn't it? What makes you think we can get there this time?"

"Look! The northwest wind is beginning to subside. The weather is very changeable now. It could turn favorable at any time. If it does, I can maneuver that short distance without risk. But, understand, I'm not necessarily recommending it. Just suggesting we think about it."

"And you, Agabus," said Julius, "what do you think?"

"I'm willing to leave it up to the Captain."

Paul spoke up, "Sirs, may I remind you that Yom Kippur passed yesterday. Common knowledge places that date as the end of the sailing season. After that, sailing becomes dangerous. If we attempt to move at all, I perceive it will be with hurt and much damage, not only to the cargo and ship but also to our lives. 'Never trust her at any time, when the calm sea shows her false alluring smile,' as Lucretius said."

Marcus jumped up so quickly he struck his head on the upper bunk. Reeling momentarily but quickly regaining his composure, he shouted, "What right does this man have to speak? Who asked his opinion? Did you? Did you? I didn't! He's a stinking prisoner. Pay no attention to him."

Julius said, "Paul knows what he's talking about. He's been shipwrecked on these waters three times. We best heed what he says."

"Ha! ha! ha! ha! Shipwrecked thrice, eh?" said Marcus. "No wonder. He's sailed with the wrong captains. I've *never* had a wreck. I don't know about you two, but I've just made up my mind. Let's start for Phoenix this afternoon."

Marcus started rolling up his chart.

"Alright by me," said Agabus.

"Not now," said Julius firmly. "We'll watch the weather a little longer."

"Go to Hades!" shouted Marcus and stormed out of the room.

At sunrise a knock was heard on the door of the officer's cabin.

"Centurion Julius, the Captain requests your presence in his cabin immediately."

Julius arose and went up on deck to the cabin. Agabus was already with Marcus.

Marcus seemed excited. "Did you notice the flags as you came up? We are graced with a south wind this morning. What did I tell you? The sea is as calm as a whisper. Let's sail now. Phoenix is only forty miles away. We could be there before noon—before the afternoon breezes start. What do you say, Centurion?"

Julius stuck his head out the door. The flags were fluttering from a gentle southerly wind. The sea waters were remarkably calm. He asked, "How long would it take to set sail?"

"No more than half an hour. Just long enough to weigh the anchors and hoist the sail. That is, if all your men are on board. Mine are."

"They are. They all ran out of money at Lasea. What about the longboat? It's still out."

"Never mind," said Agabus, "We can drag it that far . . . can't we?"

"No problem," said Marcus.

"Then, let's do it!" said Julius.

Marcus opened the cabin door and shouted. "First Mate."

"Aye, aye, sir."

"Weigh the anchors! Hoist the sails. Sail when ready."

"Aye, aye, sir!"

A flurry of activity followed. In half an hour the mammoth ship was maneuvering its way out of the harbor and turning gracefully into the placid open sea. Only tiny ripples played upon a gently heaving surface!

*God moves in a mysterious way*
*His wonders to perform;*
*He plants his footsteps in the sea,*
*And rides upon the storm.*

William Cowper

# CHAPTER THIRTEEN

## FIRST DAY OUT OF FAIR HAVENS

PAUL WATCHED THE weighing of the anchors, the sole passenger on deck at that early hour. Despite the calm weather, he was gravely anxious. He leaned back against the railing, painfully recalling an earlier voyage—one that had begun just as peacefully but had ended in disaster. In a flash storm his ship had foundered and he had floated overnight in a longboat on the open sea. His counsel now to the Captain not to sail came out of genuine dread.

His palms were sweaty, his stomach tight, his heart pounding. He gripped the railing behind him to control his trembling. His thoughts turned inward; his brow furrowed. Oblivious to his surroundings, he stared blankly ahead.

Whenever Paul meditated, his face appeared stern, as though

he were angry. At this time Paul happened to be facing toward Marcus on the other side of the deck. Marcus shouted, "Who are you scowling at, you judgmental bigot?"

Paul did not hear him. He had closed his eyes.

*I must not succumb. Must not fear. I will trust in the Lord and not be afraid. Merciful Father, here am I. I'm in grave danger. Remember me. Help my unbelief. Strengthen my faith. I am yours, O Lord—here to do your will—here to serve you. Remember your lowly child. Give me peace. In the name of Jesus."*

As he remained with his eyes closed for a few moments, he sensed the tension leaving his body. His abdomen relaxed, his shoulders sagged, his breath slowly expired. He felt joy welling up within. *Thank you, Lord.* Over his face crept a smile. Paul almost always had a faint smile on his lips, although he often was unaware of it. He wondered why people sometimes smiled at him when he had not smiled at them. That smile had returned.

Soon other passengers joined Paul at the railing and watched the maneuvering of the ship and the passing coastline. What a beautiful morning it was! Never had they enjoyed such smooth sailing. The atmosphere was silent and serene. The only noise was the cawing of sea gulls behind them and the restless flapping of the huge sail, alternately filling and failing with the bare breeze. Those attempting to look back at Fair Havens were blinded by the brilliant sparkle of the rising sun on the rippling water.

Suddenly, the voice of Marcus filled the deck:

> Now is the season of sailing; for already the chattering swallow is come and the pleasant south wind; the meadows flower, and the sea, tossed up with waves and rough blasts, has sunk to silence. Weigh thine anchors and unloose thy hawsers, O mariner, and sail with all thy canvas set.

"What was the meaning of that?" Hermes asked.

Paul was now standing among a group consisting of Hermes, Ruth, Kore, Miriam, and Agabus. He answered, "He was quoting from Leonidas. He's obviously pleased with the situation."

There was a tense moment as they approached Cape Matala for the second time. Would they again confront the stiff head wind? Since the tall cape was round and broad, it was difficult to determine exactly when they had passed it. Gradually, a long view to the west opened to their eyes, ending in the mist-shrouded point of land far away.

Kore said, "I . . . I think we made it."

People started applauding and cheering.

The existence of the cape created a wide bay, Messara Bay, on Crete's southern coastline. Phoenix and Matala were its anchor points. This time Marcus set a course close to the coastline rather than attempting to sail straight across the bay. Then he posted Erastus beside the helmsman and disappeared into his cabin.

The mess bell jangled and the first shift of diners went below for breakfast. Spirits were high, and lively conversation buzzed across the mess hall. Agabus and the ladies, along with Hermes, Paul, and Luke, sat together at one of the tables.

Ruth said to her father, "Do you think we will try to continue on to Rome or winter in Phoenix?"

"We'll have to spend the winter at Phoenix," Agabus said. "It's too late in the season to cross the open sea—that's why we're hugging the coastline. But Phoenix has its own harbor and it's a much better arrangement than Fair Havens."

"I hope so," replied Ruth. "I want to get a nice villa in the city and not have to stay on the *Kibotos* all the time." Then her face turned sad. "We might not get to grandfather in time."

Hermes turned to Paul. "I understand you strongly recommended we not leave Fair Havens. Why?"

"Well, although the weather is calm now, in this season you never can tell what it might do. I've seen it change in a wink. I think we're risking a lot just to move forty knots."

Luke said, "Excuse me, Paul. Have you noticed how still it it's become?"

Complete calmness had settled in.

"If you'll pardon me," said Agabus, "I'll go see if anything is amiss." He folded his napkin at his plate, arose, and left the mess hall. Numerous others followed him.

In a few minutes he returned and sat back down and resumed eating. "The wind has merely quit blowing," he said. "Nothing to worry about."

Paul whispered to Luke, "That's not good. This is no time to stall."

When they were through eating, they all went back on deck. On exiting the hatch, they saw all the crew members staring inland—awestruck. The sea was glassy calm and the men appeared to be gripped with a sense of dread, as though waiting before a great mystery, not knowing what to expect. Marcus stood among them with an enigmatic look on his face—a peculiar awareness of something. Erastus was the only one moving. The passengers threaded their way through them to the port railing.

Paul went up to Erastus and said, "What's going on?"

"The men are superstitious. See that tall mountain over there. That's Ida Psiloriti, the birthplace of Jupiter. They think we've been captured by him."

A lengthy span of stillness passed before anything significant happened. Gradually a large dark cloud began to crest the peak of the mountain. To the sailors and soldiers it was a sign of Jupiter himself—god of light, weather, and sky—arising to accost them. They saw themselves as small as insects and their ship as a toy before him. Flashes of lightning began to light up the cloud. The hairs on the back of their necks stood on end.

Higher and nearer loomed the lightning-pocked cloud. Rain started to fall, the wind to blow, the sky to darken. Before the seamen could react, a wind hit the sail with such force they could not reef it. It began to rip to shreds. Suddenly, they were at the mercy of the storm. The wind, blowing fiercely down the ravines and gullies of the mountain, forced them toward open sea—they could not bear up against it. A drenching rain swept across the deck and the frightened men scampered below for wet weather gear.

During this mayhem a single gigantic wave swept over the side of the ship, flooding the deck and coursing down into the hull through the open hatches.

"Aaieeeee! Save us!" cried three men as the wave swept them across the deck. The others watched helplessly. The three bounced off the special boards that filled in the railing and did not go overboard.

Marcus Hippalus, protected by nothing more than his short kilt, manned the tiller briefly while the pilot retrieved his weather gear. Even Marcus could do nothing but allow the ship to scud seaward before the wind.

After awhile a sailor cried out, "Land ho!"

A small island on their starboard could be glimpsed intermittently through the driving rain.

Marcus shouted, "First Mate, bring the ship to lee of that island."

Erastus shouted, "Trim the sails for starboard tack. Pilot, steer leeward of the island."

Sluggishly, the *Kibotos* heeled to port and moved toward the small island. In a few minutes they came under its shelter and experienced a relative calming of the waters, though the rain still fell and the wind continued to sway the mast.

"Reef the mainsail. Hold her close to the island," shouted Marcus.

As soon as Erastus had conveyed the orders, he approached Marcus and shouted to him over the roar of the wind, "Do we put in to shore?"

"Too dangerous. I'll see if there's a cove. Call Ben Uri and Priscus first."

"Aye, aye, sir."

The two quickly appeared at the helm and Agabus shouted, "Can we make it to Phoenix?"

"I can't hear you," Marcus said. "Follow me."

Marcus quickly led them to his cabin. When he opened the door, papyri documents went flying across the room. A frightened dog jumped up on him, but he struck it saying, "Down," and continued across the room to his charts without missing a stride.

Agabus said, "What's happening?"

"It's storming. Can't you see?" Marcus answered roughly.

"Can we still get to Phoenix?" asked Julius.

"Too late. We've left Crete behind. We're being driven toward open sea. Got to hurry."

He quickly unfurled and read a map. "This is Cauda. Twenty-three knots from Crete. We can't put in here. Not a cove in sight. Too deep to anchor."

"What are we going to do?" shouted Agabus.

"All we can do is drift leeward of this island as long as possible. Have about ten hours. In the meantime got to trim the ship for storm sailing. It should subside in a day or two."

The door swung open and a gust of wind and rain blew in. Erastus entered. "Sir, can we anchor or is there a cove to put in to?"

"Too deep. There are no coves here. Retard her drift and hold her steady."

"The longboat's about to sink."

"Pull it in, imbecile. Shut that door."

Erastus left and slammed the door.

Still studying the chart, Marcus said, "Cauda Island is due *Africus* (southwest) of Cape Matala. Eeeii! This means the wind is *Aquilo!*"

"The dreaded Euraquilo!" cried Julius.

Julius erupted with the Latin compound of *Eurus*, meaning East, and *Aquilo* meaning Northeast, or East-North-East, roughly a sixty-seven degree heading.

Marcus's body suddenly sagged. He eased himself down into a chair and looked up at Julius with bleary eyes. "It's happening again, isn't it?" He paused long, looking at him. "Everything's against me."

"You can pull us through this. You've got to."

With a conspicuous act of will Marcus pulled his chair up to the desk and leaned over the map. "We can't just run before the wind. We're headed straight for Syrtis Major."

"What is that?" asked Julius.

"A dangerously shallow bay by north Africa, just west of Cyrene.

Called the Ships Graveyard. If we blow into there, we'll never get out."

"Africa? That's three hundred miles away!" shouted Agabus. "I thought you said the storm would be over in a day or two."

"Let him be," said Julius. "The Euraquilo is a wind that can blow for a week. No one can predict the weather perfectly."

"You got us into this. How are you going to get us out?" shouted Agabus to Marcus.

"I don't know."

"Don't know?" echoed Agabus.

"You're Marcus Hippalus," said Julius. "You can get us out of this if anyone can. Come on, pull yourself together."

"I could trim the foresail—sail on a broad reach—aim for Sicily."

"Sail for Sicily?" mused Agabus. He did not scold this time. "But it would be dangerous this time of the year, wouldn't it?"

"It would be dangerous." Marcus turned to Julius. "It's up to you."

"Let's see what tomorrow holds."

"Can't wait till tomorrow. We're drifting rapidly. Nine more hours and we're back under the full brunt of the storm."

"Then we decide in nine hours."

Marcus sprang from his chair and headed for the door. Outside, he called, "First Mate, trim the ship to ride out the storm when we emerge from Cauda. Nine or ten hours. Jerk that tattered mainsail down. Then frap the vessel."

"Aye, sir. But we're having trouble with the longboat."

"What's the matter?"

"Chock full of water. Can't hoist it up. To put a man in it to bail would sink it."

Marcus went to the stern and looked down. "Pull it close to the stern. Let down pots to bail it out until you can get a man down in it to bail. I'm going below to check the hull."


Meanwhile, on the lower deck people were suffering from the

buffeting of the storm. When it struck, the three ladies had gone to their cabin, doused the wall sconce to avoid fire, stripped to their underwear in the mugginess, and gone to bed. In the darkness they fell asleep. The roll of the ship was terrible, even in the owner's suite which was at the axis point of the ship, and Miriam became ill. Hers was an upper bunk. Ruth woke up and made her come down and lie on her own bunk, a lower one. She provided a pot by her bedside and climbed up onto Miriam's bunk.

Ruth awakened next, when the violent motion of the ship eased before noontime. She got up, relit the sconce, and started dressing. There was a knock on the door.

"Hello, this is Luke. Are you ladies alright in there?"

"We're fine. I'll be out in a moment."

She shook Kore and said, "Kore, get up. Dr. Luke is here. I think the storm is over."

In a minute Ruth and Kore stepped outside their cabin. Luke was alone in Agabus' suite.

"Hello!" Ruth said. "Is the storm about over?"

"I don't know. The rain is still pouring down. Are you all alright? A lot of people are sick."

"Just a little queasy. Miriam is sick, though."

"Let me see her."

Ruth went back in and covered her up, and Luke came in to attend to her. In a few minutes he arose, and, wiping his hands with a towel, said, "Watch her to see that she doesn't get dehydrated. Have her drink water often and eat soup and crackers.... Ruth, would you like to accompany me to treat the ill?"

"I'll be glad to. I was getting tired of darning socks, anyway"

"No, she wasn't," said Kore. "She loved it." She laughed, then said, "Can I come too? I want to help."

"Excellent," Luke replied. "Come with me. I need to get my bag." Outside their door he said, "Watch your step."

Agabus' room was in total disarray. His chair was overturned, his documents were scattered, and the floor was drenched with seawater from the hallway.

When they reached Luke's door he said, "Remain out here.

Paul and Hermes have both been sick and the stench is not real pleasant."

"Oh," said Ruth, "I want to help them."

She and Kore pushed into the room. Seeing Hermes in his bunk with a wet rag was over his eyes, she ran over, knelt by his side, and said, "Hermes, you poor dear. Are you alright?"

He removed the rag and said weakly, "I'd rather be dead."

Ruth stroked his cheek. "You poor thing. You'll be over it shortly."

Then she went over to Paul's bunk, knelt down, and whispered "Dear Paul, I'm so sorry you're ill. But the Lord is with you." Looking up at Luke, she asked, "Are they serious?"

"Not really. Just seasick. The main thing for which we have to watch is dehydration, especially Paul with his fasting."

"Here," said Ruth. "Let me have the water. I'll offer them some."

Luke gave her a cup of water and she tenderly offered a sip to Paul. Returning to Hermes, she gently raised his head and said, "Here, drink some of this. It will do you good." Ruth looked around and said, "Erastus and Julius are not here, are they?"

"They're up with the Captain," Luke said. "Paul has a propensity toward seasickness but he always responds to my treatment. They both should be getting over it after awhile. Can we get started now? I'm taking this long strip of linen and this pot of water. When you help a person, just tell him you're ministering in the name of Jesus."

"Okay, 'in the name of Jesus,'" said Kore. "He's my friend too."

"Kore," said Ruth in astonishment, "When did you become a Christian?"

"I really haven't yet but I want to. How do I do it?"

Ruth looked imploringly toward Luke.

"You tell her, Ruth. You can do it."

Paul raised up on his elbow to watch.

Ruth turned back to her friend and said, "Kore, if you want to find Jesus, well, ah, just pray a prayer like this, 'Dear God above,

I need a Savior and I want Jesus to save me.' Then say, ah, 'I am a sinner, but I pray that you will forgive me. I believe in Jesus.' Yes, that's it. 'I believe in Jesus—that he is the Messiah and that he died on the cross for me and was raised from the dead.' Then just thank God for saving you and close by saying, 'Amen.'"

"Is that all there is to it?" asked Kore.

"That's all—if you really mean it when you pray. Are you ready now?" asked Ruth.

"Okay, here goes." Kore bowed her head and prayed, 'Dear Lord God, I want to be a Christian too. And if you will have a silly girl like me, here I am. I've done a lot of things that I need forgiveness for. I do believe in Jesus, and I want him in my life like Paul and Luke—yes, and Ruth. Amen. Oh yes," she added, her voice breaking, "thank you for saving even me."

When Kore finished, she buried her face in Ruth's embrace and wept uncontrollably. Ruth hugged her to herself. When she finally looked up, tears were still in her eyes but a smile was on her face.

Luke shook her hand and said, "Welcome to the family of God."

Paul weakly said, "Kore, come over here."

She went over to his bedside. He took her hand in his and said, "The word of God says, 'Whoever will call upon the name of the Lord will be saved.' I'm so happy that you have found Christ. Now go forth and live for him daily."

When Dr. Luke and the ladies were through treating the ill, it was past noon. They stopped by the mess hall just as two soldiers were coming out the door. "It won't do you any good," they said. "They're not serving."

They went inside anyway and Ruth asked a cook, "Why are you not serving?"

"It's too dangerous to light the fire under these conditions, Ma'am."

"Well, I'm going to see if I can fix something."

In a few minutes the three came out of the mess hall with

several short logs in their arms and carried them into the owner's cabin. Agabus watched them with curiosity. Situated in his cabin was a small wood stove, with a flue to the outside. Into this they stuffed kindling and logs and lit a fire. Ruth tended the flame while Kore and Luke went back to the mess hall for cookware and dishes as well as meat and vegetables. Within half an hour the two ladies had prepared, despite the poor conditions of the tossing ship, an appetizing stew. They set several places at Agabus' desk and went down the hall to get Paul and Hermes. Neither felt like leaving his bunk, but Luke went up on deck and brought back Erastus.

As they ate together Agabus said, "Indeed, this is tastier than anything we've yet had in the mess hall."

Luke said, "Ruth and Kore, you're both very fine cooks. Two men will be marvelously blessed to have you as their wives."

"I'm holding out for a Christian husband," said Ruth.

"I am, too," said Kore. "I like all men, but I think I like Christian men best."

Ruth just rolled her eyes.

That afternoon the *Kibotos* was a beehive of activity. Time was short and every able-bodied crewman was working feverishly. Erastus decided the waters by the island were calm enough and ordered the mess stove relit and supper prepared. Retrieving the longboat took all day. The tossing ship and bobbing boat made lowering a pot into it a game of target practice. When it came time for someone to enter the boat to finish bailing, a man took his life into his hands to do so. The hoist proved inoperative and had to be repaired before they could raise the longboat.

Another squad was bailing out the ship's hull into which seawater had poured when the wave washed over the deck. Some were operating primitive bilge pumps; but before the job was completed, it became necessary for others to help manually by lifting water out in large pots.

Still another squad was bringing up bags of grain from the

hold to the deck to build dikes around the hatches. This task Agabus watched over personally to assure that as little of his profitable cargo as possible be wasted or contaminated by the seawater.

Another squad was assigned to "frap" the ship, that is, to wrap the entire vessel under and around with hawser ropes, stretching them taut across the deck to reinforce the hull. Marcus intended to save this job until after the yard had been lowered from the mast in order to secure the yard on the deck with the frapping ropes, but circumstances dictated otherwise. A large detail of men had climbed the mast and were scampering about high up in the rigging, preparing to lower the yard. It was almost as long as the ship itself. At the height they were working the gale was gusting at speeds up to fifty knots an hour and rain was falling in torrents. Orders shouted from the deck were difficult to hear. Preparation took so long that Marcus began to doubt they would have it down before nightfall. He finally had to order the crew doing the frapping to proceed and not await the lowering of the yard. He resigned himself to laying the yard atop the frapping hawsers and securing them in place by other means.

About this time Marcus decided to have the sea anchor deployed to further retard their drift.

Erastus directed the frapping personally. First, most of the protective boarding beneath the railings was stripped away to allow the hawsers to pass under the railings. Then a diver, who had volunteered for the dangerous task, dove into the water, pulled the thick rope behind him, and passed it beneath the *Kibotos*. Others stood on the protective timbers on the side of the ship to retrieve the rope from the diver and to pass it to men on deck. This was done repeatedly and the ship was tightly wrapped from stem to stern.

When the detail finally had the yard ready to lower, Julius ordered a large contingent of soldiers onto deck to help handle the gigantic timber. In the midst of all the action the various squads—the yard squad, frapping squad, longboat squad, and bailers—were struggling in conflict with one another. Tempers flared. Men were ready to give up. The leadership skills of Marcus, Erastus, and Julius were strained to the ultimate to manage their men and keep the work progressing. Despite the delays, they got the yard down to the deck in time to secure at least half of it beneath the frapping rope. The other half was braced and tied in place by less desirable means.

By nightfall the preparation was finally completed and nothing was left to be done but to await the end of the passage from the eclipse of Cauda. Supper was served after dark—late, but warmly welcomed.

*Across the margent of the world I sped,*
  *And troubled the gold gateways of the stars,*
  *Smiting for shelter on their clanged bars;*
    *Fretted to dulcet jars*
*And silvern chatter the pale ports of the moon;*
  *With thy young skyey blossoms heap me over*
    *From this tremendous Lover*
      THE HOUND OF HEAVEN by Francis Thompson

# CHAPTER FOURTEEN

## FIRST EVENING OUT OF FAIR HAVENS, AD 60

THE EVENING MEAL was almost over. The noise of the elements outside was muffled, but the crowded mess hall was uproarious with the sound of rattling dishes and trays, swaying lamps, sliding tables and chairs, etc. A sailor arose with his plate in his hand to get a refill from the serving table when, suddenly, a surge of the ship knocked him against the wall and to the floor where he ended up covered with an urnful of hot beans. Men laughed and yelled rowdily at his mishap as he scrambled to his feet shouting expletives in return. The sound of a knife repeatedly striking a bowl gradually penetrated the hearing of the diners. It was Erastus at the head table with the junior officers. Gradually, the commotion among the men subsided.

"I want to say a few words before you leave the mess hall," he shouted. "The Captain wants me to relate to you what our current status is." Erastus was swaying back and forth as he spoke. "First, I will confirm what you probably already suspect: we are in the clutches of the Euraquilo!"

Murmurs went up all over the room. Erastus struck his bowl again. When he got control, he continued speaking at the top of his voice, "Fortunately, this morning we were able to slip behind the island of Cauda for a little relief. Unfortunately, there is no cove here where we can shelter—no anchorage—so we are just drifting. However, we took advantage of the relative calm to better prepare the ship to ride out the storm. Within the hour we will emerge from the shelter of Cauda and come back under the full brunt of the storm. No one can say how long it will last. In the meantime we must extinguish the fires in the mess ovens. Mess personnel say they have fruits and vegetables you can eat cold. You are welcome to come here anytime you want to get what's available, but there will be no regular meal schedule after this. If anyone gets sick, a physician is on board, Dr. Luke. His cabin is two doors fore of the mess hall. Are there any questions?"

"Yes, where's Hippalus? Why isn't he here?"

Several men said, "Yeah!"

"He's on deck with the pilot, watching the storm."

"Where are we headed?"

"That's hard to say. We've trimmed the ship to drift northwestward."

"Are we headed for open sea?"

"Yes."

"How long will the storm last?"

"As I said before, no one knows. Hopefully, it will subside tomorrow."

Someone shouted, "Or it might last a week."

"It could," Erastus said. "I will acknowledge we're in a real plight. For that reason I want us to appeal to Almighty God right now for help. I've asked Paul of Tarsus to come and lead us in prayer."

Paul stood to his feet at his table and led a lengthy prayer of confession and petition for help. Everyone remained solemn. Some bowed their heads. He concluded, "And now we ask you to intervene in our behalf and somehow to use this crisis for our good and for your glory. In the name of Jesus Christ we pray, Amen."

People began to converse again. Only a few left the mess hall. Erastus walked over to the table where Kore, Ruth, Hermes, Paul, and others were sitting, and sat down.

Hermes said, "You've really got your hands full. What's really happening?"

"To tell the truth, we could be in this storm for a week, ten days, who knows? Maybe two weeks. When the Euraquilo caught us this morning, it was blowing us toward Africa."

"You were concerned about that?" said Ruth. "That's hundreds of miles away."

"I know, but this is a fifty knot wind. If we just run before it, we could hit the coast of Africa in only two days. We were headed toward the Syrtis, a dangerously shallow gulf west of Cyrene. They call it the 'Ship's Graveyard.' What we've done is to change the direction of our drift by rigging the foresail."

"What direction will we be going now?" asked Paul. "I mean when we leave the lee of Cauda."

"We should be going northwest if the wind holds steady."

"Toward Sicily," said Paul. "I see now. Marcus will employ the Euraquilo to push us the direction he wants to go."

"But that's toward open sea!" said Luke.

"I know," said Erastus, "but we don't have any choice. We can't sail back to Crete—not against this wind. We're committed."

"What danger are we now in?" asked Hermes.

"Two things," said Erastus. "The first is sinking. The waves cresting the deck could inundate us, or the vessel could spring a leak from all the strain on the hull. The second danger relates to navigation. If we can't see the sky, we can't navigate. Once we leave Cauda, we won't have any idea where we are at any time, until the clouds lift."

Suddenly, the ship lurched to port and began to sway violently. Chairs were upset and dishes went clattering across the floor.

"Here we go again. Emerging from Cauda. If you'll excuse me, I must go topside," said Erastus.

"I'm going with you," Hermes said.

Erastus and Hermes stood near the helm. It was raining hard and the wind was howling loudly from the starboard side. The night was pitch dark. Two men were wrestling the tiller that connected the two paddle rudders, one of them alternately shouting, "Port. Starboard." Everyone was dressed in rain gear.

Erastus shouted to Hermes, "At the moment, the tiller is too much for one man to handle. The pilot has a man to help him. Look up there at the bow. We keep it illuminated with the running light so he can see it. His main job now is to keep the waves from breaking over the side of the deck, so he has to head right into them. See how the waves are breaking over the bow. Actually, he tries to hit them at a slightly oblique angle. The bow comes up into the waves on the starboard side and falls off to port. We're oscillating."

The two fell silent. The ship was dipping and rising, while water constantly sloshed back and forth across the deck. After awhile, Hermes shouted, "Despite appearances, I think you've got it under control. But I notice the wind is blowing from the starboard side. If that's Euraquilo—east-northeast—, then we're aimed northward—not west."

Erastus laughed. "It looks that way. But actually we're moving *that* direction." He pointed off the port side. "That's west—hopefully!"

"Huh! We're sailing sideways," said Hermes.

"That's called 'leeway.' Excuse me, I have to go check some equipment."

Erastus crouched down into a low shelter in front of the pilot and lit a lantern and then stood back up. Hermes followed him as he went around the deck checking the security of the longboat, the yard on the deck, the mast, the rigging, and the frapping.

Early the next morning the storm was still raging at full strength. In Marcus' cabin Erastus stood before the Captain, his feet spread apart for balance, for the daily briefing. Marcus was seated comfortably at his desk, a picture of perfect poise. If he had any misgivings, it was not apparent.

"Rastus, we're on our way to Rome—riding high on the trade wind. I believe I've almost whipped the elements again." He rubbed his hands together, then looked sharply into Erastus' eyes. "You don't know what the trade wind is, do you? I learned about it from my older brother. You met Felix in Alexandria, didn't you? You didn't? Well, he sails the Indian Ocean. Carries cargo to India—coral, metals, gold, silver. Brings back silks, precious stones, other luxuries. He's one of the best navigators in the world.

"To get to and from India Felix used to have to sail along the coast of Arabia and Baluchistan—you know, just as we have to sail along the Lycian coast to Rome. Ten years ago, however, the Arabians told him the secret of the seasonal winds—the monsoons. Every year in the summertime the wind blows from the southwest, then in the winter from the northeast. 'Aha!' he thought. 'Why don't I just catch those winds and blow before them instead of hugging the coast.' So the next summer my brother entrusted his ship to the southwest wind. Lo and behold, it carried him straight to India in record time. Well, that winter he caught the northeast wind back and set an all-time record. People couldn't believe it.

"That's what I mean by 'trade winds.' So I wondered, 'Does the Great Sea have trade winds too? You know what I discovered? That the dreaded Euro Aquilo is a trade wind to the west. Yesterday, I knew that the wind off Mount Ida would catch us and send us out to sea into the path of the Euro Aquilo. Now the Euro Aquilo will carry us to Syracuse in record time."

Erastus said, "That's presuming the storm will cease, isn't it? If the clouds don't lift, how can you navigate?"

"There's no need to navigate till we get to Sicily. I've just cast myself upon the trade wind. The way I've rigged the foresail, the Euro Aquilo will deliver me right on target. I have it all calculated."

"Cast yourself and us with you! Did Agabus and Julius approve of this?"

"I haven't explained it to them yet. I want to surprise them," Marcus said with a smirk on his face.

"Isn't that contrary to maritime law—to bypass the authorities?"

"Maritime smaritime," shouted Marcus, slamming his fist on the desk and half rising to his feet. "Law is made for man, not man for the law. How could Felix have discovered the trade winds if he had been a slave to law? If you ever expect to make a successful captain, you'd better learn to use the law to your advantage. You're dismissed." He pointed toward the door.

"I can't believe that," said the Second Mate. "Has the Captain thrust us into this storm on purpose?"

Erastus was conferring with the other officers in the mess hall.

"He's a maniac," shouted a junior officer. "He plotted this thing from the very beginning."

"If he plotted it, we have a right to plot a reaction," said another.

"Doesn't sound like the Hippalus I know. He's changed," said someone.

"That's because of the holy man," explained another. "Ever since Paul of Tarsus came on board, the Captain has acted peculiarly. It's as though he's in competition with him. Did you hear that when Paul warned Hippalus not to risk leaving Fair Havens, Hippalus decided to do it anyway, just to spite Paul?"

"He's no longer fit to command. Let's put the First Mate in command."

"Hold it," said Erastus. "Don't get hasty. If we do anything, let's do it right. Once, early in the voyage, the owner got so perturbed with Hippalus he ordered me to take command. He actually wrote out the order."

"What did you do?"

"I didn't accept it. This was my first assignment as a First Mate. I didn't think I was ready yet."

"Are you ready now?"

"If I had to, I could handle it."

"You could do better than him. Maybe Ben Uri's offer still stands," said the Second Mate.

In Agabus' cabin, Erastus stood with two other officers and rehearsed Marcus' words to the owner, seated at his desk. Then he said, "In light of all this, the officers of the *Kibotos* have lost confidence in the Captain. They recommend that without delay he be removed and I be commissioned in his place."

Erastus fell silent. Agabus did not speak at first. Only after an uncomfortably long delay did he finally say, without haste, "Tell me, Erastus, what exactly would you do if you were placed in charge?"

"Sir, I would continue on as we are now, awaiting the clearing of the sky, in order to be able to navigate. Achieving that, I would turn northward to the safety of Nicopolis for the winter."

"If the sky did clear, you would not continue on? You would turn back? Not very daring, are you? Tell me, what do you think is my major concern as the owner of this vessel? My foremost concern?"

"Getting the cargo to Rome in the shortest time possible."

"Exactly. Then put yourself in my shoes. Which one would make the better captain, Hippalus or you?"

Erastus could not speak.

"Gentlemen," said Agabus, "did Hippalus in so many words actually say he plotted to thrust us into this so-called trade wind?"

"No, sir," replied Erastus, "not in so many words, but that was his clear implication."

"Could you be mistaken?"

"I don't think so, sir. What else could he have meant?"

"Could he have been deceiving you—boasting to impress you— putting a good turn on a bad event?"

"I—I don't think so, sir."

"Gentlemen, I've heard your concerns and I'll look into the matter. If there is nothing else, you're dismissed."

"Try Hippalus," an officer said. "Put him on trial."

"Court martial him," said another.

"Right."

"Yes."

"Give us a chance."

"Hold an inquiry."

"Alright, you've asked for it," said Agabus angrily. "I'll call an inquiry board for this afternoon. I'm appointing to the board—ah—myself and Hermes and—ah—Dr. Luke, if they will serve. We'll meet in the dining facility at nine bells. First Mate, you inform the Captain."

"Sir, I'd rather not."

"Come on, now. Where's your boldness? Never mind, I'll do it myself."

When the inquiry was held that afternoon, their efforts at civility—at avoiding mutiny—seemed unpropitious. Circumstances for an orderly proceeding were far from favorable. The commotion and noise from the storm were overwhelming.

"Will Erastus, the First Mate, please come to the floor," shouted Julius. The Centurion had heard about the board meeting and had asserted his right to be on it as well as his prerogative to be chairman, as the official representative of the Empire. In the mess hall he sat at the head table with Agabus to his right and Luke to his left. Hermes was not on the board. Marcus sat alone at the first table, facing them. A few witnesses and onlookers were also present. Erastus came up and stood in front of the board.

Julius said, "You and the other officers of the *Kibotos* have charged Captain Hippalus with deliberately thrusting the ship into this storm without regard to the safety of the passengers and the crew. Will you state your evidence."

Erastus recounted his conversation with Marcus that morning. In his opinion Marcus had deliberately deceived everyone by claiming to sail for Phoenix while his real intention was to catch the Euro Aquilo.

"Thank you, Erastus. If you have nothing else, would you please step down. Are there other witnesses against the Captain?"

One by one the officers came to the floor and spoke.

"The shortest route to Rome is through the Archipelago, but Hippalus took us down to Crete in order to catch the Euro Aquilo."

"He was warned to winter at Cnidus but refused to do so."

"He was warned to winter at Fair Havens but refused to do so."

"He sailed from Fair Havens with the mainsail hoisted, despite the dangers of the season. When the southerly wind ceased and a storm appeared imminent, he stood motionless on deck and neglected to reef the sail until it was too late. As a result the mainsail was ripped to shreds."

"He plans not to seek port but to try to cross the open sea to Syracuse."

When there were no more witnesses, Julius ordered Marcus to the floor for cross-examining. He asked, "Did the First Mate recount your conversation with him this morning accurately?"

"He did."

"Did you intentionally deceive the owner and me in persuading us to sail for Phoenix, knowing all along we would be caught in the Euro Aquilo?"

"I did not. I was sincere in my counsel to sail for Phoenix."

"Would your resentment over my authority aboard the *Kibotos* cause you to attempt to manipulate my decisions?"

"Admittedly, I do resent your assumption of authority, yet I would not resort to deceit to influence you."

"Do you have anything to say in your own defense?"

"Yes, I do, if it pleases the board. While it is true that I have extensively studied the advantage of riding the Euro Aquilo across the open sea, I have not deliberately chosen to do so now. The only time I would intentionally seek the Euro Aquilo would be when there is no precipitation. I would not thrust us into a storm. I will confess that my conversation with the First Mate this morning sounds incriminating, but it amounted to nothing more than idle boasting. I have no pique over the charges leveled by the First Mate and the junior officers. They are not my adversaries. I feel that I am being victimized, but not by them. The elements themselves are my enemy—the weather, the wind, the storm. There is some intelligent power behind the elements, and it has been intent on conquering me for many years. Why, I do not know. I have to defend myself continually. We are in mortal combat. For many years I have been able to master my foe, but now it is asserting its revenge. And yet I shall conquer it again, if I am permitted to remain in command." Marcus shook his fist in the air.

"Well, yes," said Julius. "None of us can speak intelligently to that—ah—issue. The board is hereby adjourned to deliberate. We will reconvene at sundown. Dismissed."

"The real issue," said Agabus, as the board members sat in his cabin, "is whether Marcus intentionally deceived us in advising us to move to Phoenix. Did he have a hidden agenda?"

"Or did he deceive us," Julius said, "even in advising us to sail by Crete, as one officer suggested. His plot might go back all the way to Cnidus."

"I'm sorry," said Luke. "I can't help you. I wasn't there."

"Maybe you can help, though, in something else," said Agabus. "Marcus' hidden agenda might have been something other than the Euro Aquilo. Julius, you remember who it was that warned against sailing from both Cnidus and Fair Havens? It was Paul, wasn't it? Is it possible that Marcus was over-reacting to Paul's counsel? Dr. Luke, did Paul feel that Marcus made his decisions to sail just to spite him?"

"Yes, in fact he does. He said it looked that way both times."

"If that's true," said Julius, "it certainly shows poor judgment on the part of Marcus, but that's not what he's being charged with. The charge is intentionally thrusting us into this storm. That's the issue. Did he in fact do that?"

"Sirs," said Luke, "there is one piece of evidence that might exonerate Marcus of that charge. It's the longboat. The fact that he let the longboat trail behind the *Kibotos* from Fair Havens is solid evidence, I think, that he was anticipating nothing more than a short, calm voyage to Phoenix."

There was a sharp rap on the door. A seaman stuck his head in and said, "Agabus Ben Uri, the Captain needs to see you in his cabin right now. It's urgent."

Agabus dismissed himself and went up on deck. He had forgotten his raincoat and had to dash through the rain from the hatch to the cabin. As he ran past he noticed considerable activity at both the fore and the aft cargo hatches. Without knocking he swiftly opened the door and stepped in. He stood a moment stamping and shaking off water. Caesar barked and ran over to him. Marcus was standing, talking to the First Mate.

"What's the problem?" Agabus asked.

"We've sprung a leak. I've had to organize a brigade at both hatches to try to get ahead of the inflow." Turning to Erastus he asked, "How is it coming?"

"They're slowly lowering the level of the water, I think. The bilge pumps alone wouldn't do it, though. I had to organize brigades at both ends to dip it out."

"The cargo?" asked Agabus.

Marcus replied, "The two lowest levels of bags are probably soaked. The rest is alright for now. Come with me, I'll show you the problem."

The two men went across the deck and climbed down a ladder into the hull. Shouting crews of sailors were standing in knee— deep water filling urns and sending them up by rope. Marcus appropriated a lantern from a sailor and led Agabus through the water to the center.

"Here's the problem—here where the mast meets the keel. The planking is beginning to separate. Reach down here and feel the gaps."

Agabus hitched up the sleeve of his robe and thrust his hand under water. The pressure of seawater coursing in prevented him from actually touching the crack, but he got the idea of what was happening.

"What can we do?" shouted Agabus.

"Afraid there's not much we can do—to fix the crack. From now on we just have to try to stay ahead of the inflow. What caused it was the severe movement of the mast in the storm before we got the sail reefed. It put too much stress on the hull. I've always contended that this is the inherent danger of a single-masted ship; too much stress at one point. They need to revert to multimasted ships—at least two, maybe three—to disperse the stress. Hopefully, it won't get any worse, now that we've removed the sail and yard. Anyway, now we've got to lighten the ship. The hull must not get so low that the waves dash over the deck and through the hatches. We're doomed when that happens. What can we jettison?"

"Anything but the wheat," Agabus shouted with a pained look on his face.

"I agree," shouted Marcus. "The wheat is what we're at sea for. Besides, the grain bags in the hold help provide ballast in the storm."

"Salt water will ruin the wheat, I fear," moaned Agabus. Marcus had turned to go back to the ladder and did not hear the comment.

Throughout the afternoon, seamen scoured the ship for anything they could jettison. First went all the freight in the hold, other than the grain. Then went miscellaneous furniture, baggage, mess fixtures, footlockers, supplies, and so forth. The soldiers grudging gave up their metal shields.

Night was falling. A crowd of seamen, soldiers, and passengers was assembled in the mess hall for a continuation of the board of inquiry.

Julius called for their attention and announced, "The board has met and considered all the testimony given this morning, as well as other evidence not given.

"Left unstated was the fact that Marcus Hippalus is not the final authority on the *Kibotos*. I am, as a Centurion, according to Roman law; and I have been exercising that prerogative ever since I came aboard. Hence, it was I, not the Captain, who made the final decision to sail from Fair Havens. Therefore, the Captain cannot be held accountable for thrusting us into this storm. If anyone is responsible, I am. We contend that there were not enough weather signs for anyone of us to have foreseen the danger of moving the ship the short distance to Phoenix.

"It is true that I made my decision on the professional advice of the Captain. The board weighed the question as to whether the Captain deliberately misled me. We do not think so. Indeed, we considered evidence to the contrary. I'm referring to the fact that the Captain left the longboat in the water when we left Fair Havens, which is evidence he probably intended to sail only as far as Phoenix.

"The board does believe, though, that the Captain's advice to set sail from Fair Havens was inordinately influenced by one individual—Paul. While the owner, the Captain, and I were in a meeting at Fair Havens, Paul interrupted us and warned us *not to* sail. Looking back on it we can now see that Paul's advice was what prompted Marcus to recommend that we do set sail. Why he was negatively influenced so, by this lowly prisoner, we do not know. However, that is not a court martial offense. Nevertheless, the board does hereby issue Captain Hippalus an official reprimand for mismanagement. Other than this we will take no action in the matter. Are there any questions? If not, I hereby order that the official minutes of this proceeding be filed permanently in the ship's log. Case dismissed."

The raging Euro Aquilo continued unabated. Unseen that night, Marcus stole into the wine bin in the hold and took a small amphora of wine back to his cabin.

A loud knock sounded on the Captain's door.

"Breakfast, Captain."

Marcus pulled his legs out of the bunk and sat up, resting his head in his hands. It was the third morning out of Fair Havens. His eyes were puffy and bloodshot. His head pounded painfully. An amphora of wine lay on his crumpled rain gear on the floor with an empty mug next to it. He looked up through the glass lens above. It was still cloudy and rainy. He had overslept.

There was another knock.

"All right! Set it in the door."

A gust of wind and rain rushed in as the door opened and a young seaman in rain gear appeared, precariously balancing a mess tray on his knee with one hand while holding the door handle with the other. The floor was tossing roughly. Taking the tray in both hands he stepped haltingly through the door.

"Morning, Captain."

"Get out and shut the door, trash." Marcus waved his hand without looking up.

The sailor hastily set the tray by the door and exited.

*Another blasted court martial. I can't believe it. Why? Why? Why? If only the clouds would lift—to navigate. I could get this wheat to Rome and set a new record—six shipments in one season! If not too much is already ruined. Oh, no! The leak!*

He straightened up with a jolt. Hastily pouring and downing a swig of wine, he walked past the tray of cold food and outside to the nearest cargo hatch. Addressing one of the bailers, he said, "Sailor, what's the condition of the leak?"

"*Ou suniemi*, Captain."

"First Mate!" bellowed Marcus.

Down in the hold someone hollered, "First Mate. Captain's calling."

"Be up in a minute, sir."

Momentarily, Erastus came climbing out of the hatch.

"What's the situation with the leak, Rastus?"

"Doesn't look good, sir," shouted Erastus above the storm. "We've been pumping and baling all night but can't keep up with it. Water level's still rising. We've got to do something quick. We're sinking."

"I'll see what can be done," said Marcus and turned away, staggering slightly.

Men came streaming out of the hatches onto deck. Sailors and soldiers ran to their respective formations. Crowding two hundred men onto the rope-strewn deck was no mean feat and was complicated further by the raging storm. The rain was falling in torrents, the wind gusting erratically, the ship alternately rising and falling into mountains and valleys of brine. Just to maintain one's footing on the unstable platform was a formidable endeavor. Groups of men locked arms and swayed en masse.

Marcus appeared before them, unshaven and unkempt, alongside Julius, and roared above the elements, "We must jettison the yard to lighten the ship. It will take the concerted effort of all. The officers will direct the operation."

The yard consisted of two peeled tree trunks lashed together at their ends. Together they were almost as long as the ship itself. They still lay lashed together and securely fastened to the deck.

Erastus repeated the orders, being barely audible above the storm. As he shouted, the men looked down at the heavy yard arms. Immediately, several sailors shouted back in Greek.

"What did they say?" asked Marcus.

"They said they won't do it. If the ship sinks, the yard could save their lives. It could support forty men floating in the sea."

"Blasted idlers! Tell them they do it or face execution, every last one of them!"

Erastus said in Greek, "Look, men, if we remove this yard, the ship can rise a foot or two out of the water. It might give us just the margin we need. If we keep it, we could sink in a matter of a day or two. Maybe we can survive! But I believe our best hope is to salvage the *Kibotos* itself as long as we can. Come on, men—help me!"

Erastus began whacking at the yard's retaining ropes with a machete. Quickly, Julius did the same with his long sword, then Hermes joined them. The men watched. Marcus retired to his cabin. Erastus then started kicking crates out of the way. After a few minutes, he bowed his frame to the trunks and only barely nudged them. When he did so, though, all the men, soldiers first, then sailors, began to shout and help. Soon four hundred arms were encircling the yard and lifting it waist high. Hastily, the officers unleashed guy ropes and other rigging from the side of the ship to enable the crew to reach the edge. It took considerable time to maneuver the trees to the starboard railing. The men were huffing and sweating profusely. Finally, they were in position lengthwise above the railing.

With an "*Eis, duo, treis!*" the men heaved with all their might and the yard fell into the water beside the ship, causing the deck to catapult upward. The two joined yardarms sank beneath the waves, then bobbed back to the surface. Gradually, they trailed off into the wake of the ship.

"There goes our last hope of sailing to Rome," said Erastus.

That morning all the heavy rigging was also thrown overboard. Erastus took the precaution of sending several men up the swaying mast to remove the crow's nest, pulleys, and other projections in order to reduce the resistance of the mast to the wind. By the end of the day the tall mast was nothing but a skinny pole pointing heavenward above the deck. The water level of the *Kibotos* was back to normal but the water in the hold remained deep—and was still rising.

Over the next several days Marcus never left his cabin.

Erastus ran the ship—changing the pilots, managing the bail crews, encouraging the sick, and so forth. The water in the hold rose daily—the grain became almost totally soaked.

Erastus thought to himself, "We need to get to a port immediately. But where are we? If we are still heading westward, we're now in the very center of the Great Sea, hundreds of miles from land."

The passengers and crew suffered extensively. The terror of

survival, the stench of nausea, the continual demands on the crew, the hopeless bailing, the plague of rats fleeing the hold, the constant groaning of the ship's frame, the tossing by wind and waves, the numbing effect of the wet and cold—all combined to create a scene of confusion, anxiety, and fatigue.

One incident finally broke all hope. On the seventh day they encountered a singularly violent wind that made the sea unusually turbulent. For a short while, the *Kibotos* was tossed about like a stick in a mountain stream. The Captain's cabin on deck was especially tortured by the agitation. Suddenly, a mountainous wave crested the bow and struck the cabin. It hit with such force it dislodged Marcus' Seeing Glass from the roof and smashed it down into his cabin with a mighty crash, shattering it into a thousand pieces. A gaping hole was left in the roof.

Seamen rushed to the cabin and banged on the door. "Captain! Captain! Are you hurt?"

Getting no response, they tried to force the door open. Finally, a man scurried up the ladder to the roof, dropped down through the hole, and released the lock from within. The Captain's body was on his bunk. His dog lay whining on the floor beneath the volume of glass. The cabin was a mess. The drench of rain through the hole had already washed all the ink off the sea charts spread out on the desk, leaving a sinking feeling among those who saw it. It was their sole means of navigation.

They dreaded approaching the Captain's body. Erastus ran in, took one look at the Captain, and said, "Don't disturb him. He's drunk." Several amphora jugs rolled around on the floor. "Go fetch some sail cloth. We've got to mend that hole. Someone help me free this dog."

Just as they uncovered his body, Caesar expired. Tenderly, Erastus wrapped his bloody body in canvas and laid it in a dry corner of the room. They then stretched cloth over the opening in the roof and raised a tall pole beneath it to effect runoff. They also hauled off the mass of glass and trash from the cabin and threw it overboard. Although the repair and cleanup took most of the afternoon, the Captain never awakened.

From this experience the crew concluded that their celebrated Captain had given up. The hold was slowly filling, the ship was listing, the maps were destroyed. They had no yard, no rigging, no pulleys—in short, no mainsail. They could not make land before sinking. They, too, lost all hope.

The *Kibotos* became a ghost ship; people moved about like zombies. The optimism of the Christians, though in contrast to the general lassitude, effected no encouragement. Yet the storm continued!

Late that night a lightning storm struck. It was pitch dark save for the vibrating pulses of sheer light playing all around the *Kibotos*. Volleys of thunder cracked and exploded without interlude. The wind, waves, and rain continued unabated.

Marcus came out of his cabin carrying the wrapped body of Caesar. He did not have a shirt on and his chest was heaving.

"Oh, Cecilia, Cecilia, can you forgive me? I've failed you again. Poor, poor Caesar. Woe is me!"

He went over to the railing and slowly dropped the body overboard. Then he returned to his cabin. In a minute he emerged again, still bare-chested, with a mug in his hand, and stumbled toward the bow. The *Kobotos* was listing both to port and to bow, permitting waves to crest the bow perilously. Marcus climbed up onto the forward platform directly behind the female figurehead and planted his feet apart like the Colossus of Rhodes. Despite the rhythmic rising and plunging of the bow, he kept himself stationary by clinging with his right hand to the forward-sloping mast of the foresail while holding the mug in his left hand. His silhouette, cast by the undulating lightning, showed how exceedingly dangerous his position was. Of a sudden, he let go of the mast and beat on his chest with his right hand. The ship rose abruptly, almost tossing him into the sea, and he caught hold of the mast again. Then he began an explosive soliloquy. The pilots could hear it at the stern, his words fading in and out.

Addressing the figurehead he shouted, "Dear damsel, my silent witness, soon you will share my disgrace. Would that you had sailed more than one season, for you could have been the toast of the Empire. Henceforth, only the denizens of the deep can toast you. I drink a toast to you, Our Lady of the Deep."

He swung the mug to his lips and threw back his head. A bolt of lightning struck in front of the bow with a terrible clap. Laughing raucously, Marcus wiped his mouth with the back of his arm and stumbled down off the platform. He staggered around for awhile, then climbed back up again, this time facing aft.

"O *Kibotos* . . . *Kibotos* . . . ark, symbol of salvation. And shall you be my coffin? The first ark bore its habitants above the flood; shall you sink yours beneath it? A toast to you, Ark of the Deep."

He tossed down another swig and climbed down. After sitting for awhile on a bundle of rope, he rose to the platform again.

"Great Sea, Mare Internum, my friend of long-standing. You have borne me safely upon your bosom for many years. Has my weight now become so wearisome that you conspire with my enemy—"

A single bolt of lightning off the starboard flashed on and off repeatedly, then burst aloud with a mighty crescendo.

"I have no pique with you, nor have I ever had. Your terrors have always been my delight—your wave my rocking chair, your expanse my highway, your depths my buoyancy. My pique is with another, even the wretched wind. Will you now betray me to him? A toast to the Great Sea."

He gulped down more of the wine. Holding the mug upside down, he gazed into it, then turned and hurled it violently across the deck, shattering it against the front wall of his cabin. He again faced forward with both arms outstretched.

"Ah Wind, mighty foe! Yours is the conquest! I am defeated! . . . beaten! . . . vanquished! . . . lost! . . . The battle is over! . . . Would you could speak to me now, as I speak to you. I would ask: why have you hated me so? . . . hounded me so? . . . persecuted me so? Has there been a design to your pursuit of me? Am I so vile, so evil, so sinful that I must be chased around the world like a fugitive? Why have you sent your minion to me—the Apostle—the 'sent one'? Clever you were to clothe him with wisdom to countermand my decisions—to make him a devious traitor on my ship. Enough of that! It's all for nought now! Suffice it that he goes down with me! . . . Bah! I have nothing left with which to toast you . . . except my blood. Here's to you, you powerful Archenemy! I bid you adieu!"

Marcus stumbled downward to the bow, which was now virtually underwater but which suddenly rose high, now requiring of him an uphill climb. He grabbed onto the railing and prepared to catapult overboard. Suddenly, as the bow descended again, someone grabbed both his arms from behind and shouted, "No, you don't."

Marcus quickly shifted his weight and threw the assailant over his shoulders and up against the half-submerged railing, almost overboard. The man crouched by the railing for a moment. Marcus backed away to see who it was. "Ah ha! Julius! Just as I suspected!"

Julius rose to his feet. Momentarily, both centurions, now high in the air, were illuminated by the forward running light. Both were in kilts. Both were being heavily showered by the breakers over the bow. A crowd gathered on deck.

"Aaaaaaaaaaah!" Marcus charged Julius. Julius side-stepped and met Marcus with a shattering blow to the face, knocking out a tooth. Marcus went down and Julius danced nimbly to the opposite side of the deck.

Marcus got up and approached Julius more cautiously.

"Come on, Hippalus. You've been wanting to fight me for a long time. Let's see what you've got."

They locked onto each other with wrestling holds and grappled, as the crowd shouted approval. Moving sure-footedly amid the clutter on the deck, the two giants clung to one another, brow to brow, perspiring and grunting. The ship bobbed up and down. Abruptly Marcus drew back his head and smashed it forward against Julius' face. Julius fell down stunned, blood gushing from his nose. Instantly, Marcus picked Julius up and lifted him high above his head and hurled him over the port side of the ship.

Instinctively, Julius grabbed onto the timber braces and broke his fall. Lightning flashed, enabling Marcus to see Julius feebly pulling himself back up. Marcus turned away and wrenched loose from the deck a large rounded post. When he returned to the railing, Julius surprised him from behind and locked his arm around his neck. The club fell to the deck. Julius clung to him, squeezing with all his might. Marcus gasped for breath. He began pounding Julius' side with his elbow. With a quick jerk, he broke free from the strangle-hold.

Instantly, Marcus grabbed the club and began swinging back and forth as Julius artfully weaved and dodged. One wild blow smashed against the running light, knocking it into the sea. There was momentary darkness—until a soldier came running up with a torch. Marcus saw Julius first and delivered a stunning club blow to his head, knocking him to the deck unconscious.

"Aaaaaaaaaaah!" cried Marcus as he rushed toward Julius' body with the club over his head. Suddenly, out of the darkness swung another club that caught Marcus in the head and dropped him to the deck. It was Hermes. The fight was over.

The crowd surged toward the two figures.

"Stand back!" shouted Dr. Luke. "Let me through."

Luke went to Julius.

"Let me through," said Ruth.

She joined Luke at Julius' side. The two worked with him for a few minutes until he began to recover consciousness. He sat up and permitted them to bathe and wrap his wounds until he was finally able to stand to his feet and be helped to his cabin. The crowd applauded and followed them.

Paul was left kneeling on the deck with Marcus' bloodied head in his lap. Tears glistened on Paul's cheeks.

*Man's extremity is God's opportunity.*
Old proverb

# CHAPTER FIFTEEN

## EIGHTH DAY OUT OF CAUDA, AD 60

PAUL CARRIED A lighted lantern. Beside him, the taller Luke was carrying a medical bag. They were the only ones in the ship's darkened hallway the morning of the eighth day. Behind his scraggly white beard, Paul's face appeared gaunt—his eyes sunken. They were just walking underneath the aft staircase when water dripped on Paul's head. He glanced up to see the closed hatch door with light around its edges. The wind howled mournfully passed it. Suddenly, the ship lurched to one side slamming him up against the wall. Luke grabbed him by the arm.

"Careful there," said Luke.

"I should have been paying more attention."

They proceeded on and stopped at a door where Luke rapped sharply, then pushed it open and stepped in.

"Hello, there. Medical call," said Luke.

Though the long cabin was filled with seamen, no one responded. Most were sitting hunched over on the edges of their triple-decker bunks staring gloomily ahead. Some were trying to sleep. Others sat on the floor leaning back against the wall. Four men were rolling dice at a table in the corner beneath the room's only lighted sconce.

"You need a little more light in here," said Paul. He took a taper and from the lantern in his hand began lighting another sconce on the wall.

"Now who needs medical attention?" asked Luke.

"Over here, Doc."

Luke went over to one of the bunks and began examining a man.

"The *Kibotos* is a strong ship," said Paul aloud as he finished lighting one sconce and walked over to another. "But aren't you glad you didn't encounter this storm in a little sailboat? I heard about some men who once did.

"It took place on a deep lake in Galilee called the Sea of Galilee. Don't curl up your lips because it was a mere lake. Storms altogether as formidable as the Euraquilo sweep down on it sometimes. I'm thinking about the experience of Jesus and his twelve disciples who were sailing across that sea one night."

Paul finished lighting the sconce and walked over and set his lantern down on the dice table. The men had quit playing momentarily and were looking up at him.

"Let's hear the story," said one of them.

"Yeah, go ahead. We're listening," said a man in a nearby bunk.

"Very well," said Paul as he casually walked away from the table. "Jesus was weary, so he curled up on some sacks in the back of the boat and went to sleep. Without warning, a storm blew up on the lake. So ferocious was it that waves quickly swept over the sides of the boat. Remember that theirs was not a huge vessel like ours but only a small, open, fifteen-man sailboat.

"The disciples became frightened. They were bailing water

with all their might, but Jesus was still sleeping in the stern. He had slept through it all. Imagine!

"The fact that he wasn't helping perturbed them, so one of them shook him awake and shouted, 'Teacher, don't you care if we drown?'

"Jesus sat up. They watch as his eyes move from face to face, one by one. That's where he sees the real storm—in their eyes! He says to them, 'Why are you so fearful?' Hmm! That was a ridiculous question to ask, don't you think?

"But he adds, 'O you of little faith!' You know what happens next? Jesus stands up in the boat in the darkness. 'Risky!' you say. And so it seemed. But get this. Jesus shouts out in the darkness, 'Peace!' Then he says, "Be still!" That's right! Immediately the wind calms down and the waves cease tossing, just like that." Paul snapped his fingers. "The disciples look at one another and look at Jesus and say, 'What kind of man is this? Even the winds and the waves obey him.'

"Jesus is in this boat with us too, so we don't have to be afraid either! Trust him! . . . Dr. Luke, are you ready to go?"

"Yes, we need to move on to the next cabin."

"Hey, I enjoyed that," said a sailor.

"I did too. Come back again tomorrow, Paul."

As Paul went to get his lantern, the men were more animated than they had been when he came in. A new spirit of liveliness coursed through the room. Some jumped down off their bunks and followed the two men out the door and down the hall to the next room.

Paul repeated the story in the rest of the cabins and similar results occurred. The crowd of followers increased steadily. When they reached the last door, the soldiers inside were astonished to see their cabin fill up with men. The sailors, soldiers and passengers never tired of hearing Paul's little story.

Kore, Ruth, and Miriam were sweltering in the humidity of their cabin that afternoon. Their hair and clothing were disheveled, their robes loosely open.

"I don't want to die," said Miriam with a sob.

"Now, now," said Ruth. "It's not all that bad. We're still afloat, aren't we?"

"If this is the end," said Kore, "I'm glad we're not alone."

"Yes," said Ruth, "the Lord is with us."

"Well, yes, *he* is, of course. But I was thinking about Paul. I'm glad he's with us. He really is different, isn't he?"

"He really is," said Ruth. "But I like him."

"It's because he loves everybody so much," said Kore.

"Uh huh," said Ruth. "There's something else too. When I catch him alone, it's as though he's really not alone. It's as though he's in the presence of someone else. I think it's because he lives in the presence of Jesus—all the time. If anyone ever doubted that Jesus lives today, he needs to meet Paul.

"I don't think this storm bothers him much either—except for maybe his seasickness. I overheard a story he was telling this morning. It was about Jesus calming a storm on the Sea of Galilee, just by speaking to it. The storm had been raging but Jesus was asleep. They had to wake him up to tell him about it, but he wasn't scared at all. Jesus said to them, 'Why are you scared, you of little faith.' Well, Paul must have a lot of faith himself because he's certainly not scared. He's like Jesus in that regard. He could sleep through a storm too if he wanted to."

"When you get to thinking about it," Kore said, "Paul's in a pretty miserable condition himself, isn't he? He's an old man—he could be retired by now and taking it easy, if he wanted to. Instead, he's a prisoner and on his way to Rome to stand trial before that maniac, Nero. If he does survive the storm, he might be executed. He's also prone to seasickness. And on top of all that did you know he's fasting?"

"Yes, I know," said Ruth.

"Yet," said Kore, "despite all that he seems happy. He smiles at everyone as though he doesn't have a care in the world. I think he feels this ship is exactly the place where he ought to be at this moment. He seems perfectly content here—right at home. Can you imagine?"

That night Marcus left his cabin in the darkness, carrying a lantern in his hand. He furtively opened a hatch on the deck, slipped down the staircase to the lower deck, and went to the opening into the hold. He climbed down the ladder to the bottom of the flooded hold and felt his way through the water to the wine stock. It was relatively quiet in that portion of the ship, save for the creaking and groaning of the vessel and the sloshing of the water back and forth. The bailers were working at the far ends of the ship and did not hear him. As he was reaching under water to retrieve an amphora of wine, he heard a voice—someone speaking his name. Though he was slightly inebriated, he stopped to listen. It was the voice of Paul of Tarsus. Still, he listened.

"O Lord, I intercede in behalf of Marcus Hippalus. O, help him, I pray. He's in such misery, such darkness! How he needs you—your softening touch. I pray that you will convict him and convert him, even him, for you are not willing that any should perish but that all should come to repentance. Even now won't you send the Holy Spirit into his heart to convict him of his sins and his need of a Savior."

Marcus was shaken to the roots of his soul. He staggered back to the ladder, and Paul never knew of his presence there. Marcus drank all night but still could not sleep, for thinking about that prayer.

The next night Marcus again descended into the hold. Near the bottom of the ladder, he stopped and listened. He was vaguely disappointed. Paul was not there.

The water was higher tonight—up to his chest. He reached down and took off a sandal and with his foot searched for the wine cabinet. Finding it, he ducked under water again and retrieved a jug. As he returned to the surface he struck his head sharply on a cross beam and fell back into the water, stunned.

When he came to, he was being carried up the ladder over the shoulder of another man, larger and more powerful even than himself. At the lower deck, the huge man effortlessly lowered Marcus to the floor and turned and walked off down the hallway. Marcus watched him disappear into the semi-darkness. He wondered who he was.

"Ding, ding, ding, ding! Ding, ding, ding, ding!" The ship's bell sounded the next morning.

Ruth aroused in her bunk.

"What does that mean?" asked Kore.

Ruth yawned and said, "Sounded like assembly call. Let's go see what it is."

As they were dressing they heard someone in the hallway say, "Get up! The First Mate is ordering everyone to the mess hall right now!"

Kore said, "I wonder what Erastus is doing."

Miriam did not feel well enough to move from her bunk, but Ruth and Kore left and joined the stream of men going into the mess hall. People were quarrelsome and rude—aggravated at having to assemble so early. It was dawn on the tenth day of the storm. When Erastus had gained some semblance of order, Paul spoke up in Greek, "Men, you should have taken my advice not to sail from Crete; you would have spared yourselves this damage and loss."

He was answered with several surly remarks.

Ruth knew he was trying to establish some authority among them. She thought he looked especially radiant this morning!

"But now I urge you to keep up your courage, because not one of you will be lost."

The crowd only grew more restless and looked at one another cynically.

"Only the ship will be destroyed."

Several people looked across the room at Agabus. He appeared crestfallen.

"Last night an angel of the Lord—whose I am and whom I serve—stood beside me."

He paused. Men sat up straight and a buzz of excitement went through the room.

"He said to me, 'Do not be afraid, Paul. You must stand trial before Caesar.'"

*Amazing! He thinks that is good news,* thought Ruth.

"The angel also said, 'God has graciously given you the lives of all who sail with you.'"

Paul paused long and the room grew deathly silent. Someone whispered, "Hallelujah!"

"So keep up your courage, men, and have faith in God that it will happen just as he told me."

*They need a call to faith. Many are skeptical.*

"Oh, yes, one other thing. The angel also said, 'You must run aground on some island.'"

Immediately, Paul stepped down from the platform. He was through. At first the crowd did not know how to react. One by one they began to get up and file out of the hall. Suddenly, as quickly as someone popping the cork out of a bottle, everyone began talking at once. Some of the Christians remained behind and gathered around Paul with excitement. "God has remembered us," was the common comment among them. "Tell us how it happened," someone begged.

"Alright," Paul replied, "but while I'm here in the mess hall, would someone please prepare me some breakfast? Anything. It doesn't have to be hot."

"You're ending your fast!" Luke said. "Praise the Lord! That's the best news of all."

"Indeed. The Lord has heard my prayer. There was a private message to me from the angel that I didn't mention."

"Let's hope he remains alive until he can be converted."

Those around them did not know what they were talking about.

"He will," said Paul.

Paul's announcement marked a turning point in the lives of

the passengers aboard the *Kibotos*. Although the storm continued to rage, a sense of optimism returned. The common opinion was that the sun would appear at any time, for they deduced that visibility must certainly return to enable them to find the island Paul mentioned.

Men began to clean up—to straighten up their environment, wash themselves, comb their hair, shave, launder their clothes. "Who knows?" someone said. "There might be women on that island."

The number of ill decreased dramatically, reducing the time of Luke's rounds. Men became jovial. Laughter and horseplay returned, making the *Kibotos* a boisterous place—a virtual seafaring party! The rigors of the past ten days were quickly put behind. A prevailing topic of conversation was, "Here's what I plan to do when I get on land."

The mess hall was reopened for cold meals. Dry bread rations were brought up from the ship's store and served along with honey, crackers, pickled vegetables, salted fish, and herring. Although the stove was not relit, the mess crew mixed dough for Ruth, Kore, and Miriam to cook at Agabus' stove. The ladies welcomed the opportunity and prepared scores of small loaves of pan-fried bread to provide at least some measure of warm food to the starved crew, soldiers, prisoners, and passengers.

Mess personnel returned to carrying food and water to Marcus' cabin though they seldom found him conscious.

Erastus' job was made easier by the revived ardor of the crew. Malingerers were few. The bailing crews sang or chanted heartily while they worked. He had the hawsers girdling the ship repaired and tightened. When, on the morning of the eleventh day, the leak had lessened, some attributed it to his initiative; others recognized in it the hand of God.

Volunteers precariously scaled the mast and tied themselves in place. While they swayed back and forth in the storm, they scanned the sea for the first sight of land—or even light. None was seen— no one even so much as saw the horizon—but men vied for the chance to be the first to call out, "Land ho!", so strong was their confidence in Paul's prediction.

Paul approached Julius, Erastus, and Agabus about preaching again. With Marcus virtually out of the picture, they had no objection and permitted him to announce his meetings and meet openly at whatever hour he chose. He began holding two meetings a day in the mess hall—at daybreak and dusk.

At one of the gatherings he said, "Concerning our rescue, I have faith in God that it will happen just as he told me. 'Saving faith' is both similar to and different from this kind of faith. Saving faith is personally trusting Jesus Christ that he is all he claimed to be, that he did all he claimed to do, and that he *will* do all he claimed he will do for our salvation. In other words it is faith in the person and work of Christ Jesus."

At another meeting he said, "You might have placed faith in my vision and its message of hope for us all, but that's not enough. You must do more. You must, in your mind, sincerely approach the Lord Jesus Christ and put your trust in him personally if you want him to save you. He loves you and wants to be your Savior. Do you understand? If so, are you ready now to do it?" Paul always preached for decision.

On another occasion he said, "You may say to yourself, 'I'll watch what happens, and if it turns out the way Paul predicted, then I'll put my trust in Christ.' But if you do that, it will not be faith—it will be sight. Salvation is through faith, not sight. If you wait, you'll be like the Hebrews who demanded a sign before they would believe."

Agabus winced. He himself had adopted a wait-and-see attitude. To his credit, though, he at least had allowed Paul to read his Scripture scrolls again, which was a measurable benefit to Paul. The hours spent pouring over the Scriptures detracted from the constant rolling of the ship. Not a service was held when he did not experience the rolling. The audience was alternately above him, beneath him, tilted to the left, tilted to the right, beneath him, and on and on.

Then something happened that destroyed their new optimism. Erastus had to call a meeting of junior officers on the twelfth day.

"Men, we're running out of water! I just counted the kegs in the store, and we have only enough water for one more day at our present rate of usage. We didn't stock up enough at Fair Havens, thinking we were bound only for Phoenix. We're in a big bind. What are we going to do?"

"I know what happened," said one of the men. "We've been consuming too much water cleaning up. All that washing, bathing laundering, mopping."

"You're probably right," said Erastus. "Now, what can we do about it?"

"Catch rainwater," said someone.

"We don't have any containers," said another.

"Obviously, we need to ration what we have," offered someone.

"Will even rationing solve the problem?" asked another. "It depends on how much longer we're at sea."

A clamor of voices joined in agreement.

Some shouted, "I thought we were to be cast on an island by now."

"Yeah, that's what Paul promised."

"It's been two days since he prophesied and we haven't so much as seen the sun."

"When are we supposed to be rescued?"

"I don't know," said Erastus. "I didn't make the prediction, you know. Let's ask the one who did."

"Yeah, let's find out a time schedule for this supposed miracle. Make him prove himself."

Paul was called into the room.

"Paul," Erastus said, "we have an urgent problem. We're running out of water. We're going to have to start rationing. The question is, how much longer will we be at sea? The officers want to know if you have any idea when we'll be cast on that island you talked about. It's been over two days since you announced it."

"Sirs," Paul said, "I honestly don't know."

"Can you say whether it will be soon or late?"

"Soon, I think," replied Paul, "at least so it seemed. I don't think it will be much longer."

"Do you think we'll see land today?" someone asked.

"Maybe. I don't know."

"Tomorrow?" asked someone else.

"I can't say. We can only trust in God."

"Next month?" called someone from the back of the room, drawing guffaws from those around him.

"Men, listen," said Erastus, "It's obvious we don't have a date. Therefore, we have no choice but to ration water to the maximum extent and just hope that'll be enough. Put out the word to resort to desert rationing: no more than a quart per person per day. No more baths, no more laundering, no more mopping with potable water. Additional rations will be available only on special request to me. That should give us two more days. Let's hope that will be enough."

When news of the rationing spread, morale flickered like the dousing of live coals in a fireplace. People began to murmur.

"How much longer will the water supply hold out?"

"Why haven't we been rescued yet?"

"From what Paul said, I thought we would have been cast upon an island by now—that is, if he knew what he was talking about."

"The Christian God is no better than the Roman gods."

"Nothing but promises, promises, promises!"

People quit eating again and the number of sick soared. Attendance at Paul's meetings dropped to a handful; some of the newer Christians even stayed away.

Hastily, Paul called a meeting of the believers.

"I am not surprised at the sudden turn from the Gospel," said Paul. "Considering our fallen nature, the least problem can undermine one's resolution. We ourselves must not be ignorant of Satan's devices. I've seen it happen time and again.

"The Lord frequently tries our faith. Be aware of that. You see,

God's promise is no less sure whether it takes one day or seven. All we know for sure is that we will be rescued. Am I right?"

Several nodded their heads in agreement.

"Indeed," Paul continued, "God sometimes employs his own blessed device by delaying his promises: he does it to perfect our patience. Now is an opportunity for each of us to learn an important lesson about relating to the Father, that is, we must be patient with him. His schedule is not our schedule; he's not ruled by our calendars. We simply have to trust where we cannot trace.

"But, for the Master's glory, we must make the most of this stumbling block. If men quit coming to us, then we must go to them. I want us to spread throughout the ship like leaven in a loaf. Go forth and teach them. Teach patience. Teach them to await confidently the unfolding of God's will. Show them that patience itself is a part of faith in God. Convince them that our God *is* faithful. He will act before it's too late.

"Are there any questions? If not, then go forth in the power of the Holy Spirit. Let's pray before we go."

Staunchly, the Christians defended Paul and persistently affirmed their belief in the validity of the promise of rescue. Paul's personal optimism set a radiant example.

Still no island appeared! The next two days were living hell. Hunger, thirst, and fatigue severely strained relationships. Tempers were on edge and flared into conflict at the slightest provocation. The leadership of Erastus and the officers began to break down. They themselves succumbed to short tempers. Misery was everywhere.

During the fourteenth night Erastus was awakened by a banging on his door.

"First Mate, First Mate. You're wanted topside immediately."

Erastus hurriedly threw on his clothes and dashed to the upper deck. It was raining and pitch dark.

"Over here." The officer-on-duty was standing at the port railing. "Sir, we may be near land. Smell."

Erastus took a slow breath.

"It could be."

"Also, listen."

Erastus strained his ears. Even above the roar of the storm he could make out the strong sound of crashing waves.

"Do you hear it?"

"Yes, I do," said Erastus.

"What is it?"

"Could be another ship. Could be rocks. I think I see some breakers in the distance. Whatever it is, it's very near—I'd estimate no more than eight hundred cubits. We're moving past it! Quickly, light all the running lights. Call the trumpeter. I'll get the sounding line," said Erastus.

Erastus ran to the stern and got a special rope and weight from the storage bin beneath the tiller.

"Keep your eyes open," he shouted to the two helmsmen, "we may be near rocks or another ship."

"Aye, sir!" said the pilot.

The trumpeter began blowing intermittently. At the railing Erastus quickly tied one end of his rope to a post and lowered the weight into the water. Momentarily, he felt the weight hit bottom. His heart leaped.

"Twenty fathoms!" he shouted. "A sure sign of land."

A shout of joy went through the crowd gathering on the deck. Someone cried enthusiastically, "Land ho!"

"We're safe enough so far, but we'll need to be watchful," said Erastus.

The news spread with lightning speed and soon the deck was crowded with people. There was little to do now but wait, and everyone just stood around in the darkness chatting with one another, scarcely noticing the driving wind and rain.

Erastus called for Agabus, Julius, Paul, and other officers.

"We've just passed a point of land. What it was, I don't know: a peninsula, a reef. Whatever it was, we safely weathered it. I don't hear the breakers any more."

"Have we passed an island? What if we leave it behind?" asked Agabus.

"Sir, don't worry. I won't let that happen. I'm watching the depth of the soundings to determine the lay of the land. If I see it getting deeper again, we'll drop anchor and sit until morning. God willing we could at least send out the longboat and get help. But I suspect we're running parallel to a shoreline. Whatever it is, it's good news. Tomorrow we go ashore."

Half an hour later the sea began to get unusually choppy. People scampered below deck.

"Underwater cliffs!" shouted Erastus.

He immediately dropped his sounding line again and shouted, "Fifteen fathoms!"

As he was retrieving his line a lookout cried, "Breakers ahead!"

Erastus glanced forward on the port side, the direction of their drift. Even in the darkness he could make out the mist of waves breaking over rocks or land no more than a quarter knot ahead.

"Prepare to drop anchor!" he shouted.

Men ran toward the bow, but Erastus shouted, "No! Drop anchors from the stern. Keep the bow downwind."

LARGE        ROMAN ANCHOR

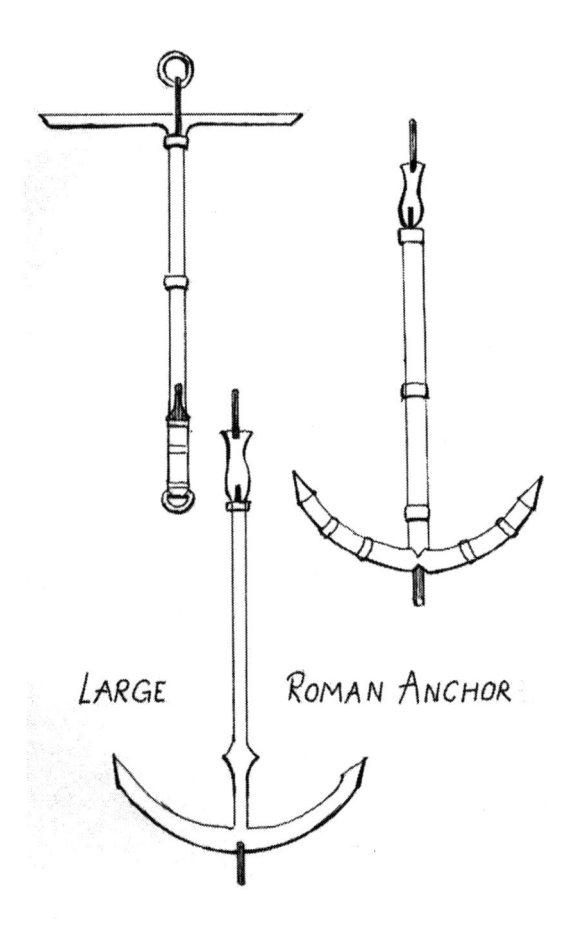

They turned and headed to the stern where they began untying the anchor hawsers from their capstans. Two huge anchors, each eight feet long and consisting of iron stocks and crowns joined together by a thick wooden beam, were stored on deck. To use the rudder ports for the anchor ropes, they first had to lift the two large paddles from the water and tie them up. Then several men lifted the heavy anchors and tossed them overboard. The windlasses spun and the hawsers grew taut but the ship continued to move.

"Sir, we're dragging anchor," shouted a seaman.

Erastus could already see boulders in the water ahead. "Quick! Strike the foresail! Release the anchors from the forward capstans! We've got to tie them at the stern!"

"Now you, you, you, you! Rush the two hawsers to the stern and tie them back there."

While Erastus watched, several sailors swiftly reeled out the bundles of rope as four men worked their way to the stern, threading the hawsers over and around the guy ropes. The task was extremely tedious in the darkness. Men cursed and swore. Erastus gravely watched the shoreline slowly bearing down on them. Finally, they reached the aft capstans, secured the hawsers in place, and tossed the loosened hawsers over the side of the ship.

Erastus shouted, "Now! Drop the forward anchors!"

Several men lifted the two anchors which were still forward and heaved them over the bow. The two hawsers trailed after the sunken anchors as the ship still sailed forward until those rope grew taut too. The great ship began faltering by fits and starts as first one and then another of the four anchors would grab the ocean bottom, then drag. Presently, they all grabbed simultaneously, causing the ship to jerk and shudder to a halt. For the first time in two weeks the mighty *Kibotos* was at rest.

Erastus sat down in the darkness and wept.

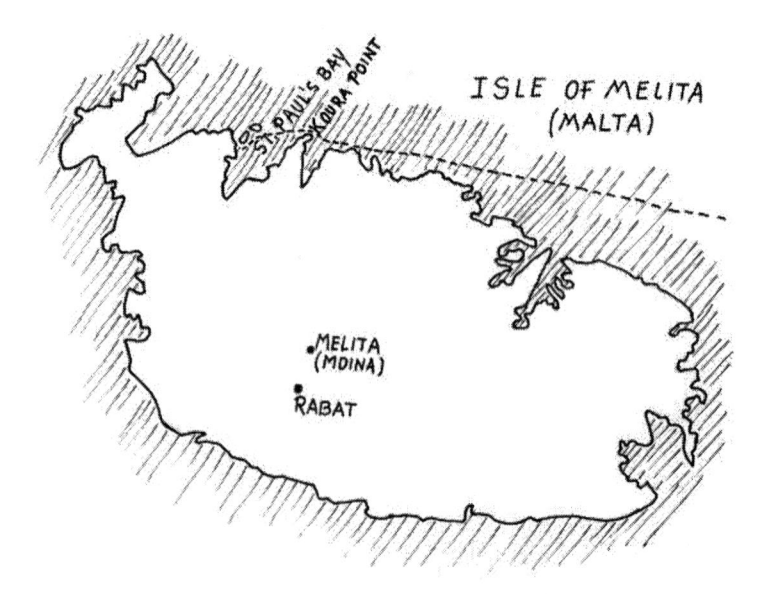

*This is the ship of pearl, which poets feign,*
  *Sails the unshadowed main,—*
  *The venturous bark that flings*
*On the sweet summer wind its purpled wings*
*In gulfs enchanted, where the Siren sings,*
  *And coral reefs lie bare,*
*Where the cold sea-maids rise to sun their streaming hair.*

*Its webs of living guaze no more unfurl;*
  *Wrecked is the ship of pearl!*
*Where its dim dreaming life was wont to dwell,*
*As the frail tenant shaped his growing shell,*
  *Before thee lies revealed,—*
*Its irised ceiling rent, its sunless crypt unsealed!*

Oliver Wendell Holmes

# CHAPTER SIXTEEN

## SHIPWRECK

FOLLOWING THE cry, "Land ho!", not a soul aboard the *Kibotos* slept for the rest of the night. The Euraquilo still blew violently, effecting a stem-to-stern rocking motion that threatened to tear the anchored ship apart. Terror gripped the crew. People scarcely noticed that the rain had reduced to infrequence.

A babel of prayers arose all over the ship—some in Latin, some in Greek; soldiers to their gods, sailors to theirs.

"O, Mars!"
"O, Poseidon!"
"O, Diana!"
"O, Aphrodite!"
"Save us!"

"Help us through the night!"

In the midst of all this, Erastus called the officers together. After a brief conference, they all spread throughout the vessel mobilizing the crew for action. Preparations needed to be made for landing. Many of the sailors resisted being pulled away from the tiny idols which they had retrieved from their baggage, but as soon as they were forced into labor, calm was restored to the ship. Julius found Erastus, conferred briefly with him, then also set about ordering his century to work.

Paul, having survived three shipwrecks, offered advice to a group of seamen on the technique of building rafts out of bunk beds. He was in a dimly lit part of the deck supervising the stacking of rafts when someone called, "Paul!"

He turned around and saw Luke hurriedly approaching.

"I've been looking everywhere for you."

"Luke! What's on your mind?"

"We've got trouble. Some officers are about to flee in the longboat."

"You must be mistaken. They're just getting it ready to launch in the morning."

"No, I overheard them plotting it."

"Let me see," said Paul.

He followed Luke to the aft of the deck cabin.

"Wait," said Luke. He held his arm out to stop Paul at the edge of the cabin. "They're just around the corner."

Paul peered around the side of the cabin into a somewhat hidden area where he could just make out the longboat dangling over the side of the ship and men climbing into it. He pulled back and whispered to Luke, "It's some of the officers. Go get Julius. I'll wait here."

Luke left and went below deck. In a few minutes he returned with Julius, followed by several soldiers with drawn swords. Paul went over and met them coming across the deck and said to Julius, "If those officers abandon ship tonight, we have no hope. Without them we can't possibly reach safety."

"Don't worry," said Julius. "They won't leave the ship."

He quickly rounded the cabin with the soldiers and caught the sailors by surprise.

"Halt!" shouted Julius.

The sailors froze. Erastus and two others were already sitting in the suspended boat.

"Where are you going?" asked Julius.

Erastus stammered, "We—ah—we were just going to lower some more anchors from the bow."

"Get out!" said Julius roughly.

When the seamen climbed out, Julius ordered the soldiers, "Cut loose the boat."

"No!" cried Erastus.

Four slashes of swords swiftly dispatched the boat into the sea. The sailors watched in dismay as their only longboat floated away.

"First Mate," said Julius, "you're under detention until daybreak. I'm hereby taking charge of the ship. Who is next in command? Call him."

Erastus called for the Second Mate. When he arrived, Julius said to him, "I'm putting the First Mate under arrest for trying to jump ship. We're taking him back to his cabin and posting a guard at his door until daybreak. You're now under my command."

"Aye, aye, sir," snapped the officer.

The soldiers led Erastus away. As they passed by Paul, Paul stopped them and said to Erastus, "Erastus, I didn't know you were among them."

Erastus hung his head and said, "I'm sorry. I'm truly sorry."

Paul placed his hand on his shoulder.

When they were gone, Julius said to Paul, "What do we do now? I haven't sailored in fifteen years."

"You'll do fine, Julius. Most of the preparations are complete now anyway. Why don't you have the mess prepare a meal for everyone before the sun comes up."

"Good idea. We'll need the nourishment."

Kore ran down the hallway to Erastus' cabin. The guard outside his door recognized her and let her enter without resistance. Erastus was lying on his back with his arms behind his head staring up at the bunk above. When Kore entered, he sat up with a jerk.

"Erastus, you poor thing. Whatever happened?"

He stood up and she rushed into his arms.

"Oh, Kore, I've made a dire mistake. I can't believe what I did."

"What on earth did you do?"

"A while ago I was preparing the longboat to launch . . . in the morning, that is. As we were rigging it one of the men said, 'Why don't we run a line to shore tonight so we can ferry the longboat back and forth with it in the morning?' I wasn't thinking. I looked ahead and saw the land only a few hundred cubits away and, oh! how I wanted to be there. Well, the soldiers caught us launching the boat and thought we were abandoning ship."

"You wouldn't have abandoned me, would you, Erastus?"

"Oh, Kore, I'm so sorry. No, I wouldn't leave you."

He began to weep.


Paul was standing at the Captain's table with Julius, Agabus, and the Second Mate. When everyone had crowded into the dining facility, Paul said, "Ladies and men, for the last fourteen days you've been in constant suspense and have gone without meals. Now I urge you to eat. You need it to survive. Don't worry, not one of you will lose a single hair from your head. The mess officer will tell you what to do."

The officer instructed them to file past the serving table and then find seats at the tables or on the floor. Paul sat down at the head table. He picked up a small loaf of warm bread and said aloud, "And now, may we all bow in prayer. Dear Lord God of heaven and earth, thank you for fulfilling your promise and delivering us to this land. Now fulfill your promise to save every life among us. Thank you for this nourishment. In Jesus name, Amen."

Paul then started eating. Encouraged by his example, everyone quickly lined up at the serving table and began filling his tray. Soon, people were crowding to the tables, and when those were full, sitting around the walls of the facility. They all began eating their fill. Loud talk and laughter resounded throughout the room.

After breakfast Julius ordered everyone onto deck. The night was still pitch dark. The Second Mate addressed the crowd, "At daybreak we hope to dock the ship . . . at least to beach her. First, though, we need to jettison all the wheat. That will lower the water level, as well as correct the tilt of the deck. Obviously, the cargo has shifted to one side in the storm. The hoists are ready and men are standing by at both hatches to supervise the project. Sailors will work the forward hatch, soldiers and prisoners the rear one. Be careful. The sacks are waterlogged. It will be dangerous. Are there any questions? If not, let's get to work."

Everyone worked at a feverish pace and by daybreak the task was completed. Though still bobbing convulsively over the rugged terrain beneath the water, the *Kibotos* had risen up out of the water appreciably and was now level.

As morning light appeared in the clouds to the east, Julius and others stood together and gazed out upon land on three sides. Despite the wind and occasional rain, they were grinning. The ship was within the mouth of a large bay. Land on their starboard side was less than a quarter knot away—the boulders Erastus had seen in the night. The furthest land they could see was about six knots away. Most of the terrain in their view was rocky and barren. Cliffs as well as low sloping hills came right down to the water's edge.

Julius asked, "Does anyone recognize this place?"

No one commented.

Erastus, who had just been freed, spoke up. "There are sea charts in the Captain's cabin. I'll fetch them."

He went over to the cabin and cautiously tried the door. It was unlocked. Opening it a crack, he saw the bearded Marcus sitting on his bunk with a mug of wine in his hand.

"I need to get the charts," said Erastus.

Marcus stood up and took Erastus by the arm. "You're not taking my charts."

"Centurion!" shouted Erastus.

Two soldiers rushed in, and with the hilt of a sword one of them knocked Marcus to the floor unconscious.

"Help me get him back into his bunk," said Erastus.

The three of them lifted Marcus and put him back into bed.

"Now restrain him."

The soldiers tied the hands and feet of Marcus to the bunk. Julius came in, followed by Paul and Luke. Seeing Marcus on the bunk, they walked over to him and stood for a moment looking down. Julius said, "How the mighty are fallen!"

"His fall is of the Lord," said Luke.

"He has fallen, only to rise again—a new man," said Paul.

The cabin was badly cluttered. Rancid food sat in trays on the floor by the door. The room reeked of urine and feces. Erastus gathered up soggy papyrus charts from the floor and laid them on the desk. One by one he unfolded the wet maps but found all the markings either washed out completely or unintelligible.

"So much for that," said Paul.

"We'll have to navigate by sight," said the Second Mate who had entered the cabin.

"I could see some crude docks around the bay," said Erastus, "but none approaching a size sufficient for the *Kibotos*. Let's go outside and see what we can see."

On deck Erastus said, "We're obviously at the mouth of a bay. We don't know how shallow the water is further inland, and any move we make will be at risk of running us aground. We're drawing two fathoms of water now. I think our only choice is to try to find the mouth of a stream, where the depth will be greater, and try to thrust the bow up into it. Let's look around."

They began to scan the shoreline downwind.

"Look," said the Second Mate. "Just beyond that peninsula. Looks like an inlet."

He was pointing straight ahead. A mist obscured the shoreline, and the group had to strain to see it.

"I can just barely make it out," said Erastus. "Maybe a cove. The waters appear relatively calm there."

The group discussed it at length. Finally, Julius said, "All right, we'll make a break toward that inlet."

It was agreed. Erastus turned to the crowd milling around on deck. "We're preparing to head for shore—toward the inlet you can vaguely see just beyond that peninsula. There seems to be calm water there. Whether we can get there or not is the question. We're likely to run aground en route. Brace yourselves. If we come to a stop, be prepared to jump into the water, but don't do so until we say. We'll still be in two fathoms of water. I want each of you now to select a partner. Pair up with someone. Whatever happens, take care of each other."

People began moving around looking for partners. Kore went up to Erastus and took him by the hand. He looked down at her and smiled. Hermes paired up with Ruth, Paul with Luke, Agabus with Miriam.

Soon, all was ready.

"Hoist the foresail," shouted Erastus. "Untie the rudders. Man the helm."

Men leaped into action. When this was done, he shouted, "Cut loose the anchors."

Axes hacked away at the thick anchor hawsers until all four of them were severed. Sluggishly, the *Kibotos* set sail. Erastus ordered a sailor to stand at the port railing and drag the lead weight of the sounding line along the sea floor. As they moved forward the man gradually took in slack from the line and called out, "Fifteen fathoms!" "Thirteen fathoms!" "Eleven fathoms!" "Ten fathoms" "Ten fathoms!" "Still holding ten fathoms!"

A lookout was positioned at the peak of the bow to watch the water, ready to sound an alarm. The *Kibotos* was slowly moving up into the bay, headed toward the peninsula at the end of a ridge.

"Look at the people standing on top of the ridge," said Julius, standing beside Erastus near the helm, with Paul and others.

"That must be the mainland," said Erastus. "The land over here on our starboard side may be an island. There's a break in the coast ahead off the starboard bow. Might be an estuary, separating it from the mainland."

They surveyed the rocky shoreline as they approached the break. Gradually, a hundred foot wide estuary between the island and the mainland opened up to their view. The water in the estuary was extremely turbulent.

"Watch out!" said Erastus to the two helmsmen. "Two seas come together there."

The bow suddenly veered precariously toward the mainland.

"I can't control her!" cried the pilot.

"Redirect the foresail," shouted Erastus.

Corrective action did no good. They were being drawn toward the dangerously towering coast like a magnet.

"We're caught in a stream!" shouted Erastus to the pilot. "The turbulence in the estuary is creating a current. Can you turn her if I strike the foresail and reduce the drift?"

"I'll try."

"Eight fathoms!" called the man with the sounding line. "Seven fathoms! Five fathoms! Closing fast."

The cliff loomed before them.

"We're going to crash!" someone cried.

To strike the rocks at their speed would deal untold tragedy.

"Three fathoms!" called the sailor.

Of a sudden, the Kibotos slid slowly to a stop. The watchman on the bow called out, "We've struck a sandbar."

For a moment no one moved. A narrow sandy beach at the foot of the cliff was only a hundred and fifty cubits away. Erastus walked up to the bow and looked down. "Hoist the foresail again and see if you can nudge the prow to port."

The sail was quickly raised but it had no effect. The pounding surf began lifting high the stern and dropping it violently back into the water.

"First Mate, we have troubles back here," called the pilot.

Erastus ran to the stern where the pilot was lifting one of the paddle rudders out of the water. Pointing down he said, "The stern is breaking up."

With the pounding of the surf and the cross action of the estuary current, the seam in the pointed stern of the *Kibotos* was opening up. Seawater was pouring into the hull.

Erastus walked over to Paul and Julius and said, "We're sinking. The stern is breaking up under the pounding. There's nothing we can do about it. We've got to abandon ship."

The three discussed the situation and agreed they had no alternative.

Paul said, "Let's get everyone off ship and to the beach as fast as possible."

Julius called out, "Let me have your attention. The *Kibotos* is sinking! We've got to abandon ship. There's no cause for panic, but please, follow our instructions. If you do, we should all be able to get to that beach safely. Remain calm now while the First Mate directs the throwing of the floats overboard."

Erastus gathered a squad of sailors and started casting the bunkbed rafts into the turbulent waters.

Julius continued, "Rope ladders will be dropped over the starboard side. I'm directing a swimmer with a rope to proceed to shore now and anchor the rope on shore. Each of us can pull himself along that rope to shore. Those of you who can swim, enter the water first but stay by the ship and hold onto the floats to keep them from drifting away. Help the non-swimmers onto the floats. There are plenty of floats for all. Don't be too hasty. Take your time. The ship won't sink for an hour or so. Don't forget the partner system; watch over your partner and take care of him. Let's all assemble on beach afterward for a head count. Wait now until the First Mate gives the signal."

Several soldiers approached Julius with drawn swords and one of them said, "Sir, it's military policy to kill the prisoners, lest they escape. Shall we proceed?"

Kore overheard them and shrieked, "No!"

"No," said Julius. He glanced toward Paul. "Spare them and let them get to shore. The cliffs will prevent them from getting away. Sergeant, round up several more soldiers and proceed to shore ahead of everyone else and apprehend the prisoners as soon as they get ashore. Take some chains with you."

Erastus shouted from the railing, "Everything is ready."

Immediately, the crowd surged toward the openings in the railing. A woman screamed. There was a splash in the sea.

"Ruth," cried Hermes.

He tore savagely through the mob to the side of the ship. Ruth had been pushed overboard. He could see her in the water entangled in the rope being towed to shore and being pulled away from the ship. Hermes ripped off his outer tunic and dived over the side. With powerful strokes he swam toward her. Just as he neared her, the rope pulled her underwater and out of sight. Hermes dived down following the rope and found her struggling to free herself from entanglement. He grabbed her by the waist and with a powerful surge lunged for the surface. When their heads broke the surface, Hermes deftly untangled the rope from around her body. Ruth sputtered and coughed.

"Dear one, are you all right?"

"I think so." She coughed a couple of times and said, "Oh, Hermes, hold me!"

Hermes was treading water, supporting both of them. He drew her tightly to his side with one arm and held her close for a few moments. Then he began gently paddling toward shore. When they reached shore, he helped her to her feet and led her back toward a sheltering overhang of the cliff, away from the wind and rain. She was shivering. He sat down in the sand with her and clasped her close to himself.

On deck the mob was uncontrollable. Paul lifted his voice over the noise and said, "Friends, there's no need to rush. God will save us all if we let him. Just put your trust in the Lord Jesus and back away from the rail a moment."

The noise subsided. People looked around at Paul and began backing away from the railing.

"Now," said Julius, "let's just proceed one at a time down the ladder, with a little more decency and order this time."

The ship's deck slowly emptied, and, ashore, groups of people were soon dragging themselves wearily up onto the sandy beach. Paul and Luke remained on board until near the end, helping people onto the ladders and over the side while speaking soft words of encouragement. Luke then assisted the aging Paul down the ladder and onto one of the last few floats available. By the time Paul dragged himself up on shore, several local inhabitants had come down to the beach to help. A survivor pointed them toward Paul. By that time the rain had ceased.

Paul stood to his feet and said, "Attention! We need to see if there are any stragglers. Would everyone please get with his partner right now."

It took a few minutes for each one to find his partner, but when that was accomplished, Paul asked, "Is anyone missing his partner?"

No one responded.

"Good, now let's all count off one at a time. One!"

People immediately picked up the count, "Two!" "Three!" "Four!" They reached two hundred seventy-five.

When no one else sounded off, Paul asked, "Is there anyone who has not counted yet? Anyone? We're one person short. Do any of you know of anyone who has not counted off yet?"

"The Captain!" called Erastus. "Has anyone seen the Captain?"

No one answered.

"He's still on board. No one untied him," he said.

By now the stern of the *Kibotos* was already underwater. It was sinking fast.

"Hermes!" called Erastus. "Let's go get Marcus!"

Hermes ran through the crowd and without stopping dived into the surf. He was unable to buck the estuary current though and swam over to the rope and started pulling himself toward the ship. Erastus was right behind him. They reached the vessel and hurriedly climbed a rope ladder to the deck where they disappeared from the view of the survivors. The ship was now listing badly to port. The crowd watched in suspense.

On board Erastus and Hermes saw the Captain's cabin already partway under water. They ran down the sloping deck to it and forced the door open. Marcus was still above water and conscious, struggling to free himself from his bunk.

"Damn the whole lot of you," Marcus boomed. "Hurry, get me loose."

Erastus and Hermes untied him. When Marcus stood up, he swayed back and forth momentarily and closed his eyes. The two jumped to his side, put his arms over their shoulders, and quickly led him from the cabin.

"Wait," said Marcus, groggily looking back, "I forgot something."

He wrestled himself free and staggered back through the water to the cabin.

"Come on! Hurry up!" said Erastus. "We haven't got long."

The deck was beginning a slow roll to port. Marcus emerged from the cabin with a mug of wine. Hermes seized the mug from him and flung it overboard.

"See here now. Who do you think you are?" said Marcus.

"Look, Captain!" said Erastus. "We're about to sink. Forget that and come on."

The two men grabbed him again and began to struggle upward against the sliding deck. The moment the three reached the edge of the deck, a great cheer went up from the crowd on shore.

"Can you climb down that ladder?" asked Hermes.

"That? No problem," said Marcus. But when he took his first step his foot slipped. Had the two men not seized him, he would have fallen into the surging waters.

"Come on back up," said Erastus. "We'll have to try this another way. Hermes, why don't you go first and help Marcus place his feet into the rungs of the ladder. I'll follow."

The three finally made it into the water where Hermes helped keep Marcus afloat at the foot of the ladder.

"I'll retrieve several floats," said Erastus.

He pulled three of the bundles of bunks together. With his knife he cut off an excess length of the rope that ran to shore and lashed the floats together. The two then struggled to get Marcus' huge frame up onto the floats. When that was done, he let them tie him on securely. Just as the two swimmers pushed off for shore guiding the floats, the *Kibotos* rolled over onto its side.

Some men started shouting across the water, "Kill him!" "Maniac!" "Hippalus caused this mess. Make him pay!"

"Better land him down shore," said Erastus.

They left the rope and guided the floats down the beach a considerable distance from the crowd. Just as they reached shore and started untying Marcus from the floats, Julius walked up with a squad of soldiers and said, "Captain Marcus Hippalus, you're under arrest for actions leading to the destruction of the *Kibotos* and its cargo."

The local delegation consisted of a matron and her son, along with several servants and neighbors. They went up to Paul and Luke, and the woman said in Latin, "How do you do? I am Estella, the wife of Publius, the governor of the island. We're here to be of help to you." She offered him her hand.

"How do you do?," he replied, as he took her hand. "I'm very glad to meet you. I am Paul of Tarsus, an Apostle of the Lord Jesus Christ. As you can see, we're quite an unkempt lot. Can you please tell us where we are?"

"You're on the isle of Malta." A murmur went through the crowd. She glanced around in surprise at their response. "Enough of that for now," she said. "You're all wet and cold. My servants have brought some dry wood to build a fire for you." She clapped her hands and the servants picked up batches of kindling and logs, piled them up in a wide area on the beach, and ignited them.

Paul talked with the members of the delegation for awhile until he saw that Marcus was safely ashore. "Excuse me for a moment," he said, "I must address the crowd again.

"May I have your attention!" The survivors began to gather around Paul. "I am happy to announce that we are safely on the island of Malta, just south of Sicily. This is Estella, wife of Publius, the Governor of the Island. She lives in a residence on the hill above us. Why not show your appreciation for her hospitality."

Everyone applauded.

"I need not remind you that a week ago, at the time of our worst extremity aboard the *Kibotos,* an angel of the Lord gave to me the promise that we would run aground on an island and that not one of us would perish." Paul paused as he struggled for self-control. When he could, he choked out the words, "Malta is that island. Two hundred seventy-six passengers were aboard the *Kibotos*—two hundred seventy-six people have been rescued, even as God promised. All praise be to our God the Father and to the Lord Jesus . . ."

Suddenly, out in the bay the ship created a great commotion as it slipped slowly underwater, sending a series of waves coursing to shore. People ran back from the water's edge. They watched the event in hushed awe.

In a few minutes Paul said, "Let's all kneel together in the sand and thank God for his delivery."

Everyone knelt, including the islanders. Paul prayed, "Dear God and Father of our Lord Jesus Christ, you offered us the promise of delivery and we trusted in you. Now you have performed your promise. This is the Lord's doing and it is marvelous in our eyes. Thank you for loving us and caring so much for us. All praise and honor be to the Lord Jesus Christ, in whose name we pray. Amen."

A chorus of "amens" went up from the sandy beach.

"Houuuu-eeee!" someone shouted, and people began spontaneously throwing their head coverings into the air, leaping up and down, and bear-hugging one another in an extraordinary show of jubilation. Even Paul got caught up in the joy, tearing open the front of his robe, slowly twirling around with both arms and his face turned heavenward, and trilling out the words "Hosanna! Hosanna! Hosanna!"

The locals first just looked on in amazement, until one of the burly sailors grabbed Estella around the waist. Her eyes bulged in surprise. The sailor caught himself, backed contritely away, and spoke something unintelligible to her. She smiled at him and said in Latin, "That's alright." Then she too joined the festivities, running to where Ruth, Kore, and Miriam were and joining her hand with theirs in a discreet Hebrew dance. The three Hebrew ladies began rapidly moving their tongues back and forth in a spine-tingling warbling sound.

At that, all the rest of the locals joined in the celebration.

The fatigued survivors were not able to linger long in the ecstatic demonstration and soon collapsed to the beach in exhaustion.

Paul, however, with exceptional energy, walked among them testifying to the saving power of Jesus and urging them to put their trust in him. "If you're willing to give your heart to the Lord, I want to ask you now to stand to your feet."

Immediately, people began rising to their feet all up and down the beach. Erastus stood up, leaving a band of sailors around him, and walked over toward Paul. Hermes was right behind him, leading Ruth by the hand.

Paul said, "Luke, will you take a third of these converts up the beach a little distance and explain to them the Way. Aristarchus, will you take another third of them down the beach and talk to them, while I talk to these around me."

Several more hours were spent on the beach, the wind howling the whole time. After extensive interviews with the new converts, Paul, Erastus, and Julius turned their attention back to Estella and conversed with her about their future. Her slaves were busily moving up and down the cliff trail on various errands. Other local people also came down to help.

Malta had few trees, and several people continually gathered driftwood and brush for the fire. After a few minutes Paul joined them. Hearing that he was a prisoner, most of the locals just dismissed him in contempt.

"Here, you," said one of the servants to him, "Bring that load over here. The fire's dying down."

Paul took the bundle over and dumped it in the middle of the fire. Flames leaped up and crackled through the brush. Paul jerked his hand back in pain. A small snake was writhing on his wrist. With a quick snap of his arm he slung the viper into the blaze, then brought the back of his hand to his mouth and sucked and spat blood. Luke quickly got a rag and wrapped the wound and Paul went away to get more wood.

The passengers thought little of the incident but the locals buzzed with conversation about it and curiously observed Paul's wrist each time he returned to the fire with wood. One of them said to Luke and others huddled around the fire, "That snake was extremely poisonous. You'll see that criminal keel over dead in a minute."

Luke quickly left the fire and met Paul bringing another load down the hill. He put his arm around Paul's shoulder and took his elbow.

"What are you doing?" said Paul, trying to shake his hands loose.

"We need to get you some treatment. That snake was very poisonous."

"Treatment, Luke? What kind of treatment? You have no bag. Don't bother, though. I've already prayed to the Father to care for me. I'll be all right."

He went on and dumped his load into the fire and went back for more. Soon, though, a native by the waterside started pointing toward Paul and shouting, "That man is a god. He is Hermes, come to visit us."

Several local people ran up to Paul, took one look at his hand, then dropped to their knees before him. "We praise you." "We worship you," they said.

"Why are you saying this?" said Paul excitedly, taking several of them by the arms and lifting them up. "I'm only a man—human, like you are. I'm a humble servant of the living God, who made heaven and earth—and this sea."

He pulled back his sleeve and showed one of the men his wrist. "God has preserved me from harm—see!—because I bring you good news, telling you to turn from worthless idols to God."

He turned around to a servant girl and said, "In the past the Lord God let all nations go their own way. Now, though, he has sent his Son, Jesus, to call all men to repentance. Believe me!"

"Oh, sir," said the girl, "You are a most honored man in our presence. We are humbled that one such as you has come to us."

She wheeled around and ran toward a distinguished-looking gentleman coming down the steep trail. She stopped him and conversed briefly with him, pointing excitedly toward Paul. The man came down to Paul, laughing jovially, and said, "My servants are very impressed with you, sir. I'm Publius, the governor of the island. I would have been here sooner, but the capitol is several miles away and I was already at work when the wreck happened.

"We've completed arrangements for accommodations for all of you. My wife and I would personally like to invite you, the ship's owner, the Captain, Centurion, and any other of your immediate party to come up to our home and be our special guests for the duration."

"That is very hospitable of you," said Paul. "I doubt the Captain will be permitted to come though. That's him, down there."

He pointed down the beach to Marcus, who was bearded, disheveled, chained, and under guard by a detachment of soldiers.

"However, can you accommodate about—ah—say, ten others of us? That's how many I would like to bring with me."

"That will be fine," said Publius with a smile. "No problem at all."

Publius began directing the evacuation of the passengers from the beach. Local residents had brought down cloaks and blankets, and they assisted the needy in getting up the steep trail. Horse-drawn coaches and wagons were lined up at the top of the cliff, on which government workers dispatched survivors throughout the island, recording the name and destination of each person as he left—some to homes, some to coastal inns, the soldiers to the island's military cantonment, and the prisoners, under guard, to a large cave near the center of the island.

Midway up the ridge trail, Publius stopped and said to Paul and the others with him, "To get to our house, we need to take this fork to the left."

The crowd ahead of them had turned up the right fork toward the waiting chariots. Publius and Luke were on either side of Paul, supporting him.

Luke said to Paul, "Do you want to stop a few minutes?"

Paul was breathing heavily. Without replying, he stopped, turned around, and looked back down at the bay. It was late afternoon. The wind had died down and the sun was beginning to break through the clouds. A rainbow had formed across the bay. While he caught his breath, he gazed wordlessly over the scene.

Luke said, "Praise God! The storm is over!"

"Yes," said Paul, "It has done its work!"

They stood silently for a few minutes longer. Paul then turned back around and started back up the trail and the others had to catch up with him. Finally, they crested the top of the ridge and found themselves at the rear of a lovely, white, single-story, palatial mansion.

"Welcome to our humble home," said Publius.

No other houses were around. They crossed a lawn and a rock patio and came to the back door of the house where a slave met them. Publius called out, "Dear, we're home."

Estella appeared at the door, wiping her hands on a dish towel. "Come right in. We've prepared accommodations for each of you and made arrangements for you to bathe. Bath towels as well as dry clothing are laid out. You're welcome to clean up while we complete dinner. It will be served in an hour and a half." She turned to the youth, now coming out the door, who had accompanied her on the beach and said, "Cicero, our son, will show you to your rooms."

"After I clean up," said Ruth, "may I help in the kitchen? For the past week I've been cooking on a heater stove on the tossing ship. It would be a joy to cook on solid ground for a change."

Kore was tugging at her sleeve. Ruth added, "You wouldn't mind if Kore and I both helped, would you?"

"Surely, both of you just come back to the kitchen when you're ready."

They all entered the house and Cicero led them from room to room as Publius followed and assigned passengers to the various rooms. When they passed by a closed door, Cicero said, "My grandfather is in there sick."

"May I visit him?" Paul asked.

"Of course," said Publius. He knocked on the door and looked in. "Papa, someone would like to meet you. May we come in?"

"Come in," said a weakened voice.

Paul entered and saw a white-haired man lying in bed beneath a pile of covers. Luke followed them into the room and said to Publius, "Dysentery?"

"I suppose so. And fever. He came down ill in the night. A physician is supposed to come look at him tonight."

"Papa, how do you feel?" asked Paul, placing a hand on his brow.

"Not good."

"I'm going to ask you to do something," said Paul. "I want you to close your eyes while I pray. Will you?"

Papa closed his eyes.

Paul prayed, "Precious God above, I ask you in the name of Jesus to heal this man of his sickness. Amen."

Paul then placed his hand over the man's brow. He said softly, "In the name of Jesus Christ of Nazareth, be healed."

The man opened his eyes. He looked around in surprise and began pushing back the covers. Paul helped him to sit up. He looked up at Paul with a smile and said, "Thank you, kind sir. But who in the world are you?"

"I am Paul of Tarsus, a slave of the Son of God, Jesus Christ of Nazareth."

Papa swung his feet out of bed. "I smell roast beef. Is Estella cooking supper? I'm starved to death."

> *I tempted all His servitors, but to find*
> *My own betrayal in their constancy,*
> *In faith to Him their fickleness to me,*
> *Their traitorous trueness, and their loyal deceit.*
> THE HOUND OF HEAVEN by Francis Thompson

# CHAPTER SEVENTEEN

## ON THE ISLAND OF MALTA

AT SUNRISE THE next morning, Hermes was outside the house, standing on the stone patio at the rear. A brilliant cloudless sky opened above him. As he stood before a low wall at the cliff's edge gazing down at the bay, the door opened quietly behind him and Ruth came out.

"Hermes," she said.

He turned around and saw her standing before the white stucco house wearing an orange robe, her auburn hair freshly washed and brushed.

"My dear one! You look so gorgeous in a Maltese robe. Come here."

She glided over to him and he took her into his arms. She smelled like orange blossoms.

"You are a picture of loveliness," he said looking into her upturned face. "You look like you slept well last night."

"I did. I feel just wonderful!"

She backed away while still holding his hand and twirled around, her tresses swinging freely and the bottom of her robe flowing bell-shaped around her bare feet.

Hermes drew her backward to himself and circled his arms around her tiny waist. The two gazed out to sea in silence for a few minutes. The view of the sunrise was exhilarating.

"Darling," he said, "if you had drowned yesterday, my heart would have died with you. When I saw you so helpless in the water, I knew for the first time how much you mean to me. What I mean to say is . . . I love you. Will you . . . will you become my wife?"

Ruth turned around and looked intently into his eyes, her green pupils, like polished emeralds in shallow ponds, moist with tears. Placing her finger upon his chin, she said, "Do you know when I first knew I loved you? It was yesterday on the beach when you prayed for Christ to come into your life. When I gave my heart to the Lord Jesus two weeks ago, I prayed that he would give me a Christian husband. You know, though, that Christ will always be first in my life. If you will have me like that, I will be yours forever."

A radiant smile broke over Hermes' face. "Dear one, I'm willing to have you under any condition."

They embraced and kissed long.

In a few minutes Publius came out the door followed by Paul. "If you're hungry," Publius said to Ruth and Hermes, "food is on the bar. We're just eating in shifts."

"Thank you," said Hermes. The two laughed at a private joke and went inside. Publius and Paul walked over to the ledge. The waters of the bay were about a hundred cubits below them. Looking down at the *Kibotos* lying visibly on its side in the water, Publius said, "You folks have added a new landmark to our scenery."

"Yes, unfortunately. Our ship must have drifted in past that peninsula across the bay the night before." He pointed to a tip of land due east. "We couldn't see it but we could clearly hear the surf dashing on the rocks."

"That's called Koura Point. Say, why was your captain arrested?"

"The Centurion charged him with causing the wreck."

"Causing the wreck? How?"

"He's being blamed for thrusting us into the storm in the first place. Two weeks ago we were on the coast of Crete, and he tried to move the ship from one anchorage on Crete to another some distance away. The storm hit us in route. I think he'll be acquitted though, since the decision had the approval of both the Centurion and the owner."

"Two weeks! You mean that storm brought you all the way from Crete! Incredible!"

"Yes! It was a grueling experience."

"I should say so . . . . Now, if you will excuse me, I must be going. The ride to headquarters in Melita takes more than half an hour. You've had a hard experience. Why don't you and your friends just remain here today and rest. I'll be back this afternoon. Tomorrow I can take you on a tour of the island if you feel like it."

"Before you leave, I'd like to find out where the prisoners from the ship are kept. I'd like to visit them."

"I had them moved to a large cave in the edge of Melita."

"That's where you're going now, isn't it? Would it be possible for Luke and me to accompany you?"

"Sure, if you feel like it. I'll have another chariot hitched up. My father is riding with me in mine, but it won't take but a second to get another one ready."

He went to the door and called, "Ho! Jarbuch, have another chariot prepared."

The two chariots traveled around the end of the bay and turned inland. The Maltese countryside was hilly and barren and ascended toward the interior of the island. At one point they crossed over some wagon ruts that had been worn in the rock in prehistoric times. From the crest of each hill they could look back and see the bay and the coastline. As Paul observed the tiny size of the island, he commented to Luke about how the providence of God had been so marvelous in permitting them to chance upon it in so vast a sea. Publius, in the chariot ahead got their attention and pointed to a high hill in the distance. Atop it they could see a city which they supposed to be Melita.

Jarbuch followed Publius' chariot along the road up the hill, into the small city of Melita, and through the narrow winding streets to the small, white, headquarters building. Publius and his father stepped out of their chariot and walked over to Paul. "Wait here while I go inside and get a soldier to take my chariot and to lead you over to the cave."

It was not far to the cave, which was located among various buildings. When they pulled to a stop on the street in front of it, they saw Julius' centurymen busily carrying bedding and supplies into the large natural opening. Julius was directing the activities.

Paul stepped out of the chariot and walked up to Julius. "Good morning, Julius, did you sleep well?"

"Paul! Luke! Yes, fine. We're bivouacked on the coast a few miles east of the bay."

"Can you tell me where Marcus is?"

"He's sleeping in the back of the cave. Go on in."

Paul walked into the cave, while Luke remained outside with Julius for a few minutes to discuss Marcus' condition. Paul found Marcus in an isolated area deep in the cave, lying on a thick folded robe on the stone floor. He was snoring loudly. A soldier bearing a spear was guarding him. He was still dressed in his kilt, bearded and smelly, his hair wild.

Paul knelt down beside him and called loudly, "Marcus! Marcus!"

Marcus aroused, snorted two or three times, opened wide his eyes, and began reaching frantically toward one side of the robe and then the other. Not finding whatever he was looking for there, his eyes darted all around the cave. He did not see the two visitors—looked right through them. He rubbed his bloodshot eyes, squinted, and finally focused on the face of Paul.

"You! Come to lead a mutiny against me, are you? Get out of my cabin. I told you I never wanted to see you again."

He started to rise to his feet but the guard knocked him back to the floor with the butt of his spear. Marcus looked at the soldier in surprise and rubbed his shoulder, then rolled over with his face to the wall and started noisily blowing his nose on the robe.

"Don't hurt him," said Paul.

Luke walked up and said, "He doesn't know where he is. He's starting withdrawal. Let's get him some clean clothes and I'll see about medicating him."

Marcus was snoring again.

The guard said, "I have orders not to let anyone else back here to see him—I mean other than you. I know you two. They're afraid someone might try to kill him. This is the first time he's awakened since we brought him here yesterday."

"We'll be taking care of him," said Luke. "Let's go get some supplies."

He and Paul left and returned after awhile with fresh clothing and food. With the help of the guard and two large men, they wrestled Marcus around to strip him, wash him, and cloth him. They wanted also to feed him, but he never fully regained consciousness.

Luke said, "He'll be like this probably for another twenty-four hours, after which he'll go into delirium tremens—not a pretty sight to see. I plan to stay with him day and night to nurse him. There's not much you can do until he comes to. Why not go back to the coast, get some rest, and return tomorrow?"

Paul left the cave and rode over to the capitol building. A crowd of Maltese people were waiting in front of the building along with Publius' father who was smiling happily. "There's Paul now," he said.

The crowd rushed over and swarmed around the chariot.

"What is this?" asked Paul good-naturedly.

"I've been telling them how you healed me yesterday."

"Permit me to clarify," Paul said to the crowd in Latin. "It was not I who healed him but rather the God and Father of my Lord, Jesus Christ of Nazareth, who did so."

"They can't understand you," said Papa. "They're barbarians."

"It sounds like you've been speaking to them, though. Obviously you know their language. Would you translate for me?"

"I'll be glad to."

Paul got out of the chariot and began talking to the crowd on the streetside. Presently, Publius came out of the building to see what was going on. On seeing Paul he decided to listen awhile and ended up remaining there for some time. Once, Paul made an effort to dismiss the crowd so that he could return to the bay to rest, but the crowd would not permit him to leave. They brought sick people to him, and one by one he healed them. Great rejoicing occurred that day in front of the Roman administration building.

By mid-afternoon, Paul was extremely weary and hungry. He finally begged leave of the crowd to eat and return to the bay, promising that he would return to preach and heal at the same place the next day.

On the way back to the coast, Paul collapsed on the seat of the chariot and slept the rest of the way. He awakened to see another large crowd in front of Publius' mansion."

"Jarbuch," said Paul to the driver, "what's going on?"

"It looks as though the slaves have brought people to see you, sir."

Jarbuch stepped down from the chariot and went over to talk to some of the men. Women and men both filled the courtyard in front of the house while children ran to and fro playing with balls and hoops. He came back and said, "They want you to heal their ill."

Young Cicero came out the front door.

Paul called him over and said, "Cicero, you speak their language, don't you?

"Yes sir, fairly well."

"Would you be willing to interpret for me? I want to speak to them."

"I'll try, sir."

"Good! Come over here."

Paul went to a low stone wall and stepped up on it.

"Step up here with me, son, so everyone can hear you."

Cicero stepped up beside him, and Paul, with his arm over Cicero's shoulder for support, began, "You have heard it said that yesterday I healed the father of Publius. Permit me to clarify. It was not my power or godliness that healed him. Rather, it was the God and Father of the Lord Jesus Christ. It was by faith in the name of Jesus that he was healed."

For an hour Paul addressed them and healed their sick. That afternoon a special bond developed between the aged apostle and the mid-teen lad. Hermes and Ruth, Erastus and Kore, also came out of the house and assisted with the management of the crowd and prayed with some of the people who spoke Latin. Estella watched from the shade of a small tree.

Paul went to the cave again the next morning. When he walked in, he found Marcus, under the watchful care of Luke and a guard, awake but moving about the darkened environment in an agitated state of mind. He did not notice Paul. He was up and down from the bunk which had been brought in for him, his hands trembling, his motions jerky, his eyes bulging.

Suddenly, he jumped up onto the bunk on his hands and knees, and shouted, "Help me. Get these rats out of here. They're all over me."

He began swatting his chest and shoulders, and sweeping his arms across his back. Paul said, "Marcus Hippalus, we love you. We're here to help you."

Marcus looked up and said, "Then help me get rid of these rats. They'll kill me."

He stopped moving and looked more closely at Paul. "You, again! Get out of here. I don't need your help. Get him away from me."

"Marcus," said Luke. "This is Paul, a servant of God. He wants nothing but good for you."

"A servant of schmad," shouted Marcus. "He's a servant of the tempest. I know him. He's here to do me nothing but harm. I've had enough of the wind and I've had enough of Paul of Tarsus. Get out. Leave me alone."

Paul meekly withdrew. He went hunting through the cave for Aristarchus. Aristarchus was a Jew from Thessalonica and had been a close associate of Paul for many years. Two years before, he had accompanied Paul to Jerusalem as an official representative of the Thessalonian church in helping transport offerings for hunger relief to the church in Jerusalem. He had been captured with Paul in Jerusalem and had been charged with the same offense as Paul: desecrating the Temple and raising an insurrection. When Paul appealed to Caesar, the authority in Caesarea decided to transfer Aristarchus' case to Rome with Paul's. Paul now found him outside the cave discussing the gospel with a group of prisoners.

When Paul walked up, Aristarchus said, "Men, you know Paul, the Apostle of Jesus. He has personally seen the Savior."

"Tell us what he is like," someone urged.

Paul took the time to explain about Christ and answer their questions.

Afterward, Paul said to Aristarchus, "If I can get you released for awhile, would you make arrangements for us to baptize here in Melita this weekend?"

"You can count on it."

"I'd like you to do most of the baptizing. The Lord has laid it on my heart to start a church here on Malta. Already I can sense the Spirit moving here in a mighty way."

Later in the morning Paul spoke to another crowd outside the administrative building, even larger than the one the previous day, and again healed many sick. When he returned to Publius' home that afternoon, he addressed a crowd that was also larger than the one the day before. At both places he announced baptismal services the next day for all who had accepted Christ as their Savior.

Early the next morning, Sunday, a crowd gathered in front of

Publius' mansion. Paul preached a long sermon, then said, "And now those who have accepted Christ Jesus or who wish to do so may follow me down to the bay where we will baptize."

Paul led them around the house and down the steep trail. Almost everyone present followed him. While the crowd milled around on the beach, several men entered the water and searched for a firm level spot where they might baptize.

Kore said to Ruth, "Do you know what? It'll be exciting to be baptized out in the water within sight of our sunken ship."

"It will! Jesus is our *kibotos*. In the same way Noah and his family were saved from the flood in their *kibotos*, we'll be saved from our sins in Jesus."

"Now then," said Paul, "I would like for the following candidates to enter the water with me first: Hermes, Ruth, Erastus, Kore, Publius and his father, and Estella."

The group waded out into the water as the crowd moved in close around them on the beach. Standing waist-deep in the water, Paul said, "The followers of Christ Jesus all baptize new converts in the same way that John the Baptist baptized. Jesus ordained it this way. He said, 'Go and make disciples of all nations, baptizing them in the name of the Father and of the Son and of the Holy Spirit.'"

He motioned for Ruth to come over to him. "Ruth, are you trusting the Lord Jesus Christ as your personal Savior?"

"Yes, I am."

"Then, in obedience to Christ's command, I now baptize you in the name of the Father and the Son and the Holy Spirit."

Paul quickly leaned Ruth back and dipped her under the water. He did the same for the others. Then he said, "I would now like to introduce you to Aristarchus."

Aristarchus had just arrived and was standing at the back of the crowd.

"For many years this man has been a close companion of mine in the work of the Lord throughout Macedonia and Asia. I have asked him to come and assist in the baptisms."

When Aristarchus waded out into the water, Paul and the

others went ashore where they were handed towels and dry robes.

Later in the day, Paul and Aristarchus were taken to Melita where another large crowd awaited them outside the headquarters. Paul again preached a powerful message. At the conclusion, he said, "Aristarchus has arranged for a baptismal service today. I now invite all of you to accompany us to the edge of town."

Aristarchus led them on a walk through the city streets to a place just outside the city walls. Beside the wall was a large natural stone depression in the ground, full of water. The city stood on a high hill and Paul looked out over the mostly barren countryside and could see the bay in which their ship had sunk and the waters of the Great Sea ringing the north side of the small island. In that location Aristarchus baptized a large crowd of soldiers, prisoners, and peasants.

Late that afternoon Paul and Aristarchus entered the dark prison cave of Marcus. Luke greeted them. Marcus was sitting on his bunk staring down at the floor. Without looking up he said in his deep bass voice, "Paul, tell me, what kind of a person am I? My life is an utter failure. My naval career is ended. I'm being taken to Rome to be tried before the tribunal. I had a chance, but I lost it. Why didn't I listen to you? I didn't have to make that stupid blunder—sailing out of Fair Havens. Why did I do it? Why am I like that?"

"Why are you like you are?" said Paul. "Do you really want to know? It's because you're running away from God."

Marcus looked up. "Running away from god? I don't see it."

"You blame God for your court martial in Britain."

"You know about that, do you? Julius must have told you. No, I don't blame a god. I don't even believe in a god. I blame only the wind. Every misfortune in my life can be traced to the action of the wind."

"Come now, the wind can't have a grudge against you. The wind is not a person, with thoughts and feelings. That's just as irrational as believing that an idol, carved by a craftsman, can have thoughts and feelings. You see that, don't you?"

Marcus stared across the cave, his brow furrowing slightly. Paul continued, "No, you're just like every man. We were all born rebels against God. We're fallen creatures. We sin against God and refuse to trust him. Sometimes we won't even acknowledge he exists, so stubborn is our rebellion. Human pride goads us to resist God.

"Yet God is real! No one's disbelief in God destroys his being—not in the least. Marcus, God loves you so much he sent his son to die for you. He's been trying to reveal his love to you. He sent me to you, and he doubtless has sent others too."

Marcus rocked backward.

"What is it?" asked Paul.

"I was just thinking of an incident aboard ship. One night when I sneaked down to the hold to the wine stock, I had to duck under water to fetch a jug. When I stood up, I struck my head on something. That was the last thing I remember—until I woke up and found myself being carried up the ladder in the darkness. I don't know who it was, but someone rescued me. He laid me gently against a wall and walked away into the darkness. You know how large I am. He carried me as easily as a mother carries a baby. I never saw him before, and I never saw him again. Could that have been God?"

"No, not God. God is a spirit. But probably it was one of his angels. An angel of that description appeared to me, too, when I was praying on the ship. It might have been the same night. Marcus, our great God is the Lord of heaven and earth, and he can do all things. He makes the sun to shine, the rain to fall, the wind to blow."

"The wind to blow? Did God send the Euraquilo? Why would he want to harm me, if he loves me as you say he does?"

"Not harm you. To get your attention. You see, he convicts us of sin, of righteousness, and of judgment."

"That's over my head. I don't see it. I don't want to talk about it anymore."

That night Paul moved into the cave among the other prisoners. Daily, throughout the winter he continued reasoning with Marcus. Many Maltese were converted to Christ and a church was formed on the island. Paul spent much time with Publius, personally training him, and eventually appointed him as pastor of the church. Every Sunday evening people came from all over the island to worship in a large assembly hall in the administration building, and Paul insisted that Publius, in addition to himself, preach at every gathering.

Erastus found another grain ship from Alexandria, the *Castor and Pollux,* the twin gods of sailors, wintering in the island's Grand Harbor at Valletta. This prominent harbor was seven knots southeast of the bay of the shipwreck. Although Erastus had sailed into Valletta several times in the years before the shipwreck, he had failed to identify the island as Malta when he was aboard the *Kibotos* because he had never before seen that part of the coast. He made reservations with the captain of the ship for transportation of his passengers to Puteoli, when it sailed again in the spring.

On a Sunday evening in early spring the next year, the new church was assembled in the large hall at the rear of the flat-roofed, administration building in Melita. The hall was packed with people, some sitting in rows of chairs, some on the floor in the aisles, some in the windows, some standing in the treed courtyard outside. Marcus sat at the back of the hall along with a number of other prisoners and soldiers. On a table and on the floor at the front was a large pile of robes, undergarments, rainwear, scarfs, and toiletries, as well as jewelry and miscellaneous personal items.

"Brothers, this is a sad day for God's people," said Publius. "Paul and his friends will set sail in the morning. We have tried to persuade Paul to remain with us; but as you know, he's under detention and must be taken to Rome to stand trial before Nero . . ."

He spoke in Latin, and Cicero, his son, interpreted in Maltese. A sadness marked the worship of the people that evening.

As the service progressed Ruth went to the front to sing a psalm, accompanied by a shepherd flutist.

> *Whither shall I go from thy Spirit?*
> *Or whither shall I flee from thy presence?*
> *If I ascend up into heaven, thou art there:*
> *If I make my bed in hell, behold, thou art there.*
> *If I take the wings of the morning,*
> *And dwell in the uttermost parts of the sea;*
> *Even there shall thy hand lead me,*
> *And thy right hand shall hold me . . .*

Marcus dropped his head and did not look up again until the song was over.

> *If I say, Surely the darkness shall cover me;*
> *Even the night shall be light about me.*
> *Yea, the darkness hideth not from thee;*
> *But the night shineth as the day:*
> *The darkness and the light are both alike to thee.*
> *For thou hast possessed my reins.*

When she finished singing, a chorus of "amens" resounded. She went back to sit with Hermes.

Publius preached a short message and then Paul rose to speak:

"Dear brothers and sisters in Christ, it is with great sadness of heart that I preach to you for the last time. Perhaps I will never see you again in this world. Nevertheless, please remember that I shall be praying for you and thanking God on every remembrance of you.

"The party of those going on to Rome tomorrow will long remember with gratitude the copious supply of personal items you have so generously showered upon us. Without them we would have been sorely disadvantaged."

He motioned to the table of gifts.

"It will be with fondness for you and gratitude to God that we remember all your extreme kindnesses and hospitality, from the very first day we chanced upon your island..."

Paul discoursed long into the night. When he finished, the friendly islanders crowded around him and his friends and smothered them with embraces, kisses, tears, and warm words of endearment and well-wishes.

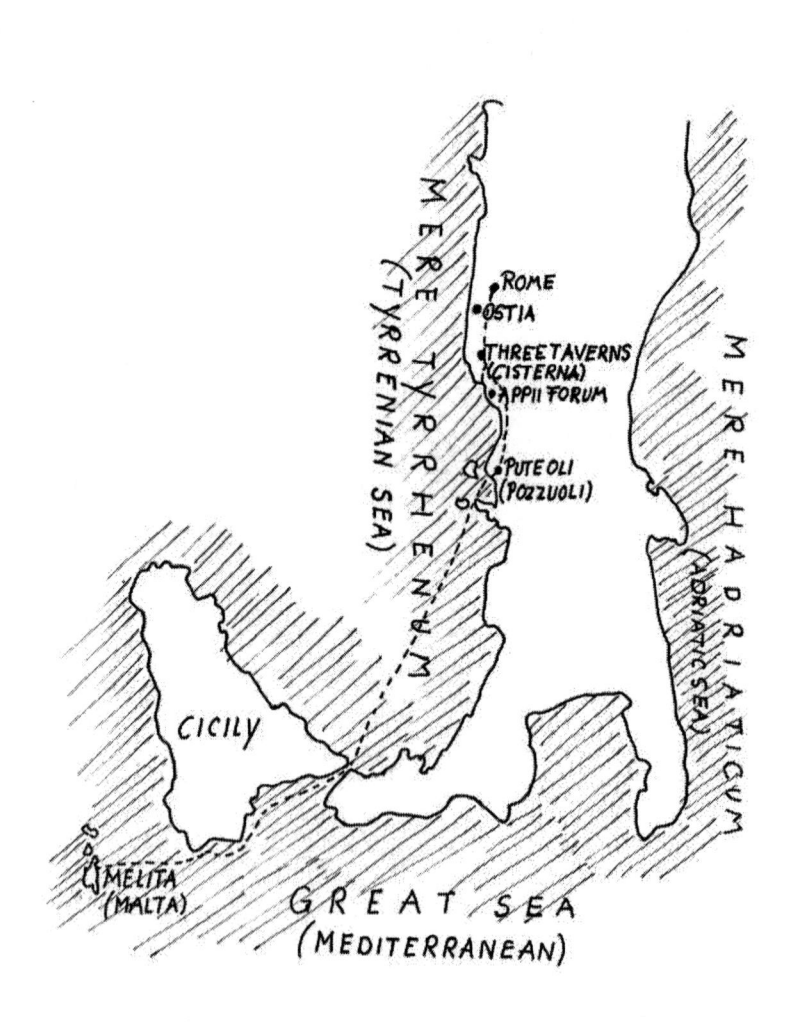

ROME
OSTIA
THREE TAVERNS (CISTERNA)
APPII FORUM
PUTEOLI (POZZUOLI)

MERE TYRRHENUM (TYRRENIAN SEA)

MERE HADRIATICUM (ADRIATIC SEA)

CICILY

MELITA (MALTA)

GREAT SEA (MEDITERRANEAN)

*Naked I wait thy love's uplifted stroke*
*My harness, piece by piece, thou has hewn from me,*
    *And smiten me to my knee;*
  *I am defenseless utterly.*
  *I slept, methinks, and woke*
*And slowly gazing, find me stripped in sleep.*
*In the rash lustihood of my young powers,*
  *I stood the pillaring hours*
*And pulled my life upon me; grimed with smears*
*I stand amid the dust o' the mounding years—*
*My mangled youth lies deep beneath the heap,*
*My days have crackled and gone up in smoke,*
*Have puffed and burst as sun-starts on a stream.*
    THE HOUND OF HEAVEN by Francis Thompson

# CHAPTER EIGHTEEN

## OUTSIDE ROME
## SPRING AD 61

AT SUNRISE THE Centurion's camp was astir with activity. Men were bathing, shaving, donning uniforms. Tents were being folded, supplies packed, and wagons loaded.

The day before, the century had arrived here at the outskirts of Rome. It had been almost two weeks since they had landed aboard the *Castor and Pollux* at Puteoli, Italy's greatest maritime city. From there the rest of the passengers had departed their various ways: Hermes to his brother's home in nearby Naples, Agabus and his companions to Rome via a coastal vessel, the *Kibotos* sailors, including Erastus, to hunt for jobs. There being a strong military presence in Puteoli, both naval and army, Julius had immediately contacted his counterpart and had arranged for land transportation to Rome. While waiting for wagons to be made available, they had spent a week in a cantonment, during which time Julius had trusted Paul to stay with the brethren of a church in the city. Finally, they had departed Puteoli and for five days had travelled the world's most famous highway, the Queen of Roads, the Appian Way, to the edge of Rome. Now they were preparing to enter the Eternal City.

Marcus was among the prisoners who were confined in a guarded compound with a temporary fence around it and a large tent in the center. He was active—but sullen, taciturn, and withdrawn.

A tall soldier appeared and set a crate of clothing on the ground just inside the gate. "Here, everyone wear these."

Several men went over to the crate and began lifting out and inspecting the assortment of shabby tan tunics.

"By Jupiter," said one of them, "they really want us to look first class when we enter Rome."

"They're filthy," said another. "Prisoners have probably been wearing them into Rome like this since the days of Julius Caesar."

"They'll probably take them away from us as soon as we've entered," said a third prisoner.

"They can have mine anytime they want as far as I'm concerned," responded the first speaker.

"Attention," cried a guard.

The prisoners merely glanced up. Julius was walking briskly up to the gate, dressed snappily in full battle array, his chain armor jingling as he walked. Paul was on his left. The two entered the compound.

"Where's Aristarchus?" said Julius.

"Over here, sir," said Aristarchus.

Julius and Paul walked over to him as Marcus, to one side, watched them out of the corner of his eye.

"How have you been faring, my brother?" asked Paul, clasping both his hands in a fraternal manner.

"Fine, thank you. The Lord has been good to me."

"Good morning, Aristarchus," said Julius. "I want you to do something for me. I want to place Paul into your keeping. He's insisting that he enter Rome with the prisoners. It's against my better judgment, but I haven't been able to talk him out of it. It will be a long march, though, and I need someone to watch over him for me. Luke would, but he won't be permitted to parade into the city with us."

"I'll be glad to, Centurion."

Julius turned to Paul. "I'd still rather you not march in. There wouldn't be anything wrong with your staying here with the baggage and coming later."

"No, I prefer to mix with the prisoners. I'm a simple prisoner myself; even when I'm free I'm still just a prisoner of the Lord. I'll do well. I appreciate your kind concern though."

"Well, I think a lot of you. Frankly, I'm indebted to you for my life—for the lives of all my men. Take care of yourself. I must be going now. Aristarchus, don't hesitate to send word to me if Paul needs help."

Julius left them and walked over to Marcus who was rolling up a sleeping mat. "And how are things with you, Captain?"

"Could be better," Marcus said gruffly without looking up. He let go of his mat, which promptly unrolled. Standing to his feet he said, "Do me a favor, Julius. Let *me* remain here with the baggage. You're willing to do Paul a favor. Why not me? I don't deserve this kind of treatment. I'm not a criminal any more than Paul is. It will be humiliating for me to walk into Rome in chains. I have many friends there."

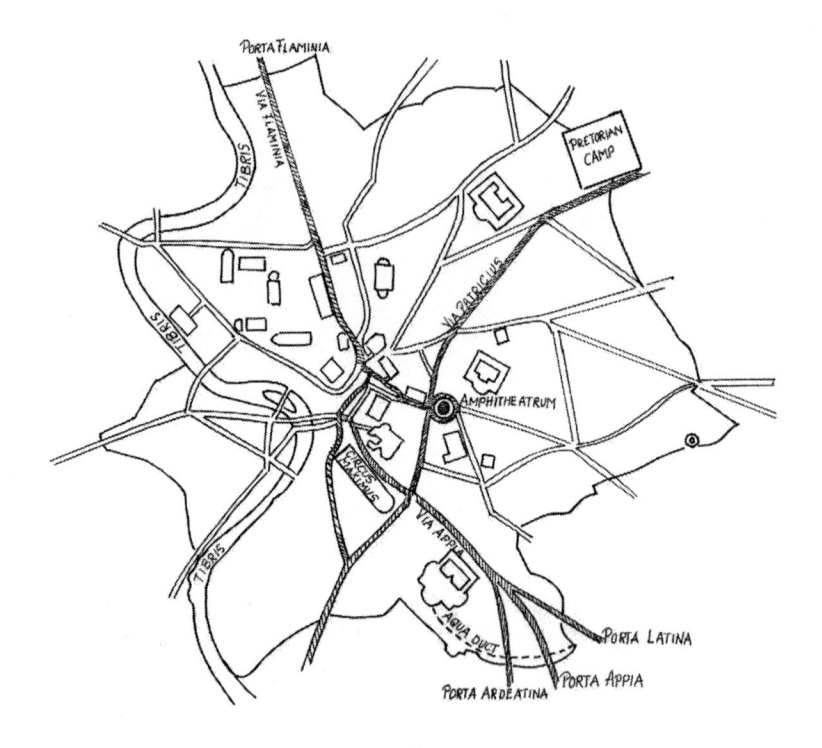

Rome

"I'm sorry, friend, I can't do that."

"This is nothing but theatrics. You and I know it. Its a farce. I don't deserve it."

"I regret it, my friend, but I have no choice."

Marcus moved in close to Julius and whispered, "Then slip me a mug of wine. I need something to calm my nerves."

"You don't need that. You haven't had anything to drink since Malta. Don't worry, though, you'll do fine."

Julius gripped Marcus' shoulder firmly with a hand and walked away, leaving Marcus standing with his hands hanging down.

As Julius left the compound, Paul and Aristarchus walked over to Marcus. Paul said, "Marcus, grace and peace to you from God our father and the Lord Jesus Christ."

"Grace and peace, huh? I certainly don't have any grace, and the only peace I'll have will be when this is all over."

"Are you familiar with this camp?" asked Paul.

"This one? Sure. This is the traditional staging area for military units entering Rome. Why?"

"Do you see that cemetery across the Appian Way?" He pointed through the row of pine trees that lined the narrow stone-paved road to their west. The famed road was already beginning to fill with wagons, chariots, and pedestrians.

Marcus looked over and winced when he saw a building among the tombstones.

"Well, continued Paul, "some of my friends pointed it out to me yesterday. You saw the Christian men who met us at Appii Forum yesterday—also, the group who later met us at Three Taverns—didn't you? They were all from a church that meets in the funeral chapel over there."

"I know," said Marcus. "I've attended there."

"Marvelous! I wasn't aware of that."

Marcus dropped back to his knees and resumed rolling up his sleeping mat. He said, "You remember my telling you about Cecilia, the friend I had fifteen or so years ago. She lived on this side of Rome and took me to the services over there several times. You say a church still meets there?"

"Yes, so they say. They've urged me to visit them. Whether or not I can, of course, depends on what Caesar does with me. I hope it will be possible, though."

"There," said Marcus, cinching a cord around his mat. He stood up. "I'd like to visit there again someday myself. They might—"

"Prisoners, assemble over here," said the chief guard from near the gate.

When all the prisoners in the compound had gathered, he said, "Men, we're coming to the end of a long sojourn together. You must agree, we've all gone through a lot. I'm not sentimental, but even I am conscious of a certain bond among us. That will come to an end today.

"Within the hour we'll be marching through the Porta Appia into the Eternal City. According to custom, this will be a Triumphal Entry. Julius, our beloved Centurion, a worthy relative of Julius

Caesar, will lead the way. You may have noticed the Julian ancestral burial place back near Bovillae when we passed it. That's where the Julian clan comes from.

"Anyway, the troops will all follow in march formation. Then come the prisoners. For the glory of our kind-hearted Julius, we want to look our best. This means for you, the prisoners, looking your worst. I want you to enter like this."

He lowered his head in a posture of humiliation. Several men laughed.

"Captain Hippalus. I want you, rather, to stand upright—proudly defiant, like this."

He modeled that posture. Marcus turned and walked away from the group.

"I'm asking you to cooperate like this to give our commander his day of glory," the guard continued. "Messengers have gone ahead to arouse the populace, and we expect thousands of Romans to give him a hero's welcome. Also, four guards will surround you as you walk, cracking whips in a menacing manner. Don't worry. Julius has ordered that none of you be touched with a whip—unless it becomes absolutely necessary."

Marcus had ambled back over to the group. He remarked to Paul, "I said this is nothing but theatrics."

All the prisoners were then chained together. A bugle sounded loudly and the chief guard shouted, "Prisoners! Fall in!"

ROMAN TRIUMPHAL CHARIOT

Julius, carrying the staff of the century's insignia and riding on a triumphal chariot borrowed for the occasion, was the first in the procession to cross into Rome over the moist pavement beneath the Porta Appia. Behind him were five trumpeters in a row, all heralding almost continuously, followed by an equal number of drummers beating cadence. Then came the one hundred armed soldiers of the century, one of the two units of the Italian cohort that had been stationed in Caesarea. Next came the motley mass of thirty-one prisoners. Julius had chosen not to bring along the baggage train with its unkempt assortment of supplies and wagons, but had left it at the assembly area with a contingent of fourteen soldiers with orders to bring it to the Praetorian Camp later in the day.

Military drums beat out a rhythmic cadence, enhanced by the united clop of hobnailed sandals on stones. A large blackbird cawed loudly as it flew over the procession and landed high up on the arch of the gate among a covey of blackbirds. Looking down on the grandeur below, they all squawked insolently. Occasionally, the crack of the whips of the four guards walking along on either side of the prisoners echoed loudly from the buildings lining the road.

The only intentional on-lookers were a handful of freedmen who had been paid to wave brightly colored pennants on sticks. Accidental on-lookers were many—impatient travelers forced to the side of the road while the troops passed.

A prisoner said under his breath, "Ha! Where are those thousands of cheering populace?"

"Yeah, who cares? Centurions are as thick as garbage flies in Rome."

Water dripped on Marcus as he walked beneath the Porta. He looked up and said to Paul, "An aqueduct passes over Porta Appia. Part of the Severiana aqueduct.

"Look. See that tall gray tenement building ahead, and off to our right. That's where my lady used to live. Jove, how I miss her."

Aristarchus said, "Paul, what are you thinking about?"

"I'm thinking about the day Christ Jesus visited Jerusalem in his triumphal entry. He entered riding on a donkey, to show his kingdom is not of this world."

"I'm thinking," said Marcus, "about the triumphal procession of Appius Drusus on the Via Flaminia after he reconquered Britain and court-martialed me many years ago. I remember I almost rushed forward to stab him. I wish I had."

Suddenly, a whip cracked loudly above their heads and they fell silent.

An hour later the procession was still valiantly moving forward. Abruptly, Julian brought the century to a halt. The wagons of their baggage train were waiting nearby beside the road. He turned his horse about and addressed the soldiers.

"Men, we're preparing to enter the Praetorian Camp through that gate ahead. The Praetorian Prefect will be on the parade field with his staff to inspect us. We will march through the gate and down an avenue to the edge of the parade field. There the prisoners will be officially turned over to the Prefect, Prefect Burrus. Then we will enter the parade field, pass in review, and finally halt before the reviewing stand. Men, be at your best. You may rest now for fifteen minutes. At ease!"

Julius then rode his horse over to the prisoners. "Paul, Aristarchus, and Marcus Hippalus. Approach me."

When they did, Julius called the chief guard and said, "Detach these men and detain them with the baggage."

Julius leaned down and whispered to Paul, "This is an act of kindness to you. You wouldn't want to experience what lies ahead for the rest of them."

The century marched through the gate and into the immaculately clean camp. Streets were laid out in exact grids and lined mostly with white, single-story, barrack and headquarters buildings. There were enough vacant fields to give a wide-open feeling to the large post. Nattily dressed troops could be seen everywhere—on errands, in training, aboard chariots, on horseback. No two or more men were ever seen walking together except they were in formation and step.

The century marched down a wide avenue in the direction of the center of the camp to a parade field. When they arrived, a fanfare of trumpets sounded from the center of the field, where were gathered several scores of soldiers adjacent to a reviewing stand draped in bright blue and red banners.

Julius called, "Century, halt."

As they stood at attention, a squad of troops marched up and halted near them.

Julius shouted, "Praefectus Praetorio, Centurion Julius Priscus of the Italian Cohort from Caesarea, relinquishing command of my prisoners."

The squad promptly surrounded the band of prisoners, took them under command, and herded them off the field. Whips cracked across their backs and heads and they cried and shouted and cursed. Instantly, the trumpets and drums struck up a martial tune and the century began marching around the parade field. It circled and came to a halt before the reviewing stand. Julius dismounted his steed, handed the reins to an aide, and stood at attention facing the stand. The drums resumed and the reviewers from the stand came down onto the field and marched up to Julius. The lead officer of the dignitaries was Burrus, Praetorian Prefect. He made a speech welcoming home the century and conferred upon Julius and others various honors and awards. Dismissal was sounded—and the brief ceremony was over.

Burrus and Julius talked amiably on the parade field for a few minutes, after which Julius led Burrus across the field to the baggage train, which was just arriving. Julius talked to the supply sergeant who in turn led them to a wagon and opened a tailgate. Three prisoners climbed down.

"Prefect Burrus," said Julius, "these are Paul of Tarsus, Captain Marcus Hippalus, and Aristarchus."

Burrus took off his helmet. He was square faced with a massive neck that joined his shaven head to his body like a stack of blocks. "Gentlemen, welcome to Rome. Julius has put in a good word for you. I want to assure you that you will be treated with the dignity due you. Paul and Aristarchus, since you have appealed to Caesar, you will be taken to the Mamertine prison by the Forum where you will be held pending further disposition of your cases. Captain Hippaulus, I had already heard about your distinguished naval career. Since you have been charged by a centurion, you will be held here at the camp pending trial before the praetorian court. Do you have any special requests before I turn you over to other guards?"

There being none, Paul and Aristarchus were put into another wagon and taken downtown. Marcus was escorted to a nearby barrack where he was given a private room with an outside door. An armed guard stood outside the room night and day.

One morning, three weeks later, the guard knocked on Marcus' door. Marcus came to the door.

Another soldier with the guard said, "I am a messenger from the praetorian court. Your trial begins in two hours. Prepare to be escorted to the court hall. Your court-appointed lawyer will meet you there."

Marcus said, "I haven't even met my lawyer. Never mind though. Also, I'm expecting a special messenger before the trial. Has anyone called for me?"

"No one that I know of."

Two hours later the guard knocked again at his door and said, "Time to go."

"Has there been anyone asking for me? A messenger?"

"None, sir."

A squad of troops escorted Marcus to another single story building. Inside, three centurions sat behind a long table. A tall, lanky civilian sat in front of them at a smaller table, to which Marcus was led. The man was his lawyer. Only a few others were present.

In the course of the trial the lawyer arose to defend Marcus:

"Gentlemen of this distinguished military court. The record of the justice administered by you is legendary, being attested by jurists all over the Empire. Therefore, it is a genuine pleasure for me to stand before you and exercise my rhetorical skills in the defense of this humble prisoner. I have every confidence that my knowledge and abilities will be properly appreciated by you, and that e're I am finished, you will feel sufficiently appraised of the facts of this man's case as to be able to exonerate him of the crimes of which he is so unjustly accused.

"Hence, I beg you cast your most sympathetic eyes upon the person of the accused. Does he look like a criminal? Of course not. He is nought but an humble citizen, striving honestly to earn his living. Perhaps he is the only son of a lowly widowed mother and sends to her the majority of his earnings that she might keep her body and soul together. You would not want to convict him and deprive him of his earning power and her of her support. Of course not. Or perhaps he is the father of a crippled son who lives for the day when his seafaring father returns home. You would not want the lad to be bereft of so upright and loving a father. Of course—"

The gavel came down. The chief judge said, "That will be enough. Thank you. You may step down."

He called the other two judges together for a whispered conference at the table. Then he said aloud, "Marcus Hippalus, the evidence that has been brought against you is most damning. We must warn you: unless you come up with a defense more convincing than that presented by your lawyer, you will be convicted and sentenced to execution. We hereby call for a fifteen minute recess."

His gavel came down again. Marcus looked back toward the outside door and saw a man signaling to him. He motioned for the man to come over. The man showed him a small sack, whereupon Marcus hastily scribbled a note and handed it to the man, who went to the chief judge standing behind the table and handed him the sack and the note. The judge sat down and read the note, then looked into the sack in his lap. It was filled with silver coins. He privately showed the other judges the contents of the bag and handed them the note. It read: "I hereby dismiss my attorney, request permission to defend myself, and request adjournment until tomorrow to have time to call witnesses. Marcus Hippalus."

At the end of the recess, the judge announced, "We grant the request of the defendant to dismiss his attorney and defend himself. We hereby adjourn court until this time tomorrow to give the defendant time to call witnesses."

He struck his gavel on the table.

The next day the court again was called to order. Present among those attending this day were Agabus Ben Uri, Julius Priscus, and Dr. Luke. Marcus said, "I call Dr. Luke to the witness stand."

"Dr. Luke, aboard the *Kibotos* in the midst of the storm that wrecked the ill-fated ship, did you, in fact, serve as a member of an inquiry board to investigate the feasibility of a court martial trying me for deliberately thrusting the ship into that storm?"

"I did."

"Who else was on that board?"

"Agabus Ben Uri, the owner of the ship, and Julius Priscus."

A buzz of conversation went through the room. The judge banged down his gavel.

"Will you please tell the court the result of that inquiry?"

"We found you not guilty of the charge. However, we did find—"

"Thank you, you've answered my question. What was the reason for your verdict, may I ask?"

"Because the decision to move the ship from Fair Havens to Phoenix was made with the complete approval of the Centurion and the ship owner."

"Are those two men present in this courtroom?"

"Yes, they are."

"Will you point them out?"

Luke pointed to Julius and Agabus.

"You entered that verdict in the ship's log that day. Can you tell he where the log is now?"

"I suppose with the ship at the bottom of a bay in Malta."

Laughter went through the courtroom.

"Thank you, Dr. Luke. You may step down. Your honors, I rest my case."

The chief judge said, "Centurion Julius, do you or Ben Uri have any objection to the contents of the testimony of Dr. Luke?"

"We have none, your honor," said Agabus.

"Then we will adjourn the trial for one hour to give the judges time to form a judgment."

An hour later the court reassembled. The chief judge announced, "We find the defendant, Captain Marcus Hippalus, not guilty of the charge of the sinking of the ship, the *Kibotos*. However, due to the fact of his drunkenness on the day of the wreck, we find him guilty of dereliction of duty and sentence him to punitive confinement at the Praetorian Camp for a period not to exceed twelve months. Court adjourned."

A month later Marcus was lying on his bunk in the barrack. A commotion occurred outside—a man calling loudly, "Yes, Centurion." He went to the window and saw Julius, Luke, and a person with a hood hiding his face. There was a rap on the door, and the guard called, "Marcus Hippalus, open to the Centurion."

Marcus opened the door and the three walked in.

"Marcus, you have visitors," said Julius.

The person pulled back his hood and shook a head of silver hair.

"Cecilia!" said Marcus.

Marcus' lady friend, of almost two decades before, stood before him, changed but not beyond recognition. She was filled out, triple-chinned, matronly, and large-bosomed—her face was plump yet soft and gentle. She had a distinguished look that seemed thoroughly out of place in a soldier's camp.

Luke said, "Marcus, Paul heard about Cecilia and asked some members of the church to search for her. They found her in Venice."

"When I heard you were here," Cecilia said, "I came as fast as I could. Marcus, how have you been?"

Marcus eyes moistened. "As good as could be expected. Are you well? You seem so."

"Yes, the Lord has cared well for me through the years. I praise his name."

Marcus turned to Julius and Luke and said, "Would you mind if we spoke alone for awhile?"

"Not at all," said Julius. "Luke, how about waiting for her outside with the guard until they're finished? I have other business to attend to."

"I'll be happy to."

When they left, Cecilia, her hands trembling, said, "I've been hearing about your glowing career down through the years. I've never ceased praying for you."

Marcus was perspiring. He said, "I suppose you're married and have grown children by now."

"No, I've never married. All this time I've been hoping . . ."

"Oh, Cecilia, I'm so sorry!"

Marcus sat down on the bed, put his face into this hands, and began sobbing aloud. Cecilia sat down beside him and took his head into her lap and stroked his hair. "Cecilia, I've ached for you so much through the years. Will you help me?"

"If I can." Cecilia was weeping.

Marcus sat up and dried his eyes but did not look into her face. "I'm a miserable man. I have been ever since I mistreated you. Do you remember the last time I saw you—in your apartment?"

"How could I ever forget?"

"No, not just my abuse of you. Before that. Do you remember that you were urging me to accept Christ? Do you remember that? That was what provoked me. No, it wasn't your fault. I felt terribly pressured from within, because I knew what I ought to do, but I refused to do it. To relieve the pressure, I resorted to the flesh. Oh, if I had it to do over again, I would have accepted your invitation."

He looked over at her. "Cecilia, is there any hope for me now? It's too late, isn't it?"

"No, it's *not* too late. Where there's life, there's hope. Look here. I've borrowed a papyrus of a portion of *Isaiah*. Read here with me, 'Come now, and let us reason together, saith the Lord: though your sins be as scarlet, they shall be as white as snow; though they be red like crimson, they shall be as wool.' And over here, 'Seek ye the Lord while he may be found, call ye upon him while he is near: let the wicked forsake his way, and the unrighteous man his thoughts: and let him return unto the Lord, and he will have mercy upon him; and to our God for he will abundantly pardon.'" Marcus, are you ready now to accept the forgiveness of God through Christ?"

"Oh, yes, I am," he responded, looking into her face. "What do I need to do?"

Cecilia instructed him briefly, and together, then, they knelt beside his bunk. Marcus prayed and accepted Christ into his life.

Paul and Marcus were standing in a large basin of water carved out in the floor in the center of the funeral chapel in the south edge of Rome. The church had been meeting in that building so long that the owners had given them permission to construct a baptistry in the floor. Julius and two armed guards stood among the large crowd of spectators around the baptistry.

"By intent, I have baptized only a few people in my lifetime," said Paul, "but I have longed for the privilege of baptizing this convert."

He then pronounced the customary formula and dipped Marcus beneath the water. Towels were given to them, and after wiping his face, Marcus said, "May I say a word?"

"Go ahead," said Paul.

They both remained in the pool as Marcus spoke:

"Many people today are running from God, but probably no one has ever run as hard as I did and yet lived to find salvation. I first heard the claim of God upon my life almost twenty years ago when my beloved fiancee proclaimed to me the gospel of Christ. At that time God brought several events into my life to convince me of the futility of the world's way and the superiority of his way. He allowed a great storm in the English channel to destroy my military career. Yet I rebelled all the more. I knew God was in it, but I claimed the elements were against me, specifically the wind. I ignored the fact that God controls the wind.

"For two decades I crisscrossed the world in my ships, defying the wind. Finally, last year God had enough of my rebellion. He allowed another storm to destroy my naval career forever: this time my ship was sunk at the isle of Malta. Afterward, Paul and others tried to convince me of a fact I already knew but was unwilling to admit—that God was pursuing me—but I wouldn't concede. I was stubborn and self-willed. At last, when Cecilia journeyed all the way from Venice to Rome just to witness to me, I finally gave up and gave my heart to the Lord. I want to say how thankful I am that God had the patience to pursue me around the world without giving up. All praise be to the name of Christ."

"The Spirit," said Paul, "has certainly loosed this man's tongue. I predict that one day the Lord will use that tongue to draw multitudes unto himself. Now, give us an opportunity to dry off and we'll hold another blessed ceremony."

When they returned, Paul conducted the wedding ceremonies of Marcus and Cecilia as well as of Hermes and Ruth.

At the reception for the two couples held afterward in the mortuary's viewing room, Agabus approached Marcus to congratulate him. Marcus took his hand, gripped it, and said, "Agabus, have you yet accepted Christ?"

Nearby, Kore spoke up. "He was baptized here last month. Miriam too."

"Yes," Agabus said, "what finally persuaded me was the fact that so many Jews in Puteoli and Rome had seen fit to accept the Lord Jesus."

Marcus turned to Kore and said, "Where's Erastus?"

"Oh, he's out sailing. Hasn't been back since we first got to Rome. I miss him."

She stuck out her lower lip and pretended to pout.

*Alack, thou knowest not*
*How little worthy of any love thou art!*
*Whom wilt thou find to love ignoble thee*
  *Save Me, save only Me?*
*All which I took from thee I did but take*
  *Not for thy harms,*
*But just that thou mightst seek it in My arms.*
  *All which thy child's mistake*
*Fancies as lost, I have stored for thee at home:*
  *Rise, clasp My hand, and come!"*

  *Halts by me that footfall:*
  *Is my gloom, after all,*
*Shade of His hand, outstretched caressingly?*
  *"Ah, fondest, blindest, weakest,*
  *I am He whom thou seekest!*
*Thou dravest love from thee, who dravest Me."*
  HOUND OF HEAVEN by Francis Thompson

# CHAPTER NINETEEN

## PUTEOLI, AD 64

THREE YEARS LATER, in the summertime, Marcus and Cecilia were relaxing at their home in Puteoli, which fronted on a paved road in the northern edge of the city. Marcus was sitting at a table reading a scroll. Cecilia was standing at the front window looking out.

"Dear, a carriage has just pulled up in front of the house. Two people are getting out. Oh! One of them is Kore! Why, she's holding an infant. I don't recognize the man."

"Wonderful! We haven't seen her in years."

There was a knock on the door and Marcus arose to answer it.

When he opened the door, he exclaimed, "Well, Erastus, you old seadog. I haven't seen you since we sailed from Malta."

"You folks, come right on in," said Cecilia. "Here, Kore, let me hold that precious bundle."

"This is little Lucius," said Kore, who seemed glad to be relieved of the burden for awhile.

"Kore, what a pleasure to see you again," said Marcus, as he embraced her. "Do you have any baggage? You're certainly welcome to stay here with us for a few days, if you desire."

"Nothing but this baby bag," said Erastus. "We just put into port here on business and have a comfortable berth on board the *Syracuse*."

"You're working on the *Syracuse* now? That's my old ship. I supervised her overhaul right here in Puteoli twenty years ago."

"Not just working. I took command of her a year ago."

"Marvelous! Congratulations! Is Decius still the owner? Still in the African grain trade?"

"Yes, she still belongs to Decius but she's no longer in the grain trade. I've been doing more or less private coastal trading between Rome and Corinth. Kore and I are on our way to Corinth now—moving back there from Rome. My father passed away recently and I inherited his estate in Corinth. We plan to move into it. Kore and the child will stay there while I ply the Adriatic."

"Ought to be a good arrangement," said Marcus. "Plenty of trade in and out of Lechaeum, and you can be at home every time you're back there."

"I'm so excited," said Kore. "I've never been in Greece. Ruth wrote that it's wonderful there. I can't wait."

She put her arm around Erastus' waist and he looked down and kissed her gently. She then took the baby from Cecilia.

"Why don't you be seated," said Cecilia, "while I heat a pot of tea?"

"I'll come with you if you don't mind."

"Surely."

"Here, dear, hold the baby."

Kore handed the infant to Erastus and followed Cecilia to the kitchen. Cecilia said, "I understand Ruth and Hermes have a child now, too."

"Two of them, and she is . . ."

They disappeared into the kitchen.

Later, over tea in the parlor, Cecilia asked, "Were you wed in Rome?"

"Yes," said Kore, "there in the church where you and Marcus were married. After the shipwreck, Erastus shipped out for Spain, and I didn't see him again until after you moved away."

Erastus took up the story: "We wrote back and forth regularly. I finally grew tired of the Spanish route, so I returned to Rome to look for a better job. That's when we were married and when I met Decius. Marcus, you've really changed."

Marcus was no longer dressed like a centurion. His hair was longer; it had whitened and now stood out thick from his head in waves, like a lion's mane. He was clean shaven and his many acne scars showed, but the rough lines had softened. A gentle smile played upon his lips.

"Erastus, since I met the Savior, I've been happier than I've ever been in my life. Much of my joy is in Cecilia. She's God's greatest gift on earth to me. I'm ever so deeply humbled that she would have me after all that went on. To me, she personifies the very essence of the grace of God toward this sinful creature."

They relaxed together and conversed throughout the afternoon. Later Cecilia prepared supper, and after eating they continued to lounge around the low dining table.

"I understand you're pastor of a church now," said Erastus. "In fact, I saw some posters around the harbor announcing your Sunday services. People everywhere are talking about you."

Marcus' face grew grave and stern, and for a moment, Erastus saw Paul in him.

"Yes, after Paul baptized me and married Cecilia and me in Rome, I had to complete my year of confinement at the Praetorian Barracks. After my release I spent almost every waking hour at Paul's apartment where he continued under house arrest. I think Cecilia began to despair of me since I was gone from home so much. Paul discipled me. The next year, after Nero released him, he sailed for Greece and brought me with him as far as Puteoli.

"Let me back up. You remember when the *Castor and Pollux* docked here from Malta? Well, at that time Paul searched out the people of the church here and Julius allowed him to spend a week with them. It so happened that several men in the church were acquainted with me, from the time when the *Syracuse* was being refurbished here. That week Paul brought them to see me, and they tried to witness to me about Christ. Well, they also told Paul they needed a pastor. Over the next two years they stayed in touch with Paul, so that when he recommended me as their pastor, they didn't hesitate to call me. I've been here ever since."

A knock sounded at the front door, and Cecilia went to answer it. She returned to the dining room and said, "Dear, it's the carriage. It's about time to go."

"Very well, love. I'll get ready."

"Go? I'm sorry. I didn't know you had an engagement," said Erastus.

"It's almost time for church," Marcus said.

"It is Sunday, isn't it?" said Erastus. "We had almost forgotten."

Kore said, "We need to return to the ship now anyway."

"No," said Cecilia. "Just come with us. There's room in the carriage for you. Besides, we meet right near the harbor and you can probably walk to your ship from there. I'll help care for the baby during the service."

A few minutes later, the five of them boarded the carriage together.

When they stopped in front of a large warehouse at the docks, they confronted a vast crowd of people milling around outside the building. It was twilight. Chariots, carriages, wagons, and saddled horses of every description were tied up all around. Marcus led them toward a front door. Men, women, and children, most of them sailors and soldiers with their families or girl friends, hailed him in an excited manner.

"Hello, Marcus."

"We're looking forward to hearing you tonight, Marcus."

"Marcus, good to see you."

Several times Marcus replied, "Wonderful to see you at church. Pray for me tonight. Let the Spirit of God prevail in our midst."

Marcus suddenly spied someone in the crowd and said to his party, "Before we go in, let me introduce you to someone." He led them over toward a youth and called, "Octavia!"

A beautiful young lady, who was apparently alone, turned and said, "Pastor Marcus."

When he came over, she embraced him. He said, "Octavia, I want you to meet Erastus and Kore. Erastus and Kore, this is Octavia, daughter to Julius Priscus."

"Marvelous!" said Kore. "Julius had told me about you."

"How are you?" said Erastus. "Where is the Centurion now?"

"He and my mother are in Augsburg now. He was stationed there two years ago."

"Why don't you come in and sit with Cecilia and our friends during the service, Octavia," said Marcus.

"But there's no more room inside," she replied. "They've shut the doors. That's why we're all standing around out here."

Marcus said, "Then let us have our own service right out here."

A large number of people gathered around him, and his tall figure towered above them.

"My friends," began Marcus, his giant voice bouncing off the buildings and wafting across the bay. Obviously, he was cut out to be a preacher. "You may wonder what message you would have heard tonight had you gained admittance into the building. I can sum it up in one word—Jesus. I am not a scholar, but I convey to you the greatest knowledge in the world—the knowledge of Jesus. I am not a rhetorician, but I seek to persuade you to come to Jesus.

"You have tried to gain admission into a building through a door, but I want to tell you about a far greater door than that. It is Jesus. Jesus said, 'I am the door: by me if any man enter in, he shall be saved.' My dear friends, I would stand here and preach until midnight if by it I thought to persuade you to walk through the door of Jesus.

"What a humble way for Jesus to present himself—simply as a door! Jesus condescends to be anything necessary that he may save people. The great men of society close their doors, but the door of Jesus is always open to whomever will choose to enter therein. Do so tonight, and find within that door peace, joy, and everlasting life . . ."

Fifteen minutes later, when Marcus prayed and dismissed the crowd, the people were slow in leaving. Many were very emotionally moved by the message. Some were weeping. Some broke into singing.

Cecilia whispered to Marcus, "I heard them begin singing inside awhile ago."

"Let's go on in," Marcus said. "I know of a side door. Come on."

When the six of them entered the warehouse, they saw people sitting on crude backless benches and standing in almost every possible spot in the building. A song service was in progress.

"Jehoshaphat!" said Kore. "Must be a thousand people in here."

The baby began to cry, and Kore rocked him in her arms and said, "There, there, sweet one, don't you cry. Everything's all right. Mommy's here."

Marcus led them to a corner office in the back. When he opened the door, they found the room full of men.

"Good evening, deacons," said Marcus. "These are Erastus and Kore, long-time friends of mine. Sorry I'm late. There was such a large number of people outside who couldn't get in, I felt led to preach a short message to them. They're still there, milling around, singing. Several accepted Christ. Would it be possible for some of you to go out and counsel with them?"

"Pastor," said a bald-headed man. "I'll send out several men. The people inside got restless, so we had them go ahead and begin the song service. Praise God, the crowd is even larger than last week. God's people have really worked this week—visiting everywhere, witnessing, promoting. They say many are ready to make public decisions for Christ tonight again."

"Excellent," said Marcus. "Now, I wonder if it would be possible for Kore and the baby to have a seat in this room during the service. We could leave the door open and she could see and hear what's going on."

"I don't see any reason why not," said the bald-headed man. "Here, Kore, you can have my chair."

Another man said, "Here, Cecilia, you and Octavia can sit here with her."

Another said to Erastus, "Hey! There's no reason for you to be apart from your wife and baby. You sit here."

"Now, let's pray together," said Marcus.

The deacons dropped to their knees and Marcus led them in a fervent prayer. Then they left the office.

When the singing, testimonies, prayer requests, and praying were over and it came time for the Bible study, Marcus stepped up onto a large packing crate set up at the end of the warehouse.

"Ahem!" he said. His great voice filled the whole building. Instantly, all noise ceased. He read the story of Jonah.

"'Jonah ran away from the Lord,' he said. "This was certainly an ill-advised act, for it brought great personal calamity upon Jonah and those with him. Peace returned only when he quit running. If holy men sometimes run from God, how much more do those who have never met God."

Marcus appeared majestic standing alone on that platform presenting the gospel in an animated fashion.

"You may now be in the process of fleeing from God. Dear friend, you can never run fast enough nor far enough to escape him. Because he loves you, he pursues you without rest. Like Jonah, I once ran from God. I ran for almost twenty years. Like Jonah, my flight put in jeopardy the lives of two hundred seventy-six ship passengers. But, like Jonah, one day I quit running and permitted God to catch me. It was the most glorious day of my life..."

## FINIS

# APPENDIX

## THE STORY FROM THE BIBLE

ACTS 27:1 (KJS) And when it was determined that we should sail into Italy, they delivered Paul and certain other prisoners unto [one] named Julius, a centurion of Augustus' band. 2 And entering into a ship of Adramyttium, we launched, meaning to sail by the coasts of Asia; [one] Aristarchus, a Macedonian of Thessalonica, being with us. 3 And the next [day] we touched at Sidon. And Julius courteously entreated Paul, and gave [him] liberty to go unto his friends to refresh himself. 4 And when we had launched from thence, we sailed under Cyprus, because the winds were contrary. 5 And when we had sailed over the sea of Cilicia and Pamphylia, we came to Myra, [a city] of Lycia. 6 And there the centurion found a ship of Alexandria sailing into Italy; and he put us therein. 7 And when we had sailed slowly many days, and scarce were come over against Cnidus, the wind not suffering us, we sailed under Crete, over against Salmone; Crete: or, Candy} 8 And, hardly passing it, came unto a place which is called The fair havens; nigh whereunto was the city [of] Lasea. 9 Now when much time was spent, and when sailing was now dangerous, because the fast was now already past, Paul admonished [them], the fast: the fast was on the tenth day of the seventh month} 10 And said unto them, Sirs, I perceive that this voyage will be with hurt and much damage, not only of the lading and ship, but also of our lives. hurt: or, injury} 11 Nevertheless the centurion believed the master and the owner of the ship, more than those things which were spoken by Paul.

12 And because the haven was not commodious to winter in, the more part advised to depart thence also, if by any means they might attain to Phenice, [and there] to winter; [which is] an haven of Crete, and lieth toward the south west and north west. 13 And when the south wind blew softly, supposing that they had obtained [their] purpose, loosing [thence], they sailed close by Crete. 14 But not long after there arose against it a tempestuous wind, called Euroclydon. arose: or, beat} 15 And when the ship was caught, and could not bear up into the wind, we let [her] drive. 16 And running under a certain island which is called Clauda, we had much work to come by the boat: 17 Which when they had taken up, they used helps, undergirding the ship; and, fearing lest they should fall into the quicksands, strake sail, and so were driven. 18 And we being exceedingly tossed with a tempest, the next [day] they lightened the ship; 19 And the third [day] we cast out with our own hands the tackling of the ship. 20 And when neither sun nor stars in many days appeared, and no small tempest lay on [us], all hope that we should be saved was then taken away.

21 But after long abstinence Paul stood forth in the midst of them, and said, Sirs, ye should have hearkened unto me, and not have loosed from Crete, and to have gained this harm and loss. 22 And now I exhort you to be of good cheer: for there shall be no loss of [any man's] life among you, but of the ship. 23 For there stood

by me this night the angel of God, whose I am, and whom I serve, 24 Saying, Fear not, Paul; thou must be brought before Caesar: and, lo, God hath given thee all them that sail with thee. 25 Wherefore, sirs, be of good cheer: for I believe God, that it shall be even as it was told me. 26 Howbeit we must be cast upon a certain island. 27 But when the fourteenth night was come, as we were driven up and down in Adria, about midnight the shipmen deemed that they drew near to some country; 28 And sounded, and found [it] twenty fathoms: and when they had gone a little further, they sounded again, and found [it] fifteen fathoms. 29 Then fearing lest we should have fallen upon rocks, they cast four anchors out of the stern, and wished for the day. 30 And as the shipmen were about to flee out of the ship, when they had let down the boat into the sea, under colour as though they would have cast anchors out of the foreship, 31 Paul said to the centurion and to the soldiers, Except these abide in the ship, ye cannot be saved. 32 Then the soldiers cut off the ropes of the boat, and let her fall off. 33 And while the day was coming on, Paul besought [them] all to take meat, saying, This day is the fourteenth day that ye have tarried and continued fasting, having taken nothing. 34 Wherefore I pray you to take [some] meat: for this is for your health: for there shall not an hair fall from the head of any of you. 35 And when he had thus spoken, he took bread, and gave thanks to God in presence of them all: and when he had broken [it], he began to eat. 36 Then were they all of good cheer, and they also took [some] meat. 37 And we were in all in the ship two hundred threescore and sixteen souls. 38 And when they had eaten enough, they lightened the ship, and cast out the wheat into the sea. 39 And when it was day, they knew not the land: but they discovered a certain creek with a shore, into the which they were minded, if it were possible, to thrust in the ship. 40 And when they had taken up the anchors, they committed [themselves] unto the sea, and loosed the rudder bands, and hoised up the mainsail to the wind, and made toward shore. taken . . . : or, cut the anchors, they left them in the sea} 41 And falling into a place where two seas met, they ran the ship aground; and the forepart stuck fast, and remained unmoveable, but the hinder part was broken with the violence of the waves. 42 And the soldiers' counsel was to kill the prisoners, lest any of them should swim out, and escape. 43 But the centurion, willing to save Paul, kept them from [their] purpose; and commanded that they which could swim should cast [themselves] first [into the sea], and get to land: 44 And the rest, some on boards, and some on [broken pieces] of the ship. And so it came to pass, that they escaped all safe to land.

28:1 And when they were escaped, then they knew that the island was called Melita. 2 And the barbarous people shewed us no little kindness: for they kindled a fire, and received us every one, because of the present rain, and because of the cold. 3 And when Paul had gathered a bundle of sticks, and laid [them] on the fire, there came a viper out of the heat, and fastened on his hand. 4 And when the barbarians saw the [venomous] beast hang on his hand, they said among themselves, No doubt this man is a murderer, whom, though he hath escaped the sea, yet vengeance suffereth not to live. 5 And he shook off the beast into the fire, and felt no harm. 6 Howbeit they looked when he should have swollen, or fallen down dead suddenly: but after they had looked a great while, and saw no harm come to him, they changed their minds, and said that he was a god. 7 In the same quarters were possessions of the chief man of the island, whose name was Publius; who received us, and lodged us three days courteously. 8 And it came to pass, that the father of Publius lay sick of a fever and of a bloody flux: to whom Paul entered in, and prayed, and laid his hands on him, and healed him. 9 So when this was done, others also, which had diseases in the island, came, and were healed: 10 Who also honoured us with many honours; and when we departed, they laded [us] with such things as were necessary.

11 And after three months we departed in a ship of Alexandria, which had wintered in the isle, whose sign was Castor and Pollux. 12 And landing at Syracuse, we tarried [there] three days. 13 And from thence we fetched a compass, and came to Rhegium: and after one day the south wind blew, and we came the next day to Puteoli: 14 Where we found brethren, and were desired to tarry

with them seven days: and so we went toward Rome. 15 And from thence, when the brethren heard of us, they came to meet us as far as Appii forum, and The three taverns: whom when Paul saw, he thanked God, and took courage. 16 And when we came to Rome, the centurion delivered the prisoners to the captain of the guard: but Paul was suffered to dwell by himself with a soldier that kept him.

MARE ADRIATICUM
(ADRIATIC SEA)
ROME
THREE TAVERNS
(CISTERNA)
ITALI
PUTEOLI
(PUZZUOLI)
GREECE
MARE TYRRHENUM
(TYRRHENIANSEA)
SICILY
MELITA
(MALTA)
GREAT S
(MEDITERRANE
SYRTIS
(SYRTUS MAJOR)

TURKEY
MYRA
RHODES
CRETE
MT. IDA
MONI VRONDISI
FAIR HAVENS
(KALI LIMINES)
CYPRUS
TYRE
NABATEANS
JERUSALEM
ALEXADRIA
PETRA
MOUTH OF THE NILE

BVG